Praise for Indra Sinha's *The Cybergypsies*

'Not only is it an exhilarating read but it is a demonstration
of why we need to read'
The Times

'A vivid exposé of a social evil, accompanied by an equally
vivid evocation of the pleasures of addiction'
Observer

'An engrossing tale of modern morality'
Face

'Truly extraordinary'
Independent

Indra Sinha was born in India and spent his childhood in Bombay and the hills of the Western Ghats. He was educated at Mayo College, Ajmer and Pembroke College, Cambridge. His work of non-fiction, *The Cybergypsies*, received widespread critical acclaim. This is his first novel. Indra Sinha lives with his wife and three children in Sussex.

THE DEATH
OF MR LOVE

INDRA SINHA

Scribner

First published in Great Britain by Scribner, 2002
This edition published by Scribner, 2003
An imprint of Simon & Schuster UK Ltd
A Viacom Company

Grateful acknowledgement is made to the following: *Blitz* newspaper; 'Main
Nashe Mein Hoon', lyrics by Shailendra, music by Shankar-Jaikishan, sung by Mukesh,
from the film *Main Nashe Mein Hoon*; 'Aye Dil Mushkil', lyrics by Majrooh Sultanpuri,
music by O.P. Nayyar, sung by Mohammed Rafi, from the film *CID*; 'Goodness
Gracious Me', lyrics by Herbert Kretzmer, sung by Peter Sellers and Sophia Loren,
from the film *The Millionairess*; *Calypso* lyrics by Mighty Sparrow.

1 3 5 7 9 10 8 6 4 2

Simon & Schuster UK Ltd
Africa House
64–78 Kingsway
London WC2B 6AH

Simon & Schuster Australia
Sydney

www.simonsays.co.uk

A CIP catalogue record for this book is available from the British Library

ISBN 0-7432-0700-9

Typeset by Palimpsest Book Production, Limited
Polmont, Stirlingshire
Printed and bound in Great Britain by
Cox & Wyman Ltd, Reading, Berkshire

Dedicated with affection and respect to

Mulk Raj Anand

who told me when I was a child to write,
and when I was grown up to write about my childhood.

'Bhalu, call this story fiction if you want, but you must write it for three reasons. First because it is true, and at its heart is that murder of forty years ago which people in India still remember. Second, because its threats* are still alive, running unbroken into the future. Third, you must reveal that the uproar and sensation of the Nanavati trial hid another monstrous crime, which remains undiscovered, its perpetrator unpunished, except by these words that you will write.'

*A slip. I was trying to type 'threads'. Phoebe claimed this was a message from Maya, received at a second seance in Brighton, after I had left for Bombay in July 1999.

PROLOGUE

Last night on Juhu beach I startled a prostitute, hard at work beneath a client in the cigarette-butt salted sand. She saw me over his shoulder and let out an ululation of pure terror. How elating that shriek was. Mostly, my fellow citizens are impervious. If they notice me at all, they don't know what they are seeing. All kinds of tricks I have tried to gather an audience. I staggered among the traffic at Kemp's Corner, but instead of the expected chorus of horns and abuse, drew a solitary beep from one rattled motorist. I climbed onto the statue of the black horse at Kalaghoda and perched behind King Edward VII, waving to the people below, but only a few looked up. I have roamed Bombay city from end to end and everywhere I meet eyes that stare through me as if I weren't there. Those who can see don't want to. They look hastily away. Well, I am not a decent sight in my blood-soaked attire, my hair curded with dried gore. A disgrace, the averted faces proclaim, father of his own misfortune. They can tell from the bottle I am carrying, whose miserable translucence proclaims it to be empty, that I am no good-hearted village drunk, driven by a harsh life and an unjust world to drown his sorrows in honest country mash. My stuff is Scotch at four hundred chips a bottle. Across its label strides the top-hatted, monocled, red-coated figure which our Indian cinema has translated into hero man 'Jahnny Walkar', screen maestro, last slurred word in comedic drunkenness. If this story ever becomes a movie, I fear it's he who will play me.

To be hated is one thing, to be ridiculed is worse. I am accused

3

of unpleasant crimes, to some of which I may even plead guilty, but I was never a figure of fun. Those who know me well could tell you that I am a quiet man, a gentle soul – if only my friends would speak up – but many of them now deny having known me. I want the chance to tell my own story, to put my side of things. Look, I am described (I am thirty-six) as 'an ageing Lothario, who maintained his sleek and deceiving looks with the help of Vasmol, "the hair darkener that keeps its promises", although this heartless seducer did not . . . He drinks foreign liquor, obtained on the black market from a bootlegger, and buys Macropolo's brown perfumed cigarettes in tins of fifty. More than forty of his gold-tipped butts were found at the scene of the crime.'

I am, it seems, a louche villain, a cynical genie of the whisky bottle, given entirely to vice, 'a symbol of those wealthy, corrupt, immoral and basically un-socialist forces which are holding the nation and its integrity to ransom'. This last is a quotation from *Blitz*, our city's beloved scandal sheet, which would like its readers to believe me capable of murder.

'Some,' writes *Blitz*, 'may attribute this sickening event to the intolerable heat of the season, but this is a mistake. Persons such as he do not share the lot of the common man. They live and move in a world of privilege. For their sins, their outrages, their crimes, they and they alone are to blame.' Please, do me a favour. The thing that happened was inexplicable, mad, and only an imbecile would blame the weather – but it was not my fault.

The heat in Bombay, in those last few weeks before the rains, is famous for driving people crazy. Such clamminess, such moisture that turns armpits into oozing swamps and crawls like insects under the clothes, such oily clinging dirt, collars and cuffs made black by an hour's wearing, such a swelter of bodies, and nights when sleep is impossible because the heat hangs like a contagion in airless rooms. In the poorest parts of the city, in chawls and shanties, there are more murders at this time of year than any other. But these are, of course, socialist areas. *Blitz* reports, 'A labourer has cut his wife's throat because she refused to make him a cup of tea. His advocate in the Sessions Court jokes that at this season the only defence is "heat of the moment".'

Even where modest incomes permit each family to have its own living space, things are no better. Across the city, people in thinly-partitioned rooms switch on their fans and open their shutters to catch the faintest breeze; but the sea has the foetid breath of a beast and its faint exhalations are soon lost in the maze of alleys. The prurient eye of *Blitz* notes, 'The young men lie on their backs and hear people going to their mating beds, and the dark snake crawls in their veins.'

The wealthy, no doubt, escape. On Malabar Hill, where the mansions and fancy apartments look out over the Arabian Sea, with servants camped outside the big front doors, chowkidars to guard each entrance and conclaves of drivers playing cards in the car parks, we siesta-ing rich seal ourselves into our air-conditioned rooms and lock out the glare, the heat and the suffering world.

On such a day, in such a room, I was lying naked on my bed, thinking of the women I had had in it. Fish-kites wheeled outside my window, and forty feet below, the sea was shouting. There were quite a few women, I will admit, but a seducer I am not. I never set out to make a woman fall in love with me. It happens naturally. I know how to be charming. Many lovers have told me, though it's hard to see while my face still carries marks of a violent struggle, that I have the looks of a film star, a firm jaw, a straight nose, thick eyebrows that frame eyes capable of great tenderness. My mouth is wide and broadens readily into a smile. In the back-streets off Mohammed Ali Road one can buy all sorts of potions which are supposed to make one irresistible to the opposite sex. A man I know used to mix a tincture of gold costing hundreds of rupees with his own semen and dab the mixture behind his ears, but such things are for the ignorant and desperate. A sincere smile costs nothing and is more effective.

Particularly galling is the suggestion (*Blitz* again) that I used drugs to get women into bed. An Anglo-Indian who calls herself 'Angela' has come forward with a pitiful story about how, ignoring her tears and wretched protestations about the trusting husband and small child at home, I cajoled her out of her underwear. These sessions — there were several — took place each time against her will and better judgement, while her moral faculty was paralysed. How could this be? She offers no explanation, other than that once, when she was 'nauseous with self-loathing', I produced a paper with a yellow powder in it and told her to take it because it would make her feel 'sparkling and alive'. Months later, on a train in South India, she overheard a sinister-looking man mention a certain yellow love philtre which, he said, when administered to a victim, would produce in her 'a feeling of lively exuberance'. It is a pity that I am in no position to mount a libel action because I know exactly who 'Angela' is and can certainly vouch for the happy gusto of her adulteries, but the only powder I recall was the stuff caked on her upper lip.

No, I never make the first move, and if I do have a reputation for walking up to beautiful women at parties and saying, 'You look lonely, would you like to dance?' simple acts of human kindness don't make me a seducer. Nor, wallah, am I a deceiver. I admit that I have often carried on more than one affair at a time, I have never pretended otherwise. Always at the outset I made it clear, 'We will be friends. We will have fun, but don't expect me to give up other friendships.' Is it my fault if some chose not to hear? I am not ready to be a husband. This is why I made it a rule only to see married women. So much the better if they had children, it made their marriages harder to leave. 'At thirty-six years old he is still a bachelor,' say my detractors, 'because no decent woman wanted to marry him.' Ah, if only it were true.

But I must not allow present troubles to get in the way of my story. Let us go back to that intolerable, steamy afternoon before the rains. The evil event had yet to happen and other thoughts occupied me as I lay on my bed, listening to the thin screaming of kites. It was four. Outside, on city streets, people were leaving footprints in the tarmac. My habit was to come home from my office at this time for a nap. Usually the sea, crying of birds and dyspeptic gurgles of the air-conditioner send me to sleep at once, but that day I was lying awake, a thin pillar of cigarette smoke rising from the vicinity of my pillow, the ashtray near my head accumulating gold cigarette-ends. I had a problem. I needed to get rid of my girlfriend . . .

Two was a mistake. I'd known it from the outset. Most of the women who come to my bed are pragmatists, they know exactly what they are doing and have their own reasons for deceiving their husbands, but Two was dangerous. She was a romantic, a thing I've noticed before in Englishwomen who, although no more inherently faithless than their Indian counterparts, have a naive belief in true love, which most Indian women, who must learn to love the strangers they marry, do not.

'I put myself in your hands,' Two said to me not very long after we met. 'I want to belong to you completely.' Normally I despise that kind of sentimentality. I should never have encouraged her.

I met Two because I was carrying on an affair with one of her best friends, to whom she bore such an uncanny and complete resemblance that they might have been twins. Both were English. They were almost exactly the same age and favoured the same look – Ava Gardner from *The Barefoot Contessa* – dark waving hair and highly arched brows above eyes that seemed to challenge men to meet them. To make confusion worse, even their names sounded alike. People constantly got them mixed up. Once, when they were still friends – before they fell out over me – they spent a whole evening at the Willingdon Club impersonating each other, flirting extravagantly in one another's names. 'My husband is away next week, do give me a ring,' breathed One, dancing with an iguana-jowled Lebanese banker, and whispered Two's number. Two smiled her sweetest smile at the High Court judge who was stroking her arm and offering to teach her Hindi, and gave him One's calling card. Little did his wrinkled and famously lecherous Lordship know, but my affair with One had already begun.

Later One came laughing up to me, bringing Two with her, and introduced us.

'I've heard all about you,' said Two, when her friend had gone off again, leaving us together. 'You've got quite a reputation.' She was still in a flirtatious mood. 'Is it safe to be seen talking to you?' Her likeness to One was startling. She had the same grey, slightly-hooded eyes, and a practised through-the-lashes stare which she probably thought of as languorous.

'Reputation is one thing, truth is another.'

'They say you can't see a woman without making a pass at her.'

'Well, what do you think? Have I made a pass at you?'

'No,' she said, 'so I expect you don't find me attractive.'

As a matter of fact I did, but not for the reasons she might have imagined. It isn't usually beauty that attracts me, but some small peculiarity. If, for example, I see a pair of thin lips, which their owner has tried to disguise by painting a voluptuous shape around them, it makes me want to find out how a woman so aware of the ugliness of her mouth will use it for kissing. The elusive thing that catches my interest needn't be physical. If I see amusement, alarm, or even contempt – it has been known – in a woman's eyes when she is talking to me, I can't help wondering what message they will convey when they are inches from mine during the love act.

Two's peculiarity was her likeness to One.

Well, of course it was irresistible. Imagine. How deep would it run? Two's kisses, would they taste like One's? One was noisy in bed, she grunted and gave little squeals. And Two? One liked the missionary position. How about Two? Well, after sex, when One re-did her face in my mirror, she would sit very upright, suck in her cheeks, raise her eyebrows and stare at herself like a haughty duchess. Two leaned forward, peered, scowling and pulling her mouth into strange quadrilaterals. But there were times when the face looking back out of the mirror could have belonged to either of them. During one of our early sessions I called Two by the name of her double. It was an easy mistake. I only realised what I'd done when I noticed the doppelganger face in the glass glowering at me. More errors followed.

Two liked to plunge her nails into my back – God knows where she had learned this unpleasant habit – and once, in bed with One, I surprised her by asking to examine her fingernails. They were chewed to the quick. She apologised and told me that for special occasions she wore false nails glued on top of the real ones. The glue wasn't very good and they were apt to lift away on sticky strings. At a smart party where plates of food were being passed round, she was appalled to see a scarlet claw circulating among the guests, stuck in a cucumber sandwich. Two would never have told such a story against herself. In fact, as I soon discovered, the chief difference between them was One's sense of humour.

When, inevitably, it became clear that I was seeing both of them, they reacted quite differently. One tried to laugh it off – most admirable, because I could tell she was hurt – but Two flew into a rage and damaged my cheek with her finger-daggers.

'What did you expect?' I demanded. It was essential to nip this in the bud. 'You knew when we met that I was seeing your friend. What made you think I'd give her up? If you're going to behave like this, I can't go on seeing you.'

She began weeping and said she was in love with me. Then she made that remark about putting herself in my hands. I should have kicked her out. Instead – why, I don't know – I softened my tone and said, 'She has fallen for me. She wants me to marry her, but you know my feelings . . .' Some minutes passed. Back in bed, the gouges on my cheek still bright with blood, Two said, 'I want to marry you too. You do realise that, don't you?'

So began a period – it did not last long, perhaps four months –

during which, if I am honest, I behaved very badly. I played them off against one another. Rivalry made them all the more ardent. Each wrote me letters which I read aloud to her rival. To each of them I insisted that the other meant nothing, that I no longer slept with her. I stopped protesting when they talked about marriage, I let each believe she was winning. I even spoke of it myself. Neither of them, of course, liked the situation. One, putting on her best brave face, said she felt sorry for Two.

'I saw Two yesterday,' One wrote to me. 'She must hate me. Her face was so hard set, her lips so tight, her hands shook when she lit a cigarette. She was coldly polite . . . You said you had to beware of her, but couldn't remember the expression you wanted so I thought of all the sayings beginning with "Beware" for you. Beware of the Dog? Beware of Pity? Beware the Ides of March? Beware of Greeks bearing gifts (bootleg whisky)? Or Christ, was it, saying "Beware of soothsayers"?'

Two wrote to me, 'Sweetheart, in these last few days something has happened and I find myself so much in love with you and so much wanting to be with you that everything else seems quite unimportant. I've never thought of myself as a particularly selfish person, but now, I want to be wholly selfish and think only of myself . . . For the first time I know what it is going to mean if we lose each other and perhaps for the first time I realise that much unhappiness has to lie ahead for someone anyway . . .'

These letters arrived within days of one another. I put them away in the cardboard box I kept under my bed for such things.

One of them had to go, but which? I had decided to drop Two, with her talent for temper and sulks, when One, without warning, upped the stakes. She came to the flat and let herself in – she had a key, Two did not – and the first I knew of her presence was when she was in my bedroom, laughing, already pulling off her clothes. Later, lying in my arms, she said she had good news.

'Tell me,' I said. I was leaning over her, affectionately tracing her lips with my finger, expecting to hear, I suppose, that her husband was going away again. He often made long trips, during which we could be free. In my mind arose the possibility of whole nights together, perhaps a run down to Goa. Instead she announced that she was pregnant.

I was horrified. I had not believed her capable of such deceit. Why had she stopped taking precautions? I hid my anger as well as I could and explained that marriage at present was impossible. She would have to be patient. Meanwhile I'd take care of things. There would be time in the future for other children.

Two was overjoyed by the news. 'She's scared of losing you,' she said. 'Hey presto, she's with child. Anyway, it couldn't be yours, could it, because you've stopped . . . you know?' There was something very vile about her triumph.

'At least *you've* nothing to worry about,' I told her. 'She won't be speaking to me again. Not after what happened.'

'What?' she demanded. 'Tell me. What happened?'

So I told her. One and I had argued. One grew angry and began yelling, 'What's got into you? Have you gone mad?'

'It's you who are mad,' I told her. 'Do you seriously expect me to marry every woman I sleep with?'

But One did speak to me again. She phoned next day to see if I had changed my mind. I said I refused to be blackmailed. I could hear her crying at the other end of the line. Then she asked in a cold voice if I realised that she would have to have an abortion.

'Do what you need to,' I replied.

There was a long silence, then she spoke my name, the name that means Love, and said, as if chiding a child, 'Darling, please come to your senses. We're talking about your child. Abortions are dangerous. They're illegal, and they're expensive. Surely you don't want to put me through that?'

'If it's a question of money,' I replied, 'I'll pay for it.'

She put down the phone.

Some weeks later I had another call from her over a crackling fading line, interrupted by loud crashes, bangs and booms, as if djinns were shifting boxes around an empty house. She said there was a thunderstorm outside. I could barely hear her voice. She informed me that she was no longer pregnant and – much of the rest was garbled by the bad connection – seemed to be alluding to an obscure legend from the past. But her last words, before she put the phone down, were perfectly clear. 'It's not unborn children, but men like you who deserve to die. I promise you, there will be retribution!'

Two arrived shortly after this, to share an evening with me – arrived with hair in rats' tails, clothes soaked from getting caught in a twilight downpour. I told her about the call.

'Retribution!' she said. 'Is she threatening to kill you?'

I told her how I'd said to One, 'What is this? A death threat? Am I in danger? Should I get a gun and keep it under my bed?'

Two laughed. Nine months passed.

And so I am drawn back, reluctantly, to the moment I have been dreading, to the sea, the crying of birds, and the heat. Lying on my bed, longing for the cool touch of fingers other than my own on my body, I wish that things had turned out differently. With One out of the way, Two has become a bore. She yatters endlessly about marriage, but unlike One, has found no way to twist my arm. I am desperate to be rid of her. I have tried to damp things down. I told her we should test our feelings by not seeing each other for a month. Reluctantly, she agreed. We are halfway through our month apart, but she writes to me every day, her letters growing steadily more desperate, about the futility of continuing in her marriage and how she can't bear the idea of life without me. She is ready, she says, to sacrifice everything, to do something drastic. Her greatest fear is that I no longer want her. Her letters repeat themselves. The last few have gone unopened into the box under my bed. Soon I will have to face Two, endure her rage, her tears and her 'something drastic'. The month is almost over and the evil moment can't much longer be deferred.

Stretched on my bed, what I do not know is that my future has already been decided. Registering a distant ring, I have no inkling of who is at the front door of my flat, is about to open the door of my bedroom, that I will have time only to snatch up a towel before I find myself staring into the black eye of a revolver, that I am already halfway through the last minute of my life.

I MAYA

THE SILVER GANESH (AMBONA, 1958)

My mother Maya, who was a storyteller – her name, aptly, means 'illusion' – used to say that writers have a special responsibility to the world because they have the power to change it. They must be careful how they tell their tales, and to whom, for storytelling is an act whose effects are incalculable and endless.

Only now as I pick up my own fountain-pen do I begin to understand why my mother never told this story herself.

It was always there. I can trace its threads in the pattern of my childhood, as far back as those evenings of the late fifties in India, when Maya was surrounded by her clever friends – artists, musicians, film-makers – in our drawing room full of candles (kept for power cuts, but used regardless) and . . . in my mind's eye I see bottles of wine, but this is the memory playing tricks. Forty years ago there were no Indian wines. Nowadays grapes may grow on the slopes of the Ambona Hills, but in those days an untouched forest covered them, and Maya's guests had to do their merry-making with whisky distilled in Bangalore and obtained, on my father's account, from the naval stores.

Music, laughter, intense discussion, this is what I remember, my mother moving round the room in a silk sari that changed colour as the light caught it, putting a record on the gramophone, pulling a book off a shelf to show someone, holding a match to an incense stick, calling to Yelliya, our surly South Indian cook, to bring the food. Dinner was rarely served before midnight. How

Maya loved those gatherings. She wore a large red kumkum dot in the middle of her forehead and this seemed to accentuate her eyes, which were dark and huge and shone with excitement as she talked. I would creep out of bed and hang, half-hidden in a curtain, watching and listening. I was always caught, of course, and dragged in my pyjamas before the company to be scolded and petted and praised, after which I would be allowed to sit for a while, with a glass of lemon squash, listening to the conversation.

Thinking of the story I have now to begin, a particular night from that time comes to mind; the night my mother told her tale of *The Silver Ganesh*. She was talking to a bear of a man with a beard that lay like a bib upon his chest. He wore the long muslin kurta that is practically a uniform for Bengali intellectuals. A twig-like pipe stuck from his hairy mouth. His name was Babul Roy and I remember thinking how funny it was that they called him 'Bubbles'. Bubbles was in those days an arty and rather unsuccessful film director and Maya was eager to tell him about her new story. (It was her screenplay period, cinema was exciting, Satyajit Ray had just released *Pather Panchali*, two of her scripts had recently made it to the screen.)

'How should we behave,' my mother was saying, 'when we don't know what the result of our actions will be? Not even don't know, *can't* know?'

'You won't catch me with this bait again,' said Bubbles, sucking on his pipe in a way that made it chuckle in sympathy. 'This is your favourite impossible question.'

Catch with this bait . . . ? Did Bubbles really say that? It seems unlikely, but is what comes to mind – my eight-year-old brain was obsessed with fishing. In any case, Maya got what she wanted, which was not an answer, but the chance to launch into her plot.

'Let's make you the hero of the story,' she said. 'One day you leave your house and, outside, find a street-boy being beaten by two policemen. They have tied his wrists to your railings and are thrashing him with lathis. He's the same age as Bhalu here, but a lot smaller. He's howling. His dirty face is streaked with tears. When they see you the policemen stop. You ask what the hell they're doing. They say they are interrogating him because they suspect he *may* be about to break into your house. You, decent soul, are outraged. You order them to release him. They grumble that people like you are the first to complain about crime, and now you're stopping them doing their job. Ten rupees shuts them up.'

'Ten rupees? I wouldn't give those bahinchods ten annas,' said Bubbles.

'Not even ten pice!' I shouted. It was a horrible story. I felt sorry for the boy. I could feel the blows of the policemen's sticks landing on *my* head and back. Bubbles, who had forgotten I was listening, was mortified. He said to me, 'Hey Bhalu, champ, you forget what I just said.'

'He already knows that word,' said my mother. 'You should hear his grandfather. My God! Every second syllable!'

My father's parents had come down from Kumharawa to visit us in Bombay before we moved to the hills. The old man complained about every bahinchod thing. The fruit, the fish, the vegetables. He quarrelled with the bahinchod dhobi and the twice-bahinchod milkman. This isn't the right moment to tell the story about the cow. After they left I missed him horribly, and Maya said she had forgotten how coarse village ways were.

'So, anyway,' she resumed, 'you take the boy inside, and tell your servants to feed him. They, of course, think you've gone mad.'

Bubbles nodded. I was fascinated by the way his pipe shot out little cannonballs of smoke, like the engines that chuffed through Ambona station.

'He eats like the starving animal he is. You ask him about his family, life on the street, but he won't talk. He doesn't trust you. What he does do is ask you for money. You give him five rupees. After he leaves, you discover that your silver Ganesh is missing.'

'And the servants say, "See, I told you so" . . .'

'Your servants urge you to report the theft,' said Maya.

'Otherwise suspicion falls on them.'

'You're angry, of course, about the statue, the boy's contempt for your kindness, but mostly with yourself for being bourgeois enough to think that one decent act can erase a lifetime's brutality. Reluctantly, you go to the police station . . .'

'While you're there the kid and his gang come back and clean out the rest of your silver . . .'

'No, no!' said Maya. Looking back, I see her trying to hide her irritation at these constant and asinine interruptions. Poor woman, she didn't know it, but she was wasting her time. Bubbles Roy would make one more lacklustre 'social' movie before diving into the popular 'filmi' culture of the sixties. Could she have looked ten years ahead and seen the titles on which his director's credit would appear – *Meri Manzil, Gawaar, Sadhu Sadhini*, and the risible but hugely popular *Sheikh Peeru* – she would not have bothered. But we are still in 1958. Everything is possible.

'No, no!' said Maya. 'Wait. A fortnight later the silver statue reappears. No one can explain how, or why. All along, the boy was innocent. You misjudged him, and now you've set the police on his back, with a real crime to bend their lathis on. You feel wretched. You must stop them. You decide to trace the boy, find him before the police do. The foolish hope revives that your kindness may, after all, have made a difference. You tell yourself fate has ordained you to do something *significant* for this child. You fantasise. You'll clothe him, make sure he has enough to eat. Send him to school. Maybe he should live under your roof . . .'

Bubbles was still nodding. Only now does it occur to me that here was the seed for his sentimental and nauseating *Gawaar* (*Yokel*, 1965, Dev Anand stars as a childless philanthropist who, against the wishes of his wife, played by Vijayantimala, adopts an orphaned village boy).

'. . . But first you must find him. You send your servants out looking. They report that he has vanished. You go yourself. But where do you start looking for one small boy in a city like ours?'

'It would make a most cinematic sequence,' said Bubbles, and began to sketch out the camera hunting through angles of light and shade in the hopeless alleys and chawls of back-street Bombay.

'Your search becomes an obsession,' my mother informed him. 'Day after day you return home defeated. You sit and brood. Then, being a storyteller, you sit down at your desk and begin to write. But in your tale it is the *boy* who creeps back to replace the statue before disappearing into the teeming back-streets. In your story too, you begin a search for the boy. Now there are two searches going on. The one in real life and the one in your story. Our movie follows both. We intercut between them . . .'

In my mind's eye I see the boy leave Babul Roy's house with its stone gateposts and creep past the wrought-iron railings where he'd been tied. His wrists are raw, circled by weals raised by the rough coir strands. He peers nervously up and down the street. Maybe the cops waited nearby, went somewhere for tea and paan, biding their time. But the coast is clear. Now that he has escaped, is no longer in the power of the black-bearded man with the weird wooden chillum, he starts to sniffle. His shoulders hurt. There is a lump on his head where the police sticks repeatedly hit. It's painful, a hillock compared to the tiny lumps raised by the sucking of lice, but his fingers can't feel it well under the matted hair. The boy begins to run, looking behind. He is afraid. The police, as they left, threatened to get him. He runs for a few hundred yards along this sedate street, its tall houses growing quietly shabbier, and reaches a main road where the traffic roars. We are near the big market. Men pushing handcarts piled with melons, wooden crates, wicker baskets of chickens, shove through a confusion of bell-jangling bikes, lorries with roped-on loads of sacks and boxes, buses with oily aromatic exhausts, swarms of black and yellow taxis. The boy calls out to a pair of Sikhs who are riding scooters side by side, each with a shalwared, dupatta'd wife side-saddle behind, clinging to his waist, the women facing each other so they can talk. All four ignore him. An old man, lifting the corner of his dhoti clear of the ground, begins to thread a route across the road. The boy darts to his side and uses him as a moving shelter. The old fellow barks at him and the boy grins. On the other side they stand together and something passes between them. I think the old man has given him a coin. The boy walks freely now, and no longer looks behind. Without my knowing how, it has become evening. I follow him along the main road, past the entrance to a busy railway station, where he stops for a moment and speaks to a beggar girl about his own age. She has a sweet face and is wearing a ragged, but clean, red dress. He wanders inside, through the throng of home-bound commuters, onto a platform where a man – he might be drunk, or perhaps dying – lies sprawled, urinating, the pool of his piss spreading away from him. The boy ignores him, skips over the yellow streams and leaves the station by a different exit, emerging onto a lesser road where traffic is passing. A few yards along a man is lying on a step outside a shop, wrapped up for the night in a dirty cotton shroud. He is coughing. The boy takes this street, passing a row of shops selling cheap gold bangles, perfume merchants – all mirrors and Islamic calligraphy – and a clinic where women with covered heads queue patiently to be seen by the compounder. Some hand-carts, like wheeled seesaws, are pulled up by the wall. Perched on the end of one of these, a pretty woman is trying to persuade her baby to drink something from a steel glass. The baby chuckles and throws the glass into the gutter. The woman reaches down, retrieves it, wipes it on her sari and tries again. The baby throws it down. The boy stops, picks up the glass. Is he going to run off with it? He hands it back to the mother. After about a mile he steps into a side lane, its first few dozen yards brightly lit, with shops on either side: cloth merchants, a shop full of pots and pans with a row of aluminium buckets hanging above its entrance, an open-front café from which film music blares, where they are frying pakoras in a huge curved pan. The boy stops, and motions with his hand to his mouth. The cook reaches down with his ladle and flips a pakora sizzling through the air. The boy catches it, cries out in pain, and the man laughs to see him juggling to save it. He continues past a bicycle repair place, a tinsmith, a shop empty save for a fat man in dhoti and vest asleep on a string bed, fingers clasped on his stomach rising and falling with the swell of his belly. Nearby, a child squatting in the gutter is setting fire to some paper, watching the burning flakes float upward. Light from a street-lamp catches her hair, haloing it golden. Further on the shops give way to a row of brick hovels, and the road surface is pitted, muddy, as though the municipality doesn't bother here. There are puddles (it must be monsoon time), his bare feet tread through the slush. He walks without hesitating, a small figure caught now and again in the glow of a street-lamp. His hand goes to his mouth, he is still eating the pakora. There is a haze of woodsmoke in the air. The lamps grow fewer, their dull spillages of light at first one, then two hundred yards apart, until at last they peter out. Now the only illumination is the dim flicker from doorways. People passing are shapes in the gloom. Five men are sitting on a string bed with their knees drawn up, backs to a brick wall, five points of orange fire in the darkness. Somewhere, dogs are snarling. The boy ducks into an alley, a few feet wide, margined by clogged gutters, that leads away between shacks made haphazardly of wood and beaten-out tin cans. Some are roofed with dry coconut fronds weighted down with tyres. Inside one of these, glimpsed by the smoky light of a kerosene lamp, a woman with a cruel face is nursing a baby. In a brighter hut, lit by a naked bulb, a man is chopping meat with a cleaver, casting lumps of flesh into a pile. Shreds hang from his fingers like snot on the nails of an inexpert nose-blower. Blood has pooled on the floor. It trickles out of the open doorway, leaks in black veins into a drain full of furry growths. I notice that where a patch of light falls through a door, the boy steps round it, passes on the shadow side. Some way ahead, a single bulb emits a feeble tobacco glow. Beyond, the alley dwindles to a muddy path and the plank-and-can shacks give way to dwellings hung with rags, plastic sheets and torn sacks. It is becoming hard to see. The boy hurries on, and then he's gone. The alley has come to an end, debouched into darkness. Blind air thick with the stench of garbage reaches my nostrils, and nearby, incongruously, the scent of cobra-jasmine. My eyes acclimatise to a wide, rubbish-strewn space, across which smoke is blowing. Weeds and broken bricks catch my feet as I cross the uneven ground towards a well of deeper darkness, a perfectly round hole in the night. It is the empty mouth of a concrete pipe, a yard across, that must have been lying here a long time, because beneath its curve a lantana bush has grown up. Moths fly up in a cloud from its tiny, bitter flowers . . .

'The poor go unheard,' my mother was saying, 'We know nothing of their lives, but they touch ours at every point. Our stories are rooted in their silence. Our characters enter bearing scars from untold tales and leave to pursue unguessable adventures. So you just can't say, "My story starts here." It's older than you. It has a thousand beginnings, each of them in someone else's life. You can't say, "It ends here." What you do reverberates after you're gone. Who knows where it ends?' She was speaking in Hindi and one phrase sticks clearly in my mind – '*Hamari kahaniyan apné aaramb sé pahlé aaramb hotin hain, aur apné anta ké baad tak jaari rahtin hain*' – 'Our stories begin before their beginnings and continue beyond their ends.' Switching to English, she added, 'Really there are no individual stories, only *the* story, coiling and weaving through all our lives.'

'What do *you* say, Bhalu?' asked Bubbles, turning to me. 'Is your mother right? Does what she's saying apply to all stories, or only to true stories? What about fiction? What about a story that deliberately tells lies? What about fairy tales?'

I thought about this for a long time, then said, 'I don't know, Uncle. What is the answer?' Bubbles laughed so much he had a coughing fit and had to give his pipe to Maya to hold. It was in her hand when she led me back to my bed. As we went I could hear Bubbles still laughing and the boom of his voice.

'What is the answer? Wah! Such innocence!'

Such innocence! It ought to be my epitaph. I was in awe of my beautiful, clever mother and it took me a long time to realise that she was not as brilliant and successful as I imagined her to be. Her aphorisms, which sounded profound to a child, and inspired loyalty enough to figure in the diaries of my student years, came gradually to seem like old lovers for whom one can remember having felt passion, but not why.

'The past is never finished with,' she once told me, 'because the present is its perpetually unfolding consequence.'

I remember all Maya's stories, but the one I loved best – it still moves and horrifies me – was *Silver Ganesh*. I don't mean the film they made of it, *Doraaha* (*Two Ways*, 1962 – not, incidentally, directed by Bubbles Roy), but the tale as told that night in Ambona more than forty years ago. It haunts me, the image of that child walking alone into the dark. For years I have followed him in dreams and in obscure byways of the waking imagination. Always, I lose him. Always, the blackness is pricked by points of wavering light and I find myself back in our candle-lit drawing room, with its book-lined walls, Persian carpets, and carvings that were once part of Goan churches and South Indian temples; back among the chink of glasses and the sweet smoke of cobra jasmine.

Maya would later claim that she had based her screenplay on something a friend had told her, and couldn't remember whether the whole thing had been invented, but in truth I no longer recall more than a few images she conjured that night for Bubbles Roy.

When I think of that boy now, it's my own memories I see.

BURNING ANGEL (LEWES/LONDON, SEPTEMBER 1998)

I was making a cup of tea in my bookshop in Lewes (if you know the High Street you would recognise it at once, it is one of those crooked timber houses made from the bones of old sailing ships, more or less opposite the castle), when the phone rang. It was Maya, to tell me about an interesting new play at the Royal Court. As an afterthought, she informed me that she was dying.

'I don't want you to make a fuss, Bhalu,' she said, not giving me a chance to interject. 'These things happen. As I was saying, it's just the author on stage talking about his visit to Palestine and the people he met. Jew and Arab both.'

'Oh!'

'If it's any good, I'll write to Zafyque. He could adapt it for Bombay—'

'Wait!'

My immediate thought was that she was testing my powers of repartee. It may seem odd to have had such a consideration at such a moment, but my mother had a wicked streak of — what? Humour? Mischief? She loved saying things to cause commotion and I could never be sure, when she behaved outrageously, whether she was being droll, or engaging in some subtle form of banter and I had missed the point. She was notorious for spiking conversations, when talking to people she disliked or who were boring her, with what she called 'durrellisms' — remarks like 'We live by selected fictions,' or 'Truth is what most contradicts itself in time'

– always adding with a sweet smile, 'Don't you agree?' She once gave my father, who prided himself on being an expert crossword solver, a cryptic clue, something like 'Backwards leaning platonic in catastrophic endgame (8–3),' and watched him puzzle over it for three months. There was of course no answer. Shortly before we moved to the forest-covered hills of Ambona, my father joined the Bombay Natural History Society and attended lectures on birdspotting. Maya found this hugely amusing. 'What's that?' she would ask, pointing to a tree, in order to hear him reply, 'Oh, just some sort of brown bird.'

She had decided that I must be educated properly, which to her meant the Russian authors. (India was in the honeymoon stage of its affair with the Soviet Union.) We had Russian children's books, and I know Russian tales – *Baba Yaga the Witch*, *The Malachite Casket*, *The Adventures of Dunno* – far better than the Brothers Grimm. At the age of eight she started me on Gorky and when I complained that *Childhood* was depressing (it opened with a funeral) she said sharply, 'Don't be so childish!' then broke into giggles and said, 'Oh, but I keep forgetting, you *are* a child!' Paradoxically, as I grew older she perfected the knack of making me feel more and more like one. All of these things were subsumed in my replies of, 'Oh!' and 'Wait!' Then I collected myself and said, 'What do you mean, these things happen? This isn't exactly an everyday occurrence.'

'I told you I don't want a fuss,' said my mother, with a testy edge to her voice. 'I was not feeling well. In my dream a burning angel folded me in its wings . . .' She allowed a silence to let this enigmatic statement sink in and then, to my astonishment said, 'Bhalu, you remember when Zafyque came to London and told us about the riots? All those years he'd lived in Bombay, it was the first time he'd ever felt unsafe—'

'Maya!'

'—the mobs were going to areas like Malabar Hill looking for Muslims. Poor Zafyque kept an iron bar by the door of his flat.'

'Oh, Zafyque is all actor,' I said sourly, remembering the visit, his insistence that we all go to see a trans-gender *Othello* in which the Moor was played by a petite actress, and how ludicrous was the scene where she smothered a hulking male Desdemona:

DESDEMONA: (*bass-voiced, blond-bearded, in striped pyjamas*)
   O, banish me, my lady, but kill me not!
OTHELLO: (*slim, wearing lacy negligée, brandishing pillow*)
   Down, strumpet!

and how Zafyque had entertained us all in the trattoria afterwards by flirting with the waitress in what he imagined to be an Italian accent. As Maya segued into memories of Bombay in the mid-fifties, when she had been a member of Zafyque's Theatre Troupe, my feelings were a mixture of irritation, worry, resentment and relief. When my mother babbled, it meant she was invoking a *tabu* and the real, forbidden subject must not be mentioned, except on her terms. Thus had it always been. We must never, for example, allude to her strange marriage. Although she had not lived with my father for twenty-five years, and had clapped eyes on him only once in the last dozen, they were still officially man and wife. In the early seventies she had followed me and my sisters to England, where we had been sent for our education, on the grounds that children should not be in a strange country without a parent, but when Suki, the youngest, graduated, she showed no sign of wanting to leave, thus effectively making sure that we also stayed. Such violent upheavals in a family do not occur without reason, but what the reason was she would never tell us, save only that after two decades of marriage she had tired of my father's irritating habit of stroking his moustache, his obsession with roses and his lack of interest in his children. She had not sought a divorce, she said, because it was unthinkable in our family. There was no more she would say on the subject, except to drop the occasional grenade.

'Your father has got a woman!' she announced once, when we were gathered for lunch at her flat. 'Homi wrote to warn me. What should I do?'

'Go back and be a wife to him?' my sister Suki suggested. She had always had a soft spot for poor old Captain Sahib. But Maya glared and the discussion was guillotined. She had never, so far as we knew, taken a lover herself, although one of her closest friends was an elderly Greek gentleman, a Mr Sefiriades, an expert in early Christian apocrypha, with whom she lunched regularly and had once joined on an over-sixties' cruise to Ephesus and Patmos, 'Separate cabins, no hanky panky'.

So I did not know what to make of this latest drama except that it was probably another false alarm. I remember her phoning once in the middle of the night screaming that the man downstairs was trying to break into her flat. In fact the poor chap was ringing her bell and banging desperately on her door to tell her she had left her bath running and it was about to bring his ceiling down.

'Anyway,' said my mother, 'I can't stay here talking, Marjorie's coming to lunch. Come and see me.' Click. Whirrr.

*　　*　　*

I reached London in the grey pigeon-light of a September dusk. Maya's flat was in one of those overheated mansion blocks round the back of Sloane Square. Coming out of the tube station I saw the Royal Court was running a play called *Via Dolorosa* and wondered if it was the one she had mentioned. I would have gone over, but the foyer was full of smart people and I was suddenly aware of being still in my bookseller's gear, baggy jumper holed at the elbows, trousers with knees like ears. I hate being conspicuous. If I had been wearing a suit and the theatre had been thronged with shabby second-hand booksellers I would still have avoided it.

I knocked and let myself into Maya's flat, and found her sitting up in bed flicking through a magazine. She was wearing lipstick, as if expecting visitors. Her eyes were made up as they had been ever since I could remember, swipes of kohl lifting the outer edges to emphasise their hugeness. I had always thought this made her beautiful when she was young; it did not seem incongruous at seventy-six, although her hair was white and there were deep lines running down either side of her mouth. She looked up, and performed a small moue of unexpected pleasure.

'So you have come.'

'Well, naturally. What did you expect?'

She offered her cheek to be kissed. I perched on her bed and held out the bunch of flowers I had bought at the tube station, a spray of freesias wrapped in cellophane.

'How lovely,' she said, not taking them. 'Put them in some water. You'll find a vase in the kitchen.'

With what adeptness she could turn me back into a small boy, stupid and awkward, always doing the wrong thing. I found a pot, sluiced some water in and stood the flowers on her bedside table.

She leaned over and wrinkled her nose. 'Wonderful. It always reminds me of *mogri*. You remember there was a wild one growing by the door in Ambona and it perfumed the whole house.'

There seemed nothing wrong with her and again I felt that familiar mixture of irritation and relief.

'Come nearer.' Her kiss settled like a fly on my cheek. 'I don't want you to be upset,' she said. 'That's not why I telephoned. But I wanted to see you. How are Katy and the lovely I & I?'

'Katy sends her love.' Our twin daughters were in Greece. I & I. Imogen and Isobel. We'd had a postcard from Crete. 'Maya, what has happened?'

She sighed and leaned back on her pillows, shading her eyes as if the light hurt them. 'Now Bhalu, please, no fuss. You know how I hate all that *blather*. As a matter of fact, I want to discuss my will.'

She must have misinterpreted my expression, because she said, 'Don't look so horrified. It's a good Hindu tradition to execute your will *before* you die. The idea is to get rid of all your *stuff*, make sure your duties are done. To depart without leaving a trace.'

'You're not departing. You've just had flu.'

'Your sisters are coming over later. We'll settle who's having what and you can start taking it away. All these things,' she said, waving her arm. 'I want them all gone.'

I looked round the shabby room, full of relics of her past. It was furnished in a stubbornly Indian manner, as if she were trying to pretend she had not spent the last quarter of a century in

England. From one corner, perched on a carved pillar, a gilded angel stared at us, its hands thrust forward cupping nothingness. Once they had held a beeswax candle to light a Goan church. Beside it, on a small table, stood a cage from which came a sudden scutter of wings. For as long as I could remember, my mother had kept bulbuls. She played old gramophone records to them, hoping that one day they might open their beaks and sing like Bhimsen Joshi. It occurred to me that these things had combined to fan her fever into a nightmare.

'I'll move the candlestick. Let me put it in the other room.'

'Take it away with you,' she said. 'I want you and Katy to have it anyway . . . Great-grandfather's case of butterflies, take that too. I'm leaving Khurram and Mumtaz in your care. Promise you'll look after them.' Her bulbuls. 'But leave them until *after* I'm gone.'

I can't bear to cage birds. If they really did outlive her, they could take their chances in the Sussex woods.

'Maya, why are you so sure that——?'

She said, 'Don't start again. I warned you not to get upset.'

'I'm not upset. I want to know what the doctor said.'

'I have already told you.' She picked up her magazine. It was one of the Indian titles – *Stardust*, *Filmfare* – she had delivered from the ABC in Southall, 'to keep track of my friends in the monkey business', by which she meant the Bombay movie industry. 'People from a time when Indian cinema could have become something worthwhile,' she used to say. 'Before all this Bollywood nonsense.' Most of the people she had known, however, Shailendra, Guru Dutt, A.K. Abbas, Bubbles Roy, were dead.

'Pan made a fuss too,' said Maya. Panaghiotis Sefiriades, her

Greek boyfriend. Extraordinary that she should have given him her news before her children. 'When I told him he urged me to pray.'

'Maya, I don't believe you've seen a doctor.'

'We Hindus don't have the comfort of the confessional and wiping the slate clean at a stroke. It isn't that simple. I have never understood the store that Christians set by sincerity of repentance. Sincerity changes nothing. It's insulting. What use is regret when one's actions are already at work in the world? I told Pan, it is not dying that frightens me, but thinking of what I've set in train. Things done, things undone.'

'You haven't seen a doctor, have you?'

She sighed. 'Honestly, Bhalu, it's impossible to discuss anything with you. As a matter of fact he was here this morning.'

'What did he say?'

'He told me what I told you.'

'I mean, what was his diagnosis? What is wrong?'

'I don't know.'

'How on earth can you not know?'

'I didn't ask. I don't want to know. I said to him, "Are you sure? Is there any possibility of a mistake?" And he said no. So that was that. That's all.'

'Surely something can be done. A second opinion, if we know what's wrong.'

'What is wrong? Why do you keep on asking what is wrong? Nothing is wrong. I'm seventy-six. Isn't that enough?'

'Grandfather lived to be ninety-six.'

'Yes and you know what they used to say in Kumharawa?' she retorted. 'That the old man lived so long because he was so fond of you. He was hanging on, waiting for your visits, which never came. And when you did go it was because he'd given up.'

My grandfather's funeral, twelve years earlier, was the last time either of us had seen my father.

'This is ridiculous,' I said, determined not to let her change the subject. 'I've never heard of a doctor making such pronouncements without a second opinion. You say he came here? What tests did he perform?'

'He felt my pulse.'

'Hardly conclusive.'

'And read my palm,' said my mother defiantly.

'My God!' I suddenly realised what she had done. 'You called in Srinuji.'

'Well, of course. I had a fever and that dream – an angel with wings of fire. I had a headache like monkeys crouched on each shoulder pounding nails into my skull. Look!' She leaned forward. 'One on this side, one on that. Little faces fringed with fur. Nasty sharp teeth. Small orange eyes.'

'Srinuji! What did he do, chant mantras over you?'

'Their nails, I fancy, punch neat holes through which ideas leak away. There are worrying blanks in my thoughts, sometimes even in sentences. A word I have known all my life is no longer there when I need it. There are gaps in memory too.'

'Let me call the doctor,' I said, getting up to do so.

'What for? I am taking Srinuji's *ghee naswaar*.'

'Oh, for God's sake. I meant your real doctor.'

'Real? You mean western? What does he know about medicine?'

'You could at least let him take a look.'

'Don't be silly,' she said. 'There is nothing he can do.'

'He could give you some pills for your headache.'

Maya hunched her shoulders and lowered her head to hide her face. Her body began to shake. It took me a few seconds to work out that she was laughing.

'Oh Bhalu, you are so funny. Pills for my headache! And please tell me, what pills will he give for my karma?'

Srinuji was her astrologer, an elderly, bleary person who moved in a pother of stars and planets, aspects, ascendants and exaltations, and was held by her in unfathomable regard. His pudding-basin belly rode on two stick legs. Trousers belted tightly just beneath the breast pocket swallowed up most of his shirt front. A scrawny neck and thrust-forward head, mouth often crimsoned by paan, gave him the air of a short-sighted but blood-thirsty tortoise with its shell on back-to-front. He had originally been her accountant, but as he aged and his interests inclined more and more to the supernatural he started offering his clients mystical as well as financial consultations. Maya took to asking his advice about her personal affairs and when my sisters and I protested she said, 'I won't allow you to laugh at him. He is a remarkable man.'

Certainly he was, and became more so. He grew the moustache and straggly beard of a tortoise patriarch, abandoned his cheap jacket and shabby overcoat (which used to make him look like one of those old Asian men you see sitting on benches in Southall, lost in baffled contemplation of their cold, grey lives), threw a shawl round his shoulders like a Himalayan baba and began wearing a necklace of rudhraksh beads wrinkled as scrotums.

Over the last few years Srinuji had come to see himself as the spiritual godfather of our family. We would receive cards at Holi, Diwali and New Year, always signed 'Srijunis'. My sisters and I learned to feel dismay whenever his name was mentioned, yet my mother had a great deal of time for him and introduced him to Panaghiotis, who also seemed to find much in him to respect.

'Pan says Srinuji is a gymnosophist,' Maya told us.

'What does he mean by that?'

'I have no idea at all,' she replied, smiling.

Never underestimate the resources of a bookseller. A quick forage through my shelves produced a tatty volume of the *OED*. (The compact edition, micrographically reproduced four-pages-to-a-page, cocked spine, bumped corners, sadly minus magnifying glass – lor, the work involved in cataloguing my so-called best stock.) The magnifying glass being lost, I deciphered the tiny text with the help of a milk bottle, found in the kitchen at the back of the shop, which had first to be rinsed and then held, half-full of water, at a tilt above the page. Of course it dripped, thereby further diminishing the book's value, but revealed that the gymnosophists were 'a sect of ancient Hindu philosophers of ascetic habits (known to the Greeks from the reports of the companions of Alexander) who wore little or no clothing, denied themselves meat and gave themselves up to mystical contemplation'; none of which shed any light on the enigma of Srinuji (who I could not imagine naked or performing yoga), nor explained his hold over my mother. Then one day the mystery was solved. I let myself in to Maya's flat and discovered them sitting on the sofa side by side. They leapt apart and I thought, Oh, surely not! Not Srinuji! But Maya explained in a rather embarrassed voice that he had asked to hear some of her poems.

'I had no idea you were interested in poetry,' I said. I had always imagined Srinuji's reading stopped at shastras and tantras and magazines like *The Urinologist*.

'Your mother is a great woman!' he exclaimed. 'It is a privilege to sit at the feet of someone who has achieved so much. Who has known the great ones of our culture.'

So that was it. A writer who had abruptly stopped work at the very edge of success and produced nothing new for twenty years had at last found an audience in this solitary fan.

'I'm afraid I have been boring Mr Srinuji with my stories of long ago,' said Maya.

He laid his hand on hers. 'Maya-ji, you are incapable of being boring.'

But there was something else, unsaid, between them . . .

Recently, he had made the baffling decision to shave off his moustache. The combination of naked upper lip and beard, a style favoured by Muslims, all but unknown among Hindus, made him more peculiar than ever.

'I won't allow you to laugh at Srinuji,' my mother had once said. Now she was sitting up in bed, laughing at me.

'You are an appalling woman.'

This seemed to strike her as even funnier. She laughed until she was sobbing, heehawing for breath, and the gasps caught in her throat and turned into a fit of coughing. 'Oh, oh, oh . . . Bhalu, you are a great fool. Just like your father – that's what he used to say.'

'All this tamaasha turns out to be only Srinuji!'

This set her off again. Eventually she found a handkerchief and blew her nose. 'Poor Srinuji. Of course! It's his fault that I am ill. He must be more careful in future. If Katy falls off her horse tomorrow, or if you catch cold, he'll be to blame.'

'Don't be silly, Mother. It's Srinuji who has made you believe, if you really do, that you are . . . that you're . . .'

'Bhalu, if you dislike tamaasha, don't create one.' (Tamaasha, used in Hindi/Urdu to signify ado-about-nothing, a stagy uproar.)

'Well, *I'm* not the one who's behaving irrationally.'

'I didn't want a fuss. I detest hysterics,' she said, picking up a hand-mirror and peering at it to check whether the kohl had run from her eyes. 'What possible good can it do, all that rushing around, hair-tearing and hullabaloo? It robs one of dignity and makes a difficult thing harder to bear.' She folded her hanky, drew one corner into a peak, licked it, and applied it to a smudge.

Was that a hint of tears? She could be such an actress. After her peculiar phone call I'd rung Katy and told her what had happened, that I was catching the next train to London and would probably stay the night with one of my sisters. 'Do you think she's really ill?' asked Katy, with the scepticism of one who had been Maya's daughter-in-law for twenty-two years.

So I looked at my mother, who had composed herself on her pillows like a small, outraged but defiant, owl.

'Sorry, Ma, no sympathy. See a proper doctor, or don't expect me to believe you're . . .'

'I'm what? What upsets you more? That word you can't utter? Or that I made the vulgar error of telling you?'

'Don't be like that.'

'I thought you'd want to come and see me. So sorry to waste your time. Mr Very Important Bookseller.'

'Oh please!' I said. Let her not start about bookselling. 'I came running, didn't I, when I got your call? But you must see, this stuff of Srinuji's, karma, palm-readings . . .'

'One day, Bhalu, you'll realise what a friend Srinuji has been to this family.'

'Ah yes, the family witchdoctor.'

'As for karma, you of all people should know what I mean.'

'I've never understood.'

'Poor boy, my karma is this room and everything in it. Which includes you . . . And now, as my eldest son, it's your duty to make sure my wishes are honoured. It's not much to ask. I'm doing you a favour by dying in England. You realise that if we were still in India you'd have to crack my skull.'

'You are incorrigible.'

'You think I'm joking? Don't tell me you've forgotten Grandfather's funeral.'

'As you please,' I said stiffly.

After this we sat in a silence broken only by intermittent and dispirited whistling from the bulbuls in their cage. Outside, it had grown dark. I went and stood at the window. From its bay I could see the lights of the theatre, the crowd on the pavement outside. A taxi with a yellow cyclops-eye turned into the square followed by another, its eye put out, which pulled up below. I wondered if it would disgorge my sisters. If they came soon I could still get a train back to Sussex. But a young couple got out.

A curious keening made me turn. Maya was humming.

'Bhalu, can you guess what's been running through my head all day?'

'No.'

'You really can't guess? Shall I tell you?'

I was expecting a line from Ghalib, or perhaps something from Tolstoy, or the Upanishads. Instead she sang: 'O doctor I'm in trouble! Well, goodness gracious me!'

Placing one finger on the point of her chin, she cocked her head, simpered, and gave an astonishing display of eye-rolling.

'My heart goes boompity boomputty boompity boomputty boompity boomputty boomboomboom . . .'

'You are a complete disgrace.'

'O from Delhi to Darjeeling I have done my share of healing
And I never once was beaten or flumm-o-o-o-o-oxed . . .'

She would sing this song to us when we were small, and had fevers, or toothache, or when we fell over and hurt ourselves.

'I remember how with *wunjab* of my needle in the *Punjab*
I cleared up beri-beri and the dreaded dysentery,
But your complaint has got me truly foxed!'

In spite of everything, my feelings rose up and overwhelmed me. I couldn't help it, I never could be cross with her for long. I put my arms round her, hugged her. She looked pleased. I said, 'Now, Mother, no more silliness. Let's talk about getting you better.'

She drew my head to her shoulder and stroked my hair as if I were a child. 'So, so serious, Bhalu,' she said. 'So stiff, so solemn. You always were, even as a little boy.'

What was I to do with her?

*   *   *

My mother had a Hindu mind, her world organised with that genius for taxonomy which has minutely subcategorised everything from music to lovemaking – she told me once that she imagined the hordes of Hindu deities arrayed in rows, each god and goddess in its own little jar, like a spice, with its own special virtue, Laxmi for money, Ganesh for luck, Saraswati for skill with the pen – but she was unorthodox to the extreme and loved to present herself as an enigma. For example, she claimed to be an atheist, but put in daily requests to Ganesh, denying that this amounted to prayer. 'It's not that I *believe* in him, it's just that my wishes always seem to be granted.'

Maya did not see such statements as contradictions, which, in any case, she regarded as trifling obstacles to understanding. We would often hear raised voices from the room she used as an office, and it would be Maya arguing *both* sides of the case with equal vehemence. If the imagined adversary was a man, she would even put on a gruff voice to make his points. When we teased her about talking to herself, she claimed that the creatures of a writer's imagination could not be counted as self, and *besides*, she was the only person she knew capable of giving her an intelligent debate.

Among the many odd things she wished me to inherit, besides bulbuls and the case of fading butterflies that had once belonged to my great-grandfather, the Kotwal, was her view of history as a cascade of consequences. She did not believe in past lives or in the conventional Hindu notion of paying in the next life for the sins of this one. For her, karma was experienced every second, here and now, because our lives are the continuously unfolding effect of all the caroming actions ever performed by ourselves and our forbears. 'We are born with free will, but are forced to expend it trying to *un-live* the lives of our predecessors.'

Maya worried about our family legends as if they still haunted us, in which case we had much to fear. To her, the stories of our selfless servant Lajju, and of Nafísa Jaan, who was killed for being too lovely to let go (the Kotwal Sahib's butterfly collection having been started for much the same reason) were not just tales of long ago but dark eddies in the blood.

'If Lajju had not picked you up and carried you despite the bullet in him, if Nafísa hadn't fallen in love, a luxury a woman in her profession could hardly afford . . .' She rarely noticed that she said 'picked *you* up', whereas the ten-year-old boy Lajju was said to have rescued from the British on a battlefield in 1858 had actually been my great-great-grandfather . . .

'If Grandfather's first wife hadn't come from a house full of smoke that ruined her lungs, she wouldn't have died young, he wouldn't have married again, and your father wouldn't have been born. If a scorpion hadn't fallen onto your father's stomach as he slept in the courtyard – the night sky in Kumharawa is really quite luminous – and stung him fourteen times because he foolishly rolled on it – but of course he was in agony, a line of punctures, like pits of fire – he would not have been rushed to Lucknow to Doctor Sahib, and wouldn't have met me. So you see, Bhalu, you owe your life to smoke and a scorpion.'

She might as well have added, since many years would intervene between that meeting and their marriage, that had the gunners on the *Scharnhorst* been more accurate, had they used their radar instead of aiming at British gun-flashes in the nacht and nebel of the North Cape, they might have sunk my father's cruiser during the war (Boxing Day 1943) and with it his as yet unimagined and unconceived heir.

She had always been a law unto herself. When it suited her she could be thoroughly old-fashioned (deciding that her will should be executed while she was still alive) but was modern enough to have abandoned my father at a time when divorce was all but unthinkable for Indian women. She had been as daring, thirty years earlier, in making a love marriage. She met my father at the house of his uncle the Lucknow doctor, and straight away set her cap at him, a most unladylike thing to do, but as she told it, she was due to start at Isabella Thoburn College, reckoned herself the equal of any man and, besides, had chosen well, for Captain Sahib had the right caste and family background with prospects that any in-laws could wish. He was about to join the Royal Indian Navy, one of the first Indians to be selected as an officer and be sent for training in England. This was 1938, and it had taken eighty years and five generations for our family to go from being rebels to loyal servants of the Crown. Maya taught me the dates of my ancestors like a history teacher rehearsing parades of kings and viceroys. I still have a school 'copy' in which she had listed, for some reason reversing conventional order:

Bhalu the Great	— *1950–?*	*You*
Captain Sahib	— *1918–?*	*Father*
Bahadur Sahib	— *1890–?*	*Grandfather*
Kotwal Sahib	— *1865–1940*	*Great-grandfather*
Bhalu the First	— *1847–1915*	*Great-great-grandfather*
Panchhazari Sahib	— *1823–1888*	*Great-great-great-grandfather*

Maya knew all their stories. I remember thinking how strange and sad it was that the familiar bugle call that floated out over the

Bombay docks at sunset (this was before we moved to Ambona), and which signalled bedtime and stories to me, was the identical sound the shivering child of a century earlier must have heard rising from the enemy lines on the eve of the battle that would alter all our destinies. Was it also his bedtime? With what stories did Lajju stop his ears? Did the boy pray for his father and Lajju not to be killed next morning? With clenched fists and tightly shut eyes, already knowing how the story ended, I used to wish backwards through time for his prayers to be answered because Maya had taught me that time is an illusion and since history, or karma, as she thought of it, exists only in what currently manifests, it can be *undone*.

'There is no past,' she said, 'because all its effects are with us now. Only appearance changes, underlying reality does not.'

No doubt this is why she called me Balachandra, and gave me the same nickname that long-ago Lajju affectionately bestowed on that other small boy, who had begged to accompany his father to war.

Bhalu, known to his playmates from an early age as Bhola Bhalu. Bhalu the Innocent. Bhalu the Fool.

'The money is equally divided,' said Maya. 'There isn't much left, but the flat will be worth a bit. My gold jewellery will go to the girls, I don't expect Katy would like it. She gets my good Kashmiri shawl. I've left the painting of the old nawab to Suki, because she loved it as a child. The clock with the silver pomegranates I thought Ninu would like. I'm leaving you my books. Try not to sell them all at once.'

'Of course not.'

'You promise?'

'If you insist.'

'My books are old friends. Many of them were *written* by old friends. Bhalu! Next door in the bookcase is Mulk's *Untouchable*. Would you mind . . . ? And while you're there,' she called after me, 'get me a rum! . . . Oh, don't be so stuffy, Bhalu. There are limes in the kitchen. Make us both one.'

So I brought her rum the way she liked it, the old Navy way, with sugar, lime-juice and hot water in a jug, and she sent me back to her bookshelves for Gorky and Ismat Chughtai, Tolstoy, Manto and Lawrence, Faulkner and Qurratulain Hyder. The piles of books mounted. She laid them out on the bed, ran her fingers with fondness over them (most, noted the bookseller's covetous eye, in their original paper jackets).

Soon she was transported back to that world she had loved and left behind. Picking up a book with a bright flourish of Urdu on the cover, she cried, 'Look at this! Majrooh's *Ghazals*! I knew him when he was beginning to make a name for himself as a lyricist in the movies. One used to meet everyone at parties. There were endless parties in those days. My God, how people drank. Everyone had told Majrooh that a poet couldn't make a living in Bombay. He was successful, but would still get depressed. People would protest, "But Majrooh sahib, you are doing so well." He would always quote a line of Kabir's: "I am selling mirrors in the city of the blind". They sing his songs still, but nobody remembers his books.'

As well as the film crowd (Charles Subramanium, who staged a bizarre public celebration of his wife's infidelities, Shankar Rao, who threw a jug of orange squash over the Education Minister for saying that Meena was a worse actress than Nargis), she had known many writers of the time.

'Hai, Qurru! We were together at Isabella Thoburn College. So young when she made a name for herself. And a woman! And look, here's Ismat, who wrote *Lihaaf* and was prosecuted by the British for obscenity. What a victory that was – delicious to think that we had stepped into the modern age while our rulers were still in the Victorian era. It took the British sixteen more years to decide that their wives and servants could be permitted to read *Lady Chatterley . . .*'

She talked and talked, about India, incidents and anecdotes, people she'd known, always about the past, the life that had ended in 1973, the year she left. Most of it I had heard before. Lately, like many old people, she had developed the habit of repeating herself, but listening to her, as she caressed her books and told their stories, I was struck by how passionately she had lived.

'Sometimes I think it would have been better if the British had never left. While they remained, they united us against them. We had purpose, a sense of destiny. So exhilarating. *Inqilaab* (revolution) was in the air, victory round the corner . . . then along came Independence and ruined everything. Partition was the Crown's final act of revenge for 1857. Bhalu, did you ever read Jyoti Bhatt's story, *Vengeance*? No? During the riots of 1947 a very, very ancient man remembers his grandfather, who'd fought in the Mutiny, describing how Hindus and Muslims stood side by side in 1857, and how the British took revenge for Kanpur, or Cawnpore as they called it, by blowing people from the mouths of cannons, forcing them to lick blood from the road – why do you think Thrice-Great had to hide in the jungle? – the old man's grandfather said that after 1857 the British worked to drive a wedge between Hindus and Muslims, and that their cruellest revenge was to pass an Act in 1903 partitioning the Hindustani language, which was a richly polyglot tongue, into Urdu and Hindi. Urdu for Muslims, Hindi for Hindus. All traces of Persian and Arabic were to be eradicated from Hindi, and of Sanskrit from Urdu. Thus the common language, which had evolved to unite us, became a tool of division. But peering out of his window at the flames and mobs of 1947, the old man concludes that his grandfather was wrong, because the last revenge of the British Sarkar was the horrifying things happening in the lane outside his door.

'Imagine, Bhalu, the lunatic irresponsibility of it. Someone draws a line on a map and one morning millions of people wake up to find themselves on the wrong side of a new border. Could no one have predicted that they would panic? Were they expected to abandon homes, fields, cattle, jobs, friends, children's education? Were the British really surprised when Hindus and Muslims who'd lived side by side for years were filled with fear, or madness, and began cutting one another's throats?

'Across the fields of blood each side stared at the other. How had one become two? Everyone had friends on the other side. Why was it happening? Gandhi went on a fast to the death and at last the killing stopped. Would it resume? Was it enough? Then – three shots in a temple garden – and Gandhi himself was gone.

'The miracle really is that we recovered. But what else? We were young, and ahead was nothing but the future. Our country had been torn in two, yet we'd build a great future in the half that was left to us. We must bring about a healing. During the fifties everything blossomed. We could reach people, talk to them, via the cinema. The first real proletarian art form. So exciting. Oh, in those days how I wrote, wrote, wrote. I was always tapping something on a typewriter. And you know, our work wasn't mere entertainment. It was dedicated to those things that nowadays sound so fustian, like justice and compassion. Above all, peace.

'We vowed that the bad times would never return, but now it is happening again in Bombay. So we failed. And who is left to speak out against it? In those days, so many people wrote on this theme. Listen to their names, even their names make a poem: Qurratulain Hyder, Ismat Chughtai, Mulk Raj Anand, Majrooh Sultanpuri, Kaifi Azmi, Krishan Chander, Khwaja Ahmed Abbas, Rajinder Singh Bedi, Firaq Gorakhpuri, Josh Malihabadi, Faiz Ahmed Faiz, Ali Sardar Jafry, and of course, the unforgettable Manto . . . If the tears of poets could heal wounds, there would be no India and no Pakistan, we would all be living in Toba Tek Singh . . .'

Writing this, and I've kept it to her part of the conversation because my own was largely interjectory, I am surprised to realise how hard all this would be to explain even to my own children, neither of whom can speak a word of Hindi, and who know little enough about life in India and Pakistan, let alone a congerie of poets and writers, most of them unknown in the West, from half a century ago. I would have to explain that Toba Tek Singh was a village in an Urdu short story by Saadat Hasan Manto, his most famous story, in which the governments of the new nations of India and Pakistan decide that having exchanged refugees, they must also exchange inmates of insane asylums.

'If we're going to talk about Manto,' said Maya, 'we ought to have another rum.'

So we sat and got quietly 'rummed-up' together – that was the old Bombay phrase – and we raised a glass to Manto's memory and Maya said he was the finest short story writer that ever lifted a pen. 'Better than Maupassant, better than O. Henry.'

Manto was a genius. It is said that, in his later days he would take a tonga (horse-drawn cab) to his publisher's office, ask for a pencil and sit there until he had written three or four stories, for which he invariably demanded to be paid on the spot. He would then take the tonga, which was waiting outside (he always hired them by the day), to the nearest liquor shop. He died aged forty-three after composing his own epitaph: 'Here, under tons of earth lies Saadat Hasan Manto, with all the secrets of storytelling buried in his breast, and the question still unresolved as to who is the better short story writer – he or God.'

'Hai,' said Maya. 'No one will ever ask that about me.'

Why then had she stopped writing? This was the big mystery of her life. She might have had success, might even have earned a place in that list of names. Whence came the bitterness that she packed so carefully along with her books and her carvings and furniture when she left India?

'You should have stayed,' I said. Then asked, as my sisters and I so often had before, 'Why did you leave?'

She was silent.

'You gave up everything, your work, your friends.'

Silence.

Why did you leave? Why didn't you go back? How many times had we asked these questions? How many different answers? . . . I didn't plan to stay on, it just happened. (Incredible. One does not lightly give up husband, friends and career.) After a while there was nothing to go back for. (Begging the question.) I thought I'd make a better career in England. (Nonsense, she was lost. She did a bit of journalism, and some writing on Indian cookery.) Once you married an English girl I knew our future would be here. (Why? There were lots of Englishwomen in India. Hadn't one of her best friends been English?)

After the twins were born, I'd suggested to Katy that we might try living in India. Maya was horrified.

'You're going to ask that poor girl to take her young babies to a country where if you want unwatered milk you have to keep a cow? Does she like cockroaches? Where will she ride in Bombay? Englishwomen have a rough time in India.'

'What about your friend?' I'd asked. 'Your English friend?'

'That's how I know.'

None of these answers stacked up. Now she sat, cradling her glass, staring into the distance. What was she thinking about? Manto? Her lost career? We were both getting drunk.

I remembered a thing Srinuji had once told me. 'Your mother

has made great sacrifices.' (Never said what these might have been.) 'She's had many disappointments in her life.' (By which I assumed he meant me.) 'Whatever I can do, in my own small way, to ease the passage,' he had added as if he were tackling an ugly case of piles, 'that I do and do gladly.'

I knew at least what Maya must have said about me: 'Bhalu is a strange boy. Nearly fifty, yet I find it impossible to think of him in other terms. So awkward, so shabby, why has he buried himself in that bookshop? He could have done something useful with his life. He grew up surrounded by books and art and I thought he could have made a life for himself in that field. Even if not as a first-rate writer, as a journalist. There is such a thing as genius in bookselling; a bookshop can be like a work of art, if the book-seller chooses his books as carefully as a novelist his characters. Unfortunately Bhalu is not a genius.'

These were all things that, at different times and with varying degrees of unsubtlety, she had conveyed to me herself.

But no one could be more disappointed with my life than me. I'm not talking about bookselling, which is a noble calling – the bookshop was the first time I'd been happy in years – I mean what happened before. The lost years. My life had been filled with Maya's stories: endless, endless stories, anecdotes, yarns, recitals, chronicles, sagas, narratives of now and then, mysteries, legends, adventures, dramas, parables, fables, tall tales, wonderful stories pulled from histories or squeezed back in again, stories, stories without end, and yet . . . as the years went by I began to feel that there was one story missing, a big story, a secret, something not being said, that had never been talked about, which nevertheless sat at the centre of our lives and had shaped them, a void bounded by other stories, a story-shaped hole into which explanations fell and vanished. This untold story corresponded in some way which I could not explain, nor begin to understand, to the hole in my own life, the gap where my destiny should have been.

For the first time, I said all this to Maya.

The room slowly filled again with silence. Even the bulbuls were quiet. They must have been asleep, little heads hidden under their wings.

At last she said, 'Bhalu, in the bedroom. The old almirah is full of files. My *work*. I was going to leave it to you anyway, but I think you should take it tonight. Look through it, then we'll talk.'

'What am I looking for?'

'Foolish!' she said. 'Do you suppose you'll find an essay entitled *Why I Left India* by Maya Sahib?'

'I don't know what to suppose. This is your idea, not mine.'

'Don't argue, Bhalu.'

'Are you feeling all right?' She was seventy-six, recovering from a temperature, and we'd had how much grog?

'It's not a question of this bit or that bit.'

'What then?'

'There are things . . .' She stopped as a new thought occurred to her. 'In music there are two kinds of notes. Those which are played. And "unstruck notes", the so-called "anhad naad". The unstruck notes are not played, but they are there, we hear them. Without them music makes no sense. It's the same with stories. You just described it. "The untold story, the story-shaped hole into which reason vanishes." Yes, I like that. I like it very much. You should consider picking up a pen, Bhalu. It's never too late, not even at your age.'

'Things such as?' I asked, trying to find patience. 'I have read all your work.'

'Things you know, things you don't. Things you know without knowing you know – this rum is twisting my tongue. In a writer's *work*, stories are never really separate. They reach out to one another. They touch, merge, diverge. They slide in and out of each other. There are stories hidden within stories, hidden in the work as a whole – a bit of this story, a piece of that. Suddenly parts of different stories combine to reveal a new, surprising tale. That's the one to look for.'

'Why do I always get the feeling that you're laughing at me?'

'Bhalu,' she said reproachfully, 'I am your *mother*.'

'As my *mother*, you were always quick to point out what a dull swamp my life had become. Why won't you talk about this?'

'You don't understand. It's not that I *won't* talk about it. I *can't* talk about it. I promised I wouldn't.'

'Who did you promise?'

She said sadly, 'There was no choice, Bhalu. We agreed. It was necessary.'

'Who agreed?' She was as maddening drunk as sober.

'Bhalu, I am so sorry . . . Over all the years, all your ups and downs, and the *drinking*,' she said, oblivious to the groggy irony of our situation, 'I prayed you were happy. No, of course I don't pray, not exactly, but I hoped . . . You had Katy, the twins.'

'What was necessary?'

'I promised your father I would not tell you, but the fact is that we agreed, your father and I – and it was the only thing we had agreed upon for years –'

'Maya!'

'— that it was necessary that you leave. The girls and I simply followed. So really, the answer to your question is that I did it for your sake.'

'My sake?' I was amazed. 'You left India for my sake? Why?' This was her revelation and it made no sense at all.

Inside the wardrobe — only Maya still called it an almirah — were nearly two-dozen box-files. Willing though I was to humour her, I would never be able to carry them on the train. I said I would ask Katy to drive me up at the weekend.

'No, no. There's no time. I have an account with a minicab firm. Phone them now. Take everything to Sussex tonight.'

Then she said, 'Bhalu, don't waste your life.'

Whether she meant this as a moral to be drawn from her own life, or as a comment on mine, I never found out, because at that moment the doorbell rang.

Sun throbbing into the bookshop's tiny kitchen. Operated kettle, found coffee, dark-clotted spoon stuck upright in the jar. Milk off. Yesterday's. Everything here just as I had left it the day before, as if the world had not changed. Mother's dying swan routine. What did she mean, she had done it for me? Sugar on the draining board, ants at it already. Stirred in three, took the mug into the bindings room, as we called it, really my lair, where Maya's files were stacked in an untidy ziggurat.

Quarter to nine. Sun leaping too sprightly off the gold-blocked lettering on Mayhew's *London Labour and the London Poor* (Cass & Co, 1967, 4 vols, reprint of the enlarged 1861–2, v.g.c). Strange that such a subject should be given so lavish a binding. I shouldn't drink. It plays havoc, and I'd promised Katy.

Last night, well after one by the time I got home to the cottage, walls washed white by the moon, no lights on. Note from Katy in the kitchen (nearly said oven), *If hungry, Shepherd's Pie in oven (not very nice I'm afraid)*. By the kettle she had left a waiting mug in which was a teabag, half-buried under a small heap of sugar and ginger-dust. My habitual bedtime guzzle. Thoughtful of her. Tiptoed into our bedroom to find, as so many times before, a lozenge of moonlight spread across the floor, Katy's head on the pillow, gentle purr of her breath (Rolls-Royce of snores). 'Why do I feel so guilty?' Lay awake with my mind racing. Garbled dreams involving exotic birds, large claw-waving crabs, my mother and a man, *a pussyistic man*, from whom, *pomploomically speaking*, I must run away and hide. I rose, still groggy, stood under the shower for twenty minutes and came downstairs to find Katy staring at the huge pile of boxes that contained Maya's *work* – she could never say 'my work' without that inflection, a self-conscious lilt followed by a minute pause, – *work* –. As Katy, in a crackling, bubbling, hissing, sputtering cacophony, prepared breakfast, I told her the whole, weird tale.

'She isn't dying,' I said, 'she's up to something.'

'What will you do with these?' Katy asked, indicating the box-files.

There was no room for them in our tiny cottage. She drove me to the bookshop and we carried them, six at a time, through the shop to the bindings room. I sat and ignored them while I opened the morning post. Bill. Bill. Junk mail selling health insurance. Bill. Letter from someone asking could I supply a set of *Household Words*. 'Editor, Charles Dickens,' the sender had written, as if I wouldn't know. Had, as it happened, volumes I, II, III, IV, V, IX and X in the original green cloth, vols XIII and XVI in half-calf. So, neither a complete nor a matching set. Still, a start. But I couldn't reach them because Maya's temple was in the way, a black pyramid at whose heart was a story-shaped chamber. Somewhere in there were the pieces I must assemble. Hot coffee abs. no effect on headthrobbing. I opened the first box.

The *work* comprised:

Several drafts, in English, of an unfinished novel, *The Cowdung Factory*, about a village whose harmony is shattered when one family acquires an apparatus for turning cowdung into gas. Maya liked to grow her tales, like pearls, round bits of grit from the real world and *The Cowdung Factory* was based on feuding families in my father's home town, Kumharawa.

Five screenplays in Hindi, of which two, *Doraaha* (*Two Ways*) and *Badnaami ka dilaasa* (*The Solace of Infamy*), had been produced.

A chaos of handwritten notes, magazine cuttings and smudgy photocopies (made by flattening book so its spine bends back on itself like a circus acrobat, and type arches up and out of a dark central gutter — ruinous to bindings, bookseller speaking here) collected in different boxes according to subject.

Themes which interested her (there were dozens, I am being selective, choosing those with a bearing on this story) included:

— the 1857 Mutiny (First War of Independence). Accounts of battles, particularly Jaura Alipur, 1858. My father's recollection of accompanying his grandfather on hunting trips in Nepal, *c*1926, with muzzle-loading muskets of the Brown Bess type as used by the rebels of seventy years earlier. A peevish note complaining that the conflict had never been properly documented by the Indian side. Even Savarkar, the Hindu revolutionary, had to rely on British sources in his account. In another file I found a news-cutting describing Savarkar's funeral procession (Bombay, 1966), led by a saffron-capped horseman, the body carried on a truck, flower-heaped, in slow procession from Dadar to Chandanwadi followed by a huge crowd, a hundred thousand people at least, including, Maya had pencilled, the film producer V. Shantaram and his 'keep', a girl called Sandhya, 'a better dancer than she was an actress'.

— the Mahratta leader Shivaji, 1627–80, whose file, a manila folder marked M.E.S. STORES, AMBONA, contained an account of the giant *ghorpats*, monitor lizards, of the Deccan plateau.

— sayings and lore collected from villagers, some of which I remembered, for example the verse people chanted as they carried statues of elephant-headed Ganesh (these were gaudily-painted clay idols, often very large) to the lake at Ambona, wading until they were in over their heads, only the statues riding the waves

Ganpati bappa morya
purjya varsha laukarya
Ganpati geley gavala
chaiin pade re amhala

until the statues would tilt, dip, and the lake softly ungarland them, widening rings of marigolds and roses on the water.

— research on the opium trade as conducted by the East India Company. An account of going with my father and 'that mad *afimchi*' Zaz Qaradaghi to an open-air concert in Poona to hear maestro Bhimsen Joshi. 'Joshi-ji was at his best, only a *little* the worse for wear. He sang his favourite raga, *Miya ki Malhar* — the critics used to say he was too fond of it.' Zaz (real name Zahir, a regular at her Ambona soirées) was the only opium addict she knew. When Zaz listened to music, he would lodge a small, gummy ball of the bitter stuff behind his front upper teeth, and swore he could *see* the sound. Maya gave a page to his description of the patterns and colours of the raga: 'I lost sense of time and place and grew aware of graceful designs that swam before my eyes, the music carving shapes, inscribing bright arabesques in the dark air before me. I remember a slash of gold, a blue blob, scarlet dots and a yellow object shaped somewhat like a frog: my mind despairs of communicating these visions.'

What a romantic she was. And what pleasure she'd had in that world of art and discourse and dandified friends, some of whom behaved as if they were living in the eighteenth century. How did this reconcile with her crusading for the poor? No contradiction. Romantics have always been drawn to revolution. It is a small step from 'Man was born free and is everywhere in chains' to 'The philosophers have only interpreted the world, the point is to change it.' Maya believed in the power of art to change things.

– Mahatma Gandhi, assorted sayings. News reporter: 'Mr Gandhi, what do you think of Western Civilisation?' Gandhi: 'It would be a good idea.' Philosophy of non-violence. Not a weapon for the weak. One must be capable of violence and *choose* not to use it. His assassination at the hands of Nathuram Godse, a Hindu nationalist and follower of Savarkar, in the garden of the Birla temple, Delhi, on 30 January 1948. Godse brought up as a strict Hindu (cf Srinuji), as a child forced to recite Sanskrit verses from the *Rig Veda* and *Bhagavad Gita*, proud of his Hindu upbringing but – one of those quirks impossible for a novelist to invent – was an addict of Perry Mason detective stories. He apparently spent the night before the assassination in loud enjoyment of *The Case of the Fan-Dancer's Horse*. Also in this file, Maya's comment on the film *Gandhi*, 'more swamiography'. A side-note that Jinnah had been played with great élan by an old acquaintance from Zafyque's Theatre Troupe.

– corruption in government service (a lot of cuttings, some quite recent). A series of articles published in a Bombay paper by a journalist who had made his name writing 'scandalographies' of Indian movie stars.

– the Bombay riots of 1993, aftermath of the Babri Masjid

business, when thirty thousand Hindu zealots, among them whole tribes of ash-smeared but otherwise naked ascetics, tore a Muslim mosque apart brick by brick because, they said, it stood on the place, the very spot where Lord Rama, incarnation of the god Vishnu, had been born. Violence then, inevitable, predictable. Riots in Bombay. In Radhabhai Chawl, a Hindu family burned to death. Hindu mobs went looking for revenge. Not just in the poor areas to which previous troubles had been confined. Went to posh localities like Malabar Hill and checked the apartment blocks for names of Muslim residents. Missing names a giveaway. In some buildings, all names were removed to protect Muslim occupants. Zafyque had come to us later that year with tales of knifings, burnings and beheadings, which horrified Maya in some intensely personal way, as if she held herself to blame.

I also found a sheaf of poems and about thirty short stories in manuscript, among them many old favourites I had known from my childhood: *Silver Ganesh*, *Nafisa Jaan* (in two versions, 'meethi', sweet, and 'teekhi', bitter), *Badnaami ka dilaasa* (*The Solace of Infamy*, several drafts, plus notes for screenplay).

Thoughts in post-rum disarray jostling and squabbling like a posse of Trafalgar Square pigeons . . .

Among the *Badnaami* material, sweet revival of old delight. A mass of notes, and photos of Johnny Walker, actor man, comic genius, my childhood favourite, Bombay's raspberry at Jerry Lewis.

JW's real name was Badruddin Jamaluddin Qazi. At the start of the fifties he'd been a conductor on a B.E.S.T (BOMBAY ELECTRIC SUPPLY TRANSPORT) bus, red with yellow lettering on the side, streaked with paan spit. Number 132. Ding-ding. Ran from R.C. Church in the naval cantonment, up past Sassoon Dock (fishwives in parrot-hued saris reeking of pomfret and Bombay Duck, the sun-dried and aptly-named sardine *Bummalo bummalo*) to the Regal Cinema, Churchgate, Marine Drive, Chowpatty Beach in a fug of sweat, tobacco, jasmine and cheap hair oil, people running along-side executing balletic last-minute leaps onto the platform, the conductor pulling them aboard. He liked an audience and would cheer up his customers with jokes and silly faces, comic solilo-quies, songs and scraps of ribaldry. The actor Balraj Sahni saw this performance (yes, in those innocent days film stars rode on buses with their public) and got him a screen test. The rest, as they say, itihaas.

Such a long time since I'd seen a Hindi movie. To hire one meant a trek to Southall or that little shop in Drummond Street, off the Euston Road – just across from the Bengali grocer where Srinuji used to buy Alfonso mangoes in season, a presentation box for my mother, always one or two gone pulpy in the straw at the bottom, packed cheekcheekcheekcheek six thousand miles away in Crawford Market, corner of Mohammed Ali Road near Victoria Terminus (boy's trail in *Silver Ganesh*), on the *other* bus route from Colaba, the noble 123, a two-cinema journey from R.C. Church through the bummalo stench to the Regal, Flora Fountain, Dhobhitalao (Washermen's Tank, stop for Metro cinemagoers) and Girgaum (through which passed the horseman, drums and multitude of Savarker's funeral procession) thence to Lamington Road, where huge hoardings, each a unique handpainted work of art, ice-cream pink heroines, villains' green faces, announced the latest films – such a pity you couldn't get them in Lewes, but once in a while I would see one at Maya's. She used to watch them with gloomy pleasure. 'The monkey business going to the dogs.'

Monkeys, orange-eyed. After her Srinuji confession, impossible to take this supposed illness seriously. Punching holes in the skull. Yes, I knew how that felt.

O my head.

Six large ones, it must have been. Maybe seven. Sisters livid. Naturally, blamed me. Bhalu up to his old tricks. Maya greeting them gaily.

'Isn't this a treat?' she cried. 'I haven't had you all together for ages. You see? I really don't mind being ill. It'll be such fun. In bed with my favourite authors. Munching chocolates. Fresh flowers every day.' Not long before her genius for infuriating her family worked its customary effect.

A man come back home from a meeting,
Catch he wife with a next man cheating . . .

Rummed-up last night in the back of the minicab, Maya's boxes rattling beside me. The driver was a chatty Trinidadian. He drove the first mile elbow on seat-back, half-turned to talk.

'I take your mother round a lot of times. She's a nice lady.'

'Where does she like to go?'

'Two three places. St John's Wood.' (Panaghiotis.) 'Harrow.' (Srinuji.) 'Couple weeks ago I take her to Peckham.' (??)

But he did not know.

Somethin on yuh mind Ah want to know
Darling why you behaving so . . .

'You like calypso music?'

'I like reggae.'

Bob Marley. 'No Woman, No Cry'. Those were the days. Before the bad times. When the twins came along, we named them Isobel and Imogen, so they became I & I. Inseparable 'I's. Twins, a theme in my life.

'Welcome to the Mighty Sparrow,' the driver was saying. 'Litta bitta sunshine from home. One of these days I'll go back, get myself a house on the beach. Not Trinidad. Tobago. People work in Trinidad, retire in Tobago . . . So, what do you do?'

'I'm a bookseller.'

'Your mother tells me she writes stories. You must be selling plenty of your mother's stories.'

Most of these exchanges took place within a few miles of her flat. He told me that he was homesick, was hoping to get back for the next North Trinidad v South Trinidad cricket match, didn't see enough – 'Lara, there's a graceful bat' – and the date of birth of his dog (Alvin, labrador, 31/3/94).

> *Pomploomically speaking you're a pussyistic man*
> *Most elaquitably full of shitification . . .*

Acute discomfort. Not just the motion, trees reeling past. The sour rum aftertaste brought back bad memories. Years ago. Fifteen at least. Pre-bookshop. That life long gone, but the shame survives. Home too often from London by the company's taxi service, too curdled to walk straight. Late-night taxis like this one weaving through nauseous country roads. Hither, yon, thither, on. Bidding the driver stop at roadside inns or (if passing through a town) at one of those Bangladeshi restaurants that masquerade as Indian, ordering with a lordly air. 'And one for my chauffeur.'

Yes, shame. Guilt. Fear, too. Katy's anger. 'Won't be a bloody doormat. I'll make my own life.' Did as well. Why be surprised?

> *Your splendiferous views are too catsarstical*
> *Too cuntimoratic and too bitchilistical . . .*

Somewhere after Gatwick, we left the motorway at the wrong exit and got lost on little back roads. Well after midnight. Open heath heaving to horizon. Oak woods in last summer leaf. Cypress besoms trying to sweep the sky of stars. Headlights picking out a sign that read 'Pennybridge Lane'.

'Boss, we are miles out of our way.'

But I didn't know either. What strange trigonometry of fate had triangulated his Calypsonian and my Indian sorrows on this night to this lane in this most English of landscapes?

The clock on the church opposite began to strike the hour. From my window I could see a cascade of roofs descending Castle Hill, bent roofs, crooked roofs, tiles of various colours. The early sun was gone. From a few chimneys smoke was trying to push upward, beaten down by a thin rain. Eleven. Maya's papers were spread out across my desk. I pushed them aside. Time to revive the kettle. Any moment now the doorbell would go and Piglet would stoop through the undersized doorway, turn, flap his umbrella in the street, snap it shut, execute a semi-military about-face and zigzag between the bookcases to my inner sanctum where, with rain dripping from a nose reddened and shined by whisky, he would ask the question he came in to ask on most mornings at this hour.

'Hello Bhalu, anything new?' This, although *a* question, was not *the* question.

'Nothing, I'm afraid.'

Eleven O'Clock Piglet, ally, confrère, semblable, my closest and probably only friend – real name Pigott – was something-or-other in the White Boar Brigade, or, as he liked to put it, 'the provisional wing of the Richard III Society', which holds that Richard is not the murderous villain everyone believes him to be. It thinks Shakespeare was trying to curry favour with Elizabeth I, whose grandpapa had defeated Richard at the Battle of Bosworth. Piglet and his friends went further and claimed Henry Tudor, not Richard, had murdered the little princes in the Tower. 'Dicky 3 didn't have a hump either,' he was always telling me. 'Shakespeare made that up too. Good drama, rotten lie.'

Piglet came in every morning to pretend he was looking for books about Richard III. Each morning feigned disappointment.

'Damn! Well, never mind . . . Charlotte?' (*This* was the question.)

'Can't,' I usually told him. 'No one to mind the shop.'

'So what? You never have any customers.'

He was right there. The bookshop was not a thriving business. It barely covered its costs, so there was nothing left to take as a salary. I was sustained by Katy, who had her own small income and ran an interior design consultancy. Thank God that even in these straitened times there were still plenty of people who could afford to pay her to scour the souks of Brighton for the ships-in-bottles, wooden ploughshares from Turkey and other bric-à-brac with which she titillated their imaginations. Thanks to Katy, my life was comfortably, reliably, humdrum: I sat, day after day, in my back room, warmed by a small log fire popping in the grate. A risk, because books lined every wall. I kept in here the more valuable volumes: bindings, worthwhile first editions. A twenty-six volume set of the *Strand Magazine* occupied a shelf above my head, good reading on quiet afternoons. Here also I kept sets of Dickens, Shakespeare, Austen, Walter Scott, whose value would be destroyed if a volume were pinched. A couple of years earlier there had been a spate of thefts. I lost a *Très Riches Heures du Duc de Berry* and a pricy *Kama Sutra* illustrated with salacious Indian miniatures. Since then there had been a mirror near the door of the back room, giving me a fish-eye view of the front shop which is where I kept modern novels and subjects that sold well – antiques, being so near Brighton – art, china, dogs and cats, horses, local history and, things being what they are, sex. People browsing there could not be seen from the road and didn't know I could see them. They often behaved oddly when they thought they couldn't be observed. One day I was amazed to see a couple – the man had his protesting girlfriend backed up against the European History, with her skirt up around her waist and I am convinced was doing, or about to do, the dirty deed when the doorbell went and she thrust him furiously away. What should one do on occasions like this? Maintain a discreet silence and enjoy? Only once since the mirror was installed did I actually see a shoplifter and then did nothing about it because, embarrassingly, it was someone I knew.

Dong *dang* DING dung. All over the town, clocks exchanging hourly reassurances. Somewhere, Piglet walking in a cloud of bells.

Charlotte was the barmaid at the White Hart. It was Piglet's custom, after he had looked in on me, to continue along the High Street to the Hart and stay there until well into the afternoon. He would drink alone if need be but preferred company. Occasionally, I was persuaded to join him, but drinking with Piglet was a bad idea. We'd invariably end up in his workshop until late, and Katy was not pleased when I came home reeking of furniture polish. Furniture polish? Yes, for Piglet, when he was not rewriting history or togging up for one of the White Boars' frequent revisionist re-enactments – the Battle of Bosworth Field as it *should* have been been fought, with a triumphant Richard bestriding the body of Henry Tudor – earned his living restoring furniture. He was a craftsman, his work was exquisite, he paid the utmost attention to period detail. Under my desk was a large cardboard box full of eighteenth- and nineteenth-century wooden planes. Piglet had bought them at an auction in Brighton so he could make his own astragals, ovolos and ogees, which, he explained, were types of moulding. The box had been there since the last time I accepted one of his invitations to Charlotte's and the bookshop stayed closed for the rest of the day.

Katy used to ask if I never got sick of sitting in an empty shop. She said we were getting old without having had any fun. After the twins went off to their university she suggested we should sell up and think about doing something exciting like living in France and keeping horses (her major interest), but I realised a long time ago that what I wanted most from life was to be left alone by it. No doubt that's why I hid myself away in a bookshop. My bookshop – well, any bookshop, but especially mine – was a complete cosmos, its books emerald tablets that mediated between the uncertain realities of the world outside and the teeming oysterbeds of the mind. It was a place to escape the real world, and in a town like Lewes, with its castle and cobbled streets, where daily life is resolutely quaint, it offered a triple escape, stories on shelves in the story of a shop in the story of a town.

It was midday before Piglet arrived to give a disappointingly perfunctory performance of his umbrella and Dicky 3 rituals.

'I've been *interviewing*.' He had decided, he told me, to take on an assistant, 'a young person keen to learn'. The employment people had sent him a girl with a stud in her tongue.

'She's not a bad sort. Just alarming when she laughs . . . I wondered if you'd like to share her.'

'Share her?'

'Yes. I only want her for a couple of days a week. She needs something else for the other days. I immediately thought of you.'

'That was kind!' I was hardly in a position to employ hands.

'I'm *writing* something,' he said grandly.

'Let me guess. It wouldn't be about a certain person, born in York in the fifteenth century, maligned and mistakenly portrayed as having a hump?'

'You know, Bhalu, people are wrong about you. You have a bright and razor-like intelligence.'

Having found for Piglet virtually everything ever written on the subject of Richard of Gloucester, it amazed me that he thought there could be anything new to say.

'Oh, it's not *scholarship*,' he said. 'Bugger all that. I'm going to the heart of the problem, like they taught us in the Army. As I see it, all the scholarship in the world won't do a blind bit of good while *that play* goes on being performed year after year.'

'Well, what can you do about that?'

'Shakespeare's Richard isn't credible. A hook-nosed hunchback casting a dirty great shadow, so that "dogs bark at me as I pass"? Where else have you seen *that*? It's Mr Punch! And no!' he said, lifting a silencing hand. 'Don't tell me that Shakespeare had never seen Punch and Judy. I know all about the *commedia dell'arte* supposedly not coming to England until 1660, but all I can say is, that's a load of bloody nonsense. Just *look* at Richard III. "I am determined to prove a villain," he's made to say and that's all he is. No *glim* of good. Alas, poor Dicky, "that slander is found a truth now, for it grows again, fresher than e'er it was".'

I had heard many of his outbursts, but never one quite so jam-packed with fragments of bard. Piglet refused to be drawn on his project.

'Poor boy,' he told me, 'you'll be amazed! "More amazed than had you seen the vaulty top of heaven figured o'er with burning meteors" . . . Charlotte?'

Later that afternoon I found among my mother's papers a large envelope which contained a story I had never seen before, called *Retribution*. It was typed on the machine she used in the late fifties and early sixties, the one with the ball of its *r* worn away to nearly nothing. *Retribution* outlined a situation, a love triangle, in which a man of overweening self-regard manipulated two women, who were so alike as to be almost twins, and got his just deserts.

The story perplexed me. Most of Maya's tales were grown round real events, often based (*Nafisa Jaan*) on episodes from our own family history, or (*Badnaami ka dilaasa* and *Silver Ganesh*) things that had happened to people she knew, but *Retribution*, narrated by a ghost, was obviously fiction. Probably it was the preliminary sketch for a screenplay: a tragic tale of adultery and murder – in those days adultery almost always carried a death sentence, at least on celluloid – with comic interludes and a fine supernatural twist. That made sense. That sounded like cinema. She had followed the same pattern with *Badnaami ka dilaasa* (*The Solace of Infamy*), which was taken up by the director Haresh Saigal, who filmed it complete with songs, dances-round-trees and all the rest of the rigmarole, riot and chilli-spice necessary to a Bombay-made 'starrer'. *Badnaami* told the story of a struggling screenwriter, played by Dilip Kumar, who falls in love with a prostitute. His friends are scandalised, but he claims to find in her a purity that others miss. He is determined to create the role that will express this. In the ensuing scandal he loses everything, wife, family, home, job, but the resulting script is his life's finest work. The day it is completed, his wife, backed by her angry brothers, throws him out. She says he must never come near her or his children again. He runs to the girl, but she informs him cruelly that she has found someone else. In this crisis, having lost nearly everything he holds dear, he abandons what is left. He gives away his remaining possessions and takes to the road as a mendicant, begging his food. His path leads him through villages and jungles, and the land opens before him in its beauty and its pain. He sees an India he has never known before. Meanwhile (of course) his wife relents and begins searching for him. One day he enters a town and sees posters advertising the latest smash hit. It's his movie. He sneaks inside without paying and catches the first few minutes, the scene where the girl delivers the film's opening theme, 'Death deceives with a blow . . .' Her face glows on the screen. His words in her mouth have the grace of poetry. He watches and listens, entranced. The titles meanwhile are rolling. As his name appears on the screen, he is thrown out of the cinema and staggers into the street, with bell-ringing cyclists swerving to avoid him. He is knocked down by a truck (the obligatory death sentence). The people who gather round are amazed to see that he is smiling. 'I knew!' he tells them. 'I knew she could do it!'

Badnaami had a modest but genuine success. The film's entry in the *Encyclopaedia of Indian Cinema* (British Film Institute/OUP, first edition 1994, slight soiling, £9.50) praises its 'remarkable portrait of rural India' and states that: 'Maya Sahib's sensitive script takes a sordid affair and turns it into an inspiring drama.'

Badnaami's hero was a flawed man whose suffering one could share, but what was Maya thinking of when she wrote *Retribution*? Her narrator was such a repellent character that it was hard to imagine anyone having sympathy with him. He feared (she makes him say) that he'd be played by Johnny Walker if the story ever became a movie. Impossible! JW specialised in good-hearted drunks, precisely what this fellow, by his own confession, was not. If anything, JW would be the man's soused and insouciant boot-legger. He'd sing a song, something like the lovely old ghazal that Mukesh sang in *Main Nashe Men Hoon*:

> *Záhid sharáb píné dé, masjid mein baith kar*
> *ya woh jagah batá dé jahán Khudá na ho.*
> If, priest, you object to my drinking in a sacred spot,
> Kindly show me to some place where God is not.

Despite all this, I could just see *Retribution* as a film. It would tell the story of a man who leads a rakish, dissolute life, until he makes the mistake of falling in love with two beautiful women at once. This pair, given their uncanny similarities, would turn out to be sisters, twins even, separated at birth by some family tragedy and unaware of one another's existence. (Making them English was of course wrong. They should be Indian, played by the same actress – Mala Sinha or Vijayantimala, who'd played a pair of doubles in *Madhumati*.) After he callously ditches the first woman, the 'obscure story from the past' mentioned in her distraught phone call would ring a bell with the second. She would contact her rival, they would discover their sisterly relationship and it would emerge that the man, or his family, had played a part in their tragedy. Together, they would plot a double revenge and the movie could conse-quently be called *Pratiphal* or, if a snappier title were wanted, *Adla-Badli*, *Adla-Badla* (*Double Justice*).

What a flick! If only they'd made it! I got quite enthusiastic. The murdered Lothario would be a challenge for . . . whom? Certainly not a stereotypical film villain. For the piece to work, it would have to be someone charming. Someone who could woo us as he had the two women. They'd seen some good in him. He was at least *honest*. Honest whatsisname. What *was* the man's name? Maya never gave him one. Why? And why call the women One and Two? So many things about *Retribution* made no sense.

But these speculations were cut short by the discovery, in the same envelope as the story, of a news clipping from *The Times of India* and a note in my mother's writing entitled *The Eel Fisher*.

This morning at dawn a cloudscape like a mountain range could be seen on the sea horizon beyond the Back Bay Reclamation. I got up early, meaning to start work, but instead went for a walk along Cuffe Parade. It's a little cooler by the sea. I was wishing, as I do all the time now, that we were still in Ambona. I know I didn't want to go there at first, but our three years there now seem like an idyll, and like every idyll since Eden, it ended badly. It is odd to be back here in Colaba, in our old flat, the one we lived in before we left the city, as if nothing had changed, when everything has. We were foolish to come back to Bombay. We should have gone far away, maybe back to Lucknow. Leaving his rose garden broke my husband's heart. Bhalu hated leaving Ambona too. His letters are filled with the excruciating trivia of boarding-school life. He gives the latest hockey scores as he did when he was eleven and first went there. I suppose I should find it endearing.

Low tide had exposed a jungle of mangroves, probed by a long concrete jetty that ran towards the outer breakwaters. Beyond was the sea spreading blue wings clear to Africa. I decided I would walk out to the end of the jetty. The swamp glittered like fever. Smells of fish and seaweed and a curious dry clicking among the mangroves. A man sitting there with a fishing rod wished me good morning. He was perhaps thirty-five years old, strongly built, and quite naked apart from a short lungi, worn like a skirt, revealing the knees. An amulet shone on the darkness of his chest. I had a feeling that I had seen him somewhere before, but thought no

77

more of it. I returned his greeting and walked on. After a little I looked back. He was still watching me.

The jetty ends in deep water, milky-green and noisy, slapping against the wall. On a floating garland, a rotting crab carcass was being picked apart by smaller relations. The outer breakwaters, which from land seem so far away, are huge ramparts, giant fingers pointing at one another. One day they will touch, shut the sea out of Back Bay, and the mangroves will be gone for ever, but on this day the sea was still pouring in through the gap, through which I could see a ship standing out to the horizon. Three years since Sybil's ship sailed. I wrote several times, but no reply. To the north was the wooded outline of Malabar Hill. Where *he* lived. Sybil used to like walking out here to the end of the pier. She would say, with that excited catch in her voice, that it brought her closer to *him*. Maybe that's what did it, thinking about Sybil and Mister Love.

When I started back, the sun was hot. The fisherman was still there. A dog was nosing at a bulging cloth bag at his feet. From time to time the pouch heaved, something in it gave a twitch. I asked what it was. The man reached in and pulled out an eel. Held it out to me. It coiled and uncoiled slowly in his hands. I had never seen one so close before. It was about thirty inches long, silvery flank, dark back shot with blue lights, a snakeish head. Its eyes were dark jewels set in gold rims. He said, 'There are lots of them here. They hide in the roots.'

The eel's mouth opened, gulped and a shudder ran all along the long body. What a pity, I felt suddenly, that such a lovely thing should die choking in this way. So I offered to buy it from him. He laughed and said, with a kind of sulky truculence, 'People like you don't eat these things. It's poor folk like me that eat them.' I said I did not want to eat it, I'd pay him to return it to the sea. He shook his head and said, 'Madam, I have to feed my family. These things aren't worth much, but I can't afford to buy one in the market. So how much will you pay?' I said I'd give him five rupees. 'That's too much, you are too generous.' 'So, are you willing?' Again he laughed. 'If I say yes, what about tomorrow? Will you also buy tomorrow's eel? And the day after? No, madam, keep your money because when it's spent I'll only have to catch another.' The eel twisted in his hands. It struck me then that I had been arrogant.

I asked if I could hold it. He said, 'It'll make your hands smell.' I didn't care, I could always wash my hands. 'You won't chuck it back?' he asked. I said I just wanted to feel what it was like to hold. He stood up and gave me the eel. It was thicker than it looked and slippery. I grasped it just behind the head and some way along the body and it went quiet and heavy in my hands, but when the mouth opened and it pulsed I could feel the muscular pull, the strength, of the thing. He and the dog were both watching me. The eel convulsed and I exclaimed, afraid it would fall. He took it from me and dropped it tail first into his pouch.

I needed to shower, but the day was so hot that even under the stream of water I could feel sweat breaking out on my body. It took ages to get the fishy smell off my hands.

Ramu laid the table, as he always does at eight o'clock sharp, an egg for Captain Sahib, boiled for exactly three minutes, puri and potato for me, our napkins neatly rolled in their silver rings, a copy of *The Times of India* laid ready. My husband picks it up and I read, across the table, the page he has just finished. This is our habit. The story was on page five.

GOPAL GODSE FREED

From Our Correspondent

NEW DELHI, Oct 13: After serving a sentence of 15 years in the Tehra Central Jail, Gopal Vinayak Godse (44), brother of Nathuram Godse, who assassinated Mahatma Gandhi on January 30, 1948, was released today. Gopal Godse was convicted of complicity in the assassination. Mr Vishnu R. Karkare, a co-accused in the Mahatma Gandhi Murder Case, who was undergoing life imprisonment in a jail in Maharashtra, was released on Tuesday on the orders of the Central Government, it was learnt in Bombay.

I must have uttered some sort of cry because Captain Sahib lowers the paper. 'Did you say something?'

I dared not reply. I must be mad. It is clear to me that I, Maya Sahib, am responsible for this news.

'How far-fetched is that, even for you?' I ask myself and an inner voice instantly replies, 'Far-fetched, is it? I'm glad you use that word. Isn't it what that bitch Noor at *Femme* once complained of in your work? "Darling, why can't you just tell it straight? Why do you always insist on making these far-fetched connections?" To which *your* rather catty response, given dear Noor's obsession to prove her descent from some obscure Mughal princess, was that tracing the ancestry of an event is no more or less inherently absurd than cherrypicking ancestors for one's family tree.'

How far-fetched is this? *Very.* Far-fetched, but unarguable. The reasoning is this. These men have been freed to carry on their rewriting of history because, as everyone predicted, it was politically impossible to keep them locked up once Mister Love's murderer had been released from prison and allowed to leave the country. It therefore follows, does it not . . . ?

'Of course it does,' says the ghost in my brain. 'It is mathematical, quadratic as anything. No release for Mr Godse and his chums if no Mister Love murderer pardoned and set free. No murderer without the murder. Therefore you are responsible for this news, because you, Maya, caused the murder.'

The eel-fisher is standing behind my husband's chair. The eyes, the voice, the sulky mouth. Suddenly, beyond any doubt, I know where I have seen him before.

'So you recognize me,' says the ghost of Mister Love.

My husband is still waiting for a reply. What can I invent?

'I thought of something funny,' I said, rather desperately.

'Share the joke?'

'I was just remembering when Ninu was little, how I used to sing her rhymes and deliberately mix up the words . . . "Sing a song of sixpence, pocket full of weasels . . ." "No, no," she'd shout. "Full of *rye*." "Pocket full of rye. Four and twenty blackbirds, baked in a samosa . . ." "*Not* samosa! *Pie!*" "Baked in a pie. When the pie was opened, the birds began to somersault . . ." "The birds began to *sing!*" "Oh wasn't that a dainty dish to set before a rhinoceros?" "No, no, Mummy," she would yell, "It's a *wrong song!*"'

But Captain Sahib's eyes were already lowered to his paper.

'You know what my mistake was?' says the ghost, with an insolent smile. 'It should have been you, Maya. It should have been you.'

With as much contempt as an immobile face can convey, I said, 'You never had a chance with me.'

'You were tempted. Admit it. What harm can it do now?'

'I don't admit it. You are a fantasist, you always were.'

'Oh, but the way you used to look at me.'

'Don't delude yourself. You could never meet a woman at a party, could you, without wanting to sleep with her? You'd meet someone new and your eyes would crawl under her clothes.'

'If you noticed, it was because you were jealous.'

'I despised you.'

He laughs. 'No. You despised yourself, because you wished it was you. You knew, didn't you, what your friends were doing? They would tell you, and you'd think, Why isn't it me? Why should they have all the excitement? You married to your dull rose-grower.'

'You are an evil man.'

'I am a dead man,' he says. 'And who's to blame?'

'You got yourself killed.'

'Not exactly. I was lying on my bed. I was trying to sleep. The doorbell rang. The first thing I saw was the gun.'

'I never liked you, but I never wanted you dead.'

'Someone did. Think about that gun. It was brought to kill me. But in court, the lawyers claimed it was carried in self-defence. They said I was dangerous, that I kept a revolver under my bed. Now Maya-ji, where do you suppose they got that idea?'

'I had nothing to do with the defence, you know that.'

'There was no gun, never was. Whisky bottles, cigarette ends, letters, all these were found under my bed, but no revolver except the one that killed me.'

'What has it got to do with me?'

'*You* know where the idea of that gun came from.'

'You are talking nonsense,' I said.

'You know I'm not. Think of Ambona. It all goes back to Ambona. Try to recall a certain day. July or August 1958 it would have been. About nine months before I was slaughtered.'

'How am I supposed to remember?' My husband had finished his egg and was wiping his mouth in that fastidious way he had, unaware that his mad wife was having an argument with a ghost.

'You know the day I am talking about. The day of the terrific storm. The children could not go out to play. They asked for a story. You chose the *wrong story*.'

'There's no such thing.'

'A story told to the wrong person at the wrong time. Why tell *that* story, Maya-ji, the agony of a woman who must lose her baby, to a woman who had just lost her baby?'

'She *asked* for that story. I tried to dissuade her.'

'And you had no power to refuse? Do you remember now? An afternoon dark as night, thunder rolling on the roof, ferocious rain. Next morning you found a large moth lying on the steps. It had been beaten to death by the heavy drops.'

'I remember that.'

'When you finished the story, your friend was crying. She asked if she might use the telephone in your room. She phoned me. Why did you interfere? Why not just leave us alone? You did not hear what I was saying to her. Did you assume I was as cruel as you? You know nothing of what I said! You just saw your friend in tears. So you prompted her, didn't you? You put those words into her head. What was it she shouted at me? "It's not unborn children but men like you who deserve to die".'

'But why,' I asked, 'why, you stupid, stupid man, did you have to sneer at her?'

'What did I say? Do you recall?'

'You said to her, "Darling, are you planning to kill me? Should I get a gun and keep it under my bed?"'

'Presto,' says the ghost. 'Please notice that the gun has just popped into existence. You see it now, don't you, Maya? All your own work. Karma flashes like lightning from cause to effect. It lights the darkness and gives us glimpses of those most terrifying truths, the consequences of our own actions. Your temper got me killed. But you didn't learn, did you? Because you did it again, to someone much crueller than me, and now you are paying for it.'

'Have you seen this?' says Captain Sahib, who has reached the item on page five. 'Gandhi's assassins are out in the world again.'

Karma is such bitter knowledge. No angel waits on the far side of death to slap a writ on me. I shall not be judged before the great white throne of *Revelation*, or have sentence passed on me in the court of Yama, or the many-pillared hall of Osiris. Karma is not reward or punishment in the next life. It's much worse than that. It's the knowledge here and now of what I have brought into being. The responsibility. And the guilt.

Bhalu, *tu salé bahut bhola hai*, you're such a fool, I told myself as I locked the bookshop early next morning and walked down to Lewes station. I had just sent a fax to a book dealer I knew in Bombay, asking him, as a huge personal favour to me, to go to the *Blitz* newspaper, if it still existed, and search in its archives for issues that covered the end of April 1959. I told him to look for any news of a murder. I did not know the name of the victim, only that he had possibly been known by the coy and unlikely title of Mister Love.

I had also decided that I would go to see Maya. I'd buy tickets for the Royal Court and surprise her. The real reason, of course, was that I wanted to question her about *Retribution* and its peculiar companion piece. If the story was intriguing, I found the note, the tale of the eel-fisher and the insolent ghost utterly baffling.

I was convinced that *Retribution* was fiction, a character sketch for a film, but *The Eel Fisher* treated it as real. Could the story be true? During the period it covered we were in Ambona, but before that we lived in Bombay. Even after we moved to Ambona my parents regularly saw their Bombay friends. I remember Sybil very well. For three summers in a row, she and her daughter Phoebe came to stay with us in Ambona. Phoebe was my best friend. Was it possible that my mother, or Sybil, or someone known to them, had been mixed up in a murder? Even caused it? Surely not. The idea was preposterous.

Who was this Mister Love, whose spectre seemed to have taken permanent lodgings in my mother's brain? Why had she chosen to represent his memory as a ghost? Apparitions are all very well in dodgy Elizabethan dramas like *Hamlet* and *Macbeth* (this is Piglet's appraisal) but what place do they have in a mid-twentieth-century tale, especially one purporting to be a true story?

Then of course there was the familiar karmic theme, hallmark of virtually all her fiction. Usually I enjoyed her excursions into the minutiae of cause and effect, but in this case my sympathies were all with bitchy Noor. For Maya to hold herself responsible for the death of Mister Love was simply absurd. Did he bear no share of blame? What about the person who took a gun to his flat and then cold-bloodedly used it? No, my mother's obsession with karma was surely a sort of mania. Some psychologist must have defined the syndrome, whose sufferers believe they are responsible for things with which they have no connection at all.

Maya had two ways to justify the karmic intrusions into her *work*. The first was a matter of dialectic. She said her doctrine of personal responsibility subverted the way history is commonly taught and received. Asoka won the Battle of Kalinga. Wellington won the Battle of Waterloo. This is what we learn. But battles are not won by kings and generals. They are the complex outcome of the individual actions of thousands of unremembered soldiers. Maya wanted the small people to recognise their importance and claim their place in history.

The second reason was ethical. Since even tiny actions have far-reaching consequences, we should be mindful of what we say and do. The problem was that this led directly to the paradox which Bubbles Roy called her 'favourite unanswerable question'. If good actions can have wildly negative effects and vice versa, how are we ever to know how to act for the best? None of this helped me make up my mind whether Maya had written about a real murder, or whether *Retribution* and *The Eel Fisher* were two parts of an elaborate fiction.

I studied the pages several times. Looking for what? Clues to her state of mind? My mother had typically Indian handwriting. Her English letter forms reflected the fact that her first languages were Hindi and Urdu, whose scripts require the pen to be lifted between letters. It was a hand typical of someone who had learned to write, as I in my turn had, with a penholder whose nib must be frequently dipped, with resultant inky blotches on thumb, index and middle fingers. I used to suck them sometimes because the ink was salty and my lips, like a dying person's, would turn cyanose. Handwriting reflects moods. If I am writing down something I don't believe in, my handwriting grows weak and skulks across the page doing its best to hide. Confident characters stride. The words in *The Eel Fisher* raced boldly across the pages without pause for reflection. Maya's manuscripts usually accumulated dozens of crossings-out as she searched for the right words. *The Eel Fisher* had nary a one. She was not inventing, not casting about for ideas, she was telling a story about which she had no doubts. Furthermore I could remember the afternoon she mentioned, when the hurricane lamps were lit (the power lines must have been brought down by the storm) and we listened to her tell the story. I even remember the story. It was the 'sweet' version of *Nafisa Jaan*.

Now other things occurred to me. If she was writing fiction, why would she have *invented* two women with virtually identical names? Unnecessary confusion. There is no need for it in the story. Why not call them Rachel and Emma? But no, they would have had the sort of names girls were given in the twenties, the kind of names you find in Enid Blyton books. Imogen and Margery, or Pat and Isobel. Why make them lookalikes? Again, there was no need.

It then struck me that, of course, a story can simultaneously be true and not true. There are many ways to dress real characters in masks, and a writer may have all kinds of motives for doing so. Thinly-disguised accounts of well-known people and events are often published as propaganda, or to generate sensation and sales.

Truth-in-a-mask could also be used to tell an important story while protecting the real people involved; to expose an injustice that would not otherwise be brought to light. One could imagine for example, a scenario where powerful interests might be able to stonewall a journalistic investigation, or quash it with a libel writ.

But to have any effect at all, fiction must be published. What had Maya done with *Retribution*? Nothing. Why write a story, show it to no one, send it nowhere, never again mention it? It was a conundrum. I could have picked up the phone, I suppose, but did not want to. My mother was very good at sending people in hot pursuit of wild-geese and (more water fowl) there was still the dying swan routine to be explained.

'Bhalu,' I told myself, 'it's not as if you have a business to run.'

I unscrewed my fountain pen and made a summary of what could be known, or reasonably inferred, from *Retribution* and its strange satellite:

Mister Love conducted indiscreet and unwise affairs with two
    Englishwomen who were alike as twins.
Each woman had cause to hate him.

He was murdered by an unknown hand.

He was maligned in a newspaper, *Blitz* (easy to check, if my contact did his stuff).

In Maya's mind his death was connected to her telling us a story one afternoon in Ambona.

There was a court case, in which someone must have been found guilty of the murder, because the murderer went to jail.

The murderer was subsequently freed and allowed to leave India, which strongly implied that he or she was a foreigner.

The freeing of Mister Love's killer made it impossible to keep behind bars the men who had plotted Gandhi's assassination.

It was a plot for a movie. It had to be.

And yet . . . what if it wasn't? Here it came again, that old uneasy feeling of stories reaching out to each other, touching, merging, diverging, stories within stories, sliding in and out of one another – myself as a being made, not of flesh and blood with a life and choices of my own, but of stories and patterns created long before my birth. 'We are born with free will, but are forced to expend it trying to *un-live* the lives of our predecessors.' (One of Maya's, of course, from the Collected Aphorisms.)

Something Maya had said the other night. She wouldn't stop talking, fixing each of us in turn with huge kohl-rimmed eyes.

'Ninu, do you remember when Bhalu hit you on the nose with a cricket bat? You were only three! I thought I'd have to report him to the police as a juvenile delinquent, but you kicked him in the eye and stabbed him in the head with a pencil. You could stick up for yourself.'

It was as though she wanted to recall every moment we had

spent together, to relive them with us. 'Suki, such a dreamy girl, always with your nose in a book, but I knew you had your head screwed on straight.'

She said, 'Bhalu, I worried about. He was always a foolish boy. Once when he was six, your father's friend Garg — oh, he was so dull, Bhalu can't really be blamed for what happened — took him to the US Club. You remember the Club, at the southern tip of Bombay with a golf course and the sea on three sides? Well, the young Gargs weren't particularly friendly and Bhalu got fed up with trailing round after them, but . . .' here she paused and impaled me with a critical eye '. . . instead of doing what any other child would have done and put up with it, he lagged further and further behind and then hid behind a bush. It was quite some time before they missed him and raised the alarm. They were worried sick. All that rough ground, snakes too, and strong tides sweeping past the point — the shores were sharp black rocks covered in crabs — but they didn't find him because by that time he was already halfway home to Cuffe Parade.'

I could actually remember this: scuffing moodily home past the fisher encampments with their big boats pulled up onto the shore of the Back Bay. I got home to find my mother dressing for yet another function to which children were not invited. She looked very glamorous that night, in a green silk sari with a gold border, and emerald eardrops. About an hour later the doorbell rang and our servant answered it. Outside I heard the voice of Garg asking for my mother. Then he caught sight of me and said, with a hatred in his voice that I shall never forget, 'Oh you wicked, *wicked* boy!'

Maya said, 'Yes, he'd come to give me the dreadful news that you had vanished – that they were searching for you in the dark with torches and the coastguard had been called out to scour the shoreline. But that's why I worry about you, Bhalu, that you'll go through your whole life running away . . .

'Oh, here's poor Sybil,' said my mother, looking through an old photograph album. 'So kind, so good, but always in some kind of trouble . . .

'And look, Bhalu, here's you and Phoebe. Taken that last summer just before they returned to England. I often wonder what became of Sybil. The letters just stopped. I always said I'd find her when I came to England. But . . .'

There we were in the photograph, a fair girl and a dark boy. We were in our garden in Ambona, with the high ridge of Bicchauda rising behind us.

By the time the train reached Gatwick, I had almost decided that I would not, after all, mention *Retribution*. Just suppose, I said to myself – and yes, it is the tiniest, remotest, unlikeliest supposition – that the story is true, the fact that she has never mentioned it can only mean she wants it forgotten, and this is hardly the time to upset her by raking up old scandal. Nevertheless, I argued, as we came clattering across the sidings at Clapham Junction, if she still maintains this ludicrous charade that she is dying, then her own philosophy of karmic storytelling *demands* that this be investigated, and for one overriding reason.

'Death deceives with a blow. The immediacy of pain disguises the deeper loss. Our own memories survive. It takes time to realise that the memories of the gone ones are lost for ever. They go, and take with them stories from childhood, anecdotes, dates, rhymes, songs, fragments of family history. But these things are not to be forgotten because what happened in the past is already shaping our unborn children's lives . . .' Her own words, from *The Solace of Infamy*.

I crossed the square to the Royal Court and bought two tickets for that evening's performance of *Via Dolorosa*. Put them in my pocket ready to flourish when Maya opened her door. I pressed the bell, expecting Maya to come to the entryphone and buzz me in. A stranger's voice answered. The door to the flat was opened by a nurse in a white uniform, who looked as unnerved to see me as I was to see her. Maya had had a fit. It must have happened during the night. Nina had found her at about eleven this morning and had rung in a panic for help. The doctor had been, and my mother was now sleeping. Nina had been trying to phone me. She'd had to go home, but would be back soon. The nurse said she was desperately sorry to give me such bad news, and I said it wasn't her fault. With the strange detachment that seems to possess one at times of crisis, I noticed that she was barefoot, and that each of her toenails was painted a different colour. She asked if I'd like to sit with my mother and offered to make me a cup of tea.

Last time I had seen Maya she was sitting up in bed reading. Now there was a needle taped to her arm and a tube running into her nose. Her face was altered, the flesh had fled from the bone. Nothing else had changed. The pile of books was still by her bed. In their cage in the corner, Khurram and Mumtaz bobbed their heads and whistled. I sat down to wait.

A little while later the nurse beckoned me out of the room and said, 'I'm sorry, but I didn't know if I should give you this. Your mother woke for a while this afternoon. She wanted to write you a note. The thing is . . . I hope you won't find it upsetting.'

She handed me a folded sheet of Maya's writing paper. It read: 'Mymy mydeardededear myyymy dedearerrer my dearearear Bhalu I I am sosorry nnot ttotoo see yoyou . . .'

When I went back into the room, my mother's eyes were open. She looked at me, smiled and said, 'Bhalu-alu-alu,' which in Hindi translates to 'Bhalu-potato-potato.'

II AMBONA

The road up into the hills weaves in a series of steep hairpins past a small temple of Hanuman, the monkey god, at which there are always flowers left as insurance by lorry drivers, who grind up and down all day in first gear. On its roof long-tailed langurs sit, nibbling fruit and regarding the passing world with wise eyes. When you reach the top, what a view it is. To the west, a gape out across a forty-mile blur of coconut groves, tribal forests, flats and swamplands. To the east, the escarpment rises still higher, the mountains assuming fantastic shapes, vast rearing domes of rock wearing the sky like a wide blue hat.

It was the beginning of 1958. My father had just announced that he was retiring early from the Navy. He wanted us to move to my mother's home-town, Lucknow, which had a climate ideal for the cultivation of roses, but Maya responded with one of her famous tantrums.

'Are you mad?' she yelled. 'I'm a writer not a dung-shoveller! The film studios are here! My friends are here! I absolutely refuse to leave!'

'But,' protested poor Captain Sahib, 'you can't grow roses in Bombay.'

One of their friends, a sculptor called Mohan Apte, came up with the answer. Why not live in the Ambona Hills? They were a six-hour drive from Bombay, less by train, and at close to four thousand feet the air was clear and dry. Roses would love it, and it was peaceful, good for thinking and writing.

'You will not be lonely,' Mohan assured my mother. 'All week long, my dear, you will work hard, and at weekends friends will come to stay. They'll be queuing up for invitations. You know how desperate everyone is to escape the city, especially in sticky weather, and the evenings are deliciously cool in the hills. You'll have parties, soirées, musical weekends. And it will be marvellous for the children.'

Mohan had a friend in the area who would keep an eye open for a suitable house we could rent.

My father was to go ahead to get things ready for us. He drove off in our old Humber, in convoy with two M.E.S. trucks carrying our furniture and belongings. With him went my two-year-old sister Suki and our ayah Shashi. Maya could hardly be expected to supervise the packing with a toddler underfoot. 'Besides,' she said, 'a child *needs* its ayah. Someone has to feed her and take care of all that *other* business.'

Emptied of our familiar things, the flat seemed vast. Nina and I, hilarious with excitement, spent our last day skidding in the corridors, went eagerly to bed and rose with the crows to hang over the balcony waiting for the Humber to return with my father's new driver, Babu, who had the reputation of being a *shikari*, a hunter. Sure enough, when he arrived, he wore a hunter's moustache and the arms that lifted our suitcases into the car were brawny enough to wrestle with pythons.

At last, we were moving, leaving the city, leaving the building that held my first memories. Goodbye to Pallonji Mansion, full of cooking smells and the laughter of servants, to Mrs Shroff in the flat above us shouting at her cook, to her little dog Cutty and the stray cats he loved to chase. Goodbye to the sickly papaya tree in the courtyard, the banana by the gate and to chowkidar Zarak Khan in his long Pathan shirt and pyjamas. Goodbye to the twang twang twang of the mattresswallah coming along the road with his cotton-fluffing harp over his shoulder, to the peanut-men of Cuffe Parade, paper cones of hot roasted nuts and savoury charcoal smoke, to Cuffe Parade and sea breezes, and the Back Bay where the fisherfolk set nets in the brown water among the mangroves and long jetties reached out through smells of salt and rot and swamp to the sea.

Babu was a movie buff and as we drove through Bombay he had a word to say about each of the films advertised on the hoardings.

'So Bhalu, who's your favourite star? Let me guess, it's . . . ?'

Correct! Who else? The funniest comic ever. In his new picture *CID*, he'd sung a song so catchy everyone was humming it.

> *Ai dil hai mushkil, jeena yahaan*
> *Jara hatt ke, jara bach ke, yeh hai Bombay meri jaan.*
> Oh heart, it's so hard to live here this way,
> Just dodge by, somehow get by, oh my life, oh my Bombay!

> *Kahin buildings, kahin traamen, kahin motor, kahin mill,*
> *Milta hai yahan sabkuchh ek milta nahin dil*
> Buildings, trams and motors, mills in every part,
> Everything, this city has, but it does not have a heart.

Babu laughed. 'Forget this song. You're no longer a Bombay-ka-babu. You're now an Ambona-ka-babu, like me.'

It was noon when we crossed the marshes at the northern edge of the city. 'I want you to keep your eyes open,' said my mother. 'Tell me if you see anything extraordinary.'

I didn't know what she meant. To me it was all extraordinary. Everything seemed magical, even everyday things like bullock carts. In the city they hauled bales and boxes and tanks of water, but here they creaked along under loads of hay and wood and leaves. The women walking by the road wore their saris in the same tail-twixt-legs fashion as the fishwives of Sassoon Dock, but on their heads they carried the strangest things: a tree branch, cowdung cakes, a pair of bicycle wheels . . .

It was late afternoon before the first of the high hills appeared, shadow-on-shadowy shapes out of the haze in the east.

Soon we were climbing, the plain dropping away. Up around hairpins that crept along the edges of precipices. Up into turns where there were lorries lying on their sides; some rusty wrecks had been there a long time. Up past the Hanuman temple with its monkeys. Up to the top with its spectacular view where we found boys selling sweets we had never tasted before, a sort of toffee studded with nuts. 'Chikkee' they called it. Babu said the district was famous for it. 'But the best is from Ambona.'

We knew the turning for Ambona was near when to southward appeared a peak that seemed to fling itself up into the air.

'Look at the mountain, children,' said my mother, turning in the passenger seat of the Humber. 'What does it look like to you?'

'It's a rabbit,' said Nina. She was five.

'No it's not, it's a ship,' I said. 'It's HMS *Hood*.'

The peak looked like the artist's impressions in my ship book of the *Hood* sinking stern first, her bows jutting into the air after the *Bismarck*'s salvo struck lucky. I was eight and, having a naval father, knew all about warships.

'It's a nose,' said my mother. 'A giant nose.'

She told us the peak had been named after a British general who had a huge snout. About a hundred and fifty years ago, he had fought the Mahrattas in these mountains.

'It's called Duke's Nose,' she said. 'Only he wasn't a duke until later. After he won a battle at a place called Waterloo.'

As we drove past its slowly altering profile I could see why it had got its name. Imagine a giant dead to the world, his head flung back, the sort of position that invites you to tickle nostrils with a straw. The bridge of the nose was a huge ridge rising out of the forest and climbing starkly to a cleft peak, on which grew a few small trees. The nostrillar side dropped sheer, thousands of feet of naked rock, and vanished from view. I kept my eyes fastened to the mountain. With every bend of the road its shape slowly changed. It became a cobra hood, mellowed to a mere cone, then turned into a bear before vanishing behind nearer hills. By the time we turned for Ambona, shadows were lengthening and the squinty rear windows of the car were filled with sunset.

We drove on between mountain shapes that were beginning to blur and be lost in the dusk,

   swam past lights of a small town, through a bazaar

      where a man was sitting cross-legged behind piles of sweets

      clang clang of drowsy bells

When I woke we were crossing a long causeway, a sort of stone bridge with nothing but darkness stretching out on either hand.

'How far now?' came the sleepy voice of my mother.

'About ten miles, madam,' the driver replied, on best behaviour in front of his new memsahib. 'We've been through Ambona. Now we go round the lake and up the hill. The last three miles, the road is rough.'

Ahead of us, outlined against a luminous sky, was a high black ridge behind which the moon was threatening to rise.

'That hill in front is Kalighat,' said Babu. 'Gets its name from a small shrine on top. They say strange things go on up there. Hey Bhalu, do you like ghost stories?'

'Don't frighten them,' said my mother.

'I'm not frightened,' I said. I was intensely interested in ghosts.

'The local name is Bicchauda — don't ask me what it means, it isn't Marathi — some village thing. Last year, about this time, a woodcutter was killed up there by a panther. He was taking honey from a beehive and the panther had the same idea. Your house is on the other side, but don't worry, the panthers won't bother you unless you keep a dog. They adore dog, for some reason.'

The road on the far side of the causeway began to twist and turn. Babu told my mother, 'They'll have supper ready for you, but I'm thinking the children will be too tired.' He turned to us, and said, 'Hey, Bhalu! Hey, Nina! Don't nod off. Want to see something special?'

He swung the car round a spur of the mountain. 'Look!'

There was the moon, hanging over a wide lake whose margins vanished into darkness.

'Stop!' my mother commanded. Babu pulled over and switched off the lights and engine. We climbed out. The lake lay glittering under the moon. Beyond, more mountains lifted dark shapes into the sky. Besides the moonsilvery water, there was no other light in the landscape. The night was soft and full of small unfamiliar sounds. Chirrings. Calls that might have been birds. I was aware of trees near us. The earth and the air had a smell I can never forget, which to this day fills me with excitement and sadness, and the longing to be back.

Soon after this, we turned off the road and began bouncing up the rough track of which Babu had spoken. At last we pulled up outside a house in whose windows an apricot glow flickered, fading in one place only to reappear in another – the servants going from room to room with oil lamps since the electricity was not yet connected. Inside was my father to greet us in a muddle of trunks, packing cases and furniture from the Bombay flat. I saw Maya's typewriter perched on a box of books. Nina and I ran from room to room of this strange new house. 'Yes, there's lots to see,' said my father, catching Nina up and giving her a hug. 'But it'll have to wait, because you're going to have supper and go right to bed.'

In the morning, everything was different. A thick mist swirled outside, making it impossible to see. We explored the house. It was a large bungalow with a steeply tiled roof and a verandah running all the way round the outside. There were many bedrooms – it was built for a large family. Maya said, 'We'll need them all when our friends come.' She was busy, directing the servants, arranging the furniture. After consultation with my father she chose a corner room, and had her desk, a long rosewood table with drawers and carved legs, moved in and her typewriter placed upon it. This was her writing room. In here she would carefully cut out and file reviews of *Badnaami ka dilaasa*, and write *Silver Ganesh*, and the bitter and sweet versions of *Nafísa Jaan*.

Our house had a sheltered courtyard in which grew papayas,

bananas, a lime bush, guava trees with smooth grey trunks, and a frangipani tree. In front was a fishpond with a fountain, a cherub whose wings had become black with mould. Round the back was a vegetable garden in which a gardener, squatting on his haunches, turning the earth with a trowel, was already hard at work. When he saw me he stopped, gave a gappy grin and said something in Marathi. I told him I didn't understand and in terrible Hindi he said, 'You boy. I have boy just like age you.'

Further up the slope, where the mist was hanging, my father planned to clear a plot of land and plant his nursery. Here he'd rear the blooms that would make him famous. The soil was a rich, voluptuous red and the air thick with the scent I had caught the night before, soft and clean, with a hint of sulphur and herbs. I wanted to start clearing the ground right away, but my father warned me on no account to go turning over rocks. The hillsides were alive with snakes. After an hour the mist began to thin. It became a bright pearly haze that was slowly suffused with gold. Then it lifted completely and I saw where we had come to live.

Our house perched halfway up a valley bounded on three sides by hills and on the fourth by a huge chasm that faced south across a gulf of air. Just visible in the distance was a bit of the lake we had seen the night before and beyond it, far away to the northwest, was a smudge that my father said was Duke's Nose, back to its old shape, but from this angle oddly reversed. Above us, the slope of Kalighat, thick with trees, climbed impossibly high into a pure blue sky. Instantly I forgot the city. Already, on that first day, I knew that this place, with its air, its earth, its birds, its animals, and its friendly bad-Hindi-speaking people, was my real, destined home.

Everyone needs to feel that they have somewhere on the earth that is uniquely theirs. This was mine. Although I never owned the land, the water, or the creatures, I knew that this was my proper place. After all these years, I still do. I still recall our three years in Ambona as the most perfect time of my life. Each of us has a true self, an inner self, the essence of the being that we are. When I imagine Bhalu's true self, he is always that eight-year-old boy.

Dhondu the gardener did all his work squatting on his haunches. He worked barefoot, big feet splayed, toes wide apart. To move forward, he'd lean to one side and lift the other leg, still bent, and waddle. With each step his body made a half turn in the opposite direction. In this way he moved stolidly through the vegetables. Dhondu always smiled when he caught sight of me and would summon me closer with cries of 'Ey-one-rey!' At least that's what it sounded like to my Hindi-tuned ears. He worked the red soil with a small mattock, mixing in cowdung, which he brought in flat dry cakes and crumbled onto the ground. I watched him scoop pits and place into them tomato seedlings with black soil clinging to their roots, and big melon seeds. He dug a network of canals and laid the hose at the top end. Water churned down, carrying bits of straw and dust before it, and spread out across the beds, turning them dark.

Our house was served by a large cistern cut into the rock high up the hill. Water was siphoned to a tap in the kitchen and we stored it in buckets and pans. It was boiled for drinking, cooled in the refrigerator and my mother said she had tasted worse. There was not enough pressure to operate a hose, so my father, fearful for his roses, installed an oil pump, which ran for two hours every morning. He himself supervised the planting and manuring of his roses, but it was Dhondu who watered them. I admired his skill with the hose. By stopping the end with his thumb, he could make a spray, and with tiny movements vary its fan, density and force. When I got to know him better, he squirted me.

Dhondu sang as he worked, mumbling words I couldn't follow. I asked our cook to translate, but the cook, Yelliya, who had come with my father from Bombay and fancied himself a cut above the locals, said, 'It's just nonsense from a nonsensical sort of person.'

> 'get planted – you hear? – in you go,
> go into the earth and make some roots
> what's that? did i hear right? hey!
> didn't i just dig a nice hole for you,
> wasn't that water i just gave you to drink?
> there's only so much i can do,
> you'll have to do your own growing'

I asked Dhondu which song it was, which film it came from. He told me – or rather I eventually understood – that it did not come from any film, but that he sang whatever came into his head. At any rate, his plants grew fast and sturdy. My first friend in Ambona was his son.

On most days Dhondu ate lunch from our kitchen – he would take his food outside and eat it sitting under a tree in the shade – but one day he announced that it was a special puja and his wife was sending lunch from the village. 'Today', he told me, 'you meet my son.' Sure enough, at midday a boy appeared from the direction of the village carrying a cloth bundle. Dhondu called me over. 'Bhalu, ey-one-rey! This is my chicken,' he said in his dreadful Hindi, standing, a picture of parental pride, with his hands on the lad's shoulders.

'This is Jula. Jula, this is Bhalu.'

The boy and I sized each other up. He was slightly smaller than me, with hair that in strands was bleached nearly blond by the sun. He wore a ragged pair of khaki shorts. The two of us watched as Dhondu undid his bundle. Inside, wrapped in leaf packages, were two chappatis, some mango pickle, a green chilli, half an onion and a dab of red halwa. Dhondu unfolded the leaves and, with sighs of satisfaction, settled down to eat.

At first I couldn't get the boy's name out properly.

'Jula.'

'No. It's Jula!'

'Jura.'

'Jula!'

'Juda.'

'No! Jula!'

'Julda.'

'Jula!'

In Marathi they have a special 'rldl' sound, the one written like an 8 lying on its side. To pronounce it the tongue must rear up, form a cobra hood in the back of the mouth, then flick forward.

'Why did he call you a chicken?'

'Not chicken, mu*raga*! Boy, mu*rldlaga*!'

Jula and I soon discovered that if he stopped trying to speak Hindi and I stopped trying to speak Marathi we understood each other much better.

'Want to play a game?' I asked.

'Sure. What do you want to play?'

'Chhupan-chhupai?'

'What's that? I don't know it.' I noticed that he had a slight lisp.

I explained the rudiments of hide-and-seek and he exclaimed, 'Oh! You mean lapandav!' We were soon running round squirting one another with the hose.

The cook scolded me, when I came in soaking, and told me that I was not supposed to mix with Jula. 'When you start school you can make friends with proper people.'

Jula didn't go to school. His regular job was keeping an eye on the village cows, which were turned out to wander the hillsides. I sometimes came across him halfway up the slope of Bicchauda, or Dagala, the next mountain towards the village. He had all sorts of ways to amuse himself and taught me the excellent game of gulli-danda, which is played with two sticks and is essentially a form of golf, although several thousand years older. Our gulli was roughly four inches long, whittled at both ends. With the danda, which was a stout stick about eighteen inches long, we would strike one end of the gulli, flipping it up into the air, and then smash it again as hard as we could, the distance of the hit being measured in *dandas*. Or we would name a distant target and see who could get there in the fewest hits. Jula and I sometimes played marbles, bending our middle fingers back towards our wrists, like medieval trebuchets, and letting fly. Jula used small round pebbles and was amazed by my glass marbles with swirling centres. His toys were simple in the extreme.

He showed me how to tear a slot in a mango leaf, and clip it to my nostrils to inhale the tang.

'Wait till the rains come,' he told me solemnly. 'Then we'll have mangoes, magic, *muzza*.'

He showed me shiny-leafed bushes covered in white stars.

'They're called karvanda, the same name as our village.' These flowers would turn into berries, he promised me, which we would enjoy hugely . . . when the rains came.

One day Jula took me home with him to a low house that smelt of smoke and cattle, with a cow tethered near the doorway. Jula's house was made of baked clay. It had a thatched roof with an extra layer of fronds lashed on to keep out the rain. Inside was dry, dark and smoky. Chickens wandered in and out. Jula's family lived, ate and slept in this one large room and his mother cooked on a small clay hearth in one corner, feeding small twigs and fragments of dried cowdung-cake into the fire beneath her pot, fanning away the smoke.

He said, 'See who's come from the big house.'

His mother folded her hands to me and asked if I would like some milk. I said I would. It tasted salty and woodsmoky, but good. Being in Jula's house did not seem as strange as it might, because the cow and the straw and smell of dungsmoke reminded me of my grandfather's house in Kumharawa.

School in Ambona was very different from the Cathedral School in Bombay where the boys were sons of doctors and lawyers and businessmen and accountants. The KGV School was for everyone. (KGV stood for King George V – his statue, a dozen years after Independence, still stood in a dusty square outside Patrawalla's General Store – but we called it KayGee Vee.) I began to learn Marathi and found that it was quite like Hindi. Lots of words were the same, one just played different games with them. Once I was used to the strange accent and that weird 'rldl' sound, neither Dhondu's songs nor Jula's chatter seemed at all hard to understand.

Of course I only saw Jula at weekends, but he would give me the latest reports of goings on at Karvanda.

'Gokul said I lost his cow and created hell. Stupid shit, I knew where she was. It was Pandri, the white one. She always gets up to that halfway grove . . . My ma sent me to pick green karvandas to make pickle. I ate so many I got a stomach ache and then I got told off . . .' It seemed the poor fellow was always getting into trouble.

I began using some of Jula's expressions and got in trouble myself. One day Shashi the ayah rushed to my mother in tears saying I had insulted her.

'How?' asked Maya.

'I can't say, madam,' the girl replied. She seemed so old and grown-up to me, but she was probably only about twenty.

So I told my mother, 'I didn't want my sisterfucker soup.'

'I beg your pardon?'

'Bahinchod.'

'I'll deal with this,' Maya told the ayah, who was still in shock. There was something wrong with my mother's face, it was twitching and her cheeks were sucking in and out.

'In future,' she said, 'get your swear words from me. That way, when you use them, you'll know exactly what they mean.'

Jula and I soon had a new friend, an Anglo-Indian boy called Ben, whom I'd met at school. His father was the stationmaster and he would sometimes let us sit in the junction box to watch the signalmen shifting the big levers that moved the trains from one track to another. They ploughed past in clouds of steam and smoke and left live coals bouncing between the rails. 'See those all?' said Ben. 'My dad says they are devils dancing.'

Ben was a year older than Jula and me. He could ride a bike and was allowed to borrow his father's bicycle, of which he was hugely proud. It was an old British Hercules with a massively strong steel frame. Ben's legs were not long enough to reach the pedals from the seat, so he rode standing up, with one foot through the frame. I sat on the crossbar and mounted thus we made bandit raids on the Ambona fruit market, swooping down to scoop a guava or an orange off the top of a neatly piled pyramid.

'Hey Bhalu, you ever gone fishing? My, what fun we'll have when the rains come.'

The rains again. I told Ben what Jula had said about mangoes and magic and *muzza*, which means 'fun', and invited him to our house. After that he came most weekends and we would roam the hills looking for Jula and make forays into the jungle pretending that we were hunting for wild animals. About two miles from our house was a cliff, a three-thousand-foot drop over which a tiger, in hot and reckless pursuit of a deer, was said to have fallen to its death. We would creep to the edge, lie on our tummies and peer down into the dizzying gulf. Even with my body pressed full length to the warm rock, I always felt my feet were rising into the air, about to tumble me over the edge. The place was called Tiger's Leap.

By our day the tigers were gone, but the hills were covered in forest — sal, teak, mango, bamboo — and full of animals. There were wolves, wild boar, deer and of course, dog-eating panthers.

We knew that Babu loved hunting, but we soon found out that he had a reputation locally as a famous shikari. We children loved hearing his stories. Out on a forest path one night, he saw two green eyes in the darkness, at the height of a man's head.

'At first, obviously, I assumed it was a ghost,' he said. 'But then I noticed that the eyes were too close together.'

Our heads bobbed in agreement. Of course.

'Babu, what did you do when you saw the green eyes?'

'Well, I lifted my gun and fired,' he said. 'There was a terrifying shriek, and this huge snake crashed down right in front of me.'

We knew this story was true because we saw the snake. Babu brought it home in my father's Humber. He opened the boot, and there it was, two large coils of brown and black python with a head like a dog's, blemished where Babu's bullet had punched a hole in it. The python smelt musty. My mother talked of having it skinned and made into a handbag and shoes. For weeks afterwards I fancied I could smell it in the car.

When he found out that we liked wandering in the forest, Babu gave us some important advice. 'If you are in the trees,' he said, 'and it's near evening, or if you come to a place that's deeply shaded, keep your ears open and if you hear a long low whistle – like this – run for your life and don't ever look back.'

The whistler was deadly. It was a flying snake, a cobra with two stubby aeroplane-like wings, which uttered its strange cry when it sighted prey. If you weren't careful it would swoop down on you out of the trees.

'How can you tell it's not a bird?' we protested.

'Birds don't make noises like that,' he said, and proceeded to imitate the calls of the forest birds: chakor, koel, bulbul, mynah, crow, drongo, did-you-do-it, shrike, kite, woodpecker.

One day he brought home two ragged balls of feathers which he'd found on the ground under a nest. Baby birds. He said a snake had probably had the rest. They took up residence in a shoebox.

Babu would feed them milk with an eye-dropper, then mash up a little meat for them and offer it to them on the tip of a finger. Within a few weeks they were glossy, plump and very tame. Babu presented them to Maya. They were her first pair of bulbuls.

Even Babu's stories seemed ordinary beside the things that Dhondu and Jula talked about. The forest was full of ghosts and goblins – it seems odd to me to use these English words – bhoots and prets, we called them, pisachas, rakshasas. There was no question but that these spirits were real. People saw them, often. Some were well known. There was Bhensachor who went round masquerading as a buffalo, 'But if you get near, pow! He attacks!' Bhensachor could change in a flash to a goat, or a wind in the trees, or a flame. All spirits were devious. A perfectly ordinary-looking man might come up to you and ask for some tobacco, but if you replied, his head would start whirling round and round and when it stopped you would be looking into a face with glaring eyes and teeth like daggers. You might be going through the forest and see a child half-hidden near a place where paths crossed, crying its eyes out. 'Don't be fooled! It's Rowlia and if you say even one word to her, her legs start lengthening and she grows and grows until she's a monster.'

Some spirits made no pretence at being human. There was a man with the head of a fish, who cried out that he was thirsty.

'If you give him water, you are done for, because his throat is as fine as a needle and he will drink a dozen pots of water before he's satisfied. Even then, instead of being grateful, he'll follow you to learn where you live and he'll steal the food from your house.'

There were many others – Jimp and Khechar, Khais and Vetal

and Satvi, Bhoochadiya and Haadal, who from the front looked like a lovely woman, but from behind was nothing but a skeleton. 'If you meet a pretty girl in the forest, first look to see if her feet are on back-to-front, for if they are, it's Haadal.'

Dhondu and Jula knew where the evil spirits congregated and from time to time held parties – the burning ghat by the lake, the small shrine on top of Bicchauda mountain. The villagers were wary of these places by day and never went near them at night.

On nights of thunder and lightning, the ghosts gambolled and played, drank and swore, told jokes and smoked, up at the shrine of the old Mother, up on top of the hill.

'But if one has the courage to go, and survives, then the ghosts and goblins are forced to grant that person's wish.'

Shashi the ayah seemed scared too.

'What lies he tells!'

One day, Jula appeared in the garden, dressed as usual in his khaki shorts, but wearing on his head what appeared to be half a boat, woven of wicker and lined with leaves.

'Don't you know anything? It's an irrla.'

'What is it for?'

'To keep the rain off, of course.'

'What rain?'

'The rain that's coming. It's going to piss down.'

That afternoon the sky clouded and there was a fierce lightning storm. We could see the flashes miles away, over Duke's Nose, which soon disappeared as a sullen cloud swept over the lake. Almost before we knew it, the rain was pelting down all around us in fat drops that exploded in the dust. Such a smell arose, a sweet woody earthy scent (Tagore called it 'the goodly smell of rain on dry ground') that cannot be imagined unless you have experienced it. Within minutes the rain was falling so hard that it blurred the landscape. It softened all the colours, mixing them with white. It was like looking through a gauze curtain. The hillsides immediately streamed with water.

After a week the quiet lake had become a sea. When we went down to the shore we could no longer see the other side, just water stretching to a cloudy horizon, and choppy waves surging in over our feet. The rains had come. Everyone was happy. Dhondu sang as he worked, wearing a larger version of Jula's rainhat.

> 'just smell the milk in the pot
> so fresh the steam is rising
> and it hasn't even been boiled,
> oh yes, this is the kind of milk
> a man needs before
> he goes off to fight the Mughals'

'Dhondu, who are the Mughals?'

'How on earth should I know? They're the people you go off to fight in songs. But the world is full of Mughals, hey Bhalu? The landlord's a Mughal. The moneylender's a Mughal. The cook, he's definitely a Mughal.'

When I think of Ambona, she is always the first one to come to mind, before Jula, Ben or any of the others. I know I have told this story chronologically, from the beginning of my time there, but that's not how it is in my memory. When I think back to those years, she is always the first one. She is there instantly. I am with her. We are at a pool on the slope of Bicchauda, with rain making rings on the surface. It's the best weather for fishing, I tell her they'll bite at anything. I am proudly teaching her everything I know, which is everything that Jula and Ben have taught me. We're after mawra, a kind of catfish. They have whiskers and like worms. Does she know how to find a worm, break it into bits and thread a hook? She looks appalled. She does not. She is eight years old, the same age as me and tanned almost as brown, with hay-coloured plaits tied up in ribbons. Her glasses have splots of mud on them.

Her mother is my mother's best friend.

Auntie Sybil — we called all our parents' friends Auntie and Uncle — sometimes spent weekends at our house in Ambona in the first months after we moved there. I used to look forward to her visits because she was cheerful and jokey, and always brought me some exciting toy, a tin aeroplane from Crawford Market, a red B. E. S. T. double-decker bus with a key sticking out of the side.

It was August. We had been living in Ambona for six months and were well and truly into the rains, on school holidays — well, all except for Jula who had no school and no holidays — when my mother told us that Auntie Sybil had been ill and was coming to stay with us for a few weeks.

'She's bringing her little girl, who's your age, so I want you to be nice to her. Take her round with you.'

I received this news with mixed feelings. Auntie Sybil was nice, and it was fun to wonder what she would bring me, but a girl?

Babu and my mother went to fetch them and took me along. Ambona station was crowded with people waiting for the Deccan Queen and loud with the cries of hawkers.

'Chayvadé vadévadé! Chayvadé vadévadé!' (tea, vadas)

'Chikkivadé! Ambona chikkivadé!' (chikki, Ambona chikki)

The grumble of the train slowing down, a comfortable, warm sooty smell, and hawkers running alongside.

'Tsai, tsai garam, garam tsai garam.' (tea, hot tea, hot-hot tea)

Among the crowd that had just got off the train was Auntie Sybil, her pale skin accentuated by dark sunglasses, looking a little lost. My mother went up to her and hugged her for a long time. To my great disappointment, she had not brought anything for me. 'This is Rosie, our ayah,' said Auntie Sybil to my mother. Standing just behind Sybil was a dumpy old lady in a long skirt who turned to the carriage and said something that sounded like, 'Commisskilly.'

Off the train climbed a girl dressed the way English children are portrayed in old books, in a floaty dress that made her look as if she had come to take tea on a lawn by the Thames. Under a straw hat tied with ribbon I saw a pointed chin, like a fox. Eyes, made huge by her glasses, of a startling grey-green and hair the colour of the grasses on the hillsides before the rains.

'Oh, isn't she lovely?' my mother sighed.

I never admitted that until a few months ago, I myself had known none of these things.

She was an amenable student. And learned fast.

We went in search of Jula and found him in his rainhat with his cows a little way up Dagala, near the village.

'What on earth is he wearing?' she wanted to know.

'Ask him,' I said.

'But I don't know how.'

So I whispered to her, and she said, 'He kaay ae?' What is that? They made a strange sight, side by side. I told Fever that the irrla, the rainhat, was lined with the leaves of the palasa tree, the flame-of-the-forest, which had been covered in red flowers when we first arrived in the hills.

We stood, surrounded by cows whisking their tails in clouds of flies. Jula had an odd habit of grabbing at the air. The cows' tails would whisk and Jula would snatch at the empty air.

Fever said, 'Whatever is he doing?'

I explained that it was just a thing Jula did and we all ran round, catching invisible flies.

Jula was as interested in Fever's umbrella as she in his rainhat. He asked her if he could open and shut it a few times. He told me that there were a couple of umbrellas in the village, but he'd never been allowed to handle one.

I asked Jula to teach Fever gulli-danda, but he said it was the wrong season. 'It's too wet. We'd lose the fucking gulli.'

We were weeks into the rains, and the hills, bare and brown when we came to Ambona, were knee-high in rough emerald grass. So Fever asked if she could wear his rainhat and she chased after us shouting a rhyme of her own invention.

'I'm the ingle-pingle-pani and I've come to take the rani,
I'm bad and I'm mean and I've come to steal the queen.'

We stayed out until it began to get dark and I said we should go home. She said, 'No, not yet.' So I took her to Karvanda where Jula's mother, who by now knew me well, received her gravely and gave us glasses of her smoky milk. Something was cooking in the pot on the chhula and Fever said, 'Mmm, that smells nice.'

Jula's mother asked me to translate and when I told her, pressed us to have some food. I tried to refuse, because I knew how poor they were, but she wouldn't allow it. She made us sit on the string bed, that they call a khaat. Fever said it sounded like 'cot'.

When Jula's mother put the plate of food in front of her, Fever said, 'He kaay ae?'

'Oh, she can speak!' exclaimed Jula's mum, delighted. She said, 'Ha bhat ani he varen. Te kalvun kha.' (It's rice and dal, mix them up and eat.)

'Can I have a knife and fork?' Fever asked, when I translated.

'Amhi kaatetsamtse vaaprit nai, hataanich jevto,' said Jula's mum, convinced that this little blonde girl could speak Marathi.

When I told Fever that they did not use knives and forks, she won my admiration by dipping her hand without hesitation into the rice. Jula's mother was equally captivated.

'Such a sweet little thing,' she said. 'Just look at those eyes. Like the brahmin's wife. Big soulful lamps. Don't forget to invite me to your wedding!' And she laughed until she started coughing, cough, cough, cough, fanning the smoke away from in front of her face, her bangles jangling.

When we left she said to me, 'Bhalu, don't get that child into mischief. Something is troubling her. You can see it in her eyes.'

I knew exactly what she meant, only it had nothing to do with eyes like the brahmin's wife. A lot of people in the hills had grey-green eyes, it was a thing peculiar to that region. It was nothing to do with eyes. I already knew what the trouble was.

Fever wanted to go fishing. I knew the good spots and where the biggest fish, the singda, mund and kolus were. Ben had shown me. Fever needed a rod, and I wanted a new one, so Ben took us to see his father.

Ben's dad was much more exciting than mine. He was a man as brown and wrinkled as a walnut, with bright blue eyes, who had once been a wrestler and still had a tremendous physique. He kept himself fit by whirling Indian clubs on the verandah of their house, and called himself a pahalvan. He put his strength down to the fact that he was part English, though by what distant derivation one was not sure. Occasionally, when he was drunk, he would sing 'God Save the Queen', which he said still sounded odd to him, because he had got so used to God saving the King.

Ben's dad did a lot of fishing for the frying pan. His wife made a catfish curry to a recipe which she said only Anglo-Indians knew.

'Come, sit, sit, all of y'all. Have something . . . Ben? Where's that boy gone? Ben, boil some water, put the pot.'

'Already done it,' Ben said.

She gave us tea sweetened with jaggery, which was hard brown bittersweet rocks of raw sugar. We watched Ben's dad trim the rods from stems of bamboo, about six feet long.

'Now,' he said, 'we need a float.' He took a peacock feather and shaved away all the glorious blue and green-gold vanes, leaving a white stem, which he cut into three-inch lengths.

To the tip of the rod he attached a line, and to the line, on a sliding knot, one of the lengths of feather stem.

'Wouldn't use rods like this at *home*,' he said to Fever. 'I'd use a proper rod, with a reel and all.'

She looked blank and it turned out that by 'home' he meant England. He had never been there, but then neither had Fever.

Next day we went with our new rods, Rosie following.

I took an empty tin for worms.

'Where do you get them? Do you buy them?'

'You'll see.' I guessed that, being a girl, she wouldn't like this. All around the pond in the grass were cowpats in various stages of decay. I showed her how to lift the drier portions. The slime below was full of writhing pink bodies.

'Ugh, I'm not doing that.'

I picked out a worm, broke it into four jerking pieces and showed her how to work one of them onto the hook.

'It's horrible,' she said. 'I feel sorry for them.'

'They don't feel anything. Anyway, each bit grows into a new worm, so throw one bit on the ground, and it's the same as setting it free. They don't mind . . . There, now you do it.'

'I can't', she said.

But I insisted. If she wanted to fish with me, she would have to bait her own hook. Rosie screamed. Fever, in her Edwardian child's frock, was on her knees in a cowpat with creatures wriggling out between her fingers.

Rosie insisted on following us everywhere, but we did our best to give her the slip. We took exceptionally difficult routes up steep places, or through thick bushes. She soon had to give up, but still she did her best to spy on us. As we neared home, we would see her standing on the verandah watching the path.

Once, returning from a tryst with Jula, we saw her umbrella bobbing behind us across the wet hillside. Later she complained to Sybil, 'Killymem, I see Misskilly playing with a dirty village boy and she was wearing his hat. Who knows what lice and what all?'

But Sybil did not want to hear. She didn't scold us and Rosie went away in a huff. I overheard Sybil saying to my mother, '. . . that woman, spying on me all the time.' I knew that Rosie went round telling our servants that Killy Memsahib was no good. Not a real Killigrew. Maybe this was why Auntie Sybil cried such a lot. She and my mother spent a great deal of time in my mother's office, talking earnestly in low voices.

'They're talking about *love* and things like that,' Fever told me, and opened her eyes very wide as if nothing more need be said.

'You know this love stuff,' I said. 'Well, um, I don't love you or anything, but I like you quite a lot.'

She cried 'Oh!' and I didn't know if I'd offended her. But she came close, put her hands on either side of my face and kissed me on my lips. 'I love *you*, Bhalu,' she said. 'You're my *best* friend. You're so clever and brave and I don't know *what* I'd do without you.'

That, I suppose, was the moment. I fell in love with her.

After that Rosie did not go out with us any more, but she seemed determined to punish us. One day I took Fever to one of my favourite places, where a stream came showering over a small cliff and formed a deep pool among the rocks.

'Look out for snakes,' I told her. The hillsides were alive with cobras driven from their holes by the rain. But it was a glorious day, one of those hot sunny days you get in the middle of the monsoon. The sun shone down through the trees and into the pool, lighting it up from within, like an aquarium.

In the pool you could find danios, long as your middle finger, striped bright blue along their silver bodies. There were comical-looking loaches to be tickled from under stones on the stream bed. We stood, still as rocks, up to our knees in water, submerging a handkerchief by its four corners and waiting for fish to swim over. We caught a dozen small fish and put them in a small zinc pail we had brought for the purpose. We intended to start our own fish tank at home. Our clothes were soon soaked, transparently clinging.

'We'll get in terrible trouble,' she said. 'We'd better take them off and let them dry in the sun.'

'What? And go around with no clothes?'

'I don't mind if you don't.'

So we took off all our clothes – I can remember thinking how pale and thin she was and how helpless that little cleft looked, where her legs joined. She saw me looking and said, 'I've never seen one of *those* before either.'

Then she had a fit of giggles and said, 'This is what it was like *before* God lost His temper.'

She walked to a nearby sal sapling, stood on tiptoes, broke off two leaves the size of dinner plates and gave one of them to me. 'And this is what He made them do *afterwards* . . .' She cocked her head and posed, leaf in place, with a knowing smile.

So we threw the leaves away and spent all the rest of that sunny afternoon bathing under the waterfall and swimming in the pool.

Back home we had just installed our captures in a large glass jar when Rosie came storming in, furious. She paraded us before Sybil, made Phoebe strip to her knickers, then pulled them down.

'See, Killymem! See! It is *all over*,' tracing the marks of sun on Phoebe's hip. She added, 'No use seeing Bhalu, he's an Indian.'

But once again, Sybil was not interested. Maya was summoned and the case put before her. She told Rosie in a voice that teetered on the edge of anger that Sybil was not to be troubled with such things. She had been very ill. She needed time to recover. Later, Rosie took our jar and emptied it, fish and all, down the drain.

My mother and Sybil spent a great deal of time together. Sybil hardly ever went out. Maya got our doctor to visit her regularly. Fever told me that the doctor had prescribed iron tablets, and I wondered what eating pellets of iron must do to Auntie Sybil's teeth. She was told to rest, so the two of them sat in my mother's office and read, often aloud to one another, and swapped family stories. The Killigrews had a history every bit as romantic as our own. They had been in India for generations. Once upon a time they had been in the opium trade. They too had fought in the 1857 war, but on the British side. My mother urged Sybil to write down these stories. They could publish them jointly. As Sybil said, there are two sides to every story but rarely are the two sides to be found in the same book. Maya said that there were in fact many more than two sides, but two sides would be enough. If reliving buried hurts could make them disappear, it would be wise to give our family histories a thorough airing.

During their last few days with us, Fever followed me around like a puppy. Ben said he knew I was in love with her, because I was always pulling her pigtails.

'One day y'all'll get married,' he said, but we knew otherwise.

'I'm never going to marry,' she told me one night.

She slept in my room and we would lie awake and talk. Our beds were side by side. We would reach out and touch hands across the gap. There was a game we played in the dark. Trailing one's fingertips over the other's arm from wrist to elbow was a 'long'. Tickling the palm was a 'little'. We'd take it in turns to give and receive these small, exquisite pleasures: 'Bhalu, do twenty longs,' 'Fever, give ten littles.'

'My mum and dad don't love each other,' she told me that night. 'That's why we came here. Mummy got ill, I used to hear her being sick every morning. She said not to tell my dad, 'cos he would be angry. She cries when she thinks no one can see.'

I couldn't imagine anyone not loving Auntie Sybil. She had been so sweet, so full of fun. Fever's dad must be a monster.

I said, 'If you don't marry then I won't either.'

She said, out of the darkness, 'I'd marry *you*, Bhalu.'

They were to leave us in September, before the end of the rains. My mother said Sybil had decided to return to England for her health, and was taking Phoebe. She did not know how long they would be gone. Phoebe was nervous. She had never been to England before. I promised I would write, giving her Jula's news, Ben's news, my news.

About a fortnight before they left a tremendous thunderstorm shook the hillsides. We could not go outside to play, so we asked my mother to tell us a story.

NAFÍSA JAAN ('SWEET' VERSION)

I clearly remember the day when Maya first told us the story of Nafísa Jaan. An afternoon dark as night, wind and rain beating on the house, oil lamps casting capering shadows (blackout caused by lightning strikes). It was too wet to do anything. Even Dhondu squatted in the shelter of the chicken-house and smoked one beedi after another. We children could not go out to play, so we were in the house, bored. My mother offered to tell us a story.

'Shivaji and the ghorpats!' I cried.

Shivaji was the Mahratta chief who had lived in these hills three hundred years before us, and spent his life fighting the armies sent against him by the Mughal emperor Alamgir and the Muslim Sultan of Bijapur. Shivaji's life was full of astounding adventures, but the best one was the way he recaptured the fort of Sinhagarh, the 'lion fortress', which was built on a huge cliff not many miles from our house. Sinhagarh had fallen into enemy hands. Shivaji wanted to take the garrison by surprise. He and his Mahrattas scoured the jungle for the biggest ghorpats (monitor lizards) they could find. Ghorpats are immensely strong and their toes cling for dear life to the rock face. Shivaji and his men tied ropes round the ghorpats' waists and set them on the cliff. The lizards began to climb the cliff. When they reached the top, Shivaji and his men swarmed up the ropes.

'You've already had that three times,' said my mother.

Sybil asked to hear *Nafísa Jaan*. Maya had written two versions of this story, the 'sweet' and the 'bitter'. Sybil wanted the 'sweet' *Nafísa Jaan*. For some reason my mother seemed reluctant.

'Not that story', she said. 'Choose another one.'

But Sybil, pale and wearing her dark glasses despite the gloom of the day, insisted. A peculiar hard expression on her face. So Maya began.

This story began a very long time ago and it has still not ended. Out of all the beginnings that one could choose, I would say that if a man called Lajju had not picked up a sword that he found lying on a battlefield in 1858, then the woman who called herself Nafisa Jaan would never have been born. And if the things that happened to Nafisa Jaan had not happened, then some of us sitting here would not have been born. Forty years after Thrice-Great, Lajju and Bhalu the First returned from the great rebellion . . . are you listening to this, Bhalu the Second?

[Yes, I am listening. Of course I'm listening. We all are. We are all there, sitting on our verandah, with the storm pressing down on us, rain hissing like knives on the roof and on the grass 'chicks' which were tied up all around the house like so many large flat irrlas. I am there with my sister Nina. Ben is there. Jula is there, curled up in a corner, smiling, though he knows not a word of English. The two ayahs, Shashi and Rosie, are there. The story is being told in English, because listening with us are our guests, my mother's friend Sybil and little blonde Fever.]

. . . the Kumharawans were still rebels. Many families, not least ours, had things to hide. Dozens of the older men had fought in Nana Saheb's army. The town was full of unwhispered secrets, but outwardly, in the havelis and courtyards and tea shops, life went on in its slow rhythms. Every winter, flights of duck arrived from across the Himalayas to honk in the marshes. In summer the bazaar filled, as it still does today, with uncouth Tibetans, come down from the mountains to sell trinkets of turquoise and silver, and the tubers of wild orchids.

Kumharawa was small, and less important than ever before in its history, but pride dictated that it should have its own squadron of cavalry. It also had a kotwal, a chief-of-police, who stood six foot six inches in his socks. The Raja, Qasim Khan, lived in a moon-palace – it was known as the Chand Mahal – which stood in huge grounds on the edge of the town. It was not a very ancient building, but it contained a zenana, in which lived the Rani and her children, two girls. Qasim Khan dearly loved his daughters but longed for a son. As a result, his wife was used to seeing a great deal of him. But then, for no very obvious reason, his visits began to tail off, and finally stopped. It was a servant who told the Rani what just everyone else in Kumharawa already knew, that Qasim Khan was spending his evenings, and some of his days, at a certain house in the oldest part of the town. In this house lived a tawaif, a singer, known as Nafisa Jaan.

> *yeh na thi hamari qismat keh wisaal-e-yaar hota*
> *agar aur jeeté rahté yehi intezaar hota*
> To be with him, that man I adored, was never to be my fate,
> And had I lived longer, all the longer I'd have had to wait

Nafisa could sing the ghazals of Ghalib in a way that destroyed your heart, yet her voice was never described as sweet. She was no Lata. Hers was, by all accounts, a harsh voice, but one capable of the most devastating honesty. She *understood* the poetry. When she sang *tere waadé par jiyee ham to yeh jaan jhoot jana*

keh khushi se mar na jaaté, agar intezaar hota

Do your promises keep me alive? If so, my life's a lie.

If I believed them I'd have died of joy, now wouldn't I?

her voice was both honey and vinegar. In one syllable she could convey sarcasm, longing, anger, love. They used to say of her that if Ghalib's words were inspired, it was she who breathed life into them. Not only this, but she could dance! She played games with the eyes that our filmi actresses could hardly dream of. And more . . . Parts of this story can't be told until some people here are older. And, no, Miss Phoebe, that doesn't mean I am concealing the truth.

A story is not like a running track. A story is a river, made by the joining of many streams. We can explore a few, but we can't turn back to trace them all. We have to choose carefully. A story is also like a road. It leads forward, but turnings constantly branch off from it. We may go down a few, but not all. Some are even dangerous. Every breath of a good story contains other stories, entering and leaving it, most of which will never be heard. That's what makes a good story good.

And now, after taking that detour, I can return to the main stream by telling you that Nafísa Jaan was herself a master of the art of storytelling. She had been trained in the kothas of Lucknow, or so it was said, for Nafísa never talked of her origins. She moved in a whirlwind of rumour. Some said she was the child of a noble Turkish family, stolen away and sold by her nurse. Others, because she could quote the beautiful love songs of Rumi's *Diwan-e-Shams* in Persian, said that her father must have been a wandering sufi poet. But the favourite story was that Nafisa was the illegitimate daughter of Mirza Ghalib himself, the child he had wanted all his life, whom in his last years he had taught to sing his poems. Ghalib was as old as the century. During the great rebellion he was living in Delhi where he witnessed the fighting and the atrocities of both sides. Nafisa could only have been his daughter if, at the time of our story, she'd been in her late thirties. But everyone who saw her described her as 'youthful'. Raja Qasim Khan, enamoured less of the verses she spoke than of the mouth that spoke them, started calling her his jaan-e-janaan, his 'life and soul', which, when this became known in Kumharawa, caused a great deal of sniggering at his expense. The truth about Nafisa's origins was, as you might expect, rather ordinary, but only two people knew it.

The Raja was quite besotted with her and was, as I have already said, soon spending all his time at her house. However flattering his attentions may at first have been, Nafisa Jaan must soon have found them suffocating. Nafisa was a unique and cultured woman. Her world was drawing rooms and music. She could flavour betel paans and conversation with equal subtlety. She could play chess. She could argue points of philosophy with maulvis and pandits. You could never accuse her of being a doormat. She was a woman born out of her time, a bright mind condemned by a society which undervalued women to a life of subservience, the work of a houri. Qasim Khan, who epitomised that society, doted on her. In her company he was no longer the dull, flabby, middle-aged, ruler-in-name of an insignificant state, but a maharaja, a nawaab, a prince with a destiny. And Nafisa, shrewd as she was clever, shamelessly flattered him.

Qasim Khan liked to think of himself as a shootin'-huntin'-fishin' man. No animal in the forest, from Almora to Kathaniya Ghat, was safe from him. The trophy room in his palace was full of deer heads, boar heads, tiger heads, that glared at you off the walls with sad glass eyes. He would shoot anything. Once, in the company of your great-grandfather, he saw a one-horned spotted deer and could not resist potting even that. The miserable trophy was mounted and sent round to our house, where our Bhalu, yes, Bhalu the Second, this Bhalu sitting here, one day found it.

[True. Exploring Grandfather's house in Kumharawa, one day I found a storeroom full of interesting things. Huge clay jars, taller than a man, with two-inch thick wooden lids. I slid one aside and saw that the jar was full of wheat. There was a metal trunk, like a large seaman's chest, filled to the top with rice. In a smaller trunk I found a neatly folded naval uniform and my father's dress sword, together with a diary which he had begun on 3 September 1939 and which petered out a few days later. In a corner was the carved wooden face of a deer, with a single antler fixed to it.]

Nafisa was not an outdoor girl, but she developed a mysterious liking for picnics. She said it was for her health, and for the same reason, she stopped granting him certain favours. Our hero used to take her to a mango grove by a lake where there stood, side by side, a small Hindu temple and a white maqbara which housed the bones of a Muslim saint. On these occasions he and his escort would ride while she was carried in a palqi because — this was her only fault — she was a rotten horsewoman.

Curiously, Nafisa constantly drew attention to this failing. She told Qasim that she wanted to learn to ride. She would go to war at his side like Rani Laxmibai. Of course neither she nor he could have known that there would be no more cavalry charges. The next battle in which anyone from Kumharawa would fight was at Ypres.

> *Nafísa, ey, Nafísa Jaan*
> *khaati hai supari-paan,*
> *chooma chaata Qasim Khan*
> *choos nikaala uska maan*
> *zameen pe thooki uski jaan*

Bhalu, shall we translate for our guests?

> Nafísa, hey, Nafísa Jaan
> loves to eat supari-paan,
> licks and kisses Qasim Khan
> sucked out all his royal pride
> spat his life out by the roadside

So sang the street urchins of 1896 (and yes, you children can chant it too, I will teach you later). The street children made this rhyme because when Qasim Khan ordered that Nafísa Jaan be given riding lessons, there was something he did not know. She had fallen in love with one of his cavalry officers. More than this, she was expecting the man's child.

Thus, some months passed and there came a point when Nafísa could no longer disguise the fact that she was going to have a child. She pleaded that she was too unwell to leave her house. The Raja wished to send his own hakim to her, but she refused. But she could not keep her news totally secret. Inevitably, tongues wagged.

When the Raja discovered Nafísa's affair, he drank himself

into a nasha, a chaos of jealous rage . . . children! Listen to the thunder in the sky above us. Hear the wind dashing rain against the house as if it wanted to wash it away. That was what the anger of the Raja was like. So, to complete the metaphor, the lightning struck. No one in Kumharawa ever learned the fate of the officer, and I too have no idea. He simply vanished. But everyone knew, or thought they knew, what had happened to Nafisa.

Nafisa Jaan, they said, heavily pregnant, her child due any day, had been obliged to leave her house and all her possessions and flee Kumharawa on foot. She had gone back, one said, to her old haunts in Lucknow. No, said another, she had been sighted in Delhi. A third said that she had travelled to Calcutta and married a rich Englishman. None of these stories were true. Nafisa Jaan never left Kumharawa.

It was night time when Nafisa's servant warned her that men were coming for her. Nafisa had no time to collect anything, let alone her precious belongings. She left her house and ran. She ran blindly through the darkness. Behind her, faintly, she could hear the pursuit. She ran till the breath was like sandpaper in her lungs and the blood was pounding in her veins. She was carrying a child in her womb, don't forget. She ran through the back lanes of Kumharawa until she came to the Shiva temple that stands opposite our house. She entered the temple and crouched behind the effigy. That is where they found her. They took her back to the palace and led her to the Raja, who struck her on the face and told her that she was going to die.

[My mother's voice at this point faltered, and we all shouted at her to continue. She looked at Sybil. 'Go on,' said Sybil, 'don't stop now.' So Maya carried on.]

Nafisa said, 'Let my baby be born. Then kill me. But don't kill my innocent child.'

He said, 'Your baby's death is not my concern.'

She knew then that there was no hope, and she said scornfully, 'It's not unborn children, but men like you who deserve to die!'

They took her down to the cellars under the palace. Down they took her, down, and down again, into the lowest basement, where the walls are supported by brick arches. In this deep dark place, they stood her in a niche. There were iron rings set in the wall and one of them unwound his turban and used it to bind her wrists to these rings.

Nafisa struggled and screamed, 'If you do this, I promise you, there will be retribution!'

But he stuffed the loose end of the turban into her mouth to muffle her screams. Then other men came with bricks and trowels and baskets of wet cement, and across the niche they began to raise a wall of bricks. Layer upon layer, higher and higher it rose, past her knees, her waist, her shoulders, her neck, until only a pair of eyes could be seen, pleading, through the vanishing gap and . . . oh my goodness, just look how dark it's become, it must be time for supper.

This was how my mother told the 'sweet' story of Nafisa Jaan.

'Bullshit!' said my friend Dost, when I told him the story many years later, in a Dongri alley darkened by blackout (the lightest thing in the street was the snowy white of his kameez). 'Your ma lifted the story of Anarkali from *Mughal-e-Azam!*'

'No, you're wrong,' I replied. 'I remember her telling that story before *Mughal-e-Azam* came out.'

I can remember everything about that evening in Ambona, the non-stop growl of rain, the glow of lamps in the house, the dark afternoon slipping gradually towards night. I remember that when my mother finished her story her friend Sybil was in tears. And that when Maya thought other people had stopped listening, she sang quietly to herself.

> *hué mar keh ham jo ruswa hué kyun na-ghar-e-dariya*
> *na kabhi janaaza uthaata na kahin mazaar hota.*
> Since I was to die disgraced, why did no river drown me?
> Then I'd have had no funeral, and no tomb built around me?

A sun so hot it burned the blue out of the sky. The hills crouched like beasts around the lake, reaching rocky tongues to the water. In our garden, the guava trees were coated with dust. Captain Sahib would no longer allow his roses to be watered during the day. He made Dhondu wait till the evening cowdust-hour before laying the hose to their roots. In Bicchauda's forest bloodsucker lizards clung to mango trunks, mouths agape, but the stifling air resisted attempts to breathe it. At this season, sixteen centuries ago, the poet Kalidas saw a cobra, maddened by heat, slide for shade under a peacock's tail.

Something happened, far away. A brief éclat, so faint, it might have been a coconut falling on the other side of the mountains; so distant that we heard only its echo, half-caught in the heat of a drowsy afternoon. A tremor ran through the rocks. Light shook. A pulse of nothingness split the world and made a hole in time. Then everything was as before, and everything had changed. It was 1959, the year Fever learned to herd cows, I stopped going to school, Jula won himself an education and we met the wild man of the hills. All these things happened within a few weeks, at the very hottest time of the year, the furnace weeks before the monsoon.

At the beginning of May my mother announced unexpectedly that Sybil and Fever were coming to stay with us again. They had returned some months earlier from their trip to England. Sybil had been feeling much better, my mother said, but the clammy Bombay weather had made her ill again.

'Phoebe will miss school so I have found her a tutor. Someone who will come here to teach her.'

'To our house?'

'Yes.' Then she added something really exciting. 'I've arranged for you to be taught here as well. Just for the rest of this term.'

As before, we all went to the station to collect them. Fever had grown taller, and her floaty dress now barely reached her knees.

'What was England like?' I asked, when we were alone. Apart from what Ben's dad had told me, I knew it only through books: Enid Blyton mostly, her stories were everywhere. We had them all, the Famous Five, the Secret Seven, the Adventure series, the Mysteries that all began with R (*Ring O'Bells, Rilloby Fair, Rat-a-tat*). I also knew the Jeeves books, and Sherlock Holmes. Maya had made me read *David Copperfield* and *Jane Eyre* – 'If Jane could practise her Hindi verbs then so can you' – and everything of Kipling's. 'One can forgive Kipling for being an imperialist,' she told me, 'because he loved India.' I admired, but did not quite understand *Stalky & Co.* and loved *The Jungle Book*, but my favourite was *Puck of Pook's Hill*, about a faraway magical place called Sussex.

'It was cold and Granny's house smells of apples,' said Fever. 'But the weirdest thing was everyone else was English.'

'What do you mean everyone *else*?'

'Well, I'm Indian,' she said.

It had never occurred to me before that she was not 'one of us'. Really, it was obvious that she had never been anything else.

✳   ✳   ✳

Fever was restless. She mooched round the house and was rude to her ayah. She took my poster paints and made a picture of a fearful hag on the bedroom wall. Rosie was furious, and Sybil apologetic, but Maya insisted it be left.

'I don't know who it's meant to be,' she said, 'but it *glows*. That child has talent.'

Sybil and Maya spent a lot of time with their heads together. They smoked incessantly. They would vanish into my mother's writing room and sit there in a fug of smoke.

Fever told me, 'Mummy isn't really ill at all. She's unhappy.'

One day Fever and I were in the garden. The window of Maya's study was open and we caught bits of what they were saying, their voices alternating . . . me reassure you, this anguish you're going through . . . often accuse myself of trying to filch sympathy which is not mine by right . . . no no, if one has a true heart, one does not stop loving people . . . unimaginable torture for those directly involved . . . you must not worry, nothing will happen . . . works itself into nausea at least once a day . . . only draws bad situations towards you . . . Maya, such terror . . . not a religious person but if prayers come to your lips say them with complete concentration and belief that you are safe . . .

Fever whispered, 'Let's go.' She seemed very upset. I could not understand why.

We went in search of Jula. The village cows and buffalos were spread out on a spur of Bicchauda, eating the ajwain that perfumes the hillsides like a double-strength oregano.

'Won't have to walk so far when the rains come,' he said. We spent the day with him, chasing the cow that liked wandering.

'Hey, Pandri! *Hamba!*'

'Teach me how to do it.'

So he taught her the calls. 'Hamba. Come here! Haik! go! Haalya! turn round! Trrru or hurroo! to make them run.'

'Can we help you take them home?'

'Sure. Then you can come to my house. Will you come? Ma'll be so pleased. She's sure to make poli. Have you tasted poli, Fever?'

She turned to me and asked, 'Can we go, please?'

I said, 'We can do anything we like.'

So Fever ran around practising cowherding.

'Do you know all their names?'

'Of course.'

'What are they then?'

'Okay, this one is Gaulan, she's sweet. The white one is Pandri. She likes wandering off. You have to keep an eye on her. This one,' (a dark cow with a white blaze on her brow) 'is Chandri, 'cos she has the mark of the moon.'

'Where does she go to?'

'Well she likes shade, so she goes up to the trees. But she has gone miles sometimes – Bicchauda, Dagala, Dinkara.'

'Dinkara, where's that?'

'As far as you can go in a day.' He pointed to a cone shaped peak that rose blue in the haze above the far slope of Dagala.

'What about the one behind it?'

'That? It has no name. It's a hill of *beyond*.'

She pointed to the palest, most distant line of mountains, a faint blue graph barely distinguishable from the sky. 'What about those?'

'Those?' said Jula. 'I don't know. I guess they are the hills of beyond and *a day*.'

*   *   *

Rosie the ayah, always on the look-out for new ways to cause trouble for us, told Maya that we had been eating meals at Jula's house.

My mother said, 'I'm happy about you going to Jula's house, but they can't afford to be feeding you.'

Jula had three younger brothers and sisters. They ran around naked, with strings round their waists, but they were better fed than some of the village children, whose swollen bellies made them look like cooking pots on stick legs.

'I usually just have milk,' I told her.

A few days later there was a man's voice outside our house.

'Haik! Trrooo!'

'. . . Grandfather will be pleased,' Maya was saying. 'His wayward daughter-in-law sees sense at last.' We were gathered in the shed next to the chickens, watching four large buffalos chew through a mound of green fodder.

'He was adamant, when they came to stay with us in Bombay. I did my best to make them comfortable, but nothing was right. The fruit was pulpy, vegetables from the bazaar lacked taste.' She did a fine imitation of my grandfather's growl. '"Call this an aubergine? You should see mine at home . . . Call this a tomato? Ours are so much juicier." Grandmother was nodding like a doll. Grandfather said he could not allow us to feed the children this inferior stuff a moment longer. He said there was nothing for it, he'd have to send us baskets from their garden. We gave them Alfonso mangoes from Crawford Market. Grandmother made a face and swore the wild tukhmi mangoes in Kumharawa had more flavour. "We'll send you mangoes from home." But the cow was the final straw.'

'Oh please tell!' said Sybil, in stitches of laughter. The first time I had seen her laugh since her illness. It suited her. She used to be such a lovely, happy lady before she got sick.

'Grandfather said "These milkmen are wretches." He had a row with the doodhwalla. Asked him did he just water the milk or also urinate in it? The poor man was most offended, although of course he *was* watering the milk. So Grandfather told us, "You must keep your own cow." I pointed out that living in a flat, we had nowhere to keep one. "What nonsense! There's a patch of grass below. You can tether it there." "But Grandfather, that's the lawn." Before they left he told me, "These Bombay cows are wretched things. I'll send you a cow from Kumharawa"'.

A woman from the village came to milk the buffalos and Maya explained why she had bought them. She had decided to distribute milk to children in nearby villages. She delivered it herself, walking through the countryside from village to village, followed by two men carrying a huge churn on a pole. Sybil accompanied her on these expeditions and sometimes Phoebe and I would tag along too. The children would run to meet us, bringing tin cups and little pots. When they drank, milk ran down their chins.

The weather was unbearably hot. Something of the mugginess of the coast seemed to have crawled up the ghats. Fever said, 'It's so different. Last year it was green. Now it's all dry.'

'That's because you came after the rains had started.'

Fever had never witnessed the change of season, the miracle that happens when the drought finally breaks.

'Listen children, I'll tell you how it will be.

'Murderous as it is now, it will get hotter. And hotter. When it seems that no living thing, human, animal or plant, can bear it any more, the first clouds will appear in the West.

'Beyond the hills, the clouds will mass like an army of chariots. The sun will falter. As the first dark outriders sweep across its face, halfway up the slopes of Bicchauda, trees will glow like jewels in a strange greenish light. Huge slow thunderclaps will ride across the valleys. Hoofbeats of approaching rain.

'The first heavy drop will hit the earth. Another drop. Another. Stamping the dust with leopard spots. The earth will sigh in relief, exhaling a strong mineral-and-herb-scented breath. The hills will vanish behind curtains of rain. Above the drumming of rain, the world will come alive with the sound of water, trickling, gurgling, pouring. Where the cracked earth lies in hollows, there will be puddles. Within hours, they will be ponds, then pools in a muddy torrent. Jula, caught on his mountain slope, will put on his irrla and caper. In Karvanda his ma and the other villagers will come out of their houses and open their arms to the pelting clouds.

'"May you never be parted from the lightning."

'The hills will turn green in one night. There'll be waterfalls. In less than a day the world we know will be gone. A six-inch high rainforest will cover the land, patrolled by red-and-black centipedes whose fangs can split shoe leather. Giant black butterflies with yellow hind wings will fly on the hill slopes.

'For two weeks, the streams will run brown as Indian Railways tea, then, as if at a prearranged signal, they'll clear and we'll see weed in the current, and tiny fish, where they come from no one knows. Crabs, black ones and yellow ones, will appear in the fields, where the women plant paddy. Halfway up Dagala mountain, there are round holes in the rock. The hill-people use them to brew liquor. They do it in March, pour in water and flowers of the mahua tree and other things, and then seal up the rocky jars with clay and straw and cowdung. When the rains come, the holes that aren't sealed will become water gardens, complete with plants and the little darting fry. Just wait, you'll see.'

This is how Maya described the onset of the monsoon.

But the rains had not yet come.

Those last baking weeks were the best time to see (and shoot) animals, because only a few waterholes still remained.

'Will you take us when you go hunting, Captain Sahib?'

She asked the question with that charming tilt of her head, to which my father, who showed scant interest in his own children, at once succumbed. So an expedition was planned. My father and Babu were going to a waterhole, a remnant of the shrunken lake, after wild boar.

We went to bed early. When we were woken, after midnight, the heat had subsided by a few degrees. It felt almost cool and we were wrapped up in the back of the jeep. Our cook, Yelliya, sat beside us, with a primus stove and a box of foodstuffs. He would make tea through the night and breakfast at dawn.

Babu drove on rough tracks through the forest, our headlights picking out black trees, leaves overhanging, branches sweeping over us so we had to duck, the jeep bouncing on ruts and around stones, raising clouds of that thick sweet red dust. For every turn, he had a new story. One track we passed led off to a small lake, extremely deep. The villagers would not go there because it was supposed to be haunted, so the fish had grown huge. You could shine a torch into the water and up they would come, monstrous shapes spiralling out of the depths. Babu said the best way to get one was to shoot it.

Yelliya grew more and more excited. 'Babu, jaanvar dekhenge jaroor? Pukka?'

'Arré yaar,' said Babu, who enjoyed jibing at the cook's superior Bombay airs, 'yeh tere ghar ke log thodi hain. Aate jaate hain. Is hi liye to jungli kehlate hain. *Timetable* thodi rakte hain!'

'What are you laughing at?' Fever whispered.

So I told her.

'Yelliya asked, "Babu, will we definitely see animals? Pukka?" and Babu said, "Arré yaar, these are not members of your household. They come and they go. Why else are they called jungli? They hardly keep to timetables."'

So we watched, and in the headlights saw a pangolin, large monkeys crashing about, several hares and a giant-squirrel leaping through a tamarind tree.

When the jeep stopped, we walked for a mile or more in darkness on a path that wove through tall grasses shining blonde in the light of our torches. Eventually we came to a place where Babu had made a hide out of dry thorn branches, near the lake where the animals came to drink.

'Be very quiet,' my father warned us. Perhaps an hour went by. I began to get hungry. My tummy rumbled.

'What was that?' whispered Captain Sahib. Fever had a fit of giggles that would not stop.

It was almost dawn, and the first smears of light appeared above the hills of beyond and a day.

Babu and my father decided to take their shotguns and go in search of jungle fowl. Fever and I didn't want to remain with Yelliya, so we went for a walk.

Even though it was so early the heat had already begun. The grasses were brittle. The forest trees were dusty, but it was cool in their shade. In a clearing we found some mahua trees, their trunks scarred where people had cut them to gather the intoxicating sap.

'If we stay still, might we see a bear?'

Maya had said that bears and wild boar often came to lick the mahua wounds. So we climbed into a nearby tree and waited. The forest was very still, all browns and ochres and yellows.

'Bhalu, there's someone else here.'

I could see nothing, in the mosaic of sunlight and leaf.

'There!'

In a patch of deep shade, by the mahua tree, was a man. Was there? The shadow pattern shifted and he was gone.

There were people in the hills whom even the villagers knew little about. Dark men who wore next to nothing and carried bows. Dhondu told me they were called Kathodis.

'You want to watch out. They're masters of magic.'

We met my father and Babu coming back through the woods with their guns and a jungle fowl for the pot. We fell in behind them and pretended that we too had guns, and took pot-shots at anything that moved. The path we were on led through a clearing, a place where lightning had felled a large tree and opened up a gap in the forest canopy. It was a place where you would often see unusual butterflies. We were almost across when Babu, who was leading, stopped so suddenly that my father almost collided with him. He held up his hand in that hunter's gesture which means, 'Hush, be quiet and still,' and, very slowly, motioned with his chin. There! In the trees at the edge of the forest, a man was standing watching us. He was dark, darker than the villagers, and appeared to be naked. For a few seconds we stared at him and he at us, then, to my surprise, my father took a pace forward with his hands respectfully folded, and called out a greeting in Marathi. The man replied, also in Marathi, and stepped forward out of the forest. I got a good look at him. He wore nothing but a small pouch. In his hand was a bow, and strung from his waistband, a dead lal-chuha, a squirrel rat. He and Babu began a conversation, too rapid to follow, but from the man's arm waving, and the cunning twisting-turning motions of his hand, he seemed to be telling us where the game in the forest had got to. I grinned and aimed my airy shotgun at him. My father angrily struck down its invisible barrel.

'He's young, he has no sense,' my father said and the man laughed and made some sort of admonishing gesture. My father gave him the bird we had shot and we went home empty-handed.

My father was enthusiastic about the cattle. He said their warm reek reminded him of his boyhood in Kumharawa, where he used to milk the cow. He talked of starting a dairy, and suggested that we could give Jula a full-time job. Maya vetoed this idea. She would have done it anyway, I can see that now, but the immediate cause was rude Mr Daruwalla, our tutor, an angular young man in a pale lemon suit who, as he taught, would stand at the window, handkerchief to his nose, staring with distaste at the dusty country surroundings.

Fever loathed lessons. A lot of the time we did sums. We also read history, but unlike me she didn't study Akbar and Aurangzeb and Shivaji. Instead he'd ask her, 'What happened in 1066? Who was the last Plantagenet?'

If Jula happened to be around during our lessons he would make faces at the window, or throw pebbles at it and run away. Mr Daruwalla would fling the shutters wide and yell, 'You ignorant little boy. Go away!'

He taught us literature too. He was reading *Macbeth* and Fever, who claimed to follow barely one word in three, was bored. One day Jula came looking for us and found Maya and Sybil at the back of the room, listening. Mr Daruwalla didn't dare shout at Jula with them there, so he said he could wait.

> When shall we three meet again
> In thunder, lightning, or in rain?

Daruwalla declaimed sonorously, giving each word its full weight in the line. I fidgeted and nudged Jula. But he was lost, caught up in a kind of rapture.

> When the hurly-burly's done
> When the battle's lost and won
> That will be e'er the set of sun . . .

When he finished, Jula clapped loudly.
'Oh my, thank you!' said Daruwalla, with heavy sarcasm.
But Maya asked Jula if he had really enjoyed the speech.
He said, 'I didn't understand a thing, but I liked the sound.' He

mimed slapping a dholak. 'It was like drums.'

It was after this that my father proposed Jula for the job with our buffalos and Maya said no. She announced that Jula must go to school.

'School's not for the likes of us,' Dhondu said, when this was put to him. 'He has to work, as I did.'

But Maya said that a school would be made in the village. She would find a teacher to begin classes. It would be free to all village children who wished to go.

She opened a ledger and wrote in it,

I. Jula.

Fever came to me looking upset. 'Something bad has happened, I don't know what.' A phone call had come from Bombay for Sybil. She took it in Maya's writing room and came out looking like a ghost. Maya instantly ran to her. 'What is it? What is it, darling?' They went back into the room. Fever applied her ear to the door. She told me, 'I didn't hear much. Something about "letters" and "shaitan". I don't know what it means.' She thought a moment. 'Could we ask your mother?'

'She'd never tell us. We're just children. We're not supposed to know anything.'

'It's horrible being *just* a child!' said Fever. Then, in that oddly precocious way of hers, 'I wish she'd pull herself together.'

'Shaitan means devil,' I said. 'A demon. Satan.'

She looked at me. 'Bhalu, you know what Jula said about the temple on the hill? Getting wishes granted? I want to go there.'

'Well, if you're not afraid of ghosts.'

'Of course not,' she said, full of scorn. 'Are you?'

'Never,' I lied. 'But there's no point, yet. It has to be at night, when there's thunder and lightning.'

The path up the side of Bicchauda wound through bleached grasses and thickets of scrub. Up and up it went, skirting the edge of a sheer basalt drop that, when the rains came, would be slick with water, with ferns growing in every crevice. Far away across the lake, the peak of Duke's Nose shimmered in the heat.

At last, in a clearing near the top of the mountain, we came upon a tiny whitewashed shrine. It was no bigger than a tea-chest and stood open. A garland of withered marigolds hung across its opening. We bent down and peered in. Mad eyes glared back at us. A flat red stone that stood upright in the earth with wide staring eyes, done in silver leaf, black dots for pupils. Nearby a tall stone rose out of the ground, daubed with vermilion. Around it were more flowers. We had seen other such stones deep in the forest, touched with red powder or garlanded with flowers. Babu said they were worshipped by the Kathodis. 'That wild man you saw, Bhalu, he's the master of the forest.' The hill tribes didn't have proper gods, they worshipped evil things, things that could harm them, hoping they would go away. So their gods were nag-devta, haiza-devta, chechak-devta: Lord Cobra, Lord Cholera, Lord Small-pox.

The shrine was different. It belonged to Jaakmata. That was her village name. The townsfolk called her Kali, or just Ma.

'We'll have to come back at night,' Fever said.

'What about the evil spirits?'

'I'm not afraid of them. They're just stories, they're not true.'

*   *   *

We didn't go back that year. Not in thunder nor in rain. What I chiefly remember of that bright blue day is not the ferocious heat nor the glorious view, it is the small things: the buzzing of insects in grass, dry rustle of leaves, shimmer of heat above the slopes. Above all, the deep, pure, clear silence. The peace.

Those three monsoons we spent in Ambona blur in my memory into one long idyll, a happiness-trap. I was growing tall and strong with all the exercise. I could ride a bike up a steep track, climb tall trees. The forest knew me. By the time they returned, that last year, 1960, I felt that I, along with the Kathodi, was its master.

Sybil, Phoebe, Rosie. No more Mr Daruwalla. Phoebe was taller, more grown up too, though it's hard to tell when you are only ten. She no longer wore those old-fashioned dresses.

When we were alone, Fever took off her glasses. She seemed more like a child without them. She said, 'Bhalu, something very bad is happening.'

'What's happening?'

'I don't know. But it's why we come here. She gets miserable. She cries a lot and quarrels with my dad. Then he gets angry and walks out looking grim. Rosie says the servants snigger about her. I can't bear it. I don't know if she'll ever get better.' She looked away, then said, 'I *hate* Rosie sometimes. She seems to take such pleasure.'

'I hate her too,' I said. 'Because she makes you unhappy.'

'Bhalu,' said Fever, with real purpose, 'I need to see them. The ghosts. Let's go and find Jula.'

Jula was at the village school during the day, learning to read and write and cowherding before and after lessons. I would still join him when I got back from my school in Ambona. Throw my satchel down, tear off my shirt and run, clad only in shorts, out into the rain.

I said, 'She wants to go to the temple.'

'What? Now?'

'No, of course not,' said Fever. 'At night. When there's a storm.'

'Are you mad?'

'No. Do the spirits really grant wishes?'

Jula said, 'Are you serious?' I thought at first he was teasing her, but he said, 'If you are, I'll take you to someone who knows.'

Following Jula, we set off up Bicchauda mountain. The path led across the familiar cow-grazing land, between karvanda bushes, round tall stands of feathery bamboo, but Jula took a fork, a faint line of beaten-down grasses, that headed into the forest. It climbed up over rock ledges and roots that jutted like steps from the hillside. Fever was soon some way behind. Even I found it hard going. The path ran into a thicket and stopped. Jula, ahead of us, had disappeared. Then we heard his whistle, and saw his head and shoulders emerge from a gap under a lantana bush. It was a track that looked as if it had been made by deer, a low tunnel through the undergrowth. Thorns nipped at us and branches pulled at our hair, but we crawled through into a clearing I'd never seen before. All around us birds began calling in alarm, *tur-r-r-rkutur-kotur-kotur* and green wings flashed in the sunlight. Another tunnel led away through more thorns before broadening so we could walk upright. There beneath our feet again was the faint animal trail. It soon began a steep descent, which ended at a dry stream bed. On the far side the forest was darker. The faint track began again, leaping up the hill at an impossible angle, lost in the gloom of trees.

'Where are we?' I asked Jula.

'We have crossed onto Dagala mountain,' he said. 'We have to go up and follow the west ridge.'

Again we began to climb, the trail leading upwards through thickets of karvanda and other trees, whose names I did not know. Around one, covered in dense panicles of yellow blossom, a flock of rosy finches was whirling, diving into the flower pads. It was a wilder forest than Bicchauda's. The trees were taller, their roots somehow gripping the precipitous ground. Dead creeper stems trailed from their branches. The forest floor was dark, but to our right we began to catch bright bursts of light through the leaves.

'No one from our village comes here,' said Jula, in a whisper. 'Not to this part of the forest. Not even the woodcutters.'

'Why not?' asked Fever, also in a whisper. It didn't seem right to talk out loud.

'They say it belongs to the evil spirits.'

'Then why do you come?' breathed Fever.

'I've only come here once. I was chasing that wretch Pandri. I lost her down below somewhere. On the other side.' He waved his arm. 'I came climbing up . . .'

It did not seem possible that such a place could be the home of anything evil.

'What's that?'

Hubbub of bees. Small dark shapes flitting round us. Jula said, 'It's a honey buzzard. After their comb.'

We looked up, but Jula said, 'They're down there.'

For the first time I realised that we were on the edge of a cliff. The trees below us were clinging to an almost sheer drop. The bees were a dark cloud fifty feet down. On a branch nearby sat their nemesis, a dark hawk-like shape, patiently waiting.

I stopped, worried about Phoebe. Suppose she fell. But she was following gamely. Jula was out of sight ahead. I found a place where an overhanging branch gave a grip and signalled that she should go in front. When she squeezed past our faces came close. She kissed me on the lips and said, 'I love you, Bhalu.'

We caught up with Jula a hundred yards later. He pointed. On a branch swaying out over hundreds of feet of air, a slender green snake with a pointy-tipped nose was lying asleep among the leaves.

'There's nothing like this on Bicchauda.'

'Oh, there is,' said Jula. 'On Bicchauda too, on the far side, away from the lake and the road. But he lives here, not there.'

'Who lives here?'

'Your Kathodi magic-man jaadugar purush.'

The path heaved itself up over a ledge into a region where trees were thickly massed, with deep shadows underneath. Where a tree had fallen the light was so bright as to be momentarily blinding. We passed a gap where a coral tree, leafless at this season, bore at its branch-tips bursts of orange flowers, around which birds were clustering. Nearby was a shelter, it could not be called a hut, woven from canes and leaves. Inside, a cooking pot lay near a small ring of blackened stones filled with still-warm ashes. He had been here, but the jaadugar purush was not at home.

Jula said, 'Well, Fever, this is your answer.'

'What do you mean?' she asked.

'He was here. He heard us coming and left. He doesn't want you going to the shrine at night.'

*   *   *

'We have to wait till there's lightning.'

'Are you mad?'

'Bhalu, will you be my friend for ever?'

'Yes, I will,' I said, feeling a kind of terror creep into me. 'But aren't you scared?'

'Yes,' she said. 'Of course I am. But I *will* do this. We have to wait for the thunder.'

We were sitting up in our beds, an arm's length from one another. I was reading.

'Why don't you get a book?' I said.

'Read me yours.'

So I went back to the beginning. My book was *Puck of Pook's Hill.* I got to the bit where Puck has finished telling the children the story of Weland, who became Wayland Smith. Now he's ready to leave. He tells them: 'I promised you that you shall see What you shall see, and you shall hear What you shall hear, though It shall have happened three thousand year . . .'

'Will you be here when we come again?' the children ask.

'Surely. Sure-ly,' says Puck. 'I've been here some time already. One minute first, please.' And he gives them each three leaves — one of Oak, one of Ash, and one of Thorn.

'If only *we* had a friend like Puck,' said Fever. 'If we were in England we could conjure him up with oak and ash and thorn.'

Over the next few days we tried with mango, karvanda and lime; with sal, mahua and palasa; mogra, purple balsam and jasmine.

On the night it happened, we went to bed as usual. I woke with a start in pitch darkness. A small hand was shaking me.

'Bhalu. Listen.'

'Fever? What is it?'

'Shh, just listen.'

Our own breathing. The beating of my heart. Then I heard it, the faintest growl. Like a panther outside the window.

'Look over there.'

From our window the sky to the west was lit up by flickerings that momentarily showed the outline of the hills. As we watched, light flared in the direction of Duke's Nose and a slim twist of energy hurled itself at the dark earth.

A sighing in the trees outside, the first touch of coolness.

'One thousand, two thousand, three thousand, four thousand, five . . . there!'

Again the low grumble, like a rumbling belly, a hungry panther.

'It's five miles away. We must hurry.'

'What's the time? You don't really want . . . ?'

'Half-past two. And yes I do. So get dressed. Quietly. Mustn't wake the old hag.'

It was a stifling night. We pulled on our thin dressing gowns and tiptoed past the room where Rosie slept. She lay on her bed, her old worn-out form covered by a thin sheet, grey hair spread out on the pillow. Please let her not wake. That time we failed to find the jaadugar purush, it had been dark when we got home. Maya and Sybil were waiting for us in a state of something like panic. They asked where we'd been, and if we had seen anyone on the mountain. 'You mustn't go out alone any more,' Sybil told Phoebe. Maya said that from now on Rosie must keep an eye on us, wherever we went.

It was not yet raining, but the moon was hidden by low clouds and the darkness was thick. Our path up Bicchauda was a faint line, the trees on either side, threatening shapes. We had a torch, but its beam only made the world beyond seem blacker. Lightning lit up the sky again, over Duke's Nose. Grotesque shadows leapt at our feet and fled up the hillside. We were frightened, but neither of us would admit it. We had protection – a string of dry red chillies from which dangled a withered lime. It came from the kitchen doorway, where Yelliya the cook had hung it to repel evil spirits. Fever was wearing Rosie's silver locket. If you pressed a catch, it flew open to reveal a calm, madonna-like portrait. 'Saint Rodenda,' Fever said. 'Rosie says it protects against the snares of the devil.'

'The devil?' I had seen his picture, horned and cloven-hoofed, with huge bat's wings. It was unnerving to think of what might be awaiting us at the top.

'Do you believe in the devil?'

'No! You don't have to, if you're a Hindu.' But I believed in rakshasas. Maybe it came to the same thing.

'Mummy believes in the devil,' said Fever. 'I heard her say that she never knew what the devil was until now.'

The path wound up a steep slope dotted with karvanda and dived into a tangle of woodland. Thick, dead creepers hung from the trees. Sal leaves waggled in the dark air.

'Fever, don't talk of devils.'

We had come to the edge of the basalt drop. Far below us, the lake lay like a sheet of hot ink. The moon emerged briefly from behind a cloud. The rock under our feet was glistening.

'Watch out,' I warned her. 'It's already rained here.'

As if in confirmation, a wind started up from the direction of

Duke's Nose, cool, with the scent of rain in it. Moments later came a big flash and the roar of an approaching downpour.

'Here. Hold my hand. The rock is slippery.'

She reached out and grabbed, almost pulling me off-balance. By the time we got across, the rain had stopped. Fifty more yards and then, in front of us, there was the glade and the little shrine, its interior in shadow, and the standing stone. An uneasy moonlight was flowing across the place. I don't know what I'd been expecting; drums maybe – we sometimes heard drumming high up on the hill, and saw a pinprick of fire – flames round which we imagined monstrous shapes dancing; slobgobbledy laughter; demons having a good time. But the glade was utterly deserted.

Fever said, sounding almost disappointed, 'There's nothing here.'

I bent down and peered into the shrine. Lightning flashed again and eyes jumped out of the darkness.

'Bhalu, there *is* something!'

'Don't be scared. It's only a stone.'

But she was staring back the way we'd come.

'Quick! Hide!' She snatched at my arm, started running towards the nearest trees. I stood still. Anything could be in the forest.

'Bhalu!' she screamed.

Just entering the glade – a pale figure caught in the lightning glare – it seemed to hang there, white and shining.

Then I ran too. Bicchauda erupted with noise. Boom crash of lightning. Chittering like many tiny, sharp-toothed voices. Thorns clawing my face, arms. Where was she? The rain began again, hard as before. Another huge flash. I saw her crouched at the foot of a big tree. She was looking at me, saying something, but whatever it was, was drowned by the thunderclap right overhead.

I shouted, 'We can't stay here.'

She stared at me. I tried to pull her up. Shouted again, 'We've got to go home.'

She shook her head. 'No! No! There's a *thing* out there!'

There came a thin shriek, choked off suddenly. Then a scream that seemed to hang on the wind.

A thick root, slick with rain, lit up by lightning flashes: this became our world. After that second scream, there were only the sounds of the storm. The root formed a kind of cave in which we huddled, pressing our backs to the tree trunk as though it were an animal and could warm us. Fever was shaking, though it was not cold. I put my arms around her and she hugged them tighter. She must have been exhausted. She laid her head on my shoulder and closed her eyes.

At some point while she slept the rain died away. The darks of the forest changed to greys. A faint pre-dawn light crawled through the trees. Menacing shapes resolved to karvanda bushes, a claw became a dipping mango branch. It seemed that we had run far into the wood, but dawn showed us the shrine no more than forty feet away. Beyond the clearing, across miles of empty air, sunlight was already touching the tops of hills across the lake.

We came slowly down Bicchauda mountain. Everything looked different in the morning light. The storm had washed the sky clean and blue as a mynah's egg. From a high ridge, we saw the sun rise behind the hills of beyond and a day.

The valley below was still in shade. But all the lights in our house were on. There were people with lamps on the hillside. My father and the servants out looking for us. Hullabaloo too, inside the house. Sybil was lying on the sofa. My mother was sitting beside her. It was the only time I have ever seen her crying. Phoebe and I stood, guilty, scared, shocked to have caused all this.

'Where did you go?' yelled Maya. 'You *wicked* children. How could you do this? We've been out of our minds.'

But Sybil came running to us. She hugged us both and kissed away our own tears. 'Thank you, thank you,' she kept repeating and I wondered why she was thanking us.

A servant came in and said, 'Madam, the ayah has not returned.'

It was several hours later, the sun was high, when they brought her in. Men from the village, carrying her. Walking behind them, a dark-skinned man wearing nothing but a loincloth. The Kathodi, jaadugar purush. What was that look he gave us as he went past?

The villagers said the Kathodis had found her, under a cliff on Bicchauda mountain. Maya translated for the benefit of Sybil and Sybil opened her mouth very wide and screamed. In that instant I knew what it was that I had seen up on top of the mountain. Rosie had followed us. She must have got up out of her bed and followed us, just as she was, in her old cotton nightdress. She had followed us up the mountain, alone in the darkness, in rain and lightning. I also knew then beyond any doubt that it had never been spite, or nastiness, with her. She really loved Phoebe. What else would have driven her up a dark, steep mountain in a storm? Poor woman. She must have been as terrified as we were. Had our shrieks unnerved her? Maybe she tried to run. She was old. She must have slipped. Slid . . . She was so much braver than we were.

Fever was inconsolable. She wept and wept. She said it was her fault. If she had not insisted . . . I didn't want to tell her what I had

163

overheard the villagers saying. They found her with her feet twisted back to front. Maybe she was a Haadal all the time.

The rest of that day remains in my memory as a bad, confused dream. The police came, a khaki-clad inspector and two constables from Ambona. Were they going to arrest us, we asked Maya. Of course not, she said. You were not to blame. For reasons which they would not explain, the police searched the entire house. They opened every drawer and cupboard and trunk. They insisted on searching my mother's writing room and spent a long time in there.

When they left at last, Maya tried to comfort us.

'Not your fault,' she said. 'An accident.' But the hand stroking my hair shook and there was something in her voice. 'It could have been you lying there.'

The coffin lay in our house, open for inspection. Rosie's old face looked so peaceful. The undertaker's skill had hidden the bruises, soothed away the hurt. The Catholic priest from Ambona came. Candles were lit.

Getting ready on the day of the funeral. My father was wearing an old suit he had bought in London during the war.

Fever, dressed in a dark dress and hat, began to cry again. She said, 'I wanted to give back her locket. I should have put it in the coffin. It's my fault.'

Maya had an idea. She said we should each give something we cherished. She found a square biscuit tin and had it washed and dried. We spread a cloth in the tin and Fever put in the locket. Ninu said that she would like to give Rosie her doll. I put in my catapult. 'Something from each of us as well,' said my mother. She and Sybil went into her writing room. When they came out the tin was sealed with sticky tape and tied up with string.

Phoebe's father arrived from Bombay. James Killigrew. It was the first time I had ever seen him. He was a tall man, with bushy eyebrows. He seemed in a bad temper, greeted my parents shortly and to his wife said barely a word. He took Phoebe into Maya's office and shut the door.

When she came out Fever was crying. She took off her glasses and wiped them on her blouse. 'Daddy says I have to go to school in England.'

'Why? You can stay here and go to school with Jula and me.'

'I'll always love you, Bhalu. Promise me that we'll always love each other, no matter what?'

'I love you too,' I whispered.

'For ever. We must love each other for ever, till we die. No matter what happens.'

It rained throughout the funeral. We buried Rosie in the cemetery in Ambona. I had never been in a Christian graveyard before. It was a scary place, green and shadowy, with its eyeless angels, people rotting under the ground, tombstones bearing the faded names of long dead English people. Tall trees cast a green gloom and dripped without stopping. The red earth was soaked, and water was flowing along the paths. Tall lilies sprouted from the graves, pink flowers on fleshy stems which, if snapped, smelt faintly of rain.

We stood under a cluster of umbrellas as the priest led prayers. When the coffin was lowered into the grave, it splashed into thick red water gathered at the bottom. Mr Killigrew and Sybil stood side by side but did not touch each other. Phoebe was on the other side of them. My mother stood next to Sybil, then came our family. I would have liked to be near Phoebe, but there was no chance.

At last it was done and the priest led his little procession away.

Phoebe and Sybil did not come back to our house. We took our farewells there at the cemetery gate. Fever and I shook hands, rather formally, while our mothers embraced. There was nothing more to say. Then her father piled them into his car, into which their suitcases had already been loaded. The last sight I had of her was a small figure, still in her hat, waving from the window of the car as it drove away, past cows grazing at the edge of the road, and turned the corner into Ambona bazaar.

My mother said, 'We've forgotten the tin.'

She started back, but Rosie's grave was covered with a two-foot high mound. Maya called to one of the gravediggers, and told him to scoop a hole. She placed the tin there and watched the man cover it with dark red Ambona soil.

She told me two days later that Sybil had telephoned to say goodbye. Killy had booked her and Phoebe on a ship to England. They sailed the same evening.

III PHOEBE

All week I had been coping with lunacy.

'It's insane,' I said to Katy, 'that there is a huge hole in the West Pier because some idiot drove a ship through the middle of it.'

Katy, who was driving me along the Brighton sea front, reached across and, good soul that she is, rested a comforting hand on my knee. 'It's something we've all got to go through.'

'It's mad that at the top of North Street there's a shop selling dildos and crotchless panties, and at the bottom is a bloody great pleasure dome, an opium eater's fantasy if I ever saw one.'

'You mustn't take it so hard,' said Katy.

'Piglet is crazy,' I said. 'He wants me to act in a play. Says I can wear a turban and robe and be some kind of spiritual adviser from the East.'

'Well, you might enjoy it,' Katy said. 'You're good at pretending to be spiritual.'

'Piglet and his friends are mad.'

'Of course he is,' said Katy. 'But he and I, and everyone else, are doing our best to cheer you up.'

Eleven o'clock Piglet. 'Bugger me, lad,' he said, 'you look like something Henry the Eighth brought up after a dish of lampreys.'

'I don't feel up to Charlotte today.'

'It's natural that you should grieve,' he said kindly.

The problem is not that I'm grieving, I wanted to say, it's that I am unable to grieve. I am too angry. Angry with myself for not believing Maya when she said she was ill. Angry with her, because – anything to avoid unseemly emotion – she'd made quite sure I didn't.

'I will be all right,' I said to Piglet. 'Just takes a while.'

'It's no good sitting here moping. Come to our rehearsal, that'll cheer you up. The play's coming along nicely . . . By the way, don't let me forget to take those.' He waved at the box of moulding planes that still sat beside my desk.

'What rehearsal?'

'I wasn't going to tell you till I'd finished it, I wanted it to be a surprise, but . . . well, you see, seeing as it's Shakespeare who caused the whole problem in the first place, I decided to take the bull by the horns. Rewrite the bloody thing.'

'Rewrite *Richard III*?'

'Shakespeare's hardly in a position to object.'

'There is the small difficulty of writing like Shakespeare.'

'Not a problem!' he said. 'The way I see it, Shakespeare wrote reams of stuff. Thirty-odd plays, poems galore. Lots of characters involved in all kinds of junketings. People and situations to meet every need. So, my plan is to lift bits and pieces from here and there. Should work perfectly well. Just have to change a few names.'

Everything was mad. The whole of Brighton was casually and charmingly raving. Its narrow bazaars – what else can the maze of lanes to the north of the Mughal Pavilion be called? – full of sibyls and seers; a man with a pink Mohican haircut fumbling a string of Tibetan prayer beads; shops selling Hindu scriptures interpreted by Rolls-Royce-owning gurus; posters offering Shaunee sun rituals, Ashanti drum lessons, Om shanti shanti

shanti. Such a thirst for gnosis. People plundering each other's cultural middens. Bric-à-brac paraded with magpie pride. And here in the middle of all this confusion was I, looking for a large birdcage, a *palace* among birdcages, for my mother's bereaved bulbuls.

Khurram and Mumtaz had arrived in Sussex, delivered by Nina. She and Katy strongly disapproved of my plan to release them. It was not only environmentally unsound, they told me, but would be cruel to Khurram and Mumtaz. Imagine them flying off, they said, assuming they remembered how to fly, thrilled to be free, only to find that birdseed doesn't grow on trees and English woods aren't centrally-heated. What would they feed on? I consulted my shelves and found a *Popular Handbook on Indian Birds* (Hugh Whistler FRS, Gurney and Jackson, 3rd ed, 1941, twenty-one plates of which six coloured, 549pp) that had been published during the Raj.

'Indians,' it unhelpfully informed me, 'frequently tame the bird and carry it about the bazaars, tied with a string to the finger or to a little crutched perch, which is often made of precious metals or jade; while there are few Europeans who do not recollect Eha's immortal phrase anent the red patch in the seat of its trousers.'

Here was the answer then. I must tote Khurram and Mumtaz round on jewelled perches. Far better than freezing their little red butts off in the woods, their Indian instincts scrambled by a world which to them would seem quite senseless. As for Eha, whoever he had been, neither he nor his wisecracks had cracked immortality.

Maya died with her books and photograph albums still piled beside her bed, and her bulbuls calling in their cage. Just before the end her eyes opened and looked carefully at each one of us in turn, as if reading our faces, and then closed and did not open again. I remember the room being filled with the scent of nagchampa, cobra-jasmine, her favourite incense, and the sound of her breathing. I was dreading the moment when a gap between those breaths would grow into a long and lengthening silence, but when it came I felt nothing. Sitting with my sisters beside her body, talking in low voices until light faded, first in the room and then in the world outside, I could not find a tear. From time to time one of us would get up to press a kiss on her forehead, kisses that grew gradually cooler until, when it was time to say goodbye, my lips in the dark touched something waxy and cold, and still I was unmoved. I left the flat and walked to a local bookshop which stayed open late, because there was a title I wanted – about fruit, or fish or something else which I have now forgotten – and it seemed a good opportunity, since I was in the area, to go and get it. I made the journey south to Sussex dry-eyed. We arranged the funeral for the weekend and placed ads in *The Times* and *Guardian*. Katy phoned the British Embassy in Athens, to ask if they could somehow find the twins, I & I, who were trekking in Crete.

I wanted something to read at the service, so I began pulling books out of the shelves. My desk vanished under old volumes published in places like Varanasi and Tirukonamalai. I was looking for things that old Hindu texts, especially the Upanishads, or 'forest teachings', say about death, the soul's journey in the afterlife and about karma, the subject on which Maya held such a peculiar and particular view. Eventually I found, shawled in dust, an old copy of the *Brhadaranyaka Upanisad* (Trs Swami Madhavananda, comm. by

Shankaracharya, 4th ed, 1965, 678pp): I marked a few verses relating to cremation and the afterlife, and sat chewing a pencil, trying to find words that would connect them to each other and to her life.

> *To the next life you go, your minds bearing traces of things you did in this, and to reap the harvest of those deeds, to this world you return.*

This of course was exactly what she did *not* believe. For her the idea of future lives was a political tool, a conspiracy encouraged by princes and politicians to prevent the masses from rising up in anger. 'Landlord Dusht Singh, who is an evil man, lives without a care in the world, whereas we . . . Never mind. He'll be reborn as a cockroach, and what a good laugh we'll have.'

She used to say that when Karl Marx made his remark about religion being the opium of the people, he was attacking neither religion nor opium. He was saying that people denied justice and forced to lead desperate lives had, *up to that point in history*, no other consolation, relief or pleasure besides religion and oblivion. There is a Hindu equivalent, which Mitra (who had been Jula) sang one night in the Bombay bazaar when we were drinking bhang (milk into which a paste of cannabis leaves, almonds and sugar has been stirred):

> *Ganga, bhang do bahin hain,*
> *sadaa rahat Siva sang*
> *bhava taran ko gang hai,*
> *jag taran ko bhang*

> Ganga and bhang are two sisters,
> who live forever with Siva,
> On Ganga we float to the world beyond,
> but bhang is this world's river.

I sat in my back room, watching mist drift across the Downs, softly erasing thorn bushes one by one. My pencil hovered over a few more passages, but I found it hard to concentrate. The wisdom of ages seemed curiously unsatisfying.

> *You may do all manner of good on earth, but actions alone will not earn you the long rest you seek, for their effects are quickly exhausted.*

Maya would say that doing 'all manner of good' is all that can be asked of a human being. The rest is nonsense: our actions have endless consequences for good and ill. She might concede (I kept forgetting she was dead) that good effects fade more quickly — how long did Mahatma Gandhi's example sustain Indian politics? — whereas evil generates its own squalid kind of immortality.

Maya sneered at the orthodox view of karma, but her own view also guaranteed survival after death, if only by default, through the continuing effects of what she had stirred up during her life. This was something which obviously troubled her. Since her death I had hardly thought of *Retribution*. The questions it posed no longer seemed very important, which was just as well, since there was no longer any way of answering them. Really, what is the point of leaving a gnomic legacy when your entire life has been devoted to telling people that they must take note of the past? But irritation was pointless. The dead are dead. Perform the rites. Let them go.

That narrow ancient path which stretches far away, I have found it at last.

My mother would have liked a pyre of sandalwood sprinkled with clarified butter and strewn with eleven kinds of jasmine, but they don't run to that sort of thing at the West London Crematorium. She should have been borne to the fire by shaven-skull brahmins chanting mantras and sutras. Instead, on the morning of her funeral the family, minus the twins, whom the Embassy in Greece had been unable to find in time, assembled outside her flat to be greeted by an undertaker with an unsuccessfully scrubbed egg-stain on his lapel, who asked, 'So it's just the one limb, then?'

'God, no, the whole body,' replied my sister, Suki, horrified, until she realised that he meant a limo.

His comment must have brought to her mind the same image as to mine, a childhood memory of a Hindu funeral by a river, pale flames stalking on a pile of logs, out of which stuck the legs of the corpse, stiff, dusted with ashes.

You go to the fire, your body its fuel, your breath turns to smoke, your desires become coals, your life becomes the sparks of that flame in which the gods offer a human being, from which arises the being of light.

From the limousine, moving slowly through the streets of London on that damp and grey Saturday morning, we could see the hearse with the coffin loaded with flowers turning ahead of us, into the Fulham Road, then into the cemetery gates. As we drove past acres of tombstones, sorrowing cherubs, angels with outstretched wings, India seemed far away and long ago, a string of bright visions teeming with people, very clear but tiny, as if seen through the wrong end of a telescope. It came to me very strongly that this was not the right place to say goodbye to her. She might not have believed, but she'd still have liked a proper Hindu funeral. Maybe she should have gone home to Kumharawa, where they'd have known not only her name, but those of her grandparents. Hundreds of people would have come to pay their last respects. She'd have had her good send-off. The old women would have made a fuss. There would have been to-do with pastes of sandal-wood and saffron, gold dust and armfuls of flowers. Between death and funeral she would never have been alone. People would have kept vigil with her, saying prayers, chatting to one another, including her in their conversations. The brahmin – it was really our duty, but I couldn't picture any of us doing it – would have muttered in her ears things she would need to know about the sights she would encounter, the words she would need to gain safe passage.

When you depart this world, you go up into the air, which opens like the hole in a chariot wheel. Through this you ascend, you rise towards the sun, which opens like the eye of a drum. Through this you ascend, you rise towards the moon, which opens like the bowl of a drum. Through this you ascend, you rise towards a world free of sorrow.

I could imagine my dead mother's mirth at all this mumbo-jumbo, picture myself addressing her smirking corpse: 'Look, if you find this *so* silly we'll just stop, shall we?' and her replying, perhaps by means of some casual poltergeist activity, 'No way, José, I want the works.' So thrice around the pyre we would have carried her, me and the incantating brahmins, before laying her on it, and I would

176

have placed grains of rice in her mouth, to sustain her soul on its journey.

You pass forth into this space, from space into air, from air into rain, from rain into the earth where you become food. This food becomes the spark of man which kindles woman's fire, and in that fire you are born again and come again into the world. Thus do you rotate between the worlds.

Yes, had we been in India, my head would have been shaved, leaving only a tassel of hair hanging down the back of the skull – the choti, as worn by Hindu boys – Grandfather used to tie my father's choti to a hook in the ceiling to stop him nodding off over his textbooks. I would have circled the pyre five times, widdershins, before setting it alight. Then I would have had to wait, enduring all the barbecue smells and sounds, until the flames had exposed my mother's skull bone and baked it brittle, after which, taking a heavy staff, I would break her head like a coconut. This duty of the eldest son – my father had fulfilled it for my grandfather, my grandfather for my great-grandfather, Great- for Twice-Great and Twice-Great for Thrice-Great, the rebel, who survived the carnage of the late 1850s to live to a ripe and cantankerous old age – is done to free the soul to begin its journey, as it says in the *Brhandaranyaka Upanisad*, along that narrow ancient path which leads to the other world. Luckily the by-laws of the Royal Borough of Kensington and Chelsea and the rules of the General Cemetery Company make this sort of thing impossible, but to maintain the spirit of the rite, I had brought along the book, from which I planned to quote bits which I thought would have either appalled, or appealed to, my mother.

*When you know the Self, good or evil no longer touch you. You do not think
'I have done a bad thing,' nor 'I have done a good thing.'*

The chapel was full. My sisters and I had not expected the
announcement in *The Times* to draw so many mourners. Most of
them were recent friends, people with whom she played bridge and
went to parties. There were a few ex-expatriates from the Bombay
Society. Some of them we knew, but hadn't seen for years. On the
way to the lectern to give my short address about my mother's life,
I saw several people I recognised. Even after four decades there
was no mistaking the turbanned profile of Joan Barboushjian –
'Pope Joan' as she had been dubbed in the fifties by the city's
literati.

*You have passed beyond good and evil and are therefore troubled no more
by what you may or may not have done.*

'My mother Maya,' I told the audience, 'called herself a Hindu,
but for her, Hinduism was a way of life, rather than a religion. She
did not believe in rebirth, reincarnation, but . . .'

I spoke of my mother's socialism, her respect for Gandhi and
her disappointment at the tawdry communal politics of today's
India. During all of this, I noticed a pair of knees in the front row.
Attractive knees, well shaped, beneath the hem of a smart skirt.
Held close together but allowed to lean gracefully a little to one
side. Their owner was staring at me, dabbing at her eyes with a
handkerchief. Someone of Maya's, or perhaps a friend of Nina's.
She smiled when she caught me looking and I dropped my eyes to
my notes.

'. . . Our ghosts may grow feebler. They may fade, but they never entirely vanish. We live on, in and through each other . . .'

Opening the book at the page where I had inserted a marker, I found to my surprise that instead of two thousand-year-old Sanskrit verses, I was staring at a page of ovolos, astragals and reverse-ogees. I had mistakenly brought *British Planemakers from 1700*.

The final contretemps. The curtains at the back of the room swung open and the coffin began to move, then stopped with a judder. Pope Joan rose from her seat, stepped arthritically forward and laid a single red rose upon its lid. As the coffin resumed its journey, my sisters came up to read poems they had chosen from Maya's work. Nina had barely begun when a strange discordant music began to be heard. The CD, which the crematorium had asked us to supply, and which I believed to be Bhimsen Joshi singing *Miyan ki Malhar*, turned out in fact to be Sebastian Prior's *Cello Concerto*, a modern work which sounds like a chorus of Tibetan singing bowls interspersed with pneumatic drills and the distant cries of crows being plucked. I consoled myself with the thought that Maya, who throughout her life had demonstrated a carefully cultivated taste for the theatrical, would have been delighted by the effect it was having on her audience. Nina, meanwhile, struggled on with a rhyme which Maya had made up.

> Do pigeons brood on pigeon pie,
> Or pigs on bacon
> As men brood on death, and immortality.

The owner of the knees was still smiling at me. She was, at a guess, in her late thirties, blonde, and alluring in the way women are when they stop being merely pretty. Beauty lies deeper, it belongs to the soul. It may not show until a person's character is fully formed, then it shines out of them. This is why young women, however attractive they may be, are very rarely beautiful. Beauty begins at forty, I used to tell Katy, whenever I caught her examining her face too closely in the mirror. After I returned to my seat I glanced over to find the blonde woman still looking at me. Who she was, I honestly could not imagine.

After the service, we waited outside to thank the departing mourners. The moustacheless Srinuji, clad incongruously for him in a suit, came up to offer his condolences.

'You knew she was ill. How?' I asked.

'She had known for some time,' he said. 'Did she not tell you about her tests at the hospital?'

'What tests?' This revelation, following my mismanagement of the funeral, cast me into deeper gloom.

'She had been feeling ill for months,' he said, frowning at me as if I had been personally responsible for my mother's illness. 'I don't understand how you could not know about it.'

'Neither do I. But she never told us.'

'Then it was her way of coping,' said Srinuji. 'Your mother was a selfless woman. She wanted to spare you worry.'

'Tell me, why have you shaved off your moustache?'

He gave me a strangely imploring look, and plucked my sleeve. 'Bhalu-ji—'

'It makes you look like a mullah.'

'Would you kindly step this way with me? Let us go and admire the flowers.'

So we strolled among the wreaths and cellophane-wrapped bouquets. He said, 'Each of us has something to hide.'

What secret could possibly involve a moustache?

'I used to be very fond of eating paan.'

True enough. Paan it was (a confection of nuts and pastes and spices wrapped in betel leaves) that had bloodied his mouth and stained his teeth. 'I had to stop, because it would spoil the beard.' He cast an apprehensive glance in the direction of his wife, who was standing talking to Katy and my sisters. 'Those paans used to contain some tobacco. You must be familiar with them.'

'I haven't tasted paan for years.' During my days at the dope den, my friend Dost used to talk about the various 'masalas' that could be used to ginger up a paan. There was, for example, the famous 'palang-tod', or 'bed-breaker' variety, that was supposed to contain a pinch of cocaine.

'I am ashamed to say that I began smoking cigarettes. Just a few. Maybe five a day. But after some time I saw that the moustache was getting stained, a little brownish below the nostril.'

So he had given up his moustache. Human after all.

Katy said to me, 'Who is that woman? She keeps staring at you.'

The blonde stranger was walking back and forth pretending to admire the floral tributes.

'I've no idea. I assumed she was a friend of Nina's.'

'No one knows who she is.'

'Whoever she is, she is rather gorgeous.'

'Yes, I saw you ogling her earlier.'

'I don't ogle. I'm too old.'

'Liar.'

Feeling our eyes on her, the woman turned and smiled. She was tall, taller than Katy, with fair hair curving neatly to her nape. A dark suit showed off her figure as she made her way towards us. Close to, one could see that she was not as young as she had first appeared. Careful make-up smoothed her skin and all but erased the tiny lines at the corners of her eyes, which were rimmed to make them larger and shadowed to accentuate their unusual grey-green, a colour that for some reason always made me think of rain. I was aware of a subtle lemony perfume, spiked, but not spoiled, by a note of tobacco.

The stranger took a deep breath and said, 'This is so strange, I really don't know where to begin. I am sorry about your mother. She and my mother were friends. Mine died five years ago, and left some things for yours. Unfortunately they'd lost touch and I had no idea where to start looking. I had given up, then I saw the notice in the *Telegraph*. So I came, and I don't know if this fulfils my mother's request, but I think perhaps I should give the things to you, because I was never meant to keep them and they may mean more to you . . .'

She stopped, tilted her head to one side, and said, 'Bhalu, you have absolutely no idea who I am, have you?'

The stranger stood smiling, waiting for a reply. As my puzzlement grew, her smile got broader. She began to affect playful impatience. She flicked her eyes up to an interesting corner of sky, pursed her lips.

'No,' I said at last, bemused. 'I'm afraid not.'

'Clue,' said the stranger. 'When we first met, you weren't very nice to me. In fact you were downright nasty. You called me names. Does that ring any bells?'

I said, 'I'm sure you're mistaken. If I had met you before I would definitely remember.'

'You made me cut up worms.'

There is a story of Nabokov's in which a man is lifted into euphoria by the glimpse of a woman he once loved but has not seen for many years. He rushes into the Berlin night where a neon sign glows in the darkness. CAN . . . IT . . . BE . . . POSSIBLE?

'Oh Bhalu,' said the stranger. 'I wish I had a feather. I could lay you out cold . . .'

I could not speak. Never mind speak, I couldn't think. Never mind think, thought requires words. What I felt was wordless but clear, like a breath of sweet air, herbs on dry hillsides, a happiness that came bubbling up by itself from some deep untroubled source.

We stood looking at one another, mouths opening and closing like the small Bicchauda fish of years ago, imprisoned in glass jars side by side, mouthing mute questions.

'No, no,' I said. 'It can't be you.'

'I feel just the same, if it's any consolation,' said the woman.

Then she did something which convinced me. She took my face between her hands and pressed a kiss to my lips.

'Aren't you going to introduce us?' said a voice at my elbow. I had completely forgotten that Katy was standing beside me.

'I'm so sorry,' said the stranger, extending a hand. 'What must you think of me? I'm Phoebe Killigrew. Your husband and I are old friends.'

'So I see,' said Katy, looking from one to the other of us. 'Well, you must come back and have drinks.'

Could it be? This elegant creature who looked as if she had stepped straight out of a Bond Street couturier? Was this the little tomboy of childhood, she of the tuggable hay-coloured plaits?

Now that I looked again, she had a pointy chin. How had I not recognised those startling eyes? Where had the glasses gone?

'I don't believe it!' I said. The severalth time.

I had often wondered what it would be like to meet her again. I had imagined throwing our arms around one another, hugging each other, as we had done when we were children. But all I could do was mumble like a fool, over and over again, 'I don't believe it. I don't believe it.' And all she said was, 'I know, I know, I know.'

Then, bizarrely, as if there were not decades of questions to be asked and answered, the three of us found ourselves talking about where she had left her car, where near Sloane Square was the best place to park, how to find Maya's flat, where Suki, in accordance with our darling mother's dying wish – 'mourning is for fools, give me a party' – had organised a kind of wake.

'See you there!' she said gaily and was gone, leaving me still uttering expressions of disbelief, watching the cling and swing of her skirt as she walked away.

Now there was a little drama. The Srinujis, who had come by bus, were proposing to walk the couple of miles to Chelsea, and had to be asked, pressed and finally begged, before they would agree to what they had wanted all along, which was to ride with us. So, ushered into the limousine by its egg-stained chauffeur we set off through the vast cemetery, its starfish avenues of lachrymose statuary spinning around us, the living at the hub of a giant wheel of death. 'Our lives are governed by patterns which resurface time and time again.' Ashes to ashes. It was in a graveyard that I had last seen her.

'Bhalu, you're trembling,' said Katy.

I said, 'I got chilled standing out there.'

But I was, truthfully, in a state of bad shock. Initial joy had given way to contradictory and baffling feelings. An analogy (the effort of a bookseller with eight hours of each day to bury his nose in his stock) might be those curious verses from the *Rig Veda* where the poet is one moment uplifted, exalted, raving in delight, but the next confesses that, 'in deep distress I cooked a dog's intestines.' By the time we had re-entered the Fulham Road and the real world of London under drizzle, I realised that what I was actually feeling was panic.

From time to time, in London, I would run into someone with whom I'd been at school in India. There were plenty of them in England and I was always amazed at how badly they had aged, a smooth-skinned boy transformed into a corpulent banker, the champion batsman now a labourworn executive with a briefcase perpetually open on his knee. Usually, after the ritual of how-dos, and what-have-yous, there was a period of silent assessment; how well or otherwise have we done vis-à-vis the other? I would explain that I had failed at film production, no, actually walked away from it in disgust after too many boozy years, and was now a happily penniless bookseller. They would smile and say that fulfilment, enjoying one's work, was the main thing, but one could see them silently giving thanks that they had ended up as somebodies who wore somebody-suits and drove somebody-cars. Suppose Phoebe, once her own euphoria had worn off, saw me as they did, a thin, greying man, in no way remarkable, nothing like the boy who'd climbed waterfalls and shot mangoes out of trees with catapults.

Maya's flat was full of people. It was the first time I had been there since the night of her death. Apart from the missing bulbuls, everything was as it had been when she was alive. The golden angel still perched on its carved pedestal. Great-grandfather's butterflies glimmered on the wall. Familiar scent of cobra-jasmine. I peeped into the bedroom, but the bed was neatly made, counterpane smoothed and tucked in at the corners. Someone had put the books back in their shelves and tidied away the photograph albums. It felt as if Maya was out shopping and would be back shortly to welcome all these old friends. I saw Panaghiotis going up to Srinuji with hand outstretched. Beyond them, Piglet, on scrubbed-and-Sunday-best behaviour, was pouring himself a hefty whisky: the first time, and probably the last, that all three would find themselves in the same room. An old lady, a neighbour in the building, came up to offer quavering condolences, but I was only half-listening, looking around the room. Srinuji and

Panaghiotis were already deep in conversation. I caught a few incense-scented phrases of Christian consolation. Srinuji was nodding, ever the sage. How stiff and composed Pan looked. What his loss was I could only imagine. He and Maya had been close.

'Arthritis,' the old lady said, peering up at me. Why she hadn't been able to come to the funeral. I must steer her towards Katy and my sisters, who had their heads together, no doubt discussing the mysterious reappearance of Phoebe.

Where was Phoebe? Had she decided not to come? But no, there she was, in the doorway. Smiling. Being greeted by my sister Nina. Exclamations. Mutual surprise, pleasure.

'It's been a terrible day,' the old lady confided. 'I've had to take an extra pill for my knees.'

Phoebe was looking about, she had not yet seen me. Nina was leading her towards Suki and Katy. I had just managed to extricate myself and was making my way across the room when my arm was grasped from behind.

'A word,' said a voice in my ear. 'My kingdom for a word.'

Piglet, wagging his whisky at me.

'Not now, Piglet.'

'You're up to something, friend Bhalu.'

Never in all the years I'd known him had I felt such irritation. I tried to move on, but he was still holding onto my arm.

'Not so fast, laddie. Who's your blonde lady chum?'

'Just someone I knew years ago.'

'Well,' he said. 'Aren't you the dark horse?'

'An old friend. Haven't seen her in years.'

I followed his eyes to where Phoebe was standing with my sisters and Katy. They were talking rapidly, in that eager way that women have when they go into conclave. Phoebe had her back to me. She was laughing, shifting her weight from one leg to the other.

'Seemed rather keen on you.'

'For heaven's sake, I haven't seen her in four decades!'

'And say,' declaimed Piglet, 'what store of parting tears were shed? Thou art an old love-monger!'

'I had given up hope,' Phoebe was saying, as we joined them. 'It was as if you'd vanished off the planet.' She gave me a bright smile. 'Mummy was in India just before she died and she tried to find your mother. Then she discovered you'd been in England all along. She was amazed. All those years. Afterwards I tried to trace your mum, but there was no sign of her in the directory.'

'No, she's ex-directory,' said Nina, as if Maya were still alive.

'They usually tell you that the number exists, before they refuse to give it to you . . .'

'She's listed under her maiden name,' Nina said, still clinging to the present tense.

'Her maiden name? Why was that?'

'She would never tell us,' said my other sister, Suki.

Phoebe said, 'But we couldn't find *any* of you.'

This was not surprising. By 1993 my sisters were both married, and Katy and I were listed as Shaw's Bookshop. 'As a matter of fact,' I interjected, 'we tried to find you too. Soon after we came to England. Back in the seventies. No sign anywhere.'

'I was abroad for a long time,' said Phoebe. 'Mummy, bless her, never had a phone.'

'So how *did* you find us?' asked Suki.

Katy said, 'Phoebe read Maya's name in the *Telegraph*.'

'Not the *Telegraph*,' said Nina. 'It must have been *The Times*, or the *Guardian*.'

'Maybe it was *The Times*,' said Phoebe.

'We *would* have put it in the *Telegraph*,' Nina persisted, 'but we thought no one of Maya's would see it.'

'She was kind. I remember her very well,' said Phoebe. 'She cared about people. Mummy loved her.' She raised her wine glass, as if to toast our absent mothers. 'It's such a shame they never met again. But I suppose they have by now. Up there having a good gossip about all of us.'

'I doubt it,' said Nina. 'Once we're dead that's it.'

In which case, I thought, why can't you bring yourself to use the past tense?

'*Khattam*. Finished,' said my sister. 'Maya was right. It's no good being sentimental. I don't believe in ghosts.'

'I believe in ghosts,' said Phoebe. 'And in my experience they're anything but sentimental.'

This caused a short silence. I said, 'Maya thought people live on through their actions.'

'Maya was full of nonsense,' said Nina.

'It's hard to believe unless it's happened to you,' Phoebe said. 'Mummy still talks to me, and I wish she wouldn't.'

The much longer silence that followed was broken by my eleven o'clock chum, who bounded forward, trotter outstretched. 'Call me Piglet. Everyone does.'

'Piglet,' I said. 'This is Phoebe Killigrew. We last saw her, what, I should think it must be more than thirty-five years ago. Ninu here would have been—'

'Poor Bhalu, he's drivelling,' said Nina quickly. She turned to Phoebe. 'I don't remember you very well. I suppose because I was so much younger and you were one of Bhalu's friends.'

'More than friends,' said Phoebe. 'Bhalu was my hero.'

'Really?' said Katy, amazed as only one could be who had lived with me for two decades.

'Last time I saw him he was a little boy, yet I recognised him at once. The moment I saw him I thought, Yup, that's my Bhalu.'

Something in the way she said *my* Bhalu.

'He used to teach me how to do things. Even nowadays, if there's something I need a man to do, I often think, I wish I had a Bhalu.'

'I wish *I* had that sort of Bhalu,' Katy said. She looked around the room. 'Did you say you were married? Is your husband here?'

After a small, uncomfortable pause Phoebe said, 'Peter couldn't come. He's at home. In Yorkshire.'

'With your children?'

Again the tiny flicker. 'We have no children.'

Another angel passed overhead.

'Yorkshire, did you say?' cried Piglet, once more unto the breach. 'Whereabouts?'

'Sorry?'

'In Yorkshire. Where do you live?'

'You wouldn't know it,' said Phoebe. 'It's a tiny place.'

'I'm sure I shall,' said Piglet. 'Our lot's often on manoeuvres up there. What's it called?'

'It's a tiny place,' she repeated. 'Not far from Richmond.'

'"Ay, ay, thou wouldst be gone to Richmond. I've had pastimes there and pleasant game," as the Bard never said. Well, did say, but not quite like that. I know Richmond. We did a Bosworth there, outside the castle. About three years ago. Perhaps you saw it?'

'Are you in the army?'

'Bodyguard of King Richard, at your service,' said Piglet. 'Man-at-arms. Halberdier, to be precise. I carry a sort of axe-on-a-pole.' He began to enumerate the troops and arms needed to re-fight various skirmishes of the Yorkist wars.

'God, how is he getting home?' Suki whispered to me.

Phoebe was listening to Piglet's lengthy descriptions of cannon, polearms and arrow storms.

'So there you have it,' he said at last. 'Now then, what's it called, your village? "Hard by York's gate let us lie, there to conquer or to die." Odds on I've bivouacked there.'

'My village?' Piglet's sottish Shakespearean bonhomie seemed to have thrown her. She was gazing at the titles in Maya's rose-wood bookcase, probably terrified that if she told him, a troop of medieval drunkards would turn up unannounced on her doorstep. 'I wouldn't call it a village really. Just our house and a couple of farms. Sleeman. You won't find it on a map.'

Rescue being necessary, and spotting the tall, turbanned figure of Joan Barboushjian, I took Phoebe's elbow and said, 'Excuse us, there's someone who knew Phoebe's mother.'

'Congratulations, Bhalu,' said Pope Joan. 'A very moving service.' Politeness or sarcasm? I couldn't tell. 'I hadn't seen a great deal of Maya lately. Pity. We're all due for the chop. Me next, I suppose.'

I introduced Phoebe and said, 'You must have known Phoebe's mother in Bombay. Sybil Killigrew?'

Pope Joan turned her pterodactyl gaze to Phoebe and said, 'Well, well. So you're Sybil's girl. You look nothing like her.'

Phoebe gave me a sly wink and we were children again, on parade before our mothers' friends.

'Do I remember Sybil? Well, of course I do! I met her several times, at Maya's, but I never knew her very well. She just vanished. One heard all sorts of stories, but . . .' She paused as if thinking better of whatever she had been going to say. 'What became of her? Did she marry again?'

'Unfortunately no,' said Phoebe. 'She never did.'

'Bhalu, my little rascally Bhalu,' said Phoebe. 'My *oldest* friend. I've waited years for this moment.'

At last we were on our own. There was so much I had been chafing to say to her, but now that I had my chance, I was tongue-tied.

'You haven't changed,' she said. 'I look at you and I can see the little boy inside, standing up on tiptoe to peep out of your eyes.'

'Here's to you!'

'To us!' she said. 'Old friends.' She touched glasses and took a long sip. She needed it as much as me. 'Yes,' she said, turning her inspection onto me. 'You're a bit gruffer, and your fingernails are cleaner than I've ever seen them, but really, you're just the same.'

'How can you tell?'

'I don't know, I just can.' She had a trick of letting her head fall a little to one side. 'In what way have *I* changed?'

'What a question!'

'Well, what's the answer?'

'Not to state the obvious but . . .'

'But . . . ?' Again that little coquettish tilt. I remembered it now. She had always done it.

'You've got rid of your glasses.'

'Yes.'

'I don't suppose anyone pulls your hair any more.'

'No.'

'You smoke.'

'Oh hell, is *that* so obvious? I was being good too, thinking I wouldn't have one while I was here.'

'It's really not important.'

'What else then?'

You've grown up, I wanted to say. What happened to you? Do you remember Ambona? Do you still climb trees? How the hell did you become such a gorgeous bloody woman?

I said, 'You're no longer a little girl.'

With rather a wan smile she said, 'Perhaps I never was.'

'Do you go back?' she asked. 'To India, I mean? There was that little boy we used to play with. Jula? I remember him very clearly. I wonder where he is now.'

I had hardly been back and had not seen Jula for the best part of thirty years, but began to tell her what I knew, how he had grown up and become Mitra, who was apprenticed to a printer and how I used to hobnob with him in the Dongri bazaar.

'Dongri? Where's that?'

'It's a Muslim bazaar in the heart of Bombay.'

She said, 'I want to hear about *you* first. Tell me about your daughters. About the bookshop.'

I had been dreading the moment when I would have to confess what a khichdi (kedgeree) I had made of my life. In the event it was surprisingly painless. Every parent finds it easy to talk about their offspring, so I described events from the twins' childhood, how Katy had taught them to ride, how proud we were of their cups and medals and school reports, and how lost we had felt when they first went off to university. Phoebe was a good listener and soon I was telling the sorry tale of my lost years – my foray into the Soho film industry, at first cheap B-features, later commercials, the boozing, late nights in The French Pub and drinking clubs – until the bookshop saved my marriage and probably my life. Nice pat phrase, that. Properly self-deprecating.

'It's a wonder the girls did so well,' I added. 'Considering that at one point I seriously thought I was an alcoholic.'

'Same silly Bhalu,' said Phoebe. 'You always did yourself down, even as a child.'

But all she'd had was the oft-told, expurgated version. Perfected in the telling. Not my shames – dark hair, cheap wine, and Pushkin – though Katy knew and had forgiven me. Nor another thing I had never told anyone. Getting home early, unexpected, one day during that same awful era, and witnessing something I shouldn't have. Something Katy never knew I'd seen. I knew how close I had come to losing her.

'You don't realise how *important* you are,' Phoebe was saying.

'Important?' It wasn't a word I'd have chosen.

'Yes, important. It doesn't mean being a boss or a big shot. It means being special to other people. Being kind. Like you were to me, when we were children . . . You don't mind, do you, if I smoke?'

Normally I can't bear people smoking near me, but I shook my head. 'No, of course not. Go ahead.'

She lit a cigarette, exhaled. 'I was thinking of that when I was listening to you in the chapel, talking about your mother. What she believed. That it's important to do small kindnesses, good things, because they carry on, they have their effects. It's quite true. People remember things for years. They don't forget.'

It wasn't quite what Maya had meant, but I was touched.

Phoebe stood swirling her wine, watching it climb in the glass, then glanced briefly across the room at Katy, who was talking to Piglet and Panaghiotis. 'I wish I'd been there,' she said. 'I wouldn't have let you get in that state.'

For a moment I didn't follow what she was talking about, but then I was horrified. 'I've given you the wrong idea,' I said. 'Katy's the gentlest soul. Not many women would have been as patient. And she supported me in giving up the London job, though it left us almost penniless. I'll always be grateful for that.'

Phoebe said quickly, 'Sorry, that was clumsy. I didn't mean to imply . . . I'm sure Katy did everything she could.'

The wake was almost over. Srinuji and Piglet were collecting glasses. Sounds of washing up emanated from the kitchen. Katy came over and lifted a plate from the mantelpiece.

'You two all right?' she asked.

'Katy's lovely,' said Phoebe. 'You're lucky. How did you meet her?'

It was soon after I finished my Sussex course, the one I'd come from India to do. Post-graduate diploma in film studies. I had a flat in Brighton and was travelling to London for interviews with film companies. To support myself I got a job in a bookshop and was put in charge of the horse, dog and cat shelves. A girl with a rather nice bottom, often jodhpur-cased (I didn't mention this bit to Phoebe) used to come in and browse the horse books. So I made a point of ordering every horsey title in every publisher's catalogue. We soon had the biggest equine section in town and I used to skim through them so I could make conversation. That's how we got to know one another. We went out for coffee, the odd meal at some cheap café in the Lanes, a walk on the beach. It was a tremendously hot summer. She took me home to meet her parents, who had a small farm on the Downs.

'That's so romantic,' said Phoebe. 'But you always were.'

'Hardly how I'd have described myself.'

'Oh, making a girl cut up worms is quite romantic, in its way.'

'When we told them we were engaged,' I said, 'her father I think was aghast, but did his best to hide it. He took me aside and asked me not to rush her into marriage. "She's so young," he kept on and on saying.'

'So when did you disappoint him?'

'We've been married just over twenty-two years. The twins had their twenty-first birthdays, just after Maya died.'

I wanted to change the subject. 'You haven't yet told me about Peter. How long have you been married?'

She said, 'Oh hell, for ever.' But her eyes were suddenly quick.

'Phoebe, do you remember Tiger's Leap?'

It was one of my most vivid memories of her, as a child during that last summer, when the shadows from the grown-up world had begun to fall across us. Late afternoon on one of those days when the rain stops and everything sings. She was standing at the edge of the cliff at Tiger's Leap, gazing into a brazen haze out of which rose an odd, conical peak. We used to joke that it was like a breast with a standing-up nipple. She took off her glasses, held her face up to the sun, closed her eyes and in the oddly grown-up manner she had acquired, said, 'I'm so happy. If anything makes me sad, I'll remember this moment.'

In the years that followed, I learned to do this myself, store up moments of happiness and hoard them against dark times.

She frowned. 'I remember all sorts of queer things. Some of it's a bit hazy. But I remember everything we did together.'

'You know, I always hoped we'd meet again.'

Dropping her voice so low that it was almost a whisper, she said. 'You *hoped*? I *knew*! I *knew* you would keep your promise.'

I must have looked blank because she added, 'You promised you would come to England and find me.'

Piglet came up and said, 'Are you going back to Lewes, Bhalu? Cadge a lift, can I?' He drifted away consulting his watch. Probably working out if he'd have time to see Charlotte.

'Time I went,' said Phoebe. 'Dare I kiss you again?'

But this time it was just a peck on the cheek. 'I'll be in touch,' she said. 'Now I've found you I'm not going to let you go.'

'Well, well,' said Katy, watching Phoebe taking her leave of my sisters. 'So that is the legendary Phoebe? I can see that she must have been very pretty, when she was young. You certainly made a big hit with *her*.'

'Oh, for God's sake, Katy, we were *children*.'

'Well, you're not a child now,' said Katy. 'No matter what your mother may have told you to the contrary.'

Srinuji was approaching to make his farewells. Odd, but now that I knew why he had shaved off his moustache, I felt almost fond of him.

'Your mother and I,' said this surprising man, drawing me aside, 'used to enjoy playing the game of moamma. Do you know it?'

I did not.

'Moamma means quandary, dilemma. The first player quotes a line of poetry, with one word missing. The second player is offered two words, both of which are apt. Which is the correct choice? To win, you have to know the language and the literature. This is a Lucknowi game. It was played in the time of the nawabs. Of course the courtiers used to play for thousands, but when I went home last year' – I had forgotten he was from her home town – 'there were five-rupee games on every street corner. One can buy the entry forms in sweet shops and bicycle shops. Forget professors of poetry, in Lucknow even rickshaw drivers want to discuss the latest moamma situation with you. I shall demonstrate with an easy example: "Na tha kuchch to *blank* tha, kuchch na hota to *blank* hota . . ." "When nothing was, there yet was *blank*, had nothing been *blank* would have been . . ." Your choice is "malik" or "khuda".'

Both words were Muslim names for God.

'I never thought to hear you talking of Khuda.' I had no idea why he was telling me all this.

'Whatever name we give to Him, the One Upstairs is the same. Would you like to play?'

'Okay,' I said.

'I'll give you a couplet of Kabir's. "Piya chaahe prem ras, raakha chaahe *blank*, ek myaan men do khadag, dekha suna na kaan." "You want to drink love's potion yet keep your *blank* preserved, but two daggers in one scabbard, no one has yet observed". Your dilemma is "jaan" or "maan".'

'Life or honour?'

'Exactly.'

'Which is it?'

'That is for you to decide.'

I told him I would think about it, but inside me rose that silent, violent joy.

How did a cowherding caterpillar, Jula, become the pupa from which emerged Mitra the printer?

Having time on my hands, I decided I would put Jula's story on paper for Phoebe. It began, of course, in Ambona, but years later, I had got to know him again under different circumstances in Bombay. If Ambona was the determining influence of my childhood, our times in the Dongri bazaar were the most exciting part of my early adulthood. Ambona and Dongri, these were the two most powerful places in my life and Jula, aka Mitra, had been there with me in both. I had never told these stories before, much less written them down. My account started as a letter, but after several days of scribbling and rubbing-out, I realised that I was really writing for myself.

After we left Ambona it was nearly six years before I saw Jula again. January 1966. I was sixteen and had just finished at my school in the north, where I was sent after you left for England. In India in those days one left school after doing more or less the equivalent of the old British O-level. At an absurdly young age, we went on to university. I was going to Saint Stephen's in Delhi, with a lot of my friends, but the next few months were my own. Maya and my father were back in Bombay, strangely enough, in the same flat we lived in before Ambona. Captain Sahib's dreams of a rose garden – remember how he loved his roses, his long lectures about hybrid tea roses called things like Doctor K. Biswas and

Deenabandhu Reverend Andrews? – had long since been reduced to a few mildewed plants that struggled to breathe in the Bombay fug. I was in the city for a few weeks, and decided to take the train up to Ambona. It would be the first time I had been back.

Indian railway stations all smell alike, of coal dust, engine grease and disinfectant, with hints of jasmine and beedi-smoke.

VT, Victoria Terminus, was thronged with villagers. Baskets of produce, eggs, aubergines, spinach, poultry wheezing in wicker cages, went bobbing by on the heads of red-shirted porters with brass licence plates bound to their right arms. I drank a tea – Indian Railways brew, thick and sweet with a hint of cardamom, and felt ridiculously happy. Even the letters AMBONA on my smudgily printed pasteboard ticket were jigging up and down, as though they were as elated as me. I was travelling third class. I used to enjoy the crowded compartments and bizarre combinations of people brought together by chance.

Bombay is like a finger pointing south into the Arabian Sea. Ambona is to the south-east but to get there, whether by rail or road, one has to go thirty miles north, before turning for the hills.

Phoebe, remember what makes that journey unforgettable? The train howls and plunges into a tunnel – darkness, muffled wheelbeats, red lamps swinging past like infernal milestones, a long, long wait before touches of light on rough rock walls signal the tunnel's end approaching fast – a glimpse of day, impressions of tawny slopes climbing away steeply and you're into the next – a roaring black mouth opens and swallows you; people's voices buzz strangely; there's barely enough light to see one's neighbours and the tunnel goes on and on until lamps flashing by almost create an illusion of floating backwards, until light again starts to sculpt the walls, then – daylight, the train swaying in sudden quiet, and in a clear breath a valley falls sheer to the right, fields dotted with hayricks a thousand feet below, the landscape stretching away to haze in the direction of the sea; half a mile ahead, the locomotive whistles, and for a moment you see it, a chuffing toy on the curve of a miniature track. Twenty-six tunnels that loop the train up and through the hills, emerging in the surreal scenery of Reversing Point, where a viaduct carries the railway across a gulf right under the outlandish shape of Duke's Nose. Not five minutes later, we are pulling into a yellow station past a sign which says, in big Marathi letters, अम्बौणे, AMBONA.

I found an auto-rickshaw at the station and told the driver to take me to Karvanda village. A long trip, but I wanted to go straight to see Jula. Nothing had changed. The town square was still there, with its statue of George V, and roofs growing grass between their tiles, same blue mountain sky. It even smelt the same.

The driver was a teenager, my own age. He drove too fast and kept glancing at me in his mirror. 'Sir, you look familiar.'

'I used to live here.'

'What's your name?'

So I told him. 'Son of a bitch,' he said, swivelling and sending the rickshaw round a corner on two wheels. 'Don't you recognise me? I was at school with you.'

His name was Razak. I remembered him now. His father used to drive a truck at the naval base. We'd been friends, until I was plucked out and sent to my posh boarding school.

'Ben went to join the Navy,' he told me. 'He's a cadet now, in

Khadakvasla.' This was the military academy near Poona.

'I'm going to see Jula,' I said, after we'd exchanged news. 'Do you know him? He must have joined a couple of years after I left. About our age, but a couple of classes lower down.'

'Bit of a dunce?'

'Actually the reverse. A clever guy. He just started late.'

'I don't know any Jula,' scattering chickens.

'From Karvanda village. His surname is Kashele.'

'Oh, you mean Mitra.'

The rickshaw put-putted across the long dam of the monsoon lake. Bicchauda rose ahead. I could smell its mineral breath. Five years, what would have changed? But nothing had changed. It was all just as I remembered. The lake at winter level, horses and sheep grazing its margins on meadows that would go twenty feet under when the rains came. Among the herds and flocks moved tiny herdsmen, their turbans little bright blobs. It was all still there. You fear that you turn round and the world will vanish, but it was as if the hills had been waiting for me to return. Look, they were saying, we have kept everything in good order. Our trees are here, the animals are here, every one of them inventoried. Everything is just as you left it, awaiting your return.

Bicchauda's forest was dry and winter-dusty, but already some trees were putting out new leaves, yellow, pale lime. Here and there were crimson bursts of palasa, the flame of the forest. Round the lake we toiled. Up there, above, was the steep rock-face where Rosie had fallen. One dark blot on memory, the one thing about Ambona I would have liked to forget. The rickshaw shuddered on, over the pass, up and around the hill, and there was the track that led to our house and the village. Still there.

Our house did not appear to have changed. It was shut up. The gates were fastened by a rusted chain. There were weeds growing through them. They had obviously not been opened for months because it was monsoon growth, long since dead and yellowed. Strange to say, I passed it without regret. I was glad not to find someone else living there.

The track grew too poor for the rickshaw. I paid it off and watched it bounce down towards the lake in a cloud of red dust, then I turned my face to the village. Up and around the spur of Bicchauda, the track twisting down through the valley and then the gentle climb up the lower slopes of the next hill, Dagala. I found myself searching the hillside, where cows and buffalos were dotted about, for a small figure in ragged shorts. From the jungle-crowned top of Dagala, a cliff fell almost sheer into forest. This was where we had climbed to look for the Kathodi. It looked impossible. How had we got up it so easily?

At last, the familiar approach. Karvanda had not changed. The houses, with their roofs of thatch and grassy tile, looked as if they had grown out of the earth, been there for ever.

News of my approach must have already reached the village, because I was escorted the last hundred yards by a crowd of tiny children. I came to Jula's house and there was his mother, coughing, wiping her eyes, bangles jingling. She had aged, was stooping like an old woman, although she must have been younger than Maya.

She came and bent to touch my feet. I stopped her.

'No, Ma, it's only me.'

So I hugged her. She put her hand on my head, closed her eyes and murmured some mantra, gave me a blessing. She said to one of the boys hanging in the doorway, 'What are you staring at? Go find Mitra, tell him Bhalu has come . . . He helps the younger children with their schoolwork,' she explained to me. 'It's the school your mother started.'

Then she asked about my mother and said she was a saint and how everyone remembered those days and wished she'd come back.

'Jula!'

I hardly recognised him. My little ragamuffin friend had grown long and thin. He wore glasses, small round-framed specs that gave him a studious air. His face broke into a huge smile and he stuck out a hand, something he wouldn't have known to do in the old days.

'Bhalu bhai!'

'What's all this Mitra business?'

'Shambhumitra. My real name. Jula's just a nickname. You know that. It means twin. When I was born I had a twin sister, but she died. My mother called me Jula to remember my sister, that she had been there too.'

But this was something I had not known.

'You must see the school. Come, come.' And he took me by the arm and led me. The schoolhouse had been completely rebuilt in brick; it had two classrooms. Jula, no, Mitra, called out and a thin young man emerged. 'This is Rameshbhai, the teacher. He has been here two years. After our first teacher left – you remember Hari Prasad?' I did not remember Hari Prasad.

'Your mother still sends the money to pay his salary. Every month.'

They wanted to show me everything. The school books, reading primers in Marathi and English, the blackboard with sums and names of plants chalked on it.

'Bhalu, it's a fine school. Twenty children now learning to read and write, and all thanks to your mother.'

But later he said to me, 'What I don't understand is why she sent you off to that fancy place.'

I did not know why either, and I dared not tell him about my school in Rajasthan, with its marble tower and carved-sandstone cricket pavilion on the steps of which, at annual prize-givings, the boys sat in their formal achkans and Rajput turbans, like rows of expensive tulips. At Jula's school the boys wore cheap blue shorts and white shirts. Somehow their mothers kept the clothes spotless, washing them with 501 Bar Soap, scrubbing them on stones to get them clean.

Jula was seventeen, but still at KayGee Vee, a year away from his matric exam. His father Dhondu was ill. He could no longer work regularly, so Jula had taken an evening job in Ambona, at a tea shop.

'The traffic is growing between Mumbai and Pune,' he said, using the Marathi names for the two places. 'We're very busy. I can make a few rupees, it all helps.'

Jula – I could not get used to thinking of him as Mitra – told me that he wanted to learn printing, so he could make school-books. 'We have to help the simple people. Your mother helped us. Now we have to help ourselves. We have to tell our real story as *we* know it.

'Look, I have written this.' He showed me an exercise book in which was written, in Hindi, the story of Shivaji, the Mahratta chieftain who had ruled these hills four hundred years earlier.

I recognised the story my mother had told. The ghorpats, giant monitor lizards . . . but there was about Mitra's artless re-telling a freshness, a robust relish; it was like his father's seedlings, firmly rooted in this good soil.

'Do you still go into the forest?'

He laughed, put his arm round my shoulders. 'Come,' he said. 'Let's go and herd some cows.'

A half-decade passed. It was 1971 and I was twenty-one. I finished college in Delhi and came to Bombay to get a job in the monkey business. Both my sisters had grown up and were at college. Maya and Captain Sahib were still in the flat in Cuffe Parade, but already there were signs that they were nearing some sort of crisis. Maya was working on a big new project, a film script, but not having a great deal of luck with it. It had been rejected by a number of directors. My father had bought some land in Lucknow and talked of building a house. He was dreaming of his gul-e-stan, and once again his talk was all roses, though by now the names were different: Patiala Durbar, Yamini Krishnamurthi, White Nun, Muzibar – strange how I remember them in their peer groups, the roses of different periods, like pop stars, or films.

One day there was a call for me. Mitra. He told me he was in Bombay, apprenticed to a printer. He'd been there just over a year.

'I can now read English not only forwards, but backwards!'

He said he had learned how to set type, reading letters back-to-front, ranging them in trays separated by little lead slugs of just the right size. Not easy, but he was mastering it.

We met at Churchgate station and took a stroll along Marine Drive to eye up the girls. Mitra had grown taller, but was still very thin. His trousers fell in a straight line from the back of his waist to his ankles. His thighs were pencils and his shirt ballooned above a waist a girl might have envied.

Later we took a bus to his printing works. A grimy back-street building in Dongri, the heart of the Muslim bazaar area. He had two more years, he said, to finish his apprenticeship. He was full of plans.

'Your mother is helping me, we shall organise a co-operative.'

With great enthusiasm he explained that, in the company they would set up, everyone who worked there, from the chief editor to the chapraasi, would get the same money.

'We will print books that the ordinary people will be able to afford. Not cheap rubbish, but good quality books. We can print our classics with explanations. We can translate foreign books. I have been going round the city, observing the condition of people here. Bhalu, you come with me. I'll show you sights in this city you've never dreamed of. People come from villages wanting work, a new life, and they find no job, just a doorstep for a pillow. So we're going to do self-help books. How to organise and lobby for clean drinking water, for electricity. And you know, Bhalu, I've learned that even the way words are used carries the stamp of class and in-built attitudes. We shall change that. Our books will open people's eyes. We'll show them that it's possible to live without caste and bigotry.'

He said it was his destiny to be plucked, a boy from a hillside, and educated. It was as if God had chosen him for a mission and made my mother the instrument of His will. 'I repeat her name with my prayers. She is a great woman. If it hadn't been for her, I would still be herding cows, or pushing a plough with an irrla on my head.'

A few weeks later he phoned again and told me to meet him at his office. 'Tonight I'm taking you somewhere special.'

It was evening, still light, with choirs of pigeons circling the rooftops. We walked through the Muslim quarter, a maze of lanes like a net flung over the hindquarters of the old city.

Eventually, we found ourselves in an unremarkable alley. A few string beds (charpays, literally 'four-foot') stood near a pair of large iron gates beyond which was a dark courtyard.

'What is this place?'

'It's Moosa's adda.'

'Adda' means 'den'. It can be applied to any spot where people, usually men, gather for a purpose. There were gambling addas, drinking addas, cock-fighting addas . . .

'What kind of adda?'

'That, you're about to discover.'

We were greeted by a young fellow, whom Mitra introduced to me as Sharfu, the house-manager, natty in tie-up frontier pyjamas and pin-stripe waistcoat. He ducked his head shyly and asked our pleasure, producing from his waistcoat pocket a small plastic bag full of little black balls. 'Chillum chahiye?'

'I have one,' Mitra replied, fetching out a short, conical clay pipe. 'But send the boy for some tea.'

'What now?' I asked.

'Nothing,' he said. 'Just sit and watch the world pass by.'

At first I was uncomfortable. It seemed strange to me that Mitra patronised such a place. It felt unsafe. He was a Hindu and this was Muslim territory.

'Bhalu bhai,' said Mitra, packing the chillum and tamping it well, 'there are some things about Bicchauda hill you never knew. Remember where Pandri the cow used to get herself lost, up where the forest began? Well, go into the jungle there. You come to a clearing where there are hundreds of plants. My father used to smoke a little, in a chillum like this one. He said it relieved the pains in his back. It wasn't good stuff. Shit really. Even looked like goat-pellets. Nothing like this.'

I felt ashamed to think of Jula's – Mitra's – father, hunched over our vegetables day after day.

'Did many people use it?'

'Many, many people. In winter, women would eat the seeds. They're supposed to keep you warm. With such hard lives, people are entitled to small pleasures, don't you agree? Specially when it's the gift of Mahadeo. Let the rich drink champagne and whisky, this is the poor man's nasha.'

He took a toke, watching me over the chillum's rim, held it down for what seemed like for ever, then, nodding his appreciation, let out a huge gush of smoke. 'It's good,' he said, when he could speak, and handed the chillum to me.

Moosa's hashish was black and soft, small balls dusted lightly with a pearly fungus. It swam you instantly to narcotic depths – Mitra swore it was at least a quarter opium – and quickened the mind, ideas, inferences, images, feelings, connecting at fantastic speed, too fast for tongues to keep up.

An hour, or maybe minutes, went by. My body felt as if it had acquired an aura of cool blue light. A huge joy surged right through the street, transfiguring it. A scrawny red cockerel on a roof opposite puffed out its chest and scraped up a hearty cry. My worries had vanished. It no longer seemed anything but natural and delightful to be sitting in this grimy alley, drinking tea. Two old Muslim gentlemen were taking a walk, neat skullcaps offset by impeccable spade-shaped beards (wagging as they talked). Their shaven upper-lips made them look Mesopotamian. A blind beggar approached. Loose curls, sightless eyes like a Homeric bard. My thoughts were scattering like the flights of pigeons above Moosa's, fighting the wind – up, up – banking and circling, in a sky that was turning royal blue. A hand grabbed at my foot and I jumped. A small boy was crawling under the bed to retrieve a marble. I watched him fire it off, bending his middle finger back as we had done when we were children. A group of ragged girls squatted in a gutter, setting light to some paper. It twisted and slowly disinte-grated into flakes of flame, that were lifted by tiny currents into the air.

The ground floor of the building across the way housed a row of small shops. Above one of these, a crude hand-painted sign announced: SAURASHTRA TRADING COMPANY and listed its items of commerce: CURRY MASALAS, DRY FRUITS, BAKELITE SHEETS, INDUSTRIAL KNIVES, SAWS & BLADES, COTTON GOODS AND YARNS. I was staring at this old building, at its architecture, the set of its windows, its rotting woodwork, layer on layer of flaking paint – the changes which had converted it to a glum chawl from what it had once been, which was a warehouse. The building seemed to speak, to narrate its history and the city's. It had been constructed on open land in 1857, the year of the Mutiny, to store the cotton crop brought from Gujerat for the new mills being built by farsighted Parsis. The alley was cheered by news that civil war had broken out in America. Suddenly the Lancashire mills wanted Indian cotton – Surat bolls – and they passed through here. The bazaars grew up later, and filled all remaining gaps. By the turn of the century, the building said, it was no longer used for cotton. Instead it held bales of cinnamon quills, black pepper, nutmeg and cloves, dried ginger, chillies, cardamoms and betel nuts. One could still smell cinammon in the air. In the fifties, the city's post-war boom led to its conversion into apartments for families of modest means. Lacking most facilities, in some cases even water and basic sanitation, it housed more than four hundred people. They lived, some families, eight or ten to a room, and each room reeked of a different spice.

'Give me one fact and a goli of Moosa's,' Dost used to say, 'and I can infer the world.'

His name was Mohammed Khan, so we called him 'Dost' after the warlord of that name. He was happy-go-lucky, despair of the local mullahs, happiest on his way into a cinema. His knowledge of the movies was impressive. He'd go several times to see a film he liked, and even some he didn't. Dost worked part time in his uncle's dhaba (small roadside restaurant) and told us he made a little bit extra running errands for the local goons. He was, so he claimed, thoroughly familiar with the undertow of city life, its rackets, black market, bootlegging trade. 'You want anything done,' he would boast, 'I can arrange it. Peacefully.' If you needed a particular part for a car, or a special make of radio, he knew which stall to visit in Chor Bazaar (Thieves' Market). The three of us developed a bantering relationship, teasing each other about girls, penis sizes, sexual experience or lack of, circumcision ditto. Mitra still had his old Jula-trick of grabbing at invisible flies, so he became 'makkhimar', fly-killer. (*Mukhomor* is Russian for fly agaric.) I, of course, was 'Bhola Bhalu'. We would go for rides on Dost's motorbike, me sitting behind him, arms round his waist, Mitra on the tail, clinging to me.

Dost's way of making joints was fascinating. His fingers were long and knuckly, like spiders' legs: he would take a cigarette and roll it between his fingertips, patiently teasing the tobacco onto his palm. Fastidiously, he would pick out and discard the long, coarse strands. Using a complex finger-yoga, he would pick up a *goli*, a pea-sized ball of hashish, skewer it on a match and toast it till it sizzled, then crumble it into the tobacco and mill the mixture with his thumb. He would take the hollow paper tube, which he had parked between two knuckles, and blow in it to fluff it out. Taking infinite pains, he would coax the tobacco back into the paper tube, scooping, twisting, tapping frequently to tamp it down. The whole Byzantine procedure might take five or six minutes, but I have seen him do it in two, in a stiff breeze that set strings of paper flags – green flags with white crescent moons – rustling above the alley.

Nights at the dope den blurred together. I remember a blind beggar who sang, accompanied by chirring glasses. One night there was quite a crowd in the alley. More charpays were brought and set in the street. A couple of men appeared, bearing a myste-rious cylindrical object, about eight feet long. They put it down and began pulling from it a long canvas tongue. Next they brought ropes and tied them to buildings on opposite sides of the alley. The loose ends were attached to the flapping canvas which lifted into the air and became a cinema screen. While these men were making the screen taut, a projector arrived on a handcart and was established in the centre of the alley, which it completely blocked. People brought out chairs from houses and soon there was a throng of excited children sitting cross-legged in the dust. The audience sat on *both* sides of the screen. With a great deal of tinny screeching from worn-out loudspeakers, the film flickered to life.

The story seemed to be about a Bombay news reporter who is being pressured to kill a story about corruption in high places. A gangster and cabaret singer were somehow involved. There was a love scene when their faces hung, blurred grey and white shapes in the darkness. At some point, a goat climbed onto my charpay and lay there chewing, watching me with malevolent yellow eyes. Every so often, blank frames blazoned with domino dots would flicker by, signifying the end of another reel and the audience would applaud. There seemed to be far too many reels. When the show was over the crowd dispersed as quickly as it had gathered. We were once again on our own.

'Well, wasn't that a lot of shit?' said a voice out of the darkness.

'You would know, I suppose,' came Mitra's voice in reply.

'When you start making movies, Bhalu,' said Dost, 'never mind the heavy social message, concentrate on entertainment.'

'No danger of that,' I said. I was not having much luck finding a job. Even Maya's introductions had produced nothing.

'Don't listen,' came Mitra's voice again. 'All arts should aim to do something for the poor. Something tangible.'

It was Mitra who had told me that my mother was working on an important project, about which she was unwilling to say much, except that, like the film we had just seen, it concerned murder and police corruption. She was having trouble selling it, Mitra said. Her kind of work was already going out of fashion.

Dost stuck up for the 'masala' movie.

'What is the use of showing reality in films, since the films can do nothing to change it?'

'You've got it round backwards. The purpose of a good film should be to educate, and thus bring about change.'

'How much do they educate? Whom do they influence?'

'Show the world as it really is, so people can recognise their own situations. They'll know what to do. Whereas your mirch-masala, what has it got to do with anything except making money?'

'That's just snobbery,' said Dost. 'You just like being miserable. Why try to make this an art versus commerce debate?'

'Just tell me,' said Mitra, growing heated, 'how many of your big all-star movies actually teach anyone anything useful?'

Dost said, 'I haven't noticed that social movies are shy of hiring big stars. Do Johnny Walker and Guru Dutt pull crowds because they play common people, or because they are stars?'

'That is not the point. The point is, what's the intention.'

Dost said, 'What do your serious film-makers really care about the audience? They're too preoccupied with breaking new ground and winning prizes at foreign film festivals. If serious cinema wants to lift the masses out of the mire, it should talk in a way people will appreciate. And human beings like to be entertained.'

I thought of Bubbles Roy, whom I had recently met again at a party at someone's house on Juhu Beach. Bubbles, who had by then given up his arty aspirations and was well and truly mired in what would become Bollywood (it was shortly after the success of *Sheikh Piru*, the life of an Indianised Shakespeare-like dramatist), told me that Maya could have been a big shot in the movies if she hadn't been so wedded to her social-karmic hobbyhorse.

'Maya has trapped herself. She passionately wants justice, and at the same time she knows that this world is deeply unjust. It's blind, random chaos. By all means try to change it, but your good works are like using a bucket to bale a sea of misery. It's why we have God, hell, heaven. So we can bear present pain. Evildoers will be reborn as worms, beggars will wake up as princes. But Bhalu, your mother refuses to accept the help of God. She fights, she struggles, she rages against the cosmos. She shows us in her work the cruelty of life. She makes us realise that there is no hope, that our only freedom is in daily struggle. All very noble, but cinema audiences don't want to hear it. Their lives are bad enough already. They want to escape, and if we love them, we should help them.'

Thus spake the erstwhile intellectual, clad in a Hawaiian shirt, and the painted houris on his arm smirked and rolled their huge eyes.

One night Dost took us to his uncle's café, the Jam-e-Jamshid, a busy mirror-lined place in a street crowded with shoppers, where kerosene lamps hissed above pyramids of oranges, grapefruits, melons. Inside the Jam-i-Jam café, a burly man was throwing pakoras into a pan, where they fizzed like fireworks. His arms were matted with hair and he dripped delicately into the cooking. We sat at a table in the street, which (the street, not the table) smelt of goats and rotting vegetables. Somehow it was marvellous. Food came, on tiny plates. As quickly as one was finished another arrived — eggs-in-batter, brains, mutton curry. The bread was rough, good for soaking up gravy rich with golden globules of mutton fat. Everything was spiced with woodsmoke. The food kept coming, plates spreading across the rough table until I couldn't eat any more. Mitra's fingers crushing powdery black hash into strands of tobacco. There was a song, a Hindi film song popular at the time, which Dost was forever singing.

Zāhid, sharāb píné dé, masjid mén baith kar,
yā wōh jagāh batā dé jahān khudā na hō . . .
Mujhkō yaarōn maaf karna, main nashé mén hoon
Let me sit, priest, in the temple with my wine-pot,
Or else show me some other place, where God is not . . .
Forgive me, friends, I'm in my *nasha*.

'Nasha' is impossible to translate. It can mean 'drunkenness', 'inebriation', 'stupor', but also has overtones of 'trance' and 'vision', with a hint of ruthless destruction. It's what got into god Siva, lord of booze, drugs, music and sex, when he threw his hat in the air and danced the end of the world.

THE WAR (BOMBAY, DECEMBER 1971)

It was 1971 and there was big trouble in East Pakistan, thousands of refugees. People said there would be war. The city was tense; there was a general blackout – thick brown paper pasted over the headlamps of cars. No cars came down our alley, and Moosa and his folk seemed happy to ply their business in a darkness broken only by the smoky orange glow of our chillums, but the area, Dongri, was a Muslim stronghold, not safe, we were warned, for Hindus. The green and white flags of Pakistan were everywhere.

On the night war finally broke out, the three of us had gone on Dost's motorbike to Haji Ali. We sat on the sea wall and watched the incoming tide encircle the white mosque in the sea. Later, we rode to Colaba. In the darkness of the blackout there was a huge traffic jam. We were stuck in a line of barely visible vehicles and got off the bike to see what was going on.

Dost lit a cigarette.

With the flare of his match, there came an exclamation from the darkness. 'Put that out!'

'Why?'

'There's a blackout. Do you want to get us killed?'

A second voice said, 'Don't you know? Pakistan has bombed our airfields. Just two hours ago.'

'Oh God, oh God,' wailed the first voice. A small man carrying a briefcase huddled in a doorway.

'Don't be foolish,' said Dost. 'Can a pilot ten thousand feet up flying at the speed of sound see a cigarette? Especially when he has got a moon to light his way.'

He gestured to where the faint crescent, a Pakistani moon if ever I saw one, hung in a clear sky.

A new voice said, 'He's a Muslim. What are you doing, hey? Showing your fucking pals up there where to drop their bombs?'

Mitra and I protested. Soon there was a furious slanging match going on. Dost ignored us all and finished his cigarette.

In a back room behind the idols in a Hindu temple in Colaba, we bought balls of soft, bitter opium. We sat on the waterfront, near the place where the last British soldiers had left India, with the stuff gummily lodged behind the upper front teeth, where the tongue could wander for an occasional lick. A chap nearby had a transistor radio tuned to the news. Pakistan had bombed Indian airfields at Amritsar, Srinagar, Avantipur, Jodhpur, Ambala, Pathankot, Agra and Agartala. In my mind I saw the enemy planes swooping across lonely airfields, the light of the horned moon glancing along their fuselages, the wail of sirens, men running in darkness.

Mrs Gandhi would broadcast at midnight. In the harbour, the rigging of the dhows was outlined in blue fire.

Midnight found us in the Hanging Gardens. Beneath us the city lay like a spilt sack of jewels. Despite the blackout, lights flickered in many buildings, greenish, blue, yellow. From some-where below came shouting and the sound of smashing glass.

'They want the lights out,' said Mitra. 'They're demanding that people observe the blackout.'

A café called Naaz had stayed open. A group of customers sat in darkness around the radio. The broadcast was postponed; Mrs Gandhi was still in a cabinet meeting. For the next twenty minutes there was a solemn music – *Raga Durga*, I think it was, played on a sarod, which ground and leapt, built on a repetitive phrase with a sudden hard note at the end of the line. Then Mrs Gandhi came on air to say that India had declared war on Pakistan.

Just before two, there was an air-raid alert over the city. We sat in the garden, staring into the sky. There was nothing left alive but the sobbing of the siren. It filled the air. The tall buildings behind us were dark shapes, eerily lit by the waning Id moon, which had become veiled in thin cloud. The noise of the siren seemed to flow between the buildings and over them, filling every crevice. The same moon was shining over the north, over the cities that had been raided, the cold desert, the soldiers at their posts. All over the north there must have been that same feeling of expectancy, and life squeezed out by the wailing of distant sirens on both sides of the border.

The war hotted up. President Nixon announced a 'tilt to Pakistan.' The USS *Enterprise* duly began steaming up the Bay of Bengal towards the disintegrating remains of East Pakistan.

We went to Moosa's as frequently as before and listened to the news on Radio Pakistan. There was little war talk in the alleys. Not surprising, in view of their traditional links to the 'enemy'. Many people, like Dost, had relatives in Karachi, and small towns dotted all the way to the borders of Iran and Afghanistan.

It was a time of parties. One heard rumours and gossip. In Hindu areas of the city, self-seeking politicians were trying to stir up resentment against the Muslims. There was wild talk of a two-pronged invasion of Bombay. An elite Pakistani force, armed to the teeth, would land from the sea, while the bazaars would spawn a ragged army of fanatics to take the defending Indians in the rear. Cynics said the real target of these rumours was Indira Gandhi and her New Congress. Her popularity, which was ebbing before the war, had soared. She was being likened in the press to Durga Ma, the Rani of Jhansi, Joan of Arc, Boadicea, or whatever other female warrior sprang to mind.

Some rumours were just ludicrous. On the Himalayan frontier, it was said, a network of first-class roads had been constructed and trucks passed continuously along them, running not on petrol or diesel but clarified butter. But the strangest tale of all originated from a tea-seller on Delhi railway station who swore that, two days before the outbreak of war in the west, he had been asked for four hundred and fifty cups of tea, which he had served to chimpanzees wearing Indian uniforms. The chimps, he was told in confidence, were trained to chuck grenades down the hatches of enemy tanks, although how they were supposed to differentiate between the two sides, no one could explain.

My father had high-ranking naval friends and one night, by which time the city had grown used to the displays of searchlights and anti-aircraft fire, I found myself at a party where a senior admiral was holding forth to a group which included an American who was introduced as the agricultural attaché from the US Consulate. 'You know what I'd do if I were C-in-C in Eastern Command?' said the sailor. 'I'd send out two submarines – badoom! badoom! – and blast the *Enterprise* to the bottom. Mrs Gandhi would have to fire me, but in private she'd clap me on the back and say "Shabaash". The American had to laugh it off, but I could see that he was itching to get to a phone and report this intelligence, if such it could be called. In the event he was still there, glass in hand, when the admiral received a phone call, put down the receiver looking shaken, and hurried away to his headquarters. Next morning we heard that our frigate *Khukri* had been sunk in the Arabian Sea by a Pakistani submarine.

There were disturbances in the moholla. Some youths had been set on and beaten by Hindus. There were reprisals. Even so, Mitra and I, Hindus both, did not believe we were at risk. Perhaps a week after *Khukri* was lost, we met Dost, as was our habit, at the adda. It was darker and quieter than usual. The alley's sole street-lamp had fallen victim to the blackout, and the scene was lit by the faint supernatural light of the moon and the demonic glow of chillums. I found myself sitting next to a person who wore the heavy woollen robe that is commonly seen in the Middle East. He acknowledged my presence with the slightest of nods and the evening faded into luxurious hypnosis.

Stars, spread thinly across a cold blue sky, the sour, exquisite stench of hashish, the acrid goat-stench of the robe beside me all joined and became one thing. I could have expressed it all in one word, if I had known the word. And the word expanded itself into a portfolio of images, none necessarily bearing any relation to any other. This was not a dirty bazaar lane in India, it was *all* bazaar lanes from *all* time. I imagined huge wooden waterwheels turning slowly in green water, and knew they were Babylonian. These goat droppings had been dunged several thousand years ago. A clamour in the distance was the same old quarrel that had been going on between men since the beginning.

Later, in the streets. About one in the morning. The area was deserted, few people about. The lanes were mostly lined by tiny shops and businesses, shuttered up for the night. Across the main road in Bhendi Bazaar, a couple of hundred yards away, life went on. You could always get something to eat, whatever time of day or night it was. There was always somewhere to sit and have tea, or kebabs. We were heading for refreshment, Mitra leading the way, Dost and I some way behind, when we came upon a group of youths revving a scooter.

Something was said, I didn't catch what.

They set upon Mitra. He disappeared in a confusion of fists and open-handed slaps. One was trying to kick him.

We ran towards them. Dost grabbed one of the attackers and threw him to one side. I was trying to pull another one away. Mitra's glasses had come off. There was blood around his nose, but he was still shouting at them.

Dost yelled, 'Stop! This guy is my friend. I take responsibility for him.'

'And who the fuck are you?'

'Put it this way,' said Dost. 'I'm called Mohammed Khan.'

'Then you're a fucking Hindu lover,' called another voice.

The man who had spoken first took a step forward. In his hand was a knife. He said, 'I don't think you're a Muslim.'

Then Dost did something incredibly brave. He stood in front of Mitra and said, 'Okay, so you have to kill me. But first look at this . . .'

He undid his pyjama string.

For a moment anything could have happened. Then one of them laughed and the tension went out of the scene.

'It's a poor fucking thing,' said Dost, re-tying his shalwar. 'There are enough people who really hate us, but you have to pick on a couple who are our friends.'

We were still there, all of us, a group of arguing youths, when the police arrived.

We were arrested and taken to the police station, where we stood (there was nowhere to sit) in a cage along with various other miscreants. Beggars, a pair of drunks, a red-eyed man who seemed demented. 'I am a Rudra, I tell you. Look at me. I am a Rudra.' From time to time he fell on the floor, and convulsed. Someone banged on the bars of the cage, but nobody came.

Several hours later, they took us out for questioning. We asked to stay together but they led Dost away first. Mitra and I were put in a room with filthy walls that had once been blue. A calendar of Ganesh hung from a nail.

A plain-clothes policeman began questioning us.

'You are Hindus. What are you doing in this area at night? Who did you come to see? What is your business here?'

'I was working late,' said Mitra. 'My friend was with me. We were walking to catch a bus . . .'

He stolidly refused to budge from this story. Eventually, when they had ascertained that he really did work round the corner, he was allowed to go.

'What about me?' I said. 'I was with him.'

'With you it's not so simple.'

I remained in the room all night. They let me out once, to visit a hole-in-the-floor which was brimming with excrement.

It was mid-morning when another policeman came to see me. He was an older man, also in plain clothes. He must have been someone important because he had an escort of two uniformed officers, and was treated with enormous deference by my previous questioner. Tea, on a tray with a plate of biscuits, was fetched for him. Would he need a tape recorder? He declined the machine and sat sipping his tea, staring at me.

At last he turned to his subordinates and asked them to wait outside the door.

'I know your family,' was the first thing he said to me.

My immediate feeling was relief. He would surely bring this nonsense to an end.

'You're troublemakers.'

My illusions vanished. He had not come to help me.

'Your mother writes propagandist rubbish. I know what she is trying to do. She should be careful. I have a file this thick!' He pounded the desk and grasped an imaginary dossier at least two inches thick. 'And now here's her son. The next generation. Why are you in this area? Don't you know we're at war?'

'This is India,' I said. 'The people who live here are Indians.'

'Are they? Do you know how many agents Pakistan has in this neighbourhood? Your father is ex-Navy. You meet some important people. People who know the movements of our ships. You meet them, then you come here. Why?'

'I was with my friend,' I said. 'He's a Hindu.'

'I know where you were the night *Khukri* was sunk,' said the policeman. 'But where were you the night *before*?'

I was silent. Dared not tell him about Moosa's.

226

'I *know* where you were,' said the policeman. 'I take an interest. I know all about you.' Count yourself lucky that I don't charge you with something a lot more serious than smoking charas with guttersnipes.'

He got up and left.

At lunchtime, my father's lawyer came and I was released.

Mitra said, 'You bastard, Dost. Your dick saved my life.'

His spectacles were mended with tape. We were sitting on the roof of our building in Cuffe Parade.

'How come you got out before either of us?' I asked him.

'Why are you surprised?' said Dost. 'It was *my* area. You know how it is with the police in this city. It's either danda or dhanda.' (Truncheons or bribes.)

'Now I owe two lives,' Mitra told me later, with a serious look on his face. 'One to your mother, now another to Dost.'

About two months after this, my mother announced, out of the blue, that she had arranged for me to do a post-graduate course in film studies at the University of Sussex in England. The term did not start until the autumn, but I was to leave immediately.

OXYMORON (SUSSEX, JANUARY 1999)

It wasn't until I'd finished writing these recollections of Jula that I discovered we didn't have Phoebe's address or phone number.

'Not *my* fault,' Katy said. 'It was *you* who had the long tête-à-tête.'

I rang my sisters. No good. Must have been an oversight. Still, she had all my information and was bound to ring soon. Weeks went by and the papers grew dusty on my desk. Mysteriously and abruptly as she re-entered it, Phoebe had once again vanished from my life.

'She must have left something. Card? Note? Scrap of paper? Something scribbled on the back of an envelope?' I said as we sat, three months later, ticking people off our Christmas card list.

'Bhalu, she hardly talked to me. It was *you* she was interested in. If you want to know, I found her attitude to me rather offensive. As if I was some sort of interloper.'

Jealousy was so much not in Katy's repertoire, that I found this little burst of pique rather flattering. The one time I had strayed, in my leery London days, she forgave me without fuss. And when she gave me cause to be jealous I felt instead only a kind of numb fascination, and never told her that I knew, or what I knew. Sexual jealousy was a stranger to our marriage (now there's an ironic choice of words), and having women squabble over me was a new experience. New, and not at all unpleasant. Bloody fool, I thought, you're deluding yourself.

Three months without a word. I had begun the long labour of

cataloguing Maya's books. Other than that, my routine went on pretty much unchanged. It would have been just before Christmas that the post brought, along with the usual crop of bills and junk, a letter from Bombay.

> *Blitz* is no longer in existence; it is now *Cinéblitz*. I went myself to their office and met a Mr Vohra, a decent man, who allowed me to see the archives. I checked all issues released during April 1959, and there was no mention of such a murder. I checked up until August, and back till January. I can assure you that there was no such murder reported as you describe.

I had forgotten my query. I could barely remember *Retribution* or why I had been so fascinated by it. Even the personal revelations of *The Eel Fisher* seemed distant to me, another of Maya's stories, an exercise in fiction using herself as a model. There had been no murder, no Mister Love. As to the mystery of why she had never returned to live in India, since her death there were going to be no answers, and it no longer seemed important.

A dark, frozen morning in early January. Well before dawn. We were sitting in the kitchen, warming our hands round mugs of tea.

'Bhalu, you'll have to get the Moron out,' said Katy. 'If Piglet's coming to lunch, I've got to get it in the oven before we go. There won't be time later.'

'What about all this?' I asked, waving an arm. It was Twelfth Night, the last day of Christmas, when decorations must finally come down and trees go to the bonfire.

'Piglet won't mind,' she said.

The cottage was still strung with streamers, tinsel, paper chains. In a corner of the living room, our Christmas tree was gently weeping needles. On a wooden chest nearby, under a string of twinkling lights, stood the crib. None of us were religious, but we'd always had the crib. The twins assembled it each year on a base of stones that signified the Judaean desert. They would make a hut of twigs woven together with bits of straw, and into it place oxen, camels, sheep, wise men and the Holy Family, clay figures they had made and painted years ago, for a school project. It was always ceremonially declared open to the music of Mendelssohn's Violin Concerto in E Minor, a custom whose origin was lost in the mists of family folklore. The story most often told was that I & I, aged perhaps eight, had been busying themselves with stones and straw, when Maya put the record on.

Isobel asked, 'Granny, why is the music so sad?'

Maya replied, 'Because Mendelssohn was a Jew.'

The twins thought the lamenting violin was a perfect music for bare stony slopes and a story that ended so tragically.

This year, our 'bacchantes', as Panaghiotis fondly called them, had come and gone. The house bore traces – discarded clothes, left-behind mobile phone, a sack full of washing – of their whirl-wind passage. They were off with friends and boyfriend, respectively.

Katy and I missed them. And Maya.

It was still dark when I went out, breath steaming, to do the business with the Moron. Katy's horse. His name, really, was Oxymoron, so-called because his feet seemed to be in constant contradiction to one another. He didn't exactly trip over them, but the next nearest thing a quadruped can manage. So we knew him, affectionately, as the Moron.

He whiffled in the darkness when he heard me coming. Knew very well I'd have a mint for him. We had got him from a rescue centre. The people said he'd been used to pull a cart and Katy said he must have been beaten a lot, because he was head shy and leery of people, especially men. When he first arrived, getting a head-collar on him was a nightmare. So I made special efforts to be nice. I'd take a pocket full of mints with me when I went to the stable, or into the field to catch him. Gradually, we became friends.

Now he let me slide the head-collar up round his nose, buckle the strap. No problem. Prehensile lips descended to my palm and lifted the sweet. His ears flicked forward, perhaps in embarrassment, as I began admonishing him in the silly voice that people seem to reserve for horses and very small children. 'Joo gonna be a gooboy today, eh? Hoozgonnabe a gooboy?' The Moron rolled his eyes, and went back to his haynet. Katy had been training him to trot and canter without skittering sideways, to approach a jump and not pull up in blowing, snorting confusion. The 'flat work', whatever it was (did the Moron have flat feet?) was followed by 'grid work', which involved setting up ever-changing combinations of jumps – poles set on oildrums – in the field and taking him through them. She had been utterly patient.

'Katy's worked hard on you, hasn't she?' I pushed his rump to spin him round, attached the lead rope and led him out so Katy could get him ready for his big day. This morning, they were going to jump in competition for the first time.

SHE: Bhalu, have you seen my good jodhpurs?

ME: No. And how many times do I have to tell you they are named after the town of Jodhpur, pronounced with a long O, as in Joe? There is no what-rot-pot-got-hot sound in Hindi.'

SHE: Get on with all your Indian pretensions. You never used to object when I called them jodhpurs — when you were trying to get inside them.

An indoor gymkhana at any time of year, but especially in the winter, is a fearsome affair. This one took place in a huge barn, with wooden walls. When we arrived, it took some doing to coax the Moron out of his trailer — almost as hard as persuading him to enter it in the first place. But after that there was not much more I could do. Katy and the Moron vanished into the warm-up. I stationed myself in the spectators' gallery, surrounded by Pony Club mothers in ultra-waxed Barbours. Once the competition got going, they grew excited and began yelling at their daughters: things like, 'Kick *on*, Samantha, kick on!' and '*Smack* him!'

Then it was Katy's turn, trim in her beige unpronounceables and black jacket. The Moron behaved impeccably. He jumped the first round like a pro. None of his old tricks: the extra stride just before a fence, necessitating a cat-like spring over the poles, or the habit of trying to run in different directions at the same time. He went clear.

The second round was against the clock. In the lead was a child whose mother, dressed as if she were going to a hunt, was very near me, and very noisy. When the Moron's turn came, I was desperate for him to repeat his earlier success. He clattered over the first two fences then did one of his strange shuffles, which must have cost several seconds. As they turned I could see Katy lean forward and talk to him, and he put his ears back and took a run at the big triple. They were haring straight towards where I was sitting. I stood up and shouted, 'Come on, Moron!'

Oxymoron glanced up, saw me and his mind must have turned instantly to mints, for he looked as if he was trying to give me a smile. It must have been then that he decided to duck out, but with a style that only he could manage. With no check of stride he teleported sideways around the fence. Katy, picking herself up from the sand floor, looked up to the gallery and mouthed, 'Thank you very much!'

'There's absolutely *no* excuse for abuse,' said the hunting woman, giving me her most disapproving glare, as I left.

On the way home, the trailer weaving behind us, Katy said, 'Bhalu, you don't hate your life, do you?'

'What do you mean?'

'Do you ever regret you married me?'

'Daft thing. Why should I?'

'Well,' she said. 'All this, the horses, living in Sussex. This is *my* life, but maybe it isn't really yours.'

'Of course it's mine. I chose it. I like it.'

'My lords, ladies and gentlemen,' cried Piglet. 'Well, lady . . . Don't know if Bhalu qualifies as a gentleman. A magnificent repast calls for like entertainment.'

We had finished lunch, and while the dishes had been cleared away, the savour of roast still hung in the air. A bottle of wine, emptied almost to the lees, stood in the middle of the table.

Piglet drew from his pocket some folded sheets of paper and put on a pair of reading glasses.

'I give you a scene from *The Real Tragedy of King Richard III.* I ask you to imagine a wild coast in Brittany. It is dark, near midnight and on a cliff-top, two sentinels stand watch.'

He read, throwing his voice.

A sea coast in Brittany

FIRST WATCHER:

   Ten is the hour that was appointed us

   To watch for ship, lately embark'd from England.

SECOND WATCHER:

   Look where it comes; sail fill'd with fretting gusts

   The black vessel shakes on Neptune's billow,

   Half the flood hath her keel cut; up and down

   The poor ship drives, delug'd, overflow'd and drown'd;

   The ruthless waves with sands and rocky shelves

   Do threaten her with wreck.

FIRST WATCHER:

   And yet she lives!

Piglet paused and drew an anxious breath. He gazed at us over the top of his spectacles, searching our faces for reactions.

'Did you really write that? ' asked Katy, full of admiration.

'Yes, in a way, no, not exactly, ' he said all at once. 'Did you like "delug'd, overflow'd and drown'd"?'

'Very much, ' I assured him.

'Did you?' asked Piglet.

'I did.'

'You're not just humouring me.'

'I'm not.'

'Oh shut up Bhalu!' cried Katy. 'Is the bloody ship wrecked or not?'

'Ah!!' said Piglet and pushed his glasses back up to their battle station.

SECOND WATCHER:

> She cannot perish having one aboard,
>
> Of such dark, secret, midnight wickedness
>
> That even Neptune's green, prodigious bowel
>
> Cannot enclose, engulf and swallow up,
>
> But like a drunkard must vomit him forth,
>
> Who's destined to a drier death on shore:
>
> James Tyrell, Knight of England, here he comes.
>
> *Enter Sir James Tyrell.*

SECOND WATCHER:

> Yea, I'd warrant him gainst drowning, though the
>
> ship were no stronger than a nutshell and as leaky
>
> as an unstanched wench.

'Spot any joins?' asked Piglet.

'Not me,' said Katy. 'Sounds just like Shakespeare always does.'

'That's because it *is* Shakespeare. Well, all but a couple of lines, humble things but mine own.'

'Which are yours?' asked drowsy Katy.

'Oh, you must tell me,' he said. 'And now please pay good

attention, because here comes the point at which history is changed.'

The point at which history is changed. Listening to Piglet. I found myself wondering why people felt such a compulsion to re-invent the past as it *ought* to have been. The Plantagenets had been gone half a millennium. The Tudors who had supplanted them were gone. The Stuarts were gone. What difference could it make now? Perhaps the wine had made me drowsy, for my mind began to wander. Into my head unbidden came something Maya had said in *The Eel Fisher*. 'These men have been freed to carry on their rewriting of history'. A statement impenetrably Mayan. I had no idea what it could mean, only that it was in some obscure way connected with why she blamed herself for the hatreds between Hindus and Muslims in Bombay.

TYRELL:

'Tis not the first time I have landed on
This unkind coast, and when I came before
Did not the awkward winds conspire to turn
Me back again unto my native clime?
What well forewarning wind did seem to say
'Seek not the scorpion's nest, nor set no footing
On that traitor's shore'? What did I then,
But cursed the gentle gusts that took me home,
And bid them blow towards these Breton rocks.
And now come I again, 'tis not the waves
And savage seas have wrecked and hammered me
From top of honour to disgrace's feet:
My shamed life in Tudor's dishonour lies.

How was it possible, that foreign hire
Could out of me extract such spark of evil?
O treason, thou art glutted, gorged and full
With guiltless blood of innocents. Edward's
Children murdered! God rest their little souls.
The most arch deed of piteous massacre
That ever yet this hand was guilty of,
For Tudor would not be their murderer,
But gave that hateful office unto me.

FIRST WATCHER:

Methinks he hath no drowning mark upon him,
his complexion is perfect gallows.

TYRELL:

The tyrannous and bloody act is done.
Dighton and Forrest, whom I did suborn . . .

'. . . And the rest you know!'

'Bravo!' I cried, when he had finished. 'So *this* is how you pin the Little Princes on Henry Tudor!'

'Exactly! For the rest of Tyrell's tear-jerking confession, it's back to the orthodox text. The way to change history,' he said, leaning towards me and holding out his glass for a refill, 'is to tell a lot of small truths, then recombine them to make a big lie . . . I have just *un-told* Shakespeare's big lie.'

He began to talk about Shakespeare's sea scenes. 'Notice how often he says "seems". The ocean "seems to pelt", "seems to cast water", the sky "seems to pelt down stinking pitch". Two different plays, mark you. I reckon old Shakespeare would get himself into a sea-ish mood, scribble down whatever struck him, and file it away. Whenever he needed a bit of sea, or storm, he'd just hoick a few lines out of his store. He's a joy to cut and paste.'

We were almost asleep in front of the fire. That feeling that your knees and shins are going to start smoking while your back is freezing. Put more logs on. Give me fire to thaw me. Piglet's voice droning about rhythm, falling, five hard beats to a line. They don't write poems like that any more. Never know, might have been paid by the line. Well, time was, poetry was sold by weight. Maya bought leather bindings by the kilo. Bindings by the yard, gleaming gold-blocked titles. Piglet flaps his umbrella vigorously, enters an old bookshop, stoops through an arch into a small room where a log fire is burning in the grate. Leather bindings gleam in the firelight. A slender, grey-haired man looks up from his reading. His brown skin and dark eyes proclaim his eastern origin. This foreigner asks politely if he can help. Piglet begins to talk about King Richard III. The sallow foreigner smiles. Piglet has entered the heart of his universe, the spider's web. 'Bhalu,' says a voice. Yes, I, Bhalu Sahib, am the spider. Bhalu, short for Balachandra. Bhalu, the bear in *The Jungle Book* – whose name the English pronounce as if he were a relative of Cat Ballou. Even Kipling spelt it that way, Baloo, but it should be pronounced with a growl, bhhhaaaalu. There's a growl in that child. Maybe he's unhappy. Are you unhappy, growling boy? Can't say I'm unhappy. Unfulfilled, could say. I drifted here. I came in on the tide, like a jellyfish and now I'm stranded in this cold and grey. Yearn I for the sun. This sun hasn't followed in his father's footsteps. Not in Great, Twice, Thrice-Great-grandfather's footsteps. Was the one that got away. Was me. The dream changes. Voices flit mockingly across. I am with Maya, who is lying on her deathbed, reading a play and laughing. Mother, at least I'm free of the curse that besets most people, of having to live by other people's ideas. Not so! That's illusion, she cries. Like me! You can't escape the past, my bhola-est of Bhalus. Not your own, nor the ever-evolving past-to-present left you by your ancestors, of whom I'm one, my small manushya, little man, says she, putting down her book. No, I say, that's why I'm here jellyfishing. You told me this yourself, Mother. To escape those very consequences. Even in this, says my mother, you are actactacting out my dododoctrine, you will spend your life trying to ununenact mine. But you can't un-enact murder, it will out. What's done can't be undone and what was done, by thunder, lightning and in rain, was murder. Yes, while they crouch, those innocents, asleep in one another's arms, their lips like four rose petals, hiding from ghosts, they do not hear the thunder crashes. Knock, knock. Knock, knock. Wake, children, with thy knocking, I would thou couldst. Something broke the surface of my dream. Katy was shaking me.

'Bhalu,' she said. 'Bhalu, wake up. Phoebe's here.'

She was just inside the front door, hovering as if uncertain of her welcome. 'Hello? I'm not interrupting? I haven't come at a bad time, have I?'

She looked quite different from last time. She was wearing jeans and a short jacket. The Downs wind had caught and disarranged her hair. She smiled at me and a small green bird flew into my heart and sang.

I said, 'No! No! What a surprise! Come in, Piglet's here.'

'You remember I told you Mummy had left Maya a bequest?' said Phoebe, taking off her jacket and hanging it on a peg beside my shabby overcoat. 'Well, I've got it with me. I was coming down this way, so I thought why not drop it off. Is that all right?'

'Yes, of course, but—'

'It was meant for your mother,' she said, smoothing her hair. 'God, I need a mirror, I must look awful . . . The logical thing is it should go to you, only . . .' She gave me an apologetic smile. 'This is going to sound weird, but before I hand it over, would you indulge an odd request?'

'I'm sure I shall,' I said. 'Bizarre, you turning up out of the blue like this.'

'I should have rung first.'

'I meant because I don't have your number. Or address. In fact, I had no way to reach you.'

'How strange.' She did that little trick with her head. 'I'm sure I gave them to you. Or someone, anyway. I'm sure I remember writing it all down.'

'Well, it's a mystery.'

Phoebe laid a hand on my arm. 'Just before we go in . . .' She leaned forward and kissed me full on the lips, just as she had at Maya's funeral. This time there was no one to see, we were pushed in among the coats. She said, gazing at me with great grey-green eyes, 'I've thought about you a lot.'

I said, 'I was worried I'd frightened you off.'

'Silly. Of course you didn't. I'm sorry I haven't been in touch. I would have, but . . .' She gave a little helpless shrug. 'You know how it is.'

'Well, you're here now,' I said, not knowing at all how it was, but still in recovery from the kiss. 'Come in. Don't say you've driven all the way from Yorkshire?'

She was still staring at me, but the smile had gone.

I said, 'It's warmer inside. I'll put some tea on. Piglet's here. He's been reading to us from his new play. Well, not exactly *his* new play, but . . .'

'Wait,' she said. 'Come outside for a moment. To the car.'

'Is this your odd request?'

'No,' she said. 'Just for a moment. I've got to explain something.'

It was a freezing afternoon, bitter as morning had been. Sun going to earth behind a stand of birches. Oxymoron in his field looked up and snorted. Pair of pigeons wing-clapping home.

Her car was parked in the lane outside the cottage. When she unlocked the boot, it lifted slowly on dampened springs. Smart car. Clean, modern-looking, especially compared to ours. In the boot was a large, squarish object draped over with a cloth.

'If Katy appears,' she said, 'I'm showing you this. It's the thing I was talking about, that Mummy left you. All right?'

'Okay, but why all the mystery? Is something wrong?'

She stood with her back to the open boot and said, 'Look, this is awkward. I've got a confession.'

'A confession?'

'I wasn't honest with you just now. About my details. You were quite right. I didn't give them to anyone.'

'But why not? Is there some problem?'

'We've only just met again. You've no idea how important this is to me. I can't bear to begin with a lie.'

'You're going to have to explain. I'm confused.'

'Bhalu, I can't give you my address, or phone number. Not just at the moment.'

'But why not?' I asked, thoroughly puzzled. 'What possible harm could there be?'

'I can't risk you contacting me.'

'Why not?'

'It's my husband. He doesn't understand. About you and me. He thinks . . . Well, never mind.'

I was staggered. It was the last thing I had expected her to say. 'But . . .' I said. 'But, Phoebe . . . What is there to understand?'

Then she made her odd request.

Katy, in the kitchen, listened glumly.

'She wants you to go *where* tomorrow?'

'To Brighton. To see a medium. That's what she said.'

'She's not going back to Yorkshire tonight then. Where is she planning to stay?'

'I don't know.'

'So Phoebe, where are you staying tonight?' asked Katy, prodding a drowsy Piglet. 'Tea, Piglet. Cake, or left-over Christmas pudding, if you prefer . . . We can't let you go to a hotel,' she said, turning back to Phoebe, who was perched rather uncomfortably on the edge of the sofa. 'You must stay here. I'll make up the spare room for you. It won't take a minute.'

'Oh no,' said Phoebe. 'Thank you, but I have friends in Kent. It's why I was down here in the first place. I saw them earlier, then came on here.'

'You've driven down this morning? It's a long way, isn't it, all the way from Yorkshire?'

'I left before dawn. It was very icy.'

'Well, if you're sure.'

'Thank you,' said Phoebe. 'But I promised I'd get back.'

'Nonsense,' cried Piglet, coming back to life. 'How can she drive back to Yorkshire tonight? It's hundreds of miles.'

'She is staying with friends nearby,' I said.

'You missed the performance,' said Piglet. 'First reading ever. An historic moment, in its way. Which reminds me, I've been meaning to tell Bhalu, I had a good shufti on the map for that village of yours. What did you say it was called?'

Phoebe said nothing, looking from Katy to me.

'Oh yes, I remember,' said Piglet. 'Sleeman. Odd sort of name. Not easy to remember, but once you do, not easy to forget. I tried looking it up. Checked on the large-scale Ordnance Survey we use for our gallivantings. Not a whisker of a Sleeman.'

'Well, the map can't record everything,' I said.

'Look, I'll run Piglet home,' Katy said. Tea finished, we were in the kitchen for a quick conference. From next door came the boom of Piglet explaining about Shakespeare's use of minor characters.

'You stay here and have your talk with Phoebe. Maybe she'd like to stay for supper. And do say she's welcome to spend the night, if she changes her mind.' She stopped, then said, 'You know, I bet she hasn't any friends in Kent. I had the feeling she just made it up on the spot.'

'She wasn't planning to stay with us.'

'Brighton is full of hotels,' said Katy. 'She might be having an affair.'

'An affair?'

'A woman of her age who dyes her hair blonde might easily be having an affair.'

'Don't be ridiculous,' I said. 'An affair with whom?'

'Someone in Brighton, of course.'

It would at least fit with the jealous husband. On balance, this seemed a not-unlikely explanation, but I did not want to believe it.

'When we left Ambona we went on a ship to England. I think it was the first one my father could get a passage on. A cargo ship. It stopped at a port somewhere north of Bombay for a week and loaded sacks of fertiliser. I used to hang over the rail watching the barges. And the stevedores sitting in the barge fishing for their lunch. They had lines they let down into the water, and up came mackerel, eels, small sharks. They'd dismember them and sizzle them with tomatoes and peppers in a big blackened pan. Rather like a large wok.'

'A karahi,' I said. We were sitting round the table having supper – had done nothing but eat all day – and Phoebe had agreed, after all, to spend the night. So much for affairs.

'Yes, I loved curries,' said Phoebe. 'I mean real Indian ones, not those ghastly English curries you used to get, full of sultanas and bits of apple. I missed good hot Indian curries. It was one of the things I got teased about, at boarding school in England. The other girls said I had an Indian accent . . . I hated England. I still do, I think.'

'Phoebe. That nursery rhyme you used to know, in Hindi. Can you still remember it?'

'Of course.'

She recited, 'Muffety Mai, dahi malai, ghaas pe baith ke khayi.' I could still hear the child in her voice.

'I always thought you sounded so English when you said that.'

'Can you guess what it means?' Phoebe asked Katy.

'It's Little Miss Muffet,' replied my wife. 'You're forgetting I've lived with Bhalu for nearly a quarter of a century.'

'I left school when I was eighteen,' Phoebe said. 'Went to art school. I was at the Slade, studying painting. Left before my finals. I often wish now I'd finished, but I wanted to get away. I was very keen to travel. In the holidays I used to stay with Mummy. She was on her own then. She'd just moved to Lincolnshire. It was a crumbly old place, but all she could afford. We didn't have much left by then. The money from my father had stopped coming. Mummy never had a job, she used to do sewing, things like patchwork. There wasn't much money. Anyway, after I left art school I went and stayed with her for a bit, then got a job in London.'

'Is that where you met your husband?' asked Katy.

'No,' said Phoebe. 'That wasn't till much later.'

'Did you have someone?' I asked. 'Boyfriend? You must have had boyfriends.'

'Oh, lots. It was the sixties, don't forget. Swinging London, the Beatles, then Flower Power. I went a bit mad, I was a dippy hippy chick. Pop festivals, pot and painting. Doesn't seem possible now, does it? You must have done all that, Katy.'

'I was too wrapped up with ponies,' said Katy, smiling. 'I tried pot a couple of times but it just sent me to sleep.'

'Don't call it "pot," call it hashish or charas,' I said, thinking that Phoebe would enjoy reading about Dongri.

'Bhalu's always ticking me off about Indian words,' said Katy. 'Don't say "jodhpurs" say "Joe'dpoors". Don't say "Himmerlayer" say "Him-ah-liar".'

'He used to do that when we were children,' said Phoebe. 'Don't say "Jula", say . . . I still can't pronounce it.'

'Juldla,' I said and they both laughed.

'I really just wanted to paint,' said Phoebe. 'Even had my own garret. But I couldn't sell much. So I did something else I'd always fancied. Got a job on a cruise ship, as a trainee purser. We sailed round the Caribbean. I ended up spending several years there.'

'Is that where you met Peter?' This was me.

'No. I had a few boyfriends, but only one I was serious about. His name was Ronnie. We lived together for a while. He was American.

It was tremendously romantic. He had a beach shack . . . well, it was a little bit nicer than that, but not much . . . on Grand Cayman. Cocktails on a beach like talcum powder. I used to wear red shoes. My trademark.'

'It sounds fun,' said Katy. 'Why didn't you marry him?'

'I got home one day and there was a strange woman sitting there. She said she was Ronnie's wife . . . I was utterly shocked. I looked at Ronnie, but he sat and said nothing. He'd lied to me. Can you imagine? The woman started yelling at me. I said, "Look, this is my home, you can't just barge in here like this. I didn't know about you." She told me to get the hell out. She just threw me out.'

'Well, you can see her point,' said Katy.

After supper we did the washing-up together. Phoebe soaped and rinsed, and made me do the drying and putting away because, as she said, 'I don't know where things go in your house.'

'That in itself feels odd,' she added. 'Because when we knew each other before, your house was mine too.'

Frotting the wretched plates till they squeaked, I said, 'I think it's time you told me about Peter.'

'Do we have to talk about him? I'd rather not.'

'Forgive me,' I said, 'but it sounds as if you aren't very happy.'

'Oh, but I will be,' said Phoebe. 'I promise you.'

The spare room was made up. Katy announced that she was going up to bed. Phoebe and I sat by the fire and talked. We compared dates. Where was I when she was at school? What had she been doing while I was in Dongri with Jula and Dost? I thought of my memoir, which was still lying on my desk in the shop. I was about to say I'd post it, but remembered just in time. 'We'll go there tomorrow and collect it.'

Phoebe's life sounded so much more adventurous than mine. She'd gone off to the Caribbean around the time I met Katy, and was dancing red-heeled fandangos on her sugar-white beach when I was going back and forth to Wardour Street, editing and finally producing cruddy low-budget travelogues.

'You must have done some travelling together,' Phoebe said.

'Well, we went to India once.'

Just after we were married, I had taken Katy to meet my father and my grandparents in Kumharawa. Maya's parents were already dead, killed in a car crash on the Delhi–Lucknow road, Kipling's Grand Trunk Road. A drunken truck driver overtaking on a bend at night. One of the hundreds of accidents that make Indian roads so dangerous. Maya, true to form, had tried to persuade us not to go. She said she had consulted an astrologer who told her that she and her family should avoid India.

'Was it Mr Srinuji?' asked Phoebe. 'And did Katy like India?'

Tempting though it was to blame Srinuji for every bit of Maya's nonsense, he hadn't then come on the scene. Kumharawa must have been a difficult experience for Katy. For all the old man's pride in his healthy village life, there was no drainage. One had to crouch in all weathers over a latrine in the corner of the garden. Turds and whey slid through a gap in the wall into a filthy ditch in the lane beyond. Water for bathing had to be drawn from the well. Katy said she *liked* India but could not imagine living there.

'We never travelled much after that,' I said. 'A few holidays in Greece.'

'But I thought your job was making travel films.'

Yes. Having failed to get one job after another, I finally found one at a small film company whose credit I had noticed on the end of a bad documentary about Singapore. I could do better, I thought. So I walked in off the street and offered to write them a film about Bombay. I talked with passion about the city tourists never see – Dongri, naturally – and hinted that I could get their cameras into a hashish den that no foreign hippy had ever visited.

They were interested, but for a different reason.

'Can you get Air India to sponsor travel for our crew?'

I said I could always try. It meant writing a letter.

'Could you get the Indian Tourist Board to put us up?'

Another letter. It was a scam, of course. The idea was to con foreign tourist ministries into funding a holiday for the 'crew', in effect, the owner of the company and his wife. This elderly couple would wave an old 16mm Bolex out of taxi-windows, shooting on 'ends of rolls' picked up cheap (guaranteeing a film whose colour leapt and jounced). Whatever appeared on the processed film was passed to me to cut. I worked on an old-fashioned movieola – nobody does it like that any more – strips of film hanging like eels from racks. The last part of the scam was getting the 'travel documentary' released as a B-feature alongside some big Hollywood movie and collecting the EDEY money, a handout supposed to be for the encouragement of British film-making, from the government.

'Shame about your Bombay film,' said Phoebe. 'You could have done such a good one too.'

'Oh, I still think of it sometimes. I love the bookshop, but it would be nice to do other things now and again.'

'Have you ever thought of going back?' she asked. 'To Bombay,

I mean?' She was staring at me in a rather myopic way. Belladonna eyes. We were both tired. It was past three.

'I did think of proposing a documentary about Ambona. I thought the BBC might be interested. We'd have the cameras out before the rains start. Show what it's like. Barren-looking. Parched. The people, all waiting for rain. Cows on the hills, paddy fields crazed with drought. The first storms. Lightning, thunder. Downpour. Water, water, everywhere. Overnight, everything green.'

'Fishing,' she said. 'Those funny rainhat things. You should do it, Bhalu. You should *still* do it. No one will have seen anything like it before.'

But the BBC turned down my idea, and me. Someone I knew said a commercials company was looking for an editor. So began my ten-year career in the twilight zone between film and advertising. I found, rather to my surprise, that the Indian film industry was regarded with derision. No one had heard of Guru Dutt, or Majrooh. The requirement of a dozen songs per film seemed absurd. Our most famous soprano, one man told me, had a voice of peculiarly agonising quality, like a drill piercing zinc sheet.

I already hated what my life had become (aaaaiieeee, what a phrase) and it was to get worse. Yes, here comes the unwholesome truth at last. *Yaaro mujhko maaf karna, main nashe men hoon.* That lyric of Shailendra's, which was a hit when I was with Mitra and Dost in Dongri, acquired new significance for me. I pursued the nasha of alcohol. With overworked voice-overs and out-of-work actors, dub-artists and piss-artists, I drank in the George, the Ship, The French Pub (I could never remember its real name) and became something of a bon-viveur. A man I met over several bottles of wine at

Macready's offered me a job producing – commercials again, of course. I had an expense account and my real work was to entertain 'creative people' from advertising agencies to lavish lunches. We practically lived in the Tate Restaurant (Château Lafite at £145 a bottle). My boss, the splendidly named Titus Golinkin used to scold me for not spending enough. 'Only four hundred quid? What's the matter, lost your appetite? Never underestimate lunch.' Here also began the late-night taxi-rides, the drunken soliloquies. This is the truth, and I still don't care to remember it.

'And girls?' said Phoebe. 'Must have been women. Isn't the film industry full of gorgeous girls? Wasn't Katy worried? I would have been.'

'Yes, it is. But . . .'

Katy was miserable, but stubbornly loyal. She threw herself into her interior design business and work with the horses. Her lovely bottom grew anvil-shaped from the hammering of saddles.

'But . . . ?'

But there was only one, I had been going to say. A secretary in an ad agency, a tall, intense girl with a fondness for Pushkin. It was the readings from *Eugene Onegin* that – at least with hindsight – had appealed to me more than her undeniably good figure or the long black hair she would sit and brush after each supper and hurried coupling in her bedsitter off the Fulham Palace Road.

'"Evening, darkening sky, and waters in quiet flood. A beetle whirred . . ."' She'd look up from the page, sigh with pleasure. The affair lasted a few weeks. Then, in a fit of 70 proof honesty, I told Katy. After which . . .

'I was never tempted,' I lied to Phoebe.

'You're a man. You must have been tempted.'

'Perhaps I'm not a very typical man.'

That other thing happened about the same time. One day I came home early. Walked into the cottage to find it filled with strange music. Exotic birdsong. Can never hear that music now without remembering. The music must have masked my footsteps. After that I decided to quit London.

'I've never been much good with women,' I said.

'Don't do yourself down. I *wish* people wouldn't do that.' There was a strange vehemence about the way she said this, but then she smiled. 'Bhalu, you're a very attractive man.'

I was far too tired to be flattered. But to complete the tellable part of the story (Phoebe by now so tired her eyes were closing), what saved me, it is clear now, was my grandfather's death. He left some money, and Maya found a way to get it out of India. My share of his legacy came to a tidy amount, even in sterling. It was Katy who found me the bookshop.

'My God,' I said. 'Look at the time!'

It was just after five in the morning.

We crept upstairs to the spare bedroom. Phoebe whispered, 'It's almost too late to sleep now.'

She sat on the bed and slipped off her shoes.

'Shall I get you a cup of tea?' I asked.

She said, 'What a sweet, thoughtful man you are. But no thanks. I'm too tired to sleep. What I'd really like is a shower.'

The shower was in a sort of tiled cupboard. The door was in our bedroom. 'You'll have to creep through.'

'I'll be very quiet.' She stood up and began to undo her jeans. 'Could I borrow a towel?'

'Of course,' I said. I came back with a bath towel and poked it at arm's length through the door. Phoebe came quickly out of the room, took it from me and wrapped it around herself. 'God, it's cold,' she said.

I was tired, perhaps I was hallucinating. I had a distinct sense of bare limbs. It was only after she vanished into our bedroom and I heard the shower, that I realised she'd had nothing on.

At six, we went for a walk through still dark woods down to a stream from which mist was rising and sat on a tree stump while the sun rose. We threw sticks into the water, and got home to find a puzzled Katy making early-morning tea.

The sea, glimpsed through a gap at the bottom of the street, looked like rows of grey knitting. It was raining, blowing spiteful cold drops down our necks. She was wearing her jacket with the collar turned up. It puffed her hair upwards and outwards around the ears, an effect I particularly like. She stopped outside a small, unremarkable house, and rang the bell.

'Bhalu, thank you for coming,' she said. 'You may think this is a lot of nonsense, but I have to ask Mummy's permission.'

The door was opened by a woman with Brasso-bright hair and a mouth like a smudged hibiscus. She introduced herself to me as Madame Stella. We were shown into a room overwhelming in its clutter. Too many pictures: dogs, Sacred Hearts, horned gods, a goddess crowned with stars, Red Indians, Hindu sages.

In the middle of the floor stood a small cloth-draped altar on which were two lighted candles, a joss-stick and a faded black and white photograph of two women: one, who looked like a young Ava Gardner, pointing at the camera; the other, in a sari, caught with her head thrown back in a cloud of laughter. Behind them was a bougainvillaea whose grey flowers, I knew, had actually been pink. The woman in the sari was my mother.

'It's a warm spring day on the inner planes,' said Madame Stella. 'Your mother is expecting you, Phoebe darling. The gentleman's mother too. Indian lady, isn't it? Chang talked to them both this morning. They said to tell you they're keeping well. It's a good time to seek guidance. There's a big spirit council going on at the moment, you see, on the Inner. Have you got my little something, dear?'

Phoebe reached in her jacket and brought out some notes.

'Yes, well I won't be a minute,' said Madame. 'You sit yourselves down. You know what to do, Phoebe dear. Show the gentleman how to get comfortable. That's it.'

She bustled out of the room with the money.

'Phoebe,' I said, 'what on earth—?'

'Shhh! I know what you're thinking,' she whispered. 'It's all right to be sceptical, you don't *have* to believe. It's just that a lot of what she says comes true.'

'You see her regularly?' I was reminded of Maya's requests, that she would never admit were prayers, to Ganesh.

'Not very often. Once every three or four months.'

Madame Stella re-entered the room. 'Your mother,' she said to me, 'wants you to listen very carefully today. She has an important message for you. Something she could not tell you when she was alive.' She settled herself into a large armchair close to where Phoebe and I sat, squeezed together on a sofa covered with a cloth that might have come from a souk in Tunis.

The medium pointed at a picture of what looked like a Sioux chief. 'This is Chang, my Chinese guide. When he comes through, you may ask questions, but I warn you, he used to be a mandarin. He was governor of a province in China. He is used to respect. He won't like it if you interrupt. And now we will hold hands.'

I glanced over at Phoebe to see how she was taking this, but she had her eyes closed; her brow wore a little frown of concentration. The medium let her own, heavily-greened lids droop, licked her lips. She smiled, then grew stern again. Unidentifiable emotions

chased one another across her face. She drew several deep shuddering breaths, and exhaled a slow chain of hiccoughs. It was fascinating, like a performance from one of Dost's masala movies. Her
head sagged, lolled towards us and a number of sighs and grunts
shook her ample body. Her tongue extruded itself from the
crimson mouth and she began to snore.

Suddenly the eyes flicked wide open, staring at the carpet, then
– this was surely a sequence lifted from a horror movie – the head
with its protruding tongue twisted slowly and fixed us with a sly
regard. The tongue slid back, emerged briefly to lick the lips, and
a deep voice with an accent more Berlin than Beijing, in fact not
unlike Peter Seller's Dr Strangelove, said, 'Welcome Phoebe,
welcome my Indian friend.' *Velcome Veebee, velcome my Indian vriend.*

'Hello Chang,' said Phoebe, in a tiny voice. Chang rolled his
eyes and fastened them on me. Phoebe's elbow dug into my ribs.

'Hello, Chang,' I said.

'The spirit council is aware of your presence.' *Zee zbirit gounzil is
avare of your brezzence.* 'Your mothers are there.' *Mozzers.*

Chang rolled his eyes and said, 'Oh, they are looking so lovely.
Two *beautiful* ladies. Oh my soul!' *Luffly. Vyootiful. Zoul.* The part
obviously called for a certain roguish gallantry.

'Phoebe, your mozzer is nearby. Yes. Yes. Yes. Yes, she is on her
vay. She is connecting viz us qvite strongly on ze vibration. She
may not appear in ze room viz us, but she is zbeaking to me . . .'

Phoebe's body, pressed tight to mine, began to quiver. I too was
trying very hard to suppress a giggle. I gave her hand a squeeze.

'Yes, Zybil, I hear you . . . vait, zere is another zbyrit here . . .
come closer, Zybil.' The other spirit must turn out to be Maya.
But apparently not, for Chang, in an imperious gubernatorial

manner shouted, 'You! Yes, you! Ze ozzer zpirit! Kindly vait your turn . . . vat's zat you say? . . . you are called Ming, and you are ze spirit guide of ze gentleman? Vell zat is excellent, Ming, qvite excellent . . . I feel sure ve shall have a uzeful talk togezzer . . . after I have zboken to Zybil . . . No, no, Ming, please! . . . please vait your turn to zbeak, I am zbeaking viz Zybil. Zybil is here now. She is in ze room viz us.'

Phoebe's body was still shaking. I pressed against her and gripped her hand tight, supposing that, like me, she was fighting not to laugh. But when I stole a glance at her, I saw that her eyes were screwed tight shut, like a child's, and her mouth was twisted in real misery.

We went to a café near the sea. One of those where Katy and I used to go, when we first met. Strange how things go in circles. We sat at a table by the window and ordered coffee. The cafés on the sea front all have big glass windows, for the view. But it was not a day for a view, a grey sea, slabs of rain hitting the window, running down in drips and drabs. Not far away was the West Pier, with the gap where the ship had gone through it. They had fixed some sort of a footbridge across. Starlings were circling above it, never still, always working the wind.

'Phoebe, what is all this about?'

She was staring at the birds as they wheeled about the pier. There must have been thousands of them, in a huge cloud that kept changing shape as it turned, lifted, dipped. One moment it was a vast ellipse, the next a galaxy with trailing starfish arms.

'Okay,' she said. 'I'd already decided to tell you. That's why I came. Brought the box. But what's in it is so very personal . . .'

'You surely don't believe Sybil was really there, just now.'

'I *know* she was there.' She lit a cigarette, still watching the pier starlings as they demonstrated the only real lesson of history. Then she sighed, and began her story.

'Bhalu, you probably don't remember how my mother used to be. She was miserable, in Ambona. I mean how she was before. She was a lovely, cheerful person. She loved going to parties, having fun. I think she found my father a bit of a stick, but they had got it worked out. Then something happened. Mummy went to pieces. That's when she kept running away to Ambona. Your mother, Maya, was hugely supportive. She would take us in, look after Sybil. And then, back we'd go to Bombay and she'd be all right for a while. I thought, that last year, that she was getting better. I don't know how things would have turned out, if we hadn't . . . Well, if I hadn't . . .'

'You're thinking of poor Rosie. It wasn't your fault. Or mine.'

She said, 'I wish I could believe that. But if I hadn't insisted on going up there . . . It has haunted me ever since. And then we were sent away. We came here.'

'And vanished,' I said.

'After India, Mummy couldn't seem to face anything. She and Daddy were separated and after a couple of years she asked for a divorce. Said she didn't want anything from Daddy for herself, but needed money for me. She'd never had any of her own. But there was a problem, because in those days as you know it was very hard to get money out of India. All our money was there.'

'I remember,' I said. 'When I flew to England all I was allowed to bring was three pounds sterling.'

'But you got your grandfather's money,' she said, with a little unreadable smile. 'Dear Daddy, despite all his family's centuries in India, or probably because of it, never understood that after 1947, the Indians really *were* in charge. He used to order officials about. Get on the wrong side of them. So we never got any money . . .'

I remembered the tall, grim figure in Ambona cemetery.

'Daddy wanted me to go back to India, to live with him, but Mummy said she would die. She said she might as well kill herself.' Phoebe did an imitation of her mother's clipped, post-war accent: '"Darling, it's better if I die, it'll make everything simpler for everyone. Then you can go to your father."'

'What happened?' I asked, remembering how charming, how gay, her mother could be, and how unhappy she'd been in Ambona.

'Daddy had a friend,' said Phoebe, 'a sort of business partner. I think they'd been together in the Army, during the war. He lived down near Cheltenham. I reckon they did some sort of deal. The money for Mummy came from him. He used to pay my school fees too. I assumed that Daddy repaid him in India. He called himself my guardian. He was tall, like Daddy. Had to stoop to enter doorways, with the sort of bright blue eyes that seem to stare through you, if you know what I mean. He thought the world of Daddy but seemed to regard Mummy as a sort of common slut. He could never manage to be polite about her. He thought she wasn't cut out to be a Killigrew. Just like the nanny, really . . . Anyway, this man didn't provide enough money for her to live on. He said she'd have to get a job. She had a bit of money from her parents, enough to buy a tiny run-down cottage in the middle of nowhere. It was up in Lincolnshire, the only thing she could afford. I used to go there during the holidays.'

'I had always imagined you living in a big house with a butler, tennis, boating on the Thames.'

'Hah! You must be joking.' She stared out of the window.

I said, 'You're watching the birds.'

'Yes. It's like flames, or water flowing. You can sit and watch it for ever. And they've *been* there for ever. Look at the pictures.'

I hadn't noticed the photographs around the walls of the café. Faded pictures, taken years ago, when the place was in its heyday. Above the pier a dark, an always-and-never-changing blur of birds.

'When I left art school I went home to my mother for a while. She was so pathetic by then. Just flashes left of her old self. With other people she could still be the life and soul, larger than life. But it was all a sham. Inside she was all eaten up. I was looking after her. I was twenty-one. I got tired of it. I wrote to my father and told him he had to do something. That even if he could abandon her, he couldn't just abandon me. That's when I went back to London. Couldn't make it as a painter so I got the job with the cruise line. Ever since the ship, when we came back to England, I fancied working on a cruise liner. I'd be a purser and look after the passengers . . .'

She broke off to light another cigarette.

'A few months went by. We were at sea when I got a telegram from Daddy saying he was coming to England. He wanted me to be there. So I replied telling him when I'd be back. And he came. He came to England.

'Mummy didn't want to let him inside the cottage. He stood on the doorstep, holding his hat in his hand. He looked so sad. He had come all the way from India. But I hugged him and brought him in. He couldn't take his eyes off me. "Is this my little girl?" he kept saying over and over. I was eleven, the last time he'd seen me. Mummy wouldn't talk to him. She shut herself in her bedroom and wouldn't come out. I think she must already have been a bit crazy, by then . . .'

'I'm sorry,' I said.

'Before Daddy left, he made me promise that I would look after Sybil. He said I should stay with her until he could sort something out. I don't know what he thought he could do. Then he left. I walked with him to the bus stop and watched until I could no longer see him waving. Until it went out of sight. I can see it now, a green bus, getting smaller and smaller. Then I just crumpled. I cried. My God, how I cried. I cried for days. And then . . . Oh God, I'm sorry, I hate to be so depressing. I need a hanky . . .

'. . . Bhalu, I disobeyed him. I ran away. I left her. I abandoned her. That's the truth. When I went back to the ship I vowed never to set foot again in England. The long and short is that I ended up in the West Indies with Ronnie. I stayed, off and on, for nearly thirteen years. That time when she turned him away, when he was so sweet and gentle – that was the last time I saw him. My dad died when I was out there.'

Rain was still pattering against the café's big sea-facing window. One sensed rather than saw the drops. The glass was a grey sheet of mist, where the warmth inside the café had steamed it up. I was experiencing the strangest sense of dislocation. Listening to her story, I felt powerfully the nearness of the past, other rain on other windows, as if one could walk out of the café and find the road to Ambona around the next corner. Phoebe leaned over and wiped a big wet circle on the glass. In a flat grey sky the starlings were still wheeling above the West Pier.

'When I came back, Mummy was still in the cottage, but the money had stopped. After Daddy died, the guardian said that there never had been any money, that he'd been doing it for Daddy. Now that Daddy was gone, and I was working, he saw no reason to continue it. We wrote letters to Daddy's bank, and his old lawyers, but for ages we didn't get a reply. Then a letter came saying that Daddy had been nearly broke and he'd sold out his share of the family business. But there wasn't much left by then, after the debts. Just his furniture and paintings, but he'd always had those. They could not understand where the money had gone. There were no other effects that could have accounted for it. Mummy had no money and she was too proud to ask me for any. Nor would she lower herself to take the government's hand-outs. It would have meant queuing at the Social Security and God forbid she should do that. She told me she was living on dandelion leaves. I said, "For God's sake, let me give you some money," but she was stubborn as anything. So I lost my temper and shouted at her. I accused her of behaving like this just to drive me crazy with worry. She picked up a knife and said, "Don't ever talk to me like that again. I hate people who shout and threaten me. And I kill people I hate".'

Phoebe looked into my eyes. 'Bhalu, something happened in India. Something terrible, that ruined things for all of us.'

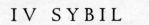

IV SYBIL

The box was of wood, stuccoed and painted with climbing roses in oranges and pinks, the shocking colours of Rajasthan. Its hinges, like the key, were corroded to rust. It stood foursquare on painted feet in a corner of my study. Inside were twenty-two diaries and notebooks, some of them leather-bound, others with coiled spines. All were filled, cover to cover, with Sybil's neat, but hard-to-fathom handwriting. A carrier bag from an English grocer contained sheaves of yellowing paper smudgily imprinted by the uneven keys of an old typewriter. Some of these, double-spaced, and bearing rusty traces of paper-clips, were manuscripts. Pressed into one notebook were a number of letters addressed to Sybil, crisp as flower petals. On top of all lay an envelope containing a handwritten note.

Moon Cottage, September 1993

My dear Maya,
If you read this, it means clever Phoebe has found you. I so regret that we lost touch after I left India. While Killy was alive India still seemed close, but that was a long time ago. I did go back once to look for you. It was earlier this year. Everything had changed. The Bombay I knew had gone and you were not there. The Navy Office told me Captain Sahib was 'out of station'. At last I made contact with Homi, who took me to lunch at Gourdon's – that at least goes on. Of

course he didn't recognise the old biddy who turned up, but after his initial consternation made a gallant recovery. He is bald and his moustache has gone grey. After a while he began to hold my hand and call me 'darling', which I very much resented. He told me of your divorce and I learned that you had followed your children to England, but that no one had heard from you in years. On my return I tried to trace you, but you have vanished. Where are you? Oh Maya, what regrets! Imagine, these last years, we might have been neighbours – sitting in the long light of English evenings, remembering how suddenly the darkness came in India. By the time this reaches you, if it ever does, I will have gone to where, as you know, I dread what awaits. You are probably the only person who can imagine. I could never talk to Phoebe about it, though I have told her some things. So many years ago, but the memories are still too awful to entertain. Maya, what I wanted to do in India, I wasn't able to do. I am leaving you my notebooks. They are all there, apart from the latest one, which I must burn, and that one other which you remember . . . I was hoping you still had it, and that, if I found you . . . Such foolishness! Ah well, now it does not matter . . .

Journals are not necessarily autobiographical and Sybil's day-to-day jottings were more often about other people than herself, but from bits and pieces in the notebooks and interleaved letters (she often kept copies of letters she wrote) I could piece together her story.

She had grown up in an unremarkable street in Croydon and was evacuated during the first years of the war. By the time it ended she was old enough to have acquired a Canadian boyfriend with whom she got roaring drunk among the crowds celebrating VE Day. The euphoria didn't last and neither did the soldier. Like many people, she found life after the war curiously flat. She'd been to a grammar school where, enthused by a fiery English teacher, she dreamed of becoming an author, but instead she found herself working in a London typing pool. Then she met Killy. In 1946 he was a dozen years older than her, in his mid-thirties, burnt brown by three years of adventuring in Burma with Orde Wingate's Chindits, for which he'd been picked because he could speak Hindustani. The Killigrews had been in India for generations. It was rumoured (Killy told her this) that they had once been in the opium trade, but nowadays dealt in cotton and machine tools. Killy was tall – two inches over six feet – with bushy up-winged eyebrows. For a big man he was a light-footed dancer. Sybil, or Billy, as he called her, felt like a waif in his arms, and was duly carried away by his tales of elephants, palm-fringed sunsets and turbanned servants. He told her stories of tiger shoots, silver

Rolls-Royces and droll maharajas. Greedy for adventure and trusting blindly in romance and fate, she agreed to accompany him back to Bombay as his wife.

Killy and Billy steamed into Bombay in a monsoon squall in the autumn of 1948. 'It won't be as you imagine,' he warned her. She was duly unprepared for the smells, smoke, noise, dirt, crowds, chaos, above all the heat, which clamped a hot, damp flannel across her mouth and nose. October is the muggiest month in Bombay. She wasn't prepared for the moisture that dribbled down her temples and made salty marshes under her arms. She knew Killy was well off, but was thrown by the sheer size of the house to which he brought her. She hadn't expected it to be so dark: endless rooms filled with heavily carved Indian furniture. The marital bed was a daunting four-poster in which, Killy said, both he and his father had been born. The walls were hung with the heads of slaughtered animals. Sybil didn't quite know how to address the servants, who greeted her with solemn deference, one immediately running to draw a bath, another to make tea. In the first months, she felt the servants' eyes following her about. One morning she discovered a room which contained an enormous billiard table. She set up the balls and chalked a cue, then looked up to meet the reproachful gaze of the head bearer.

Sybil was caught off guard by the household's strange rituals, by the fact that each morning, Killy's cook brought her the account for market, the hisaab, showing purchases of vegetables, groceries and tea. She was embarrassed weekly by the dhobi who spread the dirty washing out across the drawing-room floor, counting off items one by one before tying them up in a huge bundle which he went away balancing on his head. Tucked into her diary was a bill on smudgy yellowing paper:

Domingo Pereira
BREAD SUPPLIER
The Colaba Bakery, 165, Sassoon Dock,
Colaba, BOMBAY

Date *13/2* 19 *49*

To

PARTICULARS		Total	Rs.	As.	Ps.
	Per	*63*	*7*	*12*	
	Re				
Fine Loaves of Bread @	"				
Sweet Brown	" "				
Sandwich Bread	" "				
Whole Meal Bread	" "				
Gootlies	" "	*12*	*1*	*8*	*6*
Dinner Rolls	" "				
Cakers	" "				
Baking Charges	" "				
Total Rs.			*9*	*4*	*6*

E.&.O.E

Do Pereira

Payment Received by
Date of Payment

On it she had written, 'What the hell are Gootlies? Ask cook.'

But stranger than all of this was Killy – she hadn't expected his warning to extend to himself. She realised, after the shock of the first few months had worn off, that above all, she was lonely. Bombay was an unlovely city, its buildings peeling, stained by the rains, left unrepaired. And turbanned servants lose their charm when you catch the head bearer, or kitmutgar as Killy insisted on calling him, sitting carefully picking lice out of the folds of his turban.

Killy was frequently away visiting family businesses all over the country. When he was at home, it was off to the club with stuffy buggers who liked to play billiards after dinner and abandon the women to small talk, as if the war hadn't happened, the world hadn't changed. In England, Killy had seemed dashing. In India he seemed merely old and she felt not just younger, but inferior. Not up to the mark.

To James Killigrew and his circle, India was independent in name only. Vestiges of the Raj were everywhere. The city's streets were still known by their British names, Apollo Bunder, Ridge Road, Hornby Vellard, Marine Drive, Nepean Sea Road, Flora Fountain. *Dogs and Indians not allowed* read the sign outside the gates of the European swimming club at Breach Candy. Killy was on the club committee. When Sybil complained that the notice was outrageous – it was embarrassing enough not to be able to invite Indian friends – Killy said it had always been there. 'Relic of the old days. Just left up for tradition, really. No one takes it seriously.'

'But you *don't* allow Indians in,' she said.

'Do try to understand,' said Killy. 'It's not that we don't *want* Indians, or don't *like* Indians. It's just that it's one of the few places left for our sort of people.'

But Killy's friends were not Sybil's sort of people.

His favourite book is a hate-filled tome which had belonged to his father. It was written about seventy years ago, and purports to look a century ahead, to that most unthinkable of futures, a free India ruled by Indians. It's called *India in 1983*. Killy is pleased to call it 'a marvellously prophetic little book'. He brought it out the other night at a dinner party and read aloud: 'Out of the three hundred and sixty advanced Hindu thinkers who composed the assembly, three hundred and fifty nine had announced their intention of bringing forward bills making the practice of slaughtering cows punishable with penal servitude for life.' His English friends, even the women, shrieked with laughter. Wilmott said, 'Gandhi wanted a ban on cow-slaughter from day one of Independence.' Julia Wilmott chirped up brightly, 'But they slaughtered him instead.' This produced a silence round the table, until Killy said, 'Yes, and it was done by Hindus . . . their minds don't work like ours.' He grew morose and said, 'God help this poor country. I hope I shan't live to see 1983.'

Often in those first months he would find her crying. 'Why can't you find something to do?' Killy would ask, exasperated, as the pretty girl he had fallen for in England presented him yet again with a weeping face. 'Join a club, find a little job. Other women keep busy. Get out and about a bit. Have some fun.'

So she got out, and gradually the city came to seem less strange. Her encounter with a Bombay paanwallah made me smile.

In a niche above the pavement outside our house sits a plump, half-naked man, selling betel leaf treats called paan. The shiny, heart-shaped leaves are graded according to size and shape and strung on threads which dangle above the betelseller's head. For some reason I usually avoided his eye when I went past. But today I glanced at him and he smiled and gestured at his wares. On an impulse I decided to try one. He was delighted and called to a couple of men who were lounging nearby, to come and watch this amusing show. I began to feel quite silly standing there, in my English dress and straw hat. What if Killy, or worse, one of his friends, or God forbid, one of our servants were to see me? The paanwallah insisted on chattering at me in Hindi, of which naturally I couldn't follow a word. He put all sorts of things into the leaf, topped it off with a pinch of pink shredded coconut and grinned as I popped it in my mouth. It was rather cloying and whatever was inside turned my teeth and tongue scarlet. Afterwards I felt rather proud of myself.

Killy, besides being a member of the Breach Candy Swimming Club, belonged to most of the city's old British haunts, the Bombay Gymkhana, the Willingdon, the Royal Yacht Club. By the early fifties most of them had completed the painful process of admitting Indians to membership and Sybil met a great many of the city's wealthier inhabitants.

I have spent too many evenings in the flats of the rich crowd. The people I met were obsessed with the same ephemera from which I thought I'd escaped. Their oh-so-dull conversations revolve around business deals, the latest adulteries and the price of whisky on the black market. Some of them like to parade their wealth in front of new acquaintances like me. I have seen a tipsy businessman empty three bottles of Scotch out of a window to prove that he could afford it. I think they are all suffering from a kind of ennui. Listless women would ask me whether I'd come to India to find myself . . . The India of the streets is, I suspect, almost as much of a mystery to them as it is to me. I want to get hold of them, especially the women, whose lives seem to be spent worrying about fashion, make-up and being seen at the right parties, and shake them. I never do though. In their company a kind of laissez-faire grips me and I can do nothing to shake it off. Every time I come back from one of those wasted, frustrating evenings, I am filled with astonishment that I didn't simply walk out.

It was a relief to discover she was pregnant. At last, here was something wholly her own. She would devote herself to being a mother. But the pregnancy was difficult. Sybil was sick a lot. She longed for England and, surprising herself, for her mother. The baby was born after a labour that left her racked and disbelieving. Killy, summoned home from 'somewhere up-country', arrived in her hospital room with a fistful of flowers. She smiled feebly. By then the pain was over. She informed Killy that he had a daughter. She wanted to name the baby Barbara, but Killy insisted that she should be called Phoebe, after his mother. (For this I was grateful

273

to him; I couldn't imagine Phoebe as a Barbara.) Killy had another surprise for her. On his next visit he was accompanied by an old, dumpy woman in a faded ankle-length skirt.

> *Muffety Mai dahi malai, ghaas pe baith ke khayi.*
> *Ek badaa saa makdaa, kapdaa ko pakdaa . . .*

The child must have an ayah. Killy's old nanny had long since retired to her village in Goa, but she had sent a younger version of herself to look after the child. How could you decide this without consulting me, Sybil wanted to ask, but was grateful when the new arrival, Rosie, immediately took over the nappying, and the bottles, and the rocking to sleep, and generally began to practise the age-old lore and rigmarole of the Indian ayah.

> *. . . aur bhaag gayi Muffety Mai!*

Killy, roaring with laughter, could complete the lines. 'It's Little Miss Muffet, don't you see?'

Thus some years passed. Phoebe became a little girl. The ayah took over the hisaab and the dhobi and the responsibility of household rule. Sybil's diaries of the mid-fifties reveal a different woman. She had found friends of her own. Indian friends who shared her own tastes and guided her cultural explorations. She was no longer amazed by paanwallahs. She acquired a taste for Indian music, began to read Indian writers.

> Homi has taught me to hear how the way Indians speak
> English is actually rather beautiful, but says it is too

subtle to be enjoyed except by anyone who really knows the place. He gave me a tour of the country by accent, harsh guttural Punjabi English and light, lips-and-tongue Bengali, tongue-cracking consonants of the South. Next time Killy makes jokes about what he calls 'babu speak' I shall tell him that it is carefully-preserved eighteenth-century English, and show him the letter I found in a biography of Lord Nelson, in which Nelson, writing for a supply of water casks to be shipped to his fleet, concludes with the typical and much-sneered at babu phrase 'Kindly do the needful, and oblige.'

Killy was bemused by Sybil's new friends. 'Well, at least you're not moping around for something to do. But be careful,' he told her. 'I know these people. They always want to take advantage.'

'Of course,' her diary indignantly records, 'he's quite wrong.'

He meets someone like Homi, sees a beatnik beard and has no idea at all what to make of him. He quotes old, insulting poems by nineteenth-century bigots. He cannot begin to conceive that someone like Homi has read Steinbeck, Hemingway, Camus, Beckett, Golding, Theodore Roethke, Salinger. Killy has never *heard* of half these people. He found me reading *Catcher in the Rye* and asked if it was something by Thomas Hardy.

Sybil's friends tended to be in advertising, film or the theatre. She joined Zafyque's Theatre Troupe and went on a tour that took Miller's *Death of a Salesman* and an Indianised version of *La*

Cantatrice Chauve, a play by a new Parisian playwright, Eugène Ionesco, to Delhi, Calcutta, Madras and, curiously, Pondicherry. (Later in the diary the reason for Pondi becomes clear. Zafyque, wanting to give at least one performance of *La Cantatrice* partly in the original, needed a French-speaking audience and the only place he could think of was the old French colony. The performance evidently was peculiar, with some of the actors having 'faute de mieux', she wrote, to speak phonetically lines which they did not understand. 'The audience were very decent. Seemed to accept it as part of the overall peculiarity of the play.')

Bombay, a decade after Independence, seems to have been a most cosmopolitan city. Flotsam and jetsam cast up by the war. Some names from her diaries: Pieter 'Franzi' Bloch, Hersh Cynowicz, Josephine Tuor, Burjor Paymaster, Sir Richard and Lady Temple, Karl Bendlin, Charmain Nadim, Feisal Wahid, Faust Pinto.

> A call from the Tourist Club of India to join their Committee, and am invited to dinner and discussion at 8.30 tonight at 'Horizon View' with a Mr Pursram. Searched for Pursram in vain but found a Mr Bassam's flat open. The Consul for the Dominican Republic welcomed us in: stood hands on Grundig radiogram as big and vulgar as a cinema organ and said, 'Our dear friend Mr Bassam, a leading Arab merchant, has kindly invited us all this evening for a dance. As you know (we didn't), we never dine before eleven.' Several Arabs. I didn't know anyone. Killy kept asking, 'Well, which one invited you?' A red light was switched on and all other lights

switched off and people danced. Most eerie and I was petrified with fury! I froze into a chair under the red light and listened to the Consul for Dominica chewing peanuts. The host arrived later, lit up his radiogram with its thousand and one knobs. At dinner, leaning on the sideboard, the little mouselike Tourist Club man, Sharma, says, 'So Mrs Killigrew, how do you like dinner-dances?' 'Very much.' 'So you will ask me to some nice parties now? Cocktail parties with lots of drinks?' Ugh.

It was an era of parties. Bashes thrown by the advertising crowd, by film-wallahs who lived on the beach at Juhu, Bombay's Malibu. There always seemed to be something going on at the Willingdon. There were cocktail parties given by warriors of the Indian Navy who had gone into battle, during 1939–45, in British warships, some of which now lay at anchor in Bombay Harbour. Captain Sahib's ship, INS *Delhi* had once been HMS *Achilles* of the River Plate. Sybil took Phoebe to a lunchtime party on board and was amused when she wrote in the visitors' book, 'This ship is very nicely painted and has very nice drinks.' (About eight mango juices.) There were readings, concerts and parties without end.

Her 1957 diary described a birthday party given by a man called Subramanium, an executive with a pharmaceutical company. Sybil knew his wife, Noor. The story interested me because Noor had been one of my mother's circle. She used to come to Maya's soirées in Ambona. For some months, according to the diary, Subramanium, or 'Sub', as Noor called him, had been pleading with her to stop her dalliances. 'I am a good man. I offer you my heart, my soul, my love, my bank account.'

Noor laughed about this with her friends. 'I *always* confess when I am unfaithful, but what I could *never* tell him is that a husband can only ever be the smile on one's face. One's lover is a smile in the heart.'

'I wonder what it's like,' wrote Sybil, 'to have a smiling heart.'

Sub insisted on making all the arrangements for his 40th birthday party and personally supervised every last detail. He spent hours with his servants planning the small eats, and the feast of biryanis and pulaos. He went to Crawford Market to order the flowers, and made a call to his bootlegger for half a dozen cases of smuggled Johnnie Walker. He had his driver negotiate the narrow alley near the Fort, full of printing works and leather goods shops, to stop outside Marosa's the confectioners, where he and Noor used to meet for coffee and cake before they were married, when he was poor (Noor had never been poor). He ordered a giant cake, having first tasted to make sure that Marosa's chocolate still smelt, as it always had, of peardrops. He collected the beautifully engraved cards he had ordered a fortnight earlier and personally filled in each name in rich blue-black ink. He left nothing to chance.

When he had invited all his friends, relatives, and particularly, every one he could name of Noor's lovers, past and present, he drove his Mercedes north through Bombay's crowded suburbs and out along the coast road, skirting coconut groves through which showed glints of distant silver, till he entered the forest of the Aarey Milk Colony. It took him an hour to find the perfect spot. He nosed the great car off the road into a clearing among the pines and there attached a hose to its exhaust pipe, using a rubber kitchen glove to effect an insecure coitus.

He was found next morning – the unmistakable vehicle was one of the sights of the city – by a party of Goan picnickers. A note addressed to Noor lay on the passenger seat beside him. At the same time, his cards began arriving all over Bombay at smart apartments in Malabar Hill and Marine Drive, at villas in Juhu Beach and Marve, where the film set lived.

Charles Subramanium
cordially requests the pleasure of your company
on the occasion of his first deathday.

Noor was in bed with Bagrani when the call came, the phone brought into the room by a bearer with averted, apologetic eyes. She became hysterical and started beating Baggy with small fists, declaring that her life, too, was finished. 'How could he do this to me? I thought he was so strong, my companion.'

Sub would have died, had he not forgotten to fill the tank before setting off for oblivion. The engine coughed itself dry without pumping quite enough carbon monoxide to fill the car. He woke and found himself in hospital, and recovered in time to turn up as guest of honour at his own wake.

'Typical Sub-human incompetence,' Noor said, when she had regained her poise. 'Couldn't even kill himself properly.'

Tucked into the diary was a note, presumably in Sub's writing, which said: 'Dear Sybil, thank you for your kind well wishes. I am feeling much better today after a good rest. You asked where I scoured [*sic*?] the supplies. I have jotted down a list for you.'

*Flowers from florists at Warden Road

*Garlands near Teen Batti, Nepean Sea Road

*Mogras from Teen Batti

*Pink badami gulabs from the lanes at Crawford Market

*Panir (cheese) from Parsi Dairy Farm at Queens Road

*Kulfi (ice-cream) ditto

*Big birthday cake from Marosa's, Fort

*Samosas from that Irani café near the Metro cinema

*Chaat from Kailash Parbat in Colaba Causeway

*Rasgullas from the mithai-wallah near Kemp's Corner

*Little mawa cakes and pav from Kyani's

*Salad dressing from Rustom's, Colaba

*Ditto imported cheese, dips, meat sauces

*Dhansak from Ratan Tata Institute

*Berry Pulav from the Irani Café Brittanie at Ballard Estate

*Crockery from Chor Bazaar

*Bombay Duck (the dried fish) from Sassoon Dock

*Hilsa-fish from Crawford Market

*Fresh vegetables from Grant Road

*Vindaloo from Mrs George, a nice old Anglo-Indian lady
    in Bandra East

*Basmati rice from our local baniya

*Those wonderful paper-thin roomali rotis from a Bhopali
    chef, Gangaram, whose address I would give you, but I

have since heard that he is probably suffering from leprosy

*Badams, pistachios, cashews, walnuts from the American Dry Fruit Stores at Flora Fountain

*Sev from Vithal Bhelwala near VT station

*Kebabs from 'Bade Miyan' at Colaba. You'll always find a few big cars pulled up outside his stall

*Chicken from the goaswallahs of Crawford Market

*Sandwich ice-creams from Rustom's, Churchgate, the ones with pistachio ice-cream served between two crisp biscuits

*Alphonso mangoes from the fruit-wallahs of Breach Candy and Walkeshwar

*Firangi Johnnie Walker Scotch from the black market. Like most people I tend to use Saqi Baba in Char Null, Dongri area, but don't go there alone. Ask me and I can arrange it for you.

Among the people Sybil met through Zafyque's Theatre Troupe was my mother, Maya. Both loved reading, and shared an ambition to write. Sybil loved the new Lawrence Durrell book, *Justine*, which had burst like an exploding box of paints upon the astonished reading public. It was only just out in England but had already been pirated by Bombay's astuter pavement booksellers. Durrell was a genius, Sybil said. Never had there been such an evocation of a city as his portrait of Alexandria. Landscape tones: bruised plum, rose, burnt sienna. She could quote lengthy passages. Sybil imagined an equivalent novel set in Bombay, a thinly disguised account of the friends whose doings filled her journals. She had written the story of Sub and his death-day party, half-thinking that she could begin to weave a longer story around its characters.

Maya countered that with the exception of her hero, Manto (who alas had just died in Lahore), William Faulkner was the purest and truest writer alive. They soon became friends. Maya introduced Sybil to the city, showed her the best junk shops, haggled on her behalf in the bazaars.

To Chor Bazaar again with Maya, our taxi ploughing through crowds that mill on every pavement in the Muslim bazaar area, and spill into the street. The air is loud with hoots and the screeches of near-collisions as impatient taxi drivers seek to defy various laws of Newton. Maya took me to her favourite bookseller, a charming man who carries an air of learning. He has very white hair swept back from his forehead and his shop is piled from floor to ceiling with old leather-bound books that must have come from the libraries of departed sahibs. I found a complete set of *Decline and Fall of the Roman Empire* in gold-tooled leather. Hardly dared ask the price. But the man – his name is Sharif – picked up the pile, and said he guessed it would come to about twelve rupees. A little later when I had added a few more books, I asked again for a price. To my astonishment, he never once looked to see what any of the books were, nor opened them to check a price. He sorted two piles, leather bindings and cloth bindings, and proceeded to weigh each in a large brass scale, explaining to me that 'Leather is five rupees a seer, cloth only two.'

Maya also has a bookbinder, a little Hindu who speaks and reads no English, but somehow does the titles perfectly. To him the alphabet is just symbols, as precise and inscrutable as Chinese writing is to me.

With what huge envy I read this. A seer is just under a kilogram and five rupees in those days was perhaps worth forty pence. For a moment, I was tempted . . . But it was inconceivable that such bookdealers were still to be found in the depths of Chor Bazaar.

Sybil was captivated, as so many people initially were, by Maya's strange view of history and consequence. They swapped family stories. Under Maya's tutelage, Sybil (to Killy's surprise and pleasure) began to learn Hindi. She practised writing the script.

On a sheet of paper which also contains a pencil sketch of a dhow and a brown ring made by a cup of tea, were the following enigmatic definitions: '*dhaivat*, the song of the frog in the season of rain; *miyan ki malhar*, the song of thunder; *nívar*, wild rice; *vishálákshi*, large-eyed.'

She and Maya talked a great deal about the things they were writing, or at least hoped to write. Maya had published some short stories and by then must have been well underway with the script of *Badnaami ka dilaasa*, but said she lacked the courage to tackle anything long. Sybil was struggling with her novel about Bombay. Evidently, it would not come, because a sheet dated February 1958, tucked into her diary, lists twenty-one separate attempts, each a false start, with comments that get progressively terser:

a) One sheet typed on old Remington typewriter begins, 'As usual we found Selim's apology for a cab waiting by the sea wall . . .'

b) pp 39–68 of draft, fragment begins, 'The presence of the transmitter was disturbing . . .' *Rewrite to turn descriptive passages into dialogue.*

c) pp 1–126, in sections I to XIII typed single-spaced, 'Wind whinnied in the ropes . . .'

d) pp 1–128, typewritten carbon copy, 'As usual we found Selim's apology . . .'

e) pp 1–35, pages 11–20 missing. Begins, 'As usual we found Selim's apology for a gharry . . .'

f) One sheet, 'Grey Notebook', begins, 'When she arrived in India, the last thing on Marlene's mind . . .'

g) pp I–56, many pages missing, begins, 'India became real late one night . . .'

h) pp I–5, perforated, bound in Thakur Shipping file; 'India became real one misty dawn . . .'

i) pp I–42; 'As usual we found Selim's apology for a hansom . . .'

j) pp I–15, titled 'Meeting', begins, 'I came to India in the autumn of 1948. I had wanted to travel . . .'

k) One page, same title as (j), begins 'Gorai. Fish, eggs, rice and arak, smooth as Saqi Baba's finest . . .'

l) pp I–3, typed, paperclipped, begins, 'Salty gusts of wind whined through the rigging . . .'

m) pp I–12, typewritten, dark new ribbon, begins, 'My home is an island called Gorai . . .'

n) pp I–6, with interpolated note, begins, 'James, I am wondering how to explain everything to you . . .'

o) pp I–5, on good quality bank, begins, 'Somewhere beyond Madgaon, love begins . . .'

p) pp I–15, 2 pages missing, double spaced, begins, 'Marlene Dance fell in love on a day of rain which in her native Surrey . . .'

q) pp rough notes, mostly handwritten

r) pp I–44, double spaced, good attempt, begins, 'Jealousy is an infection of the eye . . .'

s) pp I–5, 'He lives with that awful blonde tart in the Taj . . .'

t) pp I–32, 'Two floors below, glints of light spun in the waves as they gulped at the rocks . . .'

u) pp I–68, 'As usual we found Selim . . .'

Who this Selim was, he who occupied so much of her thoughts, never became clear. Perhaps a fantasy. The horse-drawn gharries, as she called them, functioned only between the extravagant outrage of the Taj Hotel (where the blonde tart was in residence) and a loop which took in part of Colaba Causeway and a short stretch of Marine Drive. The horses were poor emaciated things, their ribs as prominent as those of the half-built dhows that lined the shore of the Back Bay.

One of the people to whom Maya introduced Sybil was the novelist Mulk Raj Anand who, when she asked for his advice on writing a Bombay novel, replied, 'I am not a novelist, I am trying to be a man. Burn your so-good poems and short stories. Give me a true picture of our poorest people.'

About a year into their friendship, Maya and Captain Sahib were planning their move to the hills. Some time towards the end of 1957, Maya and Sybil travelled up to Ambona on the train to look at the house Mohan Apte's friend had found. It was a happy trip, they seem to have laughed a great deal. Sybil had been a charming, friendly, vivacious woman. Just as quickly as any of us, she fell under the spell of the hills. Her diary, showing the undoubted influence of her favourite author, records:

> Market day. Village women bundled slimly in green and
> red saris, posing like dancers with baskets on their hips.
> They strut through the bustle, magnificent, proud crea-
> tures, wearing their poverty like rubies. Great fish with
> red gash bellies lie on black stone, foolish fish eyes
> winking at flies. Hands weigh and lift them into crushed

ice. Quails, wild fowl, guinea fowl. Partridges mewing in wicker baskets. These were the unwary, caught in basket traps baited with millet by grubby cunning boys. In the market square, a musician turns, vina on shoulder. The music exhilarates me. People throw small coins in the dust, Judas coins, dry and salty silver . . . Night pounces like a panther. On the way here I passed a sloughed-off snake skin and brought it home. The villagers believe snakes have magic powers. They hang the dry leathery thongs of skin on their houses and temple walls. Tonight there was no moon. We heard the sound of drums from the village, and the notes of a flute.

Maya plainly couldn't be doing with this sort of thing, because they had an argument.

When I read her these passages Maya grew quite cross. She said my response to India gives me away. I have a foreigner's eye, always looking for the exotic. Maya was with me in the bazaar when the musician was playing, but noticed quite different things. The village woman, whose gaudy sari caught my eye, Maya said, was quietly counting a few coins in her hand, wondering which of the many things she needed, she would have to do without. When the bus came, a number of villagers boarded it, but this woman did not. She may have had to walk five or six miles back to her home. She had already walked to market; Maya asked if I had not noticed the dust which coated her feet up to her ankles, like socks? Life for this woman, said Maya, is a daily confrontation with help-lessness. She said I must learn not simply to be satisfied with seeing the outside of things. There is nothing exotic about poverty. And Indians don't talk to one another in quaint, funny, third-class English, they have normal conversations in languages which they speak without accent, and with no mistakes. Of course I was thoroughly chastened by this tirade, but stuck up for myself by saying that it is impossible to write anything about India, at least in English, without it sounding exotic. Maya made a bet with me. She said I could choose a story, as romantic as I liked, and she would demonstrate the two ways to tell it. First, what she called the Rumer Godden way: rivers of green silk, coconuts, temple bells. Second, her preference: reality, the salt and grit of Manto. So I challenged her to tell the story of the dancing girl, Nafisa Jaan. She has promised to write two versions. One 'sweet' and the other 'bitter'.

I put down Sybil's diary, unable to read further. 'Death deceives with a blow, it disguises a deeper loss. It takes time to realise that the gone ones are lost for ever.' My mother's words, from *Badnaami*. When Maya died I was unable to cry, unable to grieve. It had taken all these months to realise that it wasn't just Maya I'd lost, but everything she knew; her memories, stories from her child-hood, snippets of family history, anecdotes, dates, rhymes, songs: precious things, which belonged to me as much as to her and which I had always left entrusted to her care. So when I reached the part of Sybil's diaries where my mother's name began

constantly leaping out at me, I found myself unable to go on. I
returned the diaries to their painted box, re-affixed its tiny
padlock and put the key away.

Next contact from Phoebe was not until March. The post brought a parcel from London. Inside was a child's book. On the flyleaf, in my mother's writing, was my name, *Bhalu Sahib, Ambona, 1959.*

'I've kept it long enough,' Phoebe's note said. 'At least it'll be in time for your grandchildren.'

A couple of mornings later she phoned the bookshop.

'Where have you been?' I asked when the pleasantries were over. 'Why these long silences?'

She apologised. Said she had been here and there. Busy. A lot on her mind. 'Anyway,' she said, 'I didn't want to hound you. Bhalu, have you read them?'

'You mean your mother's diaries?'

'Yes, of course.'

'I started,' I said, and began to explain why I had stopped.

'Bhalu, if you would *only* read them again — read them *properly* — maybe you could work out what was going on.'

'Nothing was going on,' I said. 'Nothing that would explain what you told me. At least nothing I've read so far.'

'But you haven't read everything. Please promise me you'll read the rest.'

I wanted to explain my apparent negligence, and began to tell Phoebe how I had surprised myself by becoming upset, when I read about Maya as a young woman. 'In Sybil's diaries she's almost twenty years younger than I am now.' I told her what had come to my mind, the *Badnaami ka dilaasa* speech about what the loss of a loved one really means: the loss of their stories, memories . . .

'My God,' said Phoebe at the other end of the phone, 'if that were really true, I'd be so grateful.'

So I found the little key and re-opened the box.

Sybil had tended to use large notebooks, and fill them quickly, so that there might be two, or even three, covering a single year. She must have been lonely, to have the time to fill so many cahiers, and that was on top of the endless versions of her novel – 668 pages, at a quick count – although heavily cannibalised. It was a wonder she found time for all those parties.

Soon the diaries started telling a darker story. She was trapped in a cold and failing marriage, alone for long periods in Killy's dark house. The child, Phoebe, was by now at school and the person with whom Sybil had most contact during the day was Rosie the ayah. They evidently loathed one another.

> For some time I have been convinced that Rosie spies on me. There is something almost feudal about her loyalty to Killy, whom she adores. As for me, I am a parvenue, not up to the mark. Her conversation, when she deigns to speak to me at all, is full of stories about 'Old Killymem', Killy's mother, whom she professes to have met a number of times. Old Killymem knew how to look after her sahib. When he and his friends came home at dawn from a shoot, the table would be laden with silver dishes of eggs, kidneys poached in beer, bacon, a side of beef (where did they get it from, it is virtually unobtainable nowadays), thick pork sausages (ditto). In the

evenings there were, apparently, such parties here, the men splendid in their uniforms, the women in elegant ballgowns. She makes it sound like something from a Jane Austen novel. I listen to all this nonsense, smiling, but seething inside, and point out that the world has changed. The dashing colonels and majors are as extinct as the brontosaur. But thinking about the way they lived, I am filled with incredulity. The British in India inhabited a world of their own dreaming, a vivid fantasy which at no point seemed to touch the real lives of the millions they ruled. The miracle is that the Raj lasted so long. I celebrate its death . . .

. . . Rosie has begun asking me where I go in the evenings. She comes to my room, knocks and stands in the doorway. 'Killymem,' she will say, 'last night when you came home late I was so worried. It is not safe in the city at night. You should tell me where you are going then we can telephone . . .' I wonder if she is reporting to Killy. If he is worried about me, he has never shown it, but of course he is hardly ever here to show anything. In any case, everything I do is written in these diaries, which live in a drawer of my desk. It may be that Rosie reads them when I am out. If so, Killy, you will know that I have done nothing that you, or anyone else, can reproach me with.

Less than a week after this, the diary records that on a trip to Old Man Popli's antique shop behind the Taj she saw a charming painted wooden box on legs. It would do very well for a jewellery box. It had a little hasp and was secured by a tiny padlock. She bought it, but when she got it home, she did not put her jewellery into it. She put her diaries inside and locked it, and hung the key on a chain around her neck.

Killy came home and dropped a bombshell. He was nearly fifty. It was time to recognise that the world he knew had all but vanished. He did not see a future in India for their daugher. He talked of going 'home'. But Sybil did not want to leave, and now the reason for locking her box became clear. The diary began to fill with a story she had so far dared not mention.

She had met a man. He was Indian, handsome, rich, single, utterly charming and he worshipped her.

> S and I hideously bored at the Willingdon last night. Everyone will insist that we look like twins, so we decided to swap identities. I found myself cornered by some ghastly old Lebanese banker and gave him S's phone number, which was wicked because, poor girl, her husband really is away. I was amused when she confessed she had played a similar trick on me. Later, I introduced her to L.

Something in this passage rang a loud bell. I *knew* I had heard it before. Then realised with a shock that it was part of Maya's puzzling *Retribution* story. I read on eagerly. The next few pages were full of trivia. Coffee with Homi and my mother, a trip to the Jehangir Art Gallery. Soon a new entry caught my eye.

> People say, usually women being catty, or men who are merely envious, that L is a womaniser. They complain that

if he sees a beautiful woman on her own at a party, he will go up and ask her if she'd like to dance. But this is hardly a crime. Good manners, more like, although it isn't quite how we met. It was at Noor's. I was with a small group of people and noticed him in a corner of the room. He caught my eye and smiled. A little later, he came over and said hello. We spent the rest of the evening together. He was nothing but kindness. When it was time to leave, he offered to drive me home. His car awaited. A spanking new Ambassador, he announced proudly, emphasising its brand-newness by adding that he had just taken delivery. That lapse into vulgarity was the only thing he did all evening that annoyed me, but I suppose it's flattering when someone is interested enough to try and impress you. He drove home via Marine Drive, and we got out and strolled on the sand at Chowpatty. Since then we have met a few times. Last night he took me to see a play.

Rosie, of course, was hanging around when I got home, and next morning I had a call from nosy Noor who wanted to know everything that had happened from the moment we left. She warned me to watch out. '. . . That one likes women whose husbands are away a lot.' Well, mine certainly is. It's been so long since we made love that I am beginning to feel quite unattractive. Is it surprising that I am pleased when a good-looking man notices that I am a woman?

I read this with growing excitment. Here, coming back to life in Sybil's diary, were the characters described in *Retribution*. A few pages later, there it was.

Today L asked me to lunch. He took me to Gourdon's and ordered Lobster Thermidor, which I know to be the most expensive thing on their menu. I chided him for his extravagance. His reply was that a woman like me deserved nothing but the best of everything. I am not much of one for flattery, so I tried to laugh this off. I told him that I was aware of his reputation. 'Do you believe those stories?' he asked. 'Well,' I said, 'you do a pretty good Casanova impression.' So then he looked hurt, or pretended to, and said that while he admitted to liking women, and having many women friends, there was no one in his life who was special. 'And yet I have a great need to love,' he told me. What a scream! I suppose I didn't look convinced, because then he said he would tell me a secret. I was thoroughly enjoying this performance. He leaned very close, and gazing at me with dark, defenceless eyes, he whispered that in Hindi his name meant 'love'. I couldn't hold it in a moment longer. I simply screamed. I was hooting. I laughed so hard that people at other tables were turning to stare. He sat there and smiled, giving me his hurt puppy look. 'You think I am funny?' he asked, when I had stopped laughing. I said, 'You are well named, a perfect little Narcissus, and from now on I shall call you Mister Love.'

Mister Love! So he *had* been real. And Sybil had been one of his lovers. But which? Was she One, or Two? Did it mean that the *rest* of the story was true? Mister Love in his bath towel? A black mouth that spoke a word to end his life? Mister Love had been murdered. But my enthusiasm was blunted when I recalled that, according to my man in Bombay, no such murder had been reported in *Blitz*. A far more plausible explanation was that Maya liked to base her stories on nuggets of reality, events from her own life, or those of her friends. Had she just taken the story of Sybil's love affair, Mister Love and all, and used it as the basis for a fictional murder?

On the other hand, there was *The Eel Fisher*, in which Maya seemed to blame herself for Mister Love's murder. A murder that never happened?

Love, what is it? A luxury, in marriage. Marriage kills love, does it not? Sybil confided her feelings to my mother.

> Met Maya for coffee at the Mockba. Couldn't keep it in.
> I was bursting to tell someone. I had to. I hope she was
> not shocked. It's feelings. Just feelings. It's not as if I've
> done anything. One can't help having feelings. The thing
> is not to act on them. I assured Maya that I am deter-
> mined never to reveal my feelings to L because I am afraid
> of what might happen. Maya thinks this is wise. She says
> that it is probably no more than an infatuation.

Maya told Sybil of the experience of a friend of hers, who was in love with a man who had treated her miserably – on off, off on – for years. Maya's friend yearned for this man, suffered agonies for him. One day, having returned from one of his long absences abroad, he took her to lunch. Over soup she noticed a shred of watercress stuck to his moustache. She laughed out loud. In that instant she knew that she did not love him. He was ridiculous. He was still sitting there, smiling when she pushed back her chair and left. She never saw him again.

But when Mister Love takes Sybil to lunch, there is no soup, no polished silver spoon. It's – this food is traditional Indian, you eat with your fingers, so – here, may I show you? – reaches over and presses her fingers to form a sloppy ball of rice and sauce – and now to your mouth – oh dear, chin – here, let me wash your fingers – dabs them with a napkin wetted in the rosewater bowl – does it taste nice? is it good? – brings one of her fingers to his lips, rolls them wetly over it, flicks her finger with his tongue, gently sucks – mmm, this is delicious, just like my granny used to make. Sybil experiences a sensation akin to falling. She realises that this oddly plummeting feeling is love and that she has never felt it before.

> I have a lovely secret, a special feeling, like a gift that has come to me and woken me from sleep. There's not a minute when I don't think of him, and I marvel at my own foolishness. My wild imaginings. Running off together, a whole new life. I *know* it would be absolute bliss and also *know* I am being unrealistic. I sit trying to picture his face, going over and over the same few things: every smile that showed he likes me, ditto his smallest gestures, most inconsequential remarks. This morning Phoebe was talking to me and after a while I realised I hadn't heard a word. I keep having to drag myself back to my mundane world, when really I am on a different plane. At times I feel despairing, and want to bang my head on

the table. At other times, I *know* that this is the height of happiness. When I put a record on the gramophone, every song I hear speaks directly to me, is sung for me only, carries a special message just for me. That record 'When I fall in love', L plays it twenty times running. I'll sing the words to myself even when Killy is in the room and feel oddly liberated, for my life is no longer anything to do with him. He will speak, and I look up in surprise. So much is going on in my head that I'm not aware I haven't spoken a word for hours. I no longer eat. I push away my plate, nourished by superior knowledge, armoured and invincible. I am aware constantly of my body. It is keenly alive, longing to be touched. Killy has noticed. He makes remarks. He said today that I was looking radiant. It makes him amorous. Last night he came to my room. I was expecting him and he found me ready for love, like an open flower. As I held him in my arms, I had no sense of wrongdoing, of being unfaithful to either of them. He does not know, but it was the last time. I can't make love with someone I no longer love. Last night, the lovemaking was not him and me, nor me and anyone else. It was intense, but the passion was blind, all-encompassing. He could have been anyone, everyone and everything, and I felt wholly woman.

What she had felt for Killy had not been love, could not have been, because love was this delirium. What she had felt for Killy was admiration, respect — she had mistaken it for love. In those days she was so young, so inexperienced. This was unmistakable.

The excitement, the tremulous and guilty awareness of her feelings as his fingers pressed into the small of her back when they danced together, sometimes under the eye of her husband. The yearning to melt together, to become one – she poured these feelings into her journals. She was sure that Killy would never stoop to prying, and Rosie could not pick locks. But just to be safe, she soon began attributing her emotions to a character in her novel, and for the first time, some passages were in Pitman's squigglescript. She must have felt secure, because tucked in between the pages of the diary was a faded, brown photograph of a man. He had a gentle face, with thick eyebrows, gentle eyes, and a full, curved mouth. On the back was written, in a typical Indian hand, 'With all my love, L.'

Looking for the first time at Mister Love, I felt sure I knew him from somewhere. His face seemed familiar. But I could not say from where I recognised him, or why.

For a long time Sybil resisted her own feelings and L's advances. To begin with she refused invitations to meet him alone, but her resolve gradually weakened. Mister Love had a flat near the sea at Malabar Hill. He lived with his sister, who quickly became a friend. This gave Sybil an excuse to visit him. Killy, who was spending more time at home these days, did not suspect anything; he was glad to see Sybil happy. Not that there *was* anything to suspect. Apart from feelings, which couldn't be helped, she had *done* nothing wrong. L pressed her, of course, to go to bed with him, but she constantly refused. Sybil adored L, but to her own surprise had discovered an old-fashioned respect for her wedding vows. She no longer loved Killy but she was not going to have a cheap affair.

L was so desperate, she wrote, so unhappy. All eaten up, poor boy. He thought of her every minute, begged her to see him. Spending time with her was the only thing that made his life bearable. She began to feel it was her duty to ease his suffering. There could be no harm in their meetings, so long as she *never* revealed her feelings. Poor romantic boy, he read her poems by Indian authors, so full of hyperbole they made her giggle. She enjoyed his company, she told him truthfully, and lied by saying she wanted him simply as a friend.

She was in love, but clung to her marriage. What changed her mind? Was it that a possibility which had already been dismissed as frivolous daydreaming, became real one day? L mentioned marriage. Killy was away again. Mister Love proposed a picnic. Somewhere special. They travelled in his new car through the northern suburbs to the dusty township of Borivili. He negotiated the car at walking pace through lanes bustling with people and animals until they came to a creek. A wooden fishing boat crammed with country folk took them the half mile to the far shore. Waiting for them, its bullocks patiently eating hay, was a wooden cart of the sort used by villagers. It was the first time Sybil had ever ridden in one. They creaked a mile through coconut groves and emerged into a blue-and-white dazzle of sea and sky. The beach ran from a fishing village, deserted during the heat of day, to a red sandstone hill on which crouched the remains of a Portuguese fort. Corroded cannon still pointed out to sea through tangles of lantana. The foot of the hill was whorled by the sea into caves, in which the tide left pools full of interesting creatures, 'sea urchins and starfish, little wispy shrimps and tiny pieces of coral, intricate as crystallised spittle'.

In one of these pools, lying a few inches below the surface, Sybil saw a rock imprinted with a perfect fossil leaf. Mister Love duly rolled up his sleeves, but she made him put it back again, because there were tiny animals clinging to it. They ate the picnic in a shack which, he said, belonged to one of his friends.

> The cottage was sweet-smelling and dark, the dried cowdung floor was cool and fresh and the only light in the evening, L said, would come from hurricane lamps . . . The island lay stupefied in the sun. I was aware of myriad small sounds. Gurgle and plop of mud-hoppers, incessant whine of cicadas, rustling of wind in the palms. We went swimming. I floated in my bathing costume. L said I looked like an elegant starfish.

There was no electricity, no water, just four walls and a coconut thatch roof. In this carefully chosen and well-prepared spot, he asked her to marry him, and they became lovers.

Later, they met at his flat overlooking the Arabian Sea. Her journal describes the waves teasing the rocks under his window as a joyous mating of water and earth.

> His caresses are like soft avalanches of sea. A rising tide that will submerge me. I want to open more and more for him. I am an anemone, opening out to capture, to draw into myself his fingers, tongue, all of him. Yes I want all of him and all else too, the exterior whole world. I want to take into myself the universe of outside and refashion it within my body, heal its ills, correct its faults, mend its

301

flaws, make it perfect within me, and then return this perfected world to the outside, the world born back into itself, but better than before — this is the woman's gift.

May. Hottest month of the year. The city lay suffocating under a gunmetal sky, the rains still weeks away. But Sybil was happy. She was in brightest love and her lover, love's avatar, Mister Love, was in love with her. He kept pestering her to marry him and Sybil knew that next time he asked she would say *yes*. She also realised that she must tell Killy, but the thought made her afraid. God knows what he might do. Besides, for all his neglect of her, Sybil did not want to hurt Killy. He was upset enough by the fact that she would no longer sleep with him. He did not know why. Things had changed between them, was all she would say. She no longer felt the same about him. Now that she knew their marriage was over, she sometimes looked at him, his greying head, glasses on nose, bent over a book, and felt fondness. Guilt pulled her this way and that. She did not know what to do. No one, not even her best friend, my mother Maya, knew that her relationship with L had crossed from friendship into the salt marshes of adultery.

> We meet in his flat, at times when his sister is out. No longer do we waste time talking. There is little enough time, and all of it needed. It's straight to the bedroom, eager fumblings with each other's, or our own clothes. No sooner are we naked than we fall onto the bed, lips and fingers and tongues touching, probing, sliding and slithering: it thrills me and leaves me weak with shame.

Mister Love's professions of love, each time he undressed her and she, bending down, removed his shoes as she imagined an Indian wife would, grew more ardent, but guilt-ridden Sybil would no longer give herself completely. Gently, she began turning aside his advances. Mister Love fretted. He complained that she did not love him. Didn't she *want* them to be married? She said he must understand. She could not make love to him again until things were out in the open. Which meant telling Killy. And this she still could not bring herself to do. L was behaving like a petulant child, but men are such babies, they have tantrums if they don't get what they want, especially sex. Her mind was elsewhere. Let me think and plan first, she told herself. She was worried about Phoebe. What would Killy do? She wanted the three of them, she, Phoebe and Mister Love, to be together. Of one thing she had no doubt, she had never been happier.

If this should prove to be a chimera, a false dawn, then so be it. I will count myself blessed to have enjoyed this much, to have known what love can be. One can get through life only to a point cherishing an ideal. As disillusionment sets in, the ideal sickens, infected by disappointment, frustration, agnosticism, bitterness, desperation and despair. And suddenly – when one is resigned to eking out one's lifetime in a second-rate, lonely, unfulfilled, dead, mistaken but respectable way – suddenly, with only a slight shiver of warning, one is face to face with that ideal personified, perfected more in fact than in fancy. And at that moment, and in those that follow, one says: 'This is all I have ever needed. Life didn't let me down, after all.'

Later she would copy these words into a letter she sent to her 'ideal, personified and perfected' Mister Love. She kept copies of these letters, pressed in her diary. Sometimes she wrote three a day.

Poor Sybil. It was painful for me to read her trusting words, knowing, with the hindsight of *Retribution*, what moments would actually follow. So sure was she of Mister Love's sincerity, of the genuineness of his love, that she did not quite take him seriously when he let fall, lightly, one evening, after she had again refused to sleep with him, that she had a rival.

'If you won't marry me, there are others, you know. There are others who will.'

'Which others?' she cried playfully, thinking he was teasing.

'It doesn't matter who. But I can tell you there is at least one other woman. She is not just willing, but desperate.'

'I don't believe you,' said Sybil.

'Do I have to prove it?'

He looked so serious, maybe he wasn't teasing. It wasn't surely that Anglo-Indian girl, Sybil told herself. He had assured her that was nothing but gossip. Half a dozen other names came to mind, but flim-flam, the lot of them. Then a thought struck her.

'Oh, poor love,' she said. 'I've just realised. No wonder you're in such a hurry. Don't worry, I'll save you. Just be patient a little longer.'

'What are you talking about?' demanded her paramour.

'Well, isn't it obvious? Your parents have found you another girl.'

'What rubbish.'

'And you're upset because probably she's no more prepossessing than the last one.' Laughing. Thinking of the dull woman whose photographs he had shown her. Laughing. 'No, don't deny it. Looking sulky doesn't suit you. I know how you detest arranged marriages, but don't worry, darling. I won't let her have you.'

'It's not a question of arranged marriage,' he said, by now rather irritable. Her determined good humour must have puzzled him. 'If you really must know, this other girl has more in common with you.'

'Meaning what, exactly? How is she like me?'

'I mean that she is an Englishwoman.'

This, Sybil had not expected.

'Who is she? Where did you meet her? *When* did you meet her?' But he would not say.

'Do you love her?'

'Of course not, darling. She writes to me, but her letters are not so amusing as yours. Listen, if you like I'll read you one of them.'

They were lying side by side on the bed, he naked, unsated but still hopeful, she dishevelled but still more or less clothed. Their encounters, to judge from her diary, had turned into adolescent tussles which usually ended in wrangling. As a compromise – she did not want to be cruel – she would allow him to undo her bra and play with her nipples till they were hard, to moisten his fingers between her thighs. He was hoping to arouse her. She, in no need of arousal, found other ways to ease his need.

Mister Love rolled off the bed and she heard him scrabbling underneath. He came up with a sheet of writing paper.

'Got it. Just a moment, I need my reading glasses.'

'Wait,' said Sybil. 'You shouldn't read me someone else's letter.'

He looked at her, over the rim of his glasses, as if to say, well this is what you drive me to, and read: '"Last night, when you spoke about your need to marry and the various girls you may marry, something inside me snapped and I knew that I couldn't bear the thought of you loving and being close to someone else . . ."'

It did not take long to worm out the identity of her rival. Mister Love seemed almost anxious to tell her, but the name he spoke was the last she expected to hear.

The rival was the woman she had referred to as S, her 'twin', with whom she had swapped identities at the Willingdon. Sybil's description was so close to Maya's in *Retribution*, that Maya must have based her story on Sybil's letters.

Shock subsided into anger. She had been betrayed. 'How could she?' Still she did not put the blame on him. 'She was my friend. She introduced us.' Then, as the full implications dawned, 'And she knows about *me*? About *us*?'

'I don't believe in secrets,' he said.

'What does she mean, "close to *someone* else"? The bitch! She *knows* it's me!'

'Sybil, please calm down,' said Mister Love, who must have been delighted by all this. 'You're getting it out of proportion.'

'But why didn't you tell her you've already proposed to me? *Did* you tell her?'

'Of course I did,' he said, with a bland smile.

'Then I don't understand how she could—'

'Look,' he said. 'You have nothing to worry about. I didn't encourage her. Poor girl, she is infatuated, but she means nothing to me. Not like you.'

'Do you say the same things to her?'

'Of course not!'

Ha! Liar! she thought (as her notebook records, and I, reading, silently cheered, a foolish celebration, given that I already knew the outcome), but she was ready to be mollified.

'In fact,' said Mister Love, 'S says herself that she has no chance against you.'

'Does she think we're having a contest?'

'I can't say what she thinks. Here! here!' he said. 'Listen to this. "My darling, I wish I were brilliant and witty and could write a letter to make you laugh." You see? Why does she say that? Who is she comparing herself to?'

'I don't know,' said Sybil.

'She's talking about *you*! Who else sends me such entertaining letters?'

He dived off the bed again and in a moment his voice came from somewhere underneath it. 'Listen, this is what you wrote.' He began to skim the invisible letter. '". . . couldn't make love . . . someone I didn't love . . . I'm that truthful, anyway . . ." Yes, here it is, it was when you stopped sleeping with him. "So he said I was unnatural, impossible, abnormal, prudish – an iceberg! And he was surprised because he said that when he first saw me he thought I was a nymphomaniac! Actually he was kind enough to spell it, for fear of hurting my feelings, and rather than enunciate a word like that, he started: N-I-M-F- when I stopped him . . ." See what I mean? You are so funny!'

But Sybil did not laugh.

I had been thinking about betrayal, how I had been let down so badly by someone I thought of as a friend. My mind was full of outrage. When he read my letter back to me, a needle of pain went through my heart. Only it wasn't pain, it was shame. Killy may not have been the kindest, most considerate husband, but he does not deserve to have his unhappiness mocked by the man who is cuckolding him.

The cuckolder's head popped up beside the bed and smiled, displaying a set of white teeth. 'There, my darling. No comparison. *She* knows that.'

'Wait a minute,' Sybil said. 'How does she know? How does she know about my letters? Don't tell me you've been reading *my* letters to *her.*'

'Well, of course I have,' said Mister Love.

'You read her that? About Killy?'

'Of course I didn't read that actual bit,' said her lover, quickly back-pedalling once he saw he'd upset her. 'What sort of person do you think I am? I read her harmless things, just pretty jokes, the funny way you put things. And why did I do it?' His voice rising in righteous self-defence. 'To show her how much I treasure you. To warn her not to build up dreams and raise false hopes. To make her realise that nothing could come between me and you.'

He stopped, smiled and began dancing, naked as he was, beside the bed, crooning, 'O O O you are the One the One and only, the only One for me.'

He looked so ridiculous, capering like that, with his balls and penis flopping about.

'Stop it!' I shouted. 'You sound like one of those awful songs on the Binaca Hit Parade.'

'You, darling, are the One, the One woman I have thought of marrying. To begin with it was a terrifying feeling, like falling into a trap. But how did I know it was the right thing to do? Because I missed you when you were not with me. Other girlfriends are not as much fun in bed as you are. Their conversation seems insipid. You were funny. You made me laugh. I looked forward to your letters. I found excuses to telephone you. To my disgust, I was upset when you flirted with other men. You mocked me for what you called my "mirror-worship". You called me "Mister Love".'

'You are a devil!' I exclaimed, half-horrified, half-amused. 'I don't know whether to believe you. You're playing with both of us.'

His game worked. When he climbed back onto the bed, my clothes were already coming off.

Mister Love did not deny that he had been sleeping with S. On the contrary, he made a point of telling Sybil. She was hurt, but decided that her best policy was to make light of it. 'Probably the silly boy has done it to make me jealous.' She wrote to him that he could do as he pleased. 'Your idea of marriage is getting a girl into bed. Every so often, you 'marry me'. Then, the moment my back is turned, you marry someone else! How could you? (Yes, I know I told you you could.) Please don't get married again before I can see you again . . .'

Soon she would find the courage to speak to Killy. She would reveal everything, endure his anger and there would be a final end to lies. Pressed between the pages of the notebook were several heavily worked drafts of the letter she sent a few days later to her lover, describing how he fulfilled her noblest ideal.

My dear L, I started to write to you yesterday but got ill and had to go to bed. Nothing serious. I'm so glad I got sick because when it happened I was writing a very long letter to you and I'm sure you'd have hated every word of it. It was so full of affection. It probably helped to give me a fever because bits of it kept going round in my head all night between pains. If our love should prove to be a chimera, a false dawn, then so be it. I will count myself blessed to have enjoyed this much, to have known what love can be . . .

There followed the rest of the passage from her journal, culminating in that awful moment of irony: 'Life didn't let me down, after all.'

She added, in a postscript:

S and I are so alike, we both lose weight and interest in life when we're alone. Don't be angry with me for saying this. I wish to God I were with you – Sybil.

Did Mister Love appreciate the generous spirit that made Sybil write so sympathetically of the woman who had tried to steal him away from her? I doubted it. Next time Sybil met her rival, she was sure that the other woman felt no generosity towards her.

'I saw S yesterday afternoon,' Sybil wrote to Mister Love. 'She must hate me. Her face was so hard set, her lips so tight, her hands shook when she lit a cigarette. She was coldly polite.'

Some weeks of sultry weather passed. The rains came. Sybil, yearning to believe in Mister Love's sincerity, must have had her doubts because she was still hesitating. Should she? Shouldn't she? Then she discovered something that made up her mind.

July. It was raining. She was so happy that day, the day of her good news. She bought flowers and took them round to L's flat. She let herself in with the key he had given her. (S did not have a key, she had quizzed him thoroughly about that.) Mister Love was asleep on his bed, his afternoon siesta. Before he woke up she had already pulled off her clothes and, laughing, climbed up into his arms.

Afterwards, lying with her head on his shoulder, she murmured that she had good news. 'It's something wonderful,' she said. 'Something I know you want as much as I do.'

'Let me guess,' he said, leaning up on an elbow and tracing her lips with his finger. 'Your husband is off on one of his trips. Shall we go away together, somewhere nice? The beach place in Gorai? Khandala to see the waterfalls? Wouldn't that be nice?'

'My news is much better than that,' she said, anticipating his joy when he heard it.

'Better than that? What could be better than that? Tell me.'

'I'm pregnant,' she said, and waited for his smile.

He remained silent.

'We're going to have a child,' she said, almost as if he had not understood her the first time. 'It's what you said you so much wanted.'

Still, no smile appeared on the face of Mister Love. His finger was playing around her mouth. 'A child?' he said. 'But darling, that's impossible. I thought you were taking precautions.'

'I stopped,' she said. 'When I no longer . . . with Killy. And we

313

weren't either. I stopped.' Now she was uncertain. She did not know what to make of his muted response. 'Aren't you pleased?' she tried again. 'We're going to have a child of our own.'

L's finger was abruptly withdrawn. 'It isn't the best time,' he said, rolling away. He got up and began to dress.

'Suddenly,' Sybil wrote afterwards in her diary, 'I felt naked. I *was* naked, but not until that instant had nakedness felt improper. I thought I knew him but, suddenly, there was this feeling of being a naked strumpet in a strange man's bed.'

'Of course I want to marry you,' Mister Love was saying as he stepped into his trousers. 'But this is the wrong moment.'

He began doing up the fly, one button at a time, twisting the fabric to pinch each little disc through. She must be patient. *Button.* Meanwhile she was not to worry. *Button.* He would take care of things. *Button.* There would be time in future for other children. She could not believe that she had heard this. Then of course it came to her. Relief. What a devil he was.

'You're teasing!' she said, sitting up and smiling. 'You horrible man. You've been teasing me!'

At this he gave a small smile. 'Teasing, am I? Who is teasing who around here?' 'Whom', her writer's inner voice wanted to correct, but she said nothing. 'If I am teasing, kindly tell me why did you do this? It will just cause problems.'

'What problems?' she protested, still sure that he was testing her. 'We love one another. We're not ashamed of that. Let my husband and the rest of the world say what they like.'

'You'll have to tell your husband it's his.'

'Oh, stop teasing,' she said, laughing, but no longer sure of him. 'I haven't slept with Killy since — well, several curses ago. It must have happened . . .' She stopped, recollecting that it had been the afternoon he told her she had a rival. 'Anyway it's yours,' she said. 'You know that.'

'You must tell him it is his.'

'Please my darling, don't say these things. How can I, even if I wanted to? The child is yours. It is half-Indian.'

'Then get rid of it,' said Mister Love.

She looked at him with stunned eyes. 'Darling, you can be so cruel. Don't say things you don't mean. I know you like teasing, but I beg you, don't joke about this.'

'I am not joking,' replied her Soul of Love. 'You must be crazy if you think this is a joke. You come here and announce you are pregnant. You say your baby is not your husband's. You tell me it is half-Indian. All right, I'll accept that. Half-Indian it may be, but how can I be sure it is mine?'

'My God, you are cruel. That is beneath contempt.'

She got up and began awkwardly to dress, but her fingers were shaking too much to do up the buttons.

She said, 'I don't know why you're doing this. I can't believe you mean these things. Perhaps I shouldn't have sprung the news on you, but I thought you'd be happy! This is our baby, for God's sake.' By now she was crying. 'After all, we're going to be married.'

His next words tore her heart out. 'Do you expect me to marry every woman I sleep with?'

'Do you really expect me to marry every woman I sleep with?' He turned and walked away. When she heard Mister Love speak those words, Sybil was stunned. Then, for a few blind instants, her tears turned to rage. She shouted, 'I can't believe you said that! I really can't!'

There was a bottle of water that he kept by his bed. Sybil picked it up, holding it by the neck. His back was towards her. He was standing at the window, looking out at the sea. Sybil lifted the bottle. For a moment she intended to slam it down on his head. Then she put it back and left, brushing past a tear-blurred shape that was the servant who, having heard raised voices, was hovering outside the bedroom door.

I left L's flat on Nepean Sea Road and began walking. It was raining, but it did not matter. Where I went did not matter. Anywhere would do. All places were the same. I walked up to the top of Malabar Hill, to the Hanging Gardens, where the Old Woman's Shoe stands. The tears would not stop. People were staring, so I left and walked along Ridge Road to Walkeshwar, to the temple of Hanuman. For the first time in my adult life I stood and prayed, oblivious to the fact that my prayer was to a Hindu deity. I prayed as if my heart would burst, asking for guidance, for clarity, and, I am afraid, asking that it all prove to be a mistake, that L would ring me to say that he had, after all, been teasing. I don't remember making the decision to go down the hill, but at one point on the long descent I found myself passing the Governor's House. How often had we dined there with Killy's grand friends? And what would they make of her now, this woman who never was cut out to be a memsahib, this soaked, defeated figure wandering without purpose among the common people on Chowpatty beach?

On Marine Drive she came to herself, sitting on the sea wall somewhere beyond Churchgate. The rain had stopped and the sky had cleared. The sun was setting over the sea. White-clad families out for evening strolls regarded her with curious eyes. A peanut hawker passed, his little pot of coals glowing in the deepening blue of dusk. Streaks of orange and violet over the sea, a sharp whiff of charcoal, roasting nuts: all these things she would remember for the rest of her life.

Sybil did not want to go home and had nowhere else to go. At last she stopped a taxi and went back to the house. Everything was quite normal. The ayah was trying to get Phoebe to bed, Phoebe was protesting that she wanted to wait up to see her father. Sybil said, yes of course she would read her a story. Thank God, thank God, thank God, a part of her mind kept repeating, that she had not been honourable enough to tell Killy. Thank God.

Her situation nonetheless was precarious. A pregnancy could not be hidden for long. She longed to keep the baby, but realised that Killy would never agree. What was she to do? Would he throw her out? Divorce her? Force her to have the child adopted? Unless . . . but no, that was impossible. For a woman like Noor, perhaps, with an Indian husband and an Indian lover. Or any number of women back home. But in her case, the fact of adultery could not be hidden. It came home to her that she was alone in a strange country, with no one to whom she could turn for help. She had never before needed access to large sums of money, but a large sum was needed now. The idea of abortion terrified her. Abortions were dangerous, illegal and very expensive. How could she get the money? Whom could she ask? How could she repay them?

May turned to June. Killy saw his pretty wife wandering the

house, 'all distrait', as he put it, and thought that perhaps she was suffering a nervous breakdown. It would explain why her feelings for him had changed, why she would no longer perform her conjugal duty. Nervous collapses were a common feature of British life in India. They had happened a good deal in the old days. Soldiers who could no longer bear the heat, flies and dust went 'all distrait' so frequently that a special military psychiatric hospital was opened in the small cantonment town of Deolali, in Bombay State. The condition was known as 'going doolally'.

Sybil was going doolally. Symptoms. Endless rain in the world outside. Rain inside. A feeling like the ocean welling up within, constantly jittery, on the edge of tears, unable to concentrate. The feeling that all her friends somehow *knew* about her secret shame and were avoiding her. The telephone in the house had stopped ringing. Sometimes it just would *not* stop, but the calls were all for Killy. Desperation. Looking out across the sea, glittering between squalls, and wanting to die, Sybil thought of suicide. Unable. Guilt. Thought of those left behind. The need, above all, to protect her innocent daughter. All these things she wrote in her journal, locked her box and hid the key away between her breasts.

A woman friend, whom she did not name in her journal, gave Sybil the money she needed. The same unnamed friend helped, by discreet enquiry, to find a doctor prepared to end the pregnancy. The abortionist was a European. Sybil told him she wanted to die, and he obliged by cutting her with such savage ineptitude that she bled for a week. The operation was performed in the morning. Sybil kissed Phoebe before she left for school, and took a taxi through the city's flooded streets. She had to pick her way, the last few yards, between puddles of stinking brown water. Bombay's sewers had a habit of upgushing after heavy rain. The 'clinic' turned out to be a single, insanitary room above a busy road. The doctor worked without a nurse, in fact without any assistance. Just him and Sybil in the room with damp walls which contained a table covered with a towel on which she was to lie. In a corner, on the floor, was a primus stove on which a pan of water balanced, simmering. Knives and syringes were laid out on a towel nearby. Also jars of tea and sugar and a packet of biscuits.

'I am always well prepared,' said the doctor, when, terrified but trying to be brave, she commented on this. 'We are going to be here quite some time.'

He was fair-haired, fortyish, and spoke with a strong German accent. He told Sybil that she should not worry, he had studied medicine in Berlin, before the war. Was chased out by the Nazis. He told her to remove her underwear and lie on the table.

'Don't I need to change? Properly I mean?' She had imagined green gowns, the doctor scrubbed, masked and gloved.

'No need for the top half. Just the panties.'

There was nowhere to change.

'So I won't ask what you have been doing,' he said, as she reached under her skirt to take them off. 'Don't tell me, I don't want to know. Now please, on the table.'

There was nowhere to put them, so she wadded them up and put them in her handbag. She climbed onto the table and lay stiff as a corpse. The tears began when she felt his hands on her, pulling her dress up around her waist, lifting her knees, pushing them apart. Her body shook with waves of shame and humiliation. 'Oh God,' she sobbed, 'I want to die. Please let me die.'

'Well now, that would cause me some problems,' he said in a

jovial tone. 'Please try to relax. Later, you will be fine. I have seen many ladies in your situation. Always the pretty ones, always the regret, always too late. And usually, if they are European, it is because the father was not. I am right, eh?'

He bent over her. 'It will hurt a bit,' she heard him say. 'Not for long. A few minutes. Not so bad. You must not make a noise. What we are doing is illegal.'

Where last she had been caressed by L's warm fingers, she felt the cold touch of metal.

Hours passed. She did not know how many. She lay on her back and got to know every crack in a ceiling crazed with pain. 'No risks,' he had said. 'I would like to give you an anaesthetic, but I can't. They can go wrong, and I am not equipped to deal with that.'

At some point he injected her. A long needle, directly into the womb. He hardly spoke, but Sybil could hear him humming. A tune from *Lohengrin*. He didn't tell her what might happen, so, without warning, the pain smouldering inside blazed into flame and engulfed her whole body. She began screaming and he clapped a hand over her mouth. 'Quiet! Do you want the police up here?' After a moment's panic he said, 'We need a bit of cloth. What did you do with your panties?'

She felt the fabric dragged between her teeth. 'Bite this,' he said. 'And for God's sake keep quiet.'

She felt him fumbling with his instruments between her legs and then the agony flared up again and she was gone.

In her dream Sybil was far away, on the island with L. She was lying on her back on the beach. It was hot and the sea was singing arias from Wagner. Mister Love was smiling, assuring her that everything was all right. He leaned over her and said he was just popping out for something to eat, he would be back soon.

Sybil rode back to consciousness on waves of pain. Her body was cramping, heaving like the sea, she thought, trying to cast up something on shore. From a great distance she heard the doctor's voice. 'Nearly there, nearly there now.'

She sat upright. The doctor, holding a mug of tea, was staring at something between her legs. She looked down and saw a huge clot of gore. 'Oh please, please,' she cried, 'take it away! But he said he couldn't, until the placenta came. She lay on the table waiting for eternity to pass, trying not to touch the baby.

'What happens now?' It was dark outside the room's one dingy window. Night had come, bringing more rain. Her pain had ebbed away, exposing a soul that stank like mudflats.

'Now? You go home.'

'I meant what happens to . . . ?'

He said, 'Don't concern yourself. I will dispose of it.'

'Yes, but what . . . ?' She broke off, seeing his face.

He said, 'Haven't you had enough of horror? At the end of the road, there is a facility.'

So the foetus was to be buried in the wet, stinking, municipal tip near Churchgate station. She cried at the thought of her baby flung out with the garbage. There was no relief from the rain.

For weeks she was very ill. He had hurt her inside. She dared not go to the family doctor. Her woman friend (why did she not name her, obviously it was Maya?) came to visit and took her to a clinic, which wanted to admit her. Sybil refused. They gave her drugs, which eased the pain but could not stop the nightmares. She fled to Ambona to recover, taking Phoebe with her. This was the first of the three summers they came to spend with us.

> No nightmare is worse than my daylight imaginings. For weeks after I lost her I could feel her struggling inside me. Even now I fancy that I remember her very last kick, on my left side. She wanted to be born, but poor thing, had no strength left. Phoebe's sister, I am sure she was a girl, would have been born in February.

On the date this last passage was written, she had been with us in Ambona. Now I knew why Sybil had looked so ill; why she was so withdrawn, no longer the ebullient person I had known; why Phoebe as a small child had cried behind the chicken shed; why Jula's mother had read the trouble in her eyes.

> The world is beautiful and I am empty. With other people I must put on a face. The ayah especially, she must never suspect. Maya tries to lift my spirits and for Phoebe's sake I try to be cheerful, but when I am alone, in that place

where the pain and shame and rage are gathered, I start
crying and am not able to stop. Just lately, I have found
some strength in rage. I seesaw between tears and feeling
quite murderous. Against L for his cruel betrayal, against
Killy for neglecting me, but especially against myself. I
wanted the child, but lacked courage to keep it. I should
have told them all to go to hell. Because of my weakness,
my child had a hideous death. She was entitled to the
protection of my womb, and was clawed out, to meet a
fate that I cannot bear to think of. She would have been
born in February. I keep trying to imagine what she
would have looked like. I feel as if I have done murder.

During this period, my mother told us the story of *Nafisa Jaan*. No
wonder Maya had not wanted to . . . No wonder she asked Sybil
to choose something else. Why had Sybil insisted? Was it to fuel
her rage? I read *Retribution* again. Some weeks after his contemptuous dismissal of Sybil, Mister Love had a phone call from her
on 'a crackling, fading line, interrupted by loud crashes, bangs and
booms'. She told him it was thundering. An understatement, if
she was describing that afternoon.

She informed me that she was no longer pregnant and
(much of the rest was garbled by the bad connection)
seemed to be alluding to an obscure legend from the past.
But her last words, before she put the phone down, were
perfectly clear. 'It's not unborn children, but men like you
who deserve to die. I promise you, there will be retribution!'

Sybil returned to Bombay full of trepidation. The emotional wounds caused by the abortion had not healed, but two months out of sight of her husband had made her stronger. Nevertheless she was terrified at the thought of returning to him, and to the city. What if they bumped into L in a club, or at a dance? Would her reaction betray her? But Phoebe had to go back to school and there was nothing to be done but return and face whatever lay ahead.

To Sybil's surprise, Killy was full of consideration. He was kindness itself. Never in their marriage had he been so attentive. He knew that she had been ill but not, of course, the reason. Worried by her unyielding depression, he pressed her to confide in him. His very gentleness irritated her. She told him in an outburst that she hated India, hated her life, wanted to die. She expected him to be angry, but his reaction amazed her.

Killy said he blamed himself for having neglected her. Bombay in the monsoon was hell. He suggested that she take Phoebe and go to England for a long holiday. She could stay with her parents and he would try to join them for a few weeks. Hoping she would agree, he had booked two passages on an aeroplane to England. A Super Constellation. It would be the first time in her life that she had flown. Sybil, unable to believe the best of him, thought, He means to be rid of me. Returning me like faulty goods. But as she soon discovered, she was wrong.

England, after a decade away, amazed her. It seemed so *clean*. The roads were wet and spotless, the cars and lorries moved in orderly procession. No cacophony of horns. No paanwallahs squatting in crevices in South Croydon's streets. Her parents were delighted to see her, and thrilled with the child, their granddaughter Phoebe, still wearing her Ambona tan, whom they were meeting for the first time.

They went to London Zoo, to look at the tigers.

'I suppose you have seen lots in India,' said her grandfather.

'Not tigers,' replied Phoebe. 'Leopards and wild boar, mostly.'

The grandmother said to Sybil, 'Well, she's a lovely little girl. And she'll soon lose that awful Indian singsong.'

After a few weeks, Sybil began to chafe under the fussing of her mother and the unexpressed, tight-lipped worry of her father. Then Killy arrived. He said he had taken two months' leave from the business, and she knew this must have been difficult to arrange. Killy was full of plans for their holiday. He would take her out dancing. They would revisit all their old haunts, the places 'where we did our courting'. The old-fashioned phrase made Sybil smile. They had a candlelit dinner at the little French restaurant in Soho where he had proposed. Their elderly waiter made a fuss of Sybil and said he remembered them well.

'What nonsense,' she said. 'I bet you put him up to it.'

Killy admitted that he had, and then they were both giggling. He caught up her hands in his, and said again that he regretted how he had neglected her. She knew him well enough to tell that he was sincere. Killy said he had come to realise how hard it must have been for her in India. But things would be different. He would show her, he would make amends. He reached inside his dinner jacket and produced a ticket.

'Just the two of us,' he said. 'A second honeymoon.'

A ferry ticket. They'd hire a car and drive. And in Dijon . . . In Chamonix . . . In Venice . . . Killy was wonderful. In the glorious scenery of the Alps, she forgot her sadness and acquired a tan. In her diary were two pages from a letter she had written to Maya.

. . . in Chamonix, where the peaks are the way children draw them. Wearing pointy wizard-hats of snow. K has been so kind. Not at all what I expected. I don't know what to think. I was sure our choices had been made, but now — I don't know — for the first time in months, I find myself thinking there is hope, and I'm frightened. My God, if he knew. Must be careful he doesn't see this. He knows I'm writing to you.

Later. Finally reached Venice last evening. Putting up in a small hotel in the Canareggio. K immediately wanted to go for a walk. We crossed a wide bridge into a maze of lanes and tiny canals, then found ourselves at the Bridge of Sighs. Thence via more alleys to St Mark's where we sat at a table in the square, rather chilly, and listened to the violinist at Florian's. A dark-skinned boy came up selling roses and K bought me one. I tell you, it is making me nervous. The child reminded me of the gardener's little boy in Ambona, the same huge dark eyes . . . I thought of you, your immense kindness this summer. What would I have done without you . . . We've just been out to lunch. He is still being sweet. Woe is me, I am so confused. He goes back to Bombay next week. Flying, imagine! His plan is that Phoebe and I stay in England a few weeks longer, until November. But already I think my decision is made. I'll come back. K promises things will be different. He will be at home more. We will do things together. At Christmas we will go to friends in Simla and see in the New Year. 1959. Isn't it strange, Maya, all the years I've been in India and I have never seen the Himalayas?

When the time came for him to fly back to Bombay, she did not want him to go. Freezing England now seemed intolerable.

By November, when the 'cold weather' starts in Bombay, she had recovered sufficiently to return. Would Killy have reverted to his old ways? What would happen if she met Mister Love?

But Killy was still the new, marvellous, considerate Killy. Her friends were delighted to see her, and brought her up to date with the gossip: My dear, did you hear about that madman Sub? What he did *this* time? Gradually, she began to rebuild her life.

A few weeks later, Killy whisked her off to friends in Simla. Snow and log fires. They had a good Christmas and New Year. Killy was still very solicitous and, for the first time in a decade, her marriage seemed worthwhile. By the spring, she felt restored.

Some diary entries from the new year, 1959.

January 3rd
Killy is up in arms because a report has appeared in today's papers of a 'colour bar' at his Breach Candy Club. Why he should be so surprised, I don't know, since there clearly *is* a 'no wogs' policy. *Blitz* has issued A CALL TO ALL PATRIOTS to attend a mass rally on Republic Day, the 26th. Killy says Indians are absurdly touchy about national pride and a 'demonstration' on Republic Day is a

shameless tactic to heat the blood. *Blitz* published the sign that hangs in the club, complete with strange capitalisation, which I will copy faithfully as follows:

THESE PREMISES ARE A HERITAGE OF THE EUROPEAN INHABITANTS OF BOMBAY. VESTED IN THEM FOR ALL TIME BY A TRUST DEED DATED THE 3RD FEBRUARY 1876. ONLY THEY AND THEIR GUESTS OF EUROPEAN ORIGIN TO WHOM THEY EXTEND THE PRIVILEGE ARE ELIGIBLE FOR ADMISSION.

January 6th
The Dalda Writing Contest has been won by someone called Coralie Atzenweiler. I wonder if Maya knows her. The contest has a ridiculous ring, when you know that Dalda is a white cooking fat rather like sloppy lard. The absurd names continue into the consolation prizes, with a Mr D. D. Dhanjikanjibarfiwala among the winners.

January 10th
SIXTY YEARS AGO. 1899: CRIME OF PASSION. A terrible tragedy is reported from Bandora, near Bombay. Captain Iremonger, of the Durham Light Infantry, was shot by an engineer named Gregory, on the staff of the Great Indian Peninsular Railway. Mr Gregory afterwards shot his wife dead and blew out his own brains. Captain Iremonger lies in a precarious condition. Jealousy, says the *Central News*, is alleged to

have been the motive of the crime, Mrs Gregory having been constantly in the company of the captain.

January 24th
Poor old Killy. Today's news is quite surreal. *Blitz* has printed an open letter from the Mayor of Bombay about Breach Candy, full of fine-sounding phrases and honest outrage. Killy gloomily says he can see the time coming when Indians will have to be allowed to join. 'Depressing thought, isn't it?' I don't find it so, but am so grateful to Killy for his wonderful transformation that I don't have the heart to argue. Killy read me part of a letter one of his members had planned to send to *The Times of India*. 'Dear Indians, We know you love us very much. So much that you want to do everything we do, and be with us all the time, wherever we are. We love you very much too. All we ask is somewhere we can be by ourselves now and again.'

A person calling himself 'Vox Populi' has written to Prince Philip about the 'colour bar'. But Philip and the rest of the British establishment are apparently still reeling from the fact that the Russians have sent something called a Sputnik into space.

January 31st
Nehru's daughter, Indira Gandhi, is to be President of the Indian National Congress. Is it possible that one day a woman could even be Prime Minister?

February 14th

Hitchcock's new film *Vertigo* comes here in April. He is quoted as saying, 'Suspense is like a woman; the more left to the imagination, the more the excitement.'

March 20th, 1959

What a desperate business in Tibet. The Dalai Llama [*sic*] has fled to India with thousands of his monks. His favourite saying is: 'For as long as space endures, And for as long as living beings remain, Until then may I too abide, To dispel the misery of the world.'

April 18th, 1959

With Killy and Phoebe to the Excelsior to see *Limelight*. *Vertigo* is on at the Regal. We can't take Phoebe. But *Tom Thumb* is on next week at the Metro and Killy says we can all go and see that together. We are a proper little family and I am happy again for the first time in years.

April 27th, 1959

Lunch at Bombelli's. Played U and Non-U with Zafyque and Jo. What a relief! I am predominantly U.

On this day, Sybil's diaries came to an abrupt and startling stop.

Phoebe phoned me to say she was in London, and asked me to meet her at her hotel. Didn't say why. We ate lunch in a strange underground dining room, black walls decorated with lacquered oriental birds. She seemed nervous and picked at her starter – some sort of salad – a finely sliced tomato and sprig of basil in a splash of oil.

'Nine seventy-five for that? Bit steep, isn't it?'

'Just as well it's my treat,' she said. 'I know booksellers are always broke.'

'Not all booksellers. James Heneage isn't broke. Just this one.' I was making my delighted and unaccustomed way through a ginger soup accompanied by tiny prawn dumplings.

Phoebe said, 'That reminds me, I've got you a little present.' Leaning forward she added in a mysterious whisper, 'But I can't give it to you till later. Don't let me forget.'

She was wearing one of those sun dresses that seems designed to reveal more than it covers. Optimism, I thought, is dressing for summer in May. Last time I saw her, it had been mid-winter. After which, another mysterious silence.

She said, 'I loved reading about Jula, but I can't get used to him being called Mitra. And Dost. Did I get his name right? Dost? To rhyme with toast?'

'Nearly.' She should have used the soft dental 'd' and 't', but these sounds don't exist in English.

There was an awkwardness between us this time which hadn't

331

been there before. I guessed she was thinking about her mother's diaries. Was she regretting having asked me to read them? They were so intimate and painful. And came to that shocking full-stop. Shocking at least to me, because I knew what had happened next. Or thought I knew. It was impossible to be sure.

The conundrum was this: I was now sure that *Retribution* had been inspired by Sybil's diaries. The diaries stopped on April 27th 1959, the day on which, and according to *Retribution*, Mister Love had been murdered. But my man had checked the *Blitz* archive back to January and forward to August. No such murder had been recorded. Had Maya, elaborating on Sybil's 'murderous' feelings, concluded *Retribution* with a fictitious murder? That was one possibility. On the other hand, if the murder was invented, why was Maya so specific about the date? Why did Sybil, on that very day, abandon her diary for ever? And why, within a few days more, did she take Phoebe out of school and flee to Ambona with Rosie and the hastily appointed Daruwalla?

Phoebe thought something had happened in India to ruin her parents' lives. I assumed she knew about Sybil's failed love affair, and her abortion. But the diaries said nothing about murder. The question was, should I?

'I liked the description of the hashish bazaar,' Phoebe was saying. 'But I find it odd to think of you there.'

So far, although she must have been burning to question me, she had carefully avoided any mention of the diaries. I decided that I wouldn't bring the subject up. For my part I was wondering why there had again been such a long silence before she contacted me. The air between us fairly shimmered with ghosts. That's what a ghost is, Maya used to say, an unanswered question.

'I wasn't always a stick-in-the-mud,' I said.

'I told you before, you shouldn't run yourself down. You're a fascinating, exciting man.'

Her eyes held mine above the napkin she lifted to dab at her mouth. To my great astonishment she did not appear to be joking.

'Sure you're not getting me mixed up with someone else?' When we were children she had been my loyallest supporter. Not since then had I received such unstinting regard from any female. And last time we met she had backed me in among the coats and kissed me.

'I predict that one day soon you're going to surprise yourself,' she said. 'Would you mind signalling the waiter?'

The man duly materialised from the darkness between a pair of lacquered dragons to remove our plates. Phoebe poured wine. My glass was still nearly full, hers empty. Her third, at least. She reached into her handbag and fished out a gold lighter.

'Do you mind? I know I shouldn't, between courses, but . . .'

She lit her blasted cigarette — I hate the damned things — her unease was palpable, and catching. What was the problem? Why had she asked me so suddenly to lunch? Was it really her mother's forty-year-old diaries? Or some other reason? Maybe I should have asked after her husband, or said, 'Isn't it time you told me where you live?' There was so much about her I didn't know.

'One day I'd like to eat with you in that café,' said Phoebe. 'In the street with the vegetable smell. It could hardly be more different than this.' I realised she was still talking about my report on Jula. 'Your mother was a writer. Have you ever considered it yourself? Writing something, I mean. Could you do it?'

As a matter of fact I had. Every bookseller worth his salt

thinks he can do as well as the authors whose works line his walls. We see what people buy, we have a nose for what sells. Why not?

'So what's it about, your story?'

Again those childhood mannerisms, leaning her head a little to one side before she said something, closely scrutinising my lips as I replied. They now seemed peculiarly intimate.

'*Was* it about? I haven't touched it in years.'

It was the tale of a man much like me, who, in his mid-forties, finds himself longing for a bit of adventure (being a bookseller I made him a book-*keeper*). One day he sees an advertisement for a correspondence course on how to become a private detective and on a whim sends off for it. As the lessons arrive, each teaching a different skill – how to shadow a mark without being spotted, how to eavesdrop on conversations, how to grub for evidence in people's garbage, how to steam open envelopes and carry out dead letter drops – he practises on his neighbours and friends, with ludicrous and, finally, devastating results.

'It sounds fun,' she said. 'Why did you give it up?'

'It's still in a drawer somewhere.'

The waiter reappeared, flourishing magnificent platters, black porcelain with gold chinoiserie, each bearing the artistically arrayed minimum that could be called a meal: hers was fish of some sort, halibut perhaps, steamed in little lettuce parcels, mine a tagine of lamb with lemon and olives.

'Well,' she said, when we had replenished our glasses and were addressing the tiny portions. 'What drives your man? *Fundamentally.*'

I was forced to ponder this. I had the character, a few incidents and even a notion for an ending, but most of the story was still a bright mist. I planned to have my hero narrate his story in that downbeat first-person style which is de rigueur for serious private dicks, but what *drove* him? I had never been quite sure. 'Love,' I said, taking a stab at it. 'Love, I suppose, *fundamentally*.'

She said, 'Everyone writes about love. Maybe you should try something more interesting.'

'Like what?'

'Revenge,' she said. 'Maybe he wants to take revenge.'

'He's not that sort of character.' I couldn't imagine my manqué detective wanting revenge on anyone. 'There's not much humour in revenge.'

'That isn't what I meant.' She leaned over and speared an olive from my plate. Licked it, then held it for a moment between her teeth before sucking it in and crunching.

'Bhalu, what I mean is a story not about revenge, but written *to avenge*.'

'I don't follow.'

'All right. Let's take your bookseller. Book-*keeper*. One day he finds out that, many years ago, something very evil was done to a person he loved. Something unforgivable. A cruel, heartless crime, that destroyed her life. But the crime never came to light, and the criminal was never punished. So you go back to investigate.'

'Wait a minute,' I said. 'How many years ago? Goes back where? And *who* goes back?' Here it came at last, her mother's diaries. But what a tortuous way to bring the subject up.

'Doesn't matter how long,' she said. 'What happened was so evil that it can *never* be forgotten, or forgiven. It must be punished.'

She means Mr Love's cruelty, I was thinking. But her mother's diaries stopped before the end of the story. Phoebe obviously doesn't know that Mister Love was killed for his sins.

'But Phoebe, what if the man – or woman, of course – who did this vile thing is dead?'

She said sharply, 'What makes you think it was a woman?'

Only then did it occur to me that I had never given any thought to the question of *who* had murdered Mister Love.

The exquisite but ephemeral meal was over. We resisted the ninja-like waiter's attempts to tempt us with chocolate comma, blueberry coulis, blackberry mousse and a melting cheese which, he said, was a species of vegetarian Brie. Our coffee was spiced with cardamom and cost more than an entire meal at the sort of cafés I frequented in Lewes. Phoebe sat twisting her napkin. She was not wearing her wedding ring, I noticed. The awkwardness of earlier once more interposed itself.

'Thank you for the excellent meal,' I said. 'I don't often eat like this. In fact I've *never* eaten like this.'

Phoebe seemed to come to a decision. She leaned forward and said, 'Bhalu, I've got to tell you. I've been desperate to see you. I mean, on our own.'

'Really?'

I cursed myself for sounding so gauche. The impossible thought occurred that she might be going to kiss me again.

'Yes, really. You see, there's something I want to tell you. I don't know whether I should. I've been struggling.'

'If you want to, you should,' I said.

'Can I?'

'Of course.'

'*Anything?*'

'Anything at all.'

She sighed. 'That's what I thought. You know, Bhalu, we are twin souls. We're joined by fate. Don't you feel it too?'

She reached out and took my hands. 'I'm sure it's not by chance that we met again. What happened to us, when we were children – it binds us. Do you see that? Our lives are wound round one another's.'

As a child she'd had hay-coloured plaits, incapable of retaining a ribbon, no matter how tightly, intricately knotted. Poor luckless Rosie used to get annoyed when she came home without them. The Ambona hills must have been littered with her scraps of satin. Today her hair fell softly to the neck and was cut in that style still favoured by women who grew up in the sixties, a fringe that gets in the eyes. What was she like as a young woman? We had missed the best years of each other's lives.

'Bhalu, other people don't understand. Katy thinks I'm a threat to her.' She brushed her fingers over my forehead. 'Don't frown. Grey at the temples suits you, by the way.'

'Nonsense!'

'No, you're sitting there with your mouth open, ready to tell me I'm wrong, but I'm not. Women have instincts and mine is that Katy doesn't like me. Not one little bit. Maybe she thinks I'll try to take you away from her. But she's wrong. I already *have* you. We already have each other. We've belonged to each other since we were eight years old. You're the truest, deepest friend I ever had. But we've become strangers. I'm so afraid you won't feel the same about me.'

I held her hands. Here was the cause of our awkwardness. We both so badly wanted to prove that our childhood friendship could and would effortlessly translate to the present that we daren't open up, reveal our new grown-up selves, in case we discovered after all that we had nothing in common. And I'd thought it was just me who worried about this, who feared that the adult I had become betrayed the promise of the child I had been. She was right. We were bound, and we were strangers. Certainly I very much wanted to know her. Despite the long hiatus, she was precious to me in the way that people are who have loved each other with the absolute commitment of small children.

'I had this feeling,' said Phoebe, 'that I could tell you anything. *Anything* at all and you wouldn't be judgmental. I feel that you wouldn't think the worse of me . . .'

'I can't imagine . . .'

'Bhalu, suppose I proved to be the sort of person you wouldn't want to associate with?'

'I associate with Piglet, so I don't think you've much to worry about,' I said, not sure where this was going. 'Are you trying to tell me you've done something bad?'

'No,' she said. 'At least, not yet.'

She gave a deliciously wry smile, one that began with lips pursed like a rosebud and widened slowly into a grin.

Searching her face for a clue, and finding nothing except the now fading smile, I realised again how much I had missed. I had not known her during the years that formed her face and could only guess at what might have incised the laughter lines at the corners of her eyes and the creases that ran either side of her mouth – but her eyes, grey flecked with green, were the eyes I had known as a child.

'Have you ever had an affair?'

This took me completely by surprise.

'No,' I lied. 'Have you?'

Whatever she might have said next was stifled by the approach of our waiter, all in black to match the crypt-like dining room.

Afterwards, she took me to her suite, a sumptuous white-on-white apartment done out in what purported to be Corfiot style with a four-poster bed engulfed in clouds of muslin. There was nowhere to sit, except a sort of step where the floor dropped into a bay window, so we sat on the bed.

She said, 'Bhalu, you must have guessed I didn't bring you here just to have lunch.'

'No? What, then?'

I hoped she had missed the tiny catch in my voice. Stupid to imagine, wrong to think . . . but I'd been aware of her all through the meal – her perfume, the graceful lacuna between her breasts as she leaned to lift that olive, the curl of her tongue taking a lick at it – and she'd asked if I'd ever . . .

She took my hand. 'It's so hard to believe. All these years apart, but the feelings are all still there.'

'My God,' I said, 'you are trembling.'

'Bhalu, I'm very afraid about . . . what I'm doing here with you. It's probably a bad idea. Whatever happens, I don't want it to spoil things.'

She stared at me with those strange eyes from my childhood. I could feel my doubts dissolving, animal stirrings. I was ready to betray.

'Oh, I don't think it will,' I said.

'I told you, I feel as if I can trust you with anything. Can I?'

'Of course you can.'

She released my hand, dipped into her bag and pulled out a thick notebook with a green and yellow cover. 'I brought this. I want you to read it. It's Mummy's last journal. From 1993.'

The notebook lay on the bed between us. I was floundering in a swamp of what I informed myself was relief, but which felt a great deal like regret.

Phoebe took a breath. 'Oh God, Bhalu, I feel so terrified about this. What will you think? This journal begins in England, and there's lots of things in it. But it ends during a trip she made to India, about six years ago. She wouldn't tell me why she was going. And when she came back she wouldn't say why she'd been. A couple of months later she died, and I found this by her bed.'

Desire ebbs so painfully slowly.

'Shall I take it with me?'

'No,' she said, 'I want you to read it now. Just the last few pages. I daren't risk anyone else seeing them. I should have burnt it.'

'Why, what's in it?'

'You've read the diaries?'

'Yes.' I had still not told her about *Retribution*.

'You know my mother had an affair . . . it ended badly. She had an abortion.'

'Yes, I'm sorry.'

'I've never had anything like that – an adulterous affair, I mean – so I don't know, forgive me . . . I wondered if you . . . ? The man was murdered.'

An electric panic surged up my spine. At a stroke, the whole enormity of what *Retribution* meant was made clear. It had been true. In which case, everything connected with it was true . . . and Maya had taken the blame for his death on herself.

'How do you know this?' I asked at last.

'Mummy told me. And it's in here.' Tapping the notebook with a long fingernail.

'Bhalu, I'm very afraid that I know who murdered him.'

The Arabs are sitting on the sea wall laughing in the rain. They are mostly from Dubai, dusty sons of the desert, and come here every year at this time to marvel at the monsoon. Shankar, the room waiter, told me this. He says the staff don't like them because they are dirty and let their children urinate on the floor and shit in cupboards, but the hotel puts up with it because they tip well, hundreds of rupees a time and pay over the odds for everything. For a moment just now I thought I saw L sitting on the wall among them. In an instant it all came back, the ammoniacal taint that clung to me in those months after his murder, the constant terror that I would be uncovered. I thought I should never get over it, but in time it became less terrible and, I suppose, though I did not count how many years it took, there came a day when I woke up and it was not the first thing on my mind.

I came back to India for three weeks and find three days hard to stand. The days waste away as they did when I first arrived in 1948. The smells, the mustiness, the damp heat, the unfresh beds, the sourness in the bread, all the parts of the whole taintedness are still here. I feel the same frustration as evening arrives; the fan churns up hot air, and one is cramped uncomfortably on a screwed-up bed pretending to read, while another day whiles into night with nothing achieved.

Perhaps L has returned to haunt me. After all, isn't that why I'm here, to lay the ghost, as once the man? Shankar, the room boy, has just brought me a bottle of whisky. Also two bottles of soda. There is rust under the rim where he flipped the cap off. He placed his hand on his heart, bowed and backed from the room. He has a caste mark right in the middle of his forehead. A large red dot. A bullet hole, like the one that killed L.

They are drumming now, down below. This is the first time I've watched the moon rise in India since I was with Maya in Ambona. God, Indian whisky is disgusting. Why did I come back? My joke in London was that I would bring presents for such as may still remember me, and stay just long enough to buy presents to take back. Phoebe said, 'You're not a pedlar, carrying gifts and goods backwards and forwards for other people.' No, I had another mission. My 69th birthday present will be to free myself from the nightmare people, from the last of them. I said to myself, 'I will go to India and find Maya. We will go back to Ambona together. Maya will know how to do what must be done.' Thirty-nine years ago, I left this place. Now I want to go to *The Times of India* and read the old papers to relive what I felt then. Pain, dread of exposure. I could almost hear S, my rival in love, gloating: 'You really thought you'd got away with it, didn't you, Sybil, dear?' L was dead but they would not let the story die. They poked and foraged and pried and came very close, but never did learn the truth, and when there was nothing left to report, his ghost started appearing all over the city.

Even now, at this solemn remove of time, it comes back, the flickery hysteria I felt when I read that L's ghost had been seen walking near the flat in Nepean Sea Road. Two nights after this debut it appeared again, this time at Flora Fountain. The sightings multiplied. In Memonwada Street, near Chor Bazaar, it accosted a man on his way to the Chicken-moholla Mosque. It mounted the statue of the black horse at Kalaghoda and sat smirking behind Edward VII. It alighted from a train at VT station and dissolved into a flight of pigeons. A professor from the University spotted it smoking a cheroot on the steps of the Asiatic Library. It was seen making obscene gestures on the forecastle of a naval destroyer and simultaneously begging from passing cars at Kemp's Corner. On its first outing L's spectre wore a sober business suit, but by the end its costume was invariably a blood-stained bathtowel. It was at about this time that street hawkers all over the city began selling copies of the towel L was wearing when he died, printed with his name in big blood-dripping letters. His real name, of course, not 'Mister Love' which was my pet name for him, which only Maya and I knew. What a bitter misnomer. He never missed a chance to tell me, as I assume he told all the other pretty married women who were his accustomed prey, that in Hindi his name meant 'love'.

Maya, how ironic that I should come here to look for you – sent by Zul in guise of an angel – only to learn that you have been living in England for years. How did we lose touch? We were close as sisters, 'les inséparables' — isn't that what Sub used to call us? But afterwards I hated all and everything to do with India, yes even you, Maya. Impossibly far away it seems — Ambona, hills crouched under flights of rain that summer, when I told you about my botched love affair, my fear of Killy finding out; to be unfaithful was bad enough, but with an Indian? And that was before L's death. I told you how, when I found I was expecting L's child I went to him imagining his joy, and said, 'Here is our child, that you wanted.' His face, upon which no smile appeared. His cold-hearted reply, my disbelieving tears, then the contemptuous, unforgivable suggestion that I pass it off as my husband's. God, how he must have despised me. Even then, he had another insult to hurl. 'Get rid of it. Do you expect me to marry every woman I sleep with?'

Well, now there is nothing left. We shall not meet again in this life. My hope lay in being released. My dear Maya, you will surely be astonished to get this letter from me — it must be thirty years since my last. Oh Maya, what regrets. And what irony that I should come all the way here to find you. My dearest Maya, I can just imagine your amazement to get this letter from your old friend Sybil Killigrew, much less a letter written from Bombay even though it must go back to find you in England and O God the thought of going back appals me, the work I came for undone, and if you are wondering what am I doing here, I came looking for you, sent by angelic Zul in disguise because there was something that I decided I must do and only you could help me. But Christ, you are not here. Dearest Maya, well, here am I, good old Sybil K, scouring the stinking midden that is Bombay looking for you and it turns out all along that you are in England, and separated too, so Homi Mehra tells me. Old age alas has not improved him. Maya is in England, he said, but no one knows where, no one has heard from her in years. So be it. Tomorrow I will go alone to Ambona to look for it . . .

Well I went and the directions I have carried locked in my brain for nearly forty years were no use. No use at all. I need you Maya, but what directions will find you? Look, here's an empty bottle. If I go out on the balcony and throw it hard enough – put a message in it first, it would have about as much chance of finding you – will it reach the sea?

Didn't. Bottle made foul racket, banged off car, smashed in gutter. I ducked back and turned off my light. They will blame it on the Arabs. Sybil K performs familiar Houdini act. Writing in darkness. The moon is still up, but hard-faced, mean, and very high. Can't see, can hear. Waves bursting on the sea wall, drunken words racing across the page. In the dark, their voices can come back to me. L and his child murdered within a year, skull of the father passed around in court, to see the path of bullets, corpse of the fledgling tipped in refuse bin.

What mangled mind survived that loved you both?

Child, speak. I have come back — a wave or two of sea from where you were conceived. Make contact with me tonight; the touch of mind at most is all I need to be released. By your sea, in sound of surf and with your father who is with you, release you me so that I can end this play. Child unborn, by your consent alone, I can be sent to sleep. Blot out the rest. I never found love in this world that measured mine . . . I am the cavern and the roaring seas; history and the span of time. I kill my young when occasion suits.

Garbage, speak! You, who ended in the Churchgate trash thrown out by the refugee from Hitler — no mercy — he escaped Hitler but he did not spare you. By our joint consent you perished by knife, passed to the waiting garbage heap.

Deal as you will. The devil does not beg. God deals in love, but I in death. Should you be lenient, I'll kill you both again. L didn't love me. He told me so. And other people too. When you use someone in the name of love, you deserve to be murdered.

By surf & stinking sea six bullets and a knife, remember me, Nepean Sea, Prem Ahuja and his child, remember me. Because I was not loved I killed. I AM YOUR RETRIBU-TION !

V SHAITAN

Phoebe's eyes never once left my face as I read her mother's last journal. When I looked up I would catch her gazing at me, almost in terror. She fumbled once for a cigarette, but put it away again, unlit. When I reached the black waves of self-hatred in which Sybil was drowning, her writing growing erratic, the letters larger and crazier, the pen slashing, making jagged loops, stabbing at the paper, I grew more and more fascinated and horrified; until, when the words had swollen, so monstrous and misshapen that it took barely three of them, sprawling across the paper, to fill up a line, there came an earth-heaving shock, dumbfound astoundment and the world's walls collapsed.

'Oh God!' she cried. 'Look at your face! Well, now you know!'

Yes, now I knew.

Phoebe was terrified that her mother had been a murderess. This struck me as so ludicrous that I burst out laughing.

'Phoebe. Phoebe, darling, your mother didn't kill him.'

Here I am after all, hugging her, cuddling her, pressing kisses onto her rainy cheek.

'Darling Phoebe, listen to me,' I said. 'I know that Sybil *says* she killed him. I know you *think* she did. But she didn't! She can't have.'

The truth was so much stranger. So bizarre, so overwhelming, that I didn't know how to tell her.

Phoebe was crying, making small snivelling sounds. Her nose was starting to run, but she didn't seem to be aware of it. Déjà vu.

Thus I had found her once, crouching among the chickens. I kissed her cheek again, and let her go.

'Don't cry, my dear, darling Phoebe,' I said. 'Look, I'm going to show you. I'm going to prove that your mother was completely innocent.' I picked up the notebook, and opened it to where the writing ended, in huge stark capital letters. She shook her head from side to side, like a child.

'Just here. You see? She finally names Mister Love. She gives us his real name . . .'

I stopped. The sight of that name again stopped my breath. Surely, surely, I was thinking, this is impossible. It could not have been. Phoebe leant against the white, upholstered bedhead, staring at me with wet eyes, saying nothing at all.

'Phoebe, if that name meant anything to you, you'd know that Sybil didn't kill him. Not a chance. Couldn't in a million years have killed him. Phoebe, I *know* who Mister Love was. I *know* who killed him. *Everybody knows.* It happened when I was away at boarding school. A huge scandal. In all the papers. Listen . . .'

I told the story, as far as I could remember it. The rich Sindhi seducer, the English wife of an Indian naval officer. The jealous husband going to the playboy's flat. Shooting him. The scandal and sensation of the trial. I could still hardly believe that the story told in *Retribution* referred to this shooting, because if it did, it meant that Phoebe's mother and mine had been entangled (incredible thought) in the most notorious case ever to come before an Indian court: the trial of Commander Kawas Nanavati of the Indian Navy for the killing of Prem Bhagwandas Ahuja.

Phoebe heard me out in silence, her face expressionless, a strange response to my good news.

When I stopped talking, she said, 'I'm sorry, but that doesn't make sense. Because if that's true, then tell me Bhalu, why was my mother being blackmailed?'

Blackmailed?

She began to cry again, and wouldn't stop. The violence of her grief was appalling. What could I do? I hugged her to me and felt the great snorting sobs shaking her body, pumping her ribcage, flattening her breasts against me. Please, Fever, stop, shhh, shhh, shhh. I pressed my mouth to her cheek and then to her mouth but still she would not stop. I was quite helpless. Her cries sounded like those of a small, desperate animal, sobbing, crying, uttering little squeals and astonished screams of pain.

Footsteps came to the door of the room – stopped – went away again. It occurred to me that someone from the hotel thought I was injuring her. But no, in that case they would have knocked. Whoever came to the door had decided that the sobs and cries were pure pleasure, that I was royally fucking her in this palatial bed. And recalling how, only an hour earlier, I had been daydreaming about some such outcome, I realised how utterly sad it was that I knew nothing about the woman I was holding in my arms, nothing at all.

In the end she grew quiet, gave a sigh, then found a small smile and said, 'You called me Fever.'

'You didn't *really* believe your mother murdered Mister Love?'

'What else could I think? She says so, doesn't she? She says she killed him. It's unambiguous. For years, almost as long as I can remember, I'd known we had to leave India because her lover had been murdered and she was being blackmailed. But I never really understood *why*. Something to do with letters she'd written him. I found the notebook after she died. Six years ago. And then it all made obvious, horrible sense. She was blackmailed because she had murdered her lover.'

'You'd known all this, about the murder and the blackmail, since . . . when? Since you were a child?'

She gave me a rather sad smile. 'If it weren't for you, my darling Bhalu, I would never have had the chance to be a child.'

'Oh Bhalu, I nearly forgot your present.'

She reached into her handbag and brought out a tiny Indian lacquer box. Inside was a lump of a dark aromatic substance.

'I thought we could try it together,' she said. 'Oh, of course, you need cigarettes. Here, use mine.'

She sat watching me as I performed with unsteady fingers. It was at least twenty years since I'd rolled a joint. I felt rather foolish doing it.

'Prem,' she said, rolling the word around her tongue, tasting it. She rhymed it with 'hem'. It should have rhymed with 'shame'.

'So why did she call him Mister Love?'

'Because "prem" in Hindi means "love",' I told her, tapping a mixture of tobacco and hashish, Dost-fashion, back into the tube of the cigarette. I still couldn't believe it. The Nanavati murder.

It was tantalising. I remembered so little about it, apart from the bare outline, but knew it was huge and important.

I said, 'Tell me about this blackmail.'

Phoebe flicked her gold lighter. Drew deeply on the joint and exhaled in a gush.

'My mother used to tell me things. She couldn't talk to my dad,

354

so I was her confidante. It's why I used to like coming to stay with you, because then she would tell your mother instead.'

'What did she tell you?'

Another deep drag. Holding. Smoke flaring from her nostrils. 'She'd say things like . . .' She mimicked her mother's dipped accent.

'"He's got some letters I wrote. I shouldn't have written them, it was so *stupid* of me, but how could I ever imagine . . . ? He's got the letters, and that's that. I tell you this, darling, you must keep it a secret. No one must know. I don't know what will become of us. He wants a thousand rupees, another thousand, and I told him, 'I haven't got it. There's no more. You've bled me dry.' He said – this man said, 'You can get it from your husband,' and I said, 'You know I can't ask him.' And he said, 'Well, get it from one of your other *friends*.' You should have heard the leer in his voice, the filthy beast. But there's no one I can ask. I've spent the allowance that Daddy gives me, I can't ask Maya again. And I can't pay your school fees again, darling, and maybe this time they'll kick you out. I can't pay the cook because they've taken everything. I daren't tell your father. How can I go on living like this? Tell me. How can I . . . ?"'

Within days of Mister Love's death the phone calls began. 'A matter of procedure. A quick visit to my office should sort it out.' At his office, 'Madam, is this your handwriting? Can you confirm that you wrote these letters? Thank you, that is all.'

A month later, there was another call. 'Madam, it seems we have something more to discuss. Unfortunately, copies of your letters were made. Official records. Such things can easily fall into the

355

wrong hands. To make sure that certain people behave as we would all wish, it is necessary . . . you understand . . .'

'"No, darling, I daren't let your father find out. I daren't, I just daren't. You don't understand, you're just a child. He would *kill* me. Yes, he would. He'd take you away from me. He'd send you to boarding school and you'd be miserable. You don't want that, do you? If you tell your father, he'll take you away from me and he'd never let me see you again. But I have to pay this man, or . . ."'

Whose threats did Sybil whisper into her helpless daughter's ear? Phoebe said she did not know. She thought he was an official. Her mother had never mentioned a name. He must have been close to the investigation, or the court case, to have got hold of Sybil's letters to Ahuja. A policeman maybe. Or a court officer. He had copies of her letters and had started by threatening to show them to Killy if she did not co-operate. He wanted a lot of money. She could afford it, rich foreign bitch, rich foreign husband. Sybil knew she ought to tell Killy, but she could not. For the first time in years they had begun to find happiness together. She could not bear to hurt or humiliate him. She had to lie. And for the second time in two years Sybil found herself in desperate need of money. She sold possessions. She invented essential trips that she never made, and necessary items that she never bought. She stole from Killy. But the blackmailer was never satisfied.

'Mrs Killigrew?' The cold voice on the phone. 'You have broken your word. The package is not here as agreed. Do I have to point out the conseqences?'

'"Money, Phoebe darling. That's what this man wants. More

356

and more money. And I said – I went to his office in tears, imagine how hateful to cry in front of that monster – I said, 'I haven't got any left, because you've taken it all.' And this time he said, 'The lawyers in the case know about your letters. They have no plans to use them, but how long can I keep this out of the papers? Someone will talk and that is why I am trying so hard to help you. But if you can't pay, dear lady, we can maybe come to some *other* arrangement?' I think you know what he meant, don't you? I don't have to spell it out. I just ran from his office in disgust, and that's why I'm so desperate, you see, but I can't go to your father and I can't go back to Maya. She's already helped me as much as she can. Oh darling, don't cry, I don't want *you* to be upset, you're the only person I can talk to. You're so calm, so wise, you fill me with strength. You're my tower. You're the only reason I can go on. I'm going to tell you a secret. You must never tell anyone. Will you? Promise? So let's dry that face . . ."

'Then,' said Phoebe, 'she'd tell me some other appalling thing. Like how horrible it was to lose her baby. Bhalu, she told me all about that, in the most awful detail. And what she'd felt like when her lover was murdered. She'd tell me these things and I had to listen, and try to be strong for her, and suggest things she could do. We sat and plotted together. She'd say, "You're my best friend. You are like a deep well. I can drop my secrets into you and know that they will never come up again." But I heard a voice inside me screaming, "No, no, don't tell me these things! I can't help you, Mummy, because I'm only a child".'

I thought of the little girl who so desperately wanted to visit the temple on top of the mountain, to make her wish come true.

The afternoon was wearing on. We had smoked another two

hashish-laced cigarettes, lying side by side on her bed as we talked. The mixture of wine at lunch and dope had made me drowsy. She murmured, 'I feel so much lighter. Thank God. Thank you, Bhalu. Knowing it wasn't her. I knew you'd help me!'

She got up on one elbow, leaned over me and pressed her mouth on mine. Don't fool yourself, it's the booze, I thought, melting under the heat of her breath. Anyway, she's kissed me like this before. She is impulsive and affectionate, and it doesn't mean a thing. But this time her eyes were closed and her tongue flickered at my clamped-tight lips. Surrender was inevitable. I too shut my eyes, and our tongues played naughty, joyous games. I could taste the wine in her mouth and one of her breasts was squashed against me, pressing a hard nub of nipple into my ribs.

She rolled away onto her back and reached for a cigarette.

'I met him once,' she said, directing a cloud of smoke into the bed's fairytale canopy. 'I mean the man who was blackmailing her.'

'What!?' The agony of thwarted lust.

'It must have been him. He picked me up once from school. An Indian man, in a car. It was a very hot day. He said that he was a friend of Mummy's and that she had asked him to take me to a place where we would go swimming. He said Mummy would be joining us later. So I went with him.'

She moved back onto her elbow.

'At first I thought we were going to Breach Candy, but of course he was Indian. We drove up to the top of Malabar Hill. Do you remember Bombay, Bhalu? And there is the road that goes down towards Chowpatty beach? Well, the car took that road, but after a while, it turned off to the right, down a private drive that led down towards the sea. The man told me that this was the

Governor's House. But he had access to it. There was a small beach there. Did I know how to swim? I said not very well. So he said he would teach me. He had brought a swimming costume for me. It wasn't mine. I was scared. He said I could change in the car. He himself stripped off behind a towel. He was wearing black trunks.'

'Why do you think he was the blackmailer? Couldn't he just have been a friend of Sybil's?'

'He wasn't,' she said. 'I know because when I got home Mummy was having hysterics. Rosie had been left waiting at the school gate. She brought home a note for Mummy. It said, "I have taken your kitten off to drown".'

'Bastard.'

'Yes, but that wasn't the only reason.'

'Why? What did he do to you? Did he touch you?'

'No,' she said. 'He told me a story. We were swimming in the water and he was holding me, with one hand under my tummy. We were looking back to the shore. There were big gardens, sloping up to the road, quite a way up the hillside. The man started telling me about a murder that had happened in one of the bazaars. Like the place where Jula and you used to go. A woman was stabbed to death. The man who did it cut her head off. He took it in a bag and walked across Bombay. Then he threw the head over a wall. It got stuck in a hedge, and one of the gardeners found it. My man – that is, the man who had taken me swimming – pointed up the hill to a thick hedge. He said that was where the head had been found. He asked me to be sure and tell my mother the story.'

Something occurred to me. I said, 'Was this just before you came to us, the third year? It would have been 1960.'

'I don't know,' she said. 'I can't remember. After that she said I must never be out of Rosie's sight.'

'Yes. How worried they were that day we went with Jula, to look for the Kathodi. Do you remember?'

She said, 'The best part of my childhood was being with you, away from it all.'

'No wonder they were so worried. They said the ayah must never let us out of her sight. And then the night we went up to the temple we thought she followed us because she was nosy. But what if she'd been *told* we were in danger?'

She said, 'I can't think about that, Bhalu.'

But I could. And it came back to me, the darkness, excitement and terror of that night. The ghostly figure, lit up in the lightning glare. The falling scream.

'Fever, suppose her death wasn't an accident.'

'I hate him,' said Phoebe. 'All my life I've hated him.'

At her behest I made another joint. I was holding it, staring up into the muslin clouds above when Phoebe scuffled her feet and I heard the clunk of shoes hitting the floor. Suddenly there was a foot pointing at the canopy. She lowered the leg, holding it stiff, like a dancer, then raised the other till it was vertical. Her legs were long and beautifully-shaped and when she lifted them up, her dress fell back to her hips.

'I can understand that,' I said, scarce able to breathe.

'Mummy's love affair went wrong. Her baby was scraped out of her alive. God, do you wonder why I never wanted one? Then her lover was murdered. Enough suffering, surely, for one woman. But no. Along comes this man, who knows most of this horrible story.

Does he show sympathy? He does not. Does he try to protect her? He does not. Instead he gets out his thumbscrew. And he methodically begins to torture a woman who was already half mad with grief and guilt.'

Her leg was still in the air. I handed her the joint and the leg came slowly down.

'But that wasn't all of it, Bhalu. You know what was worse?'

'Nothing could be worse.'

'Actually, darling, it was what he did to my father. And me. Daddy wasn't having affairs with people. Nor was I, till . . .'

Phoebe jumped up and knelt beside me. 'Put this thing out,' she said. 'I feel so strange.'

She looked up, laughed, then straddled me and bent so low that her hair touched my face. 'God, how I love you.'

I thought she was about to kiss me again, but she frowned, and with her face still inches from mine, said, 'Bhalu, that man. Don't you understand? He's still out there somewhere. He's old and rich, from all the money he extorted from people during his vile career. I can never forgive him. Never. I used to dream of killing him. I wanted to cut his ears off, and slit his eyes. Now I just want to see him, meet him face to face. Bhalu, I want to find him. You must help me. I want you to come to Bombay with me and find him. Say you will, darling. Please?'

Her mouth was lowering to mine when she gave a little retch, straightened up and said, 'I feel ill.'

She stood up. Swayed. I caught her, made her lie down and began folding back the cover on the far side of the bed.

'Can't sleep with clothes on,' she said. 'Undress me.'

'But . . .'

'Silly. Nothing you haven't seen before.'

So I put my arms under her shoulders and lifted her up. The dress was wriggled off. Unfastened her bra. Warm breasts, heavy. Nipples not erect. Slim body. Appendicitis scar. Hadn't had that when she was eight, or nine, or however old we'd been, under the waterfall, in Eden.

She lifted up her hips. I drew the damp scrap down her thighs. Katy was wrong. Phoebe had no need for hair dye.

She was already asleep. Breathing harshly through the nose. Since leaving the lunch table, eight hours had somehow passed. It was well past eleven. Too late to catch the last train? Not if I left immediately. After a moment's thought, I took off my shoes and socks. Paused. Then I took off my trousers and shirt and climbed into the huge bed. Christ, what the hell was I doing? What would I say to Katy in the morning? Well, nothing had happened. Almost nothing. A yard at least, between me and Phoebe. Nothing *would* happen. I would just sleep. Lying awake in the darkness, listening to Phoebe's little drunken snores, reliving the moment of that extraordinary revelation, everything that followed, I realised that she hadn't once mentioned her husband. I knew almost nothing about her.

Why did I get into bed with her?

Get hold of a video of *Basic Instinct* and run the opening sequence. Just the titles. If you get to the woman in the blonde wig with the icepick, you have gone too far; you need only the title sequence, when the screen is all shifting light and shadow. Close your eyes, and listen to the music.

It's an eerie, uneasy music, full of beauty and warning. It hints

362

that you are getting into something beyond your ken, beyond your control. You struggle to free yourself, but the music is strong, its sweetness pulls you back; there is no way out, you are lost.

She was still asleep when I woke. I washed as quietly as I could in the bathroom. Not wanting to disturb her, I told myself, but in truth I was anxious to escape. Had to rummage in her toilet bag for toothpaste. Facial scrub. Shower creme. A foil wrapper containing three condoms. I crept out, wrote a note to thank her for lunch (!) and tell her that I had borrowed Sybil's journal. 'Don't go running off to India,' I wrote. 'I am going to find out as much about this whole business as I can.'

I didn't see anyone on the way out of the hotel. Dawn was just breaking above South Kensington. Victoria deserted, the train to Lewes empty. I sat daydreaming. If she hadn't drunk so much . . . hadn't smoked that hash . . . where the hell had she got it, anyway? . . . what might have . . . ? As if I needed to ask. I knew *exactly* what would have bloody well happened. Okay, then answer the other question. Had she meant it to happen? What had *she* wanted? She'd certainly kissed me as if she meant it. Wait. Recollect the kiss. Warm, long, wet. In detail, please. Flowery bouquet, warm, rolled on the tongue. Full bodied, definitely. Fruit, melon topped with strawberry, saw them later, remember, hadn't had those when she was nine. Smooth finish with hints of honey and tobacco. Yes, she'd meant it. Condoms. No doubt at all. And God, those legs . . . damn it, more questions. Innocent? How could it be? No longer a child, was she? The legs, I was yearning to stroke them. And then . . . 'Undress me,' she said. 'Nothing you haven't seen before . . .' She could not have been unaware of the effect she was having on me.

Gazed fascinated at that channel which, last time I saw it, had been innocent, like a cleft in smooth, bare rock. Now, a watercourse widened and deepened by many rainy seasons, it fell half-hidden through dense scrub. So much for metaphor. Strangely, during lunch when I looked into her décolletage I had thought of the ravine that separates Bicchauda from Dagala. Phoebe as embodiment of the Ambona hills.

Must put Phoebe out of my mind. Think of Katy and be glad nothing *had* happened. I loved Katy. She was a good soul. Kind. Loving. Supportive. Just as attractive, in her own way, as Phoebe. Think of something else.

Thank God the train was empty.

I forced myself to open Sybil's journal. Mad words leapt out.

. . . Prem deserved it. The innocent suffered. The baby should not have been murdered. How much you love, so much shall be returned to you, in like measure. My measure is altogether more generous and less carping than yours, all those of you who thought you knew me, and put me on trial for thirty years or more. Answer for it . . . Answer.

Prem Ahuja. I had almost forgotten him. What Sybil and Maya had been mixed up in, all those years ago. Testament to Phoebe's intoxicating power: a nasha so powerful that it had almost made me forget that sensational discovery.

Poor Sybil. Thirty years passed and brought her no peace. What was it that sent her so suddenly, so mysteriously, back? Then I noticed that inside the front cover was scrawled, in the same crazy handwriting as the final ravings, 'This is Sybil Killigrew's Last Journal.' In my tumescent delirium, it did not occur to me until later to wonder how Sybil herself could have known.

Sybil's Journal, June 28th, 1993

Yesterday I started scraping the paint off the planks in the kitchen. I thought I would strip them bare, down to the wood, then polish them to make them glow.

I scraped paint all morning. There were several layers. Lime green. Under that, brown. And beneath that a dark blue. My arm hurt and by lunchtime I was crying with the pain. I went into the drawing room and lay down. Smell of damp everywhere. I thought, I want to give up. Let me just die now. When a knock came at the door I thought it must be the postman.

Standing outside was a friend I had not seen for thirty years. Zul Lalvani. He used to be a documentary film producer. Zul must be my age, or older, but he looked more or less the same as he always did. His feet were clad in dapper little handmade shoes and the rest of him in a suit in which every stitch was put in by hand. He was, in a word, immaculate. Zul! How had he found me? I was so delighted.

He said, 'Billy! My dear Billy! Do you realise your friends have been searching for you for thirty years?'

'My goodness, Zul!' I cried. 'How can you not have changed?'

Zul said, 'Don't be fooled, Billy. It's hair dye.'

Then I realised that I was standing in my dressing

gown, which had flakes of paint all over it, like multi-coloured dandruff. The scraper was sticking out of a pocket.

I said, 'Zul, I can't ask you in. I am so ashamed. The house is not fit for you to see.'

'Oh come now, Billy,' he said, stepping past me. 'Isn't that why I'm here?' Then he walked, room by room, through my rotting house, but instead of seeing all the bad things – the patches of damp, and the place where the floorboard is missing – he saw all the beauties, the possibilities. He saw at once, without my having to tell him, that the absurd loft could be converted to a studio. I started to explain all the things I had started doing (the unfinished painting in the hall, patchwork walls, made by sticking on scraps cut from magazines and books of wallpaper samples) and he never once told me I was stupid, or misguided, as Phoebe does when she comes here (when she deigns to come here). He approved of all my ideas and said it would be beautiful when it was finished.

We went into the kitchen and there was the half-scraped wall. I said, 'I did hope to finish it today, and I did try hard. But I'm so tired. I can't do any more.'

He said, 'Billy, I know exactly what to do. Now you sit down, right over there, and I'll make you a cup of tea.'

When he brought the tea, he was wearing an apron. He looked so silly with it on over his smart suit, it made me laugh.

He said, 'This won't take a tick. Leave everything to

me. Just sit here and drink your tea, and don't you worry about a thing.'

He cleaned the house from top to bottom. He spent hours. He did everything. I even heard scraping from the kitchen and got up to see what he was doing. He had just finished scraping the wall, and was rubbing some oil into the planks to give them a shine.

When he had finished, the house looked immaculate.

Then he said, 'Now Billy, you've got to look after yourself. We can't have you going and getting ill. You must eat properly.'

There was nothing in the house but a tin of peaches, one with a dent in, that I found on the bargain shelf at the supermarket.

I said, 'I'm sorry, Zul, I've nothing to give you. I was going to go to the shop tomorrow.'

He took the apron off and said, 'Now you wait here and relax. I'll be back in a jiffy.'

When he had gone I panicked. Suppose he was really disgusted and wouldn't come back. But an hour later I heard his footstep and he was whistling a tune. He came through the door laden with shopping bags.

'Just ran up the road,' he said. 'This should do us nicely.'

And while I sat in the kitchen he busied himself; the copper pans were shining, scoured till they shone. He made a risotto and whisked up a zabaglione, which was always my favourite. He'd even thought of wine. I hadn't tasted wine in years.

Over dinner he said that he had a project that he

wanted me to do. It was a documentary film, about lone-liness, and he wanted me to write the script. I said I would be delighted, but I hadn't done anything of that sort before. He said it didn't matter. He said, 'Some of us were sitting around, back in Bombay, talking about things. And when this idea came up, I thought of you.'

'But how did you know where to find me?' I asked.

'Ah,' he said. 'We Bombaywallahs know how to get things done.'

So then I became frightened. 'If you can find me, anyone can,' I said.

Zul said, 'Billy, that old business was over and done with years ago. Nobody remembers it now. You should come back to Bombay and see for yourself. All your old friends are still there.'

'Yes,' I said. 'And he's there too. The one who hounded me.'

'Him?' said Zul, with a contemptuous laugh. 'These days that fellow is nothing. Nothing! You should confront him and ask for all your money back. He would have to give it. Otherwise we shall expose him.'

When we'd finished eating he insisted on doing the washing up. He wouldn't let me lift a finger. Then he said, 'My dear, I have to get back to London tonight, but I shall be back very soon. In the meanwhile, here is an advance on the project.'

He handed me a wad of notes. I remember he used to carry large sums of money around with him. We would go to listen to singers, and sometimes, if there was one whose singing pleased him, or whom he fancied, he would peel off notes and throw them at her feet. The roll of money was all fifty-pound notes. It must have been thousands of pounds.

'I can't accept this,' I said.

'Oh yes you can,' he said. 'You will soon be starting work on that project of mine, and this will hardly cover your costs.'

I was so grateful. I poured out my feelings. I said that I had not thought that anyone cared about me, or what had happened to me. They had forgotten. I had been part of their lives for a while, and had just vanished. He had changed everything. He was like an angel, sent from heaven to help me.

He said, 'Billy darling, you need have no such worries. Your friends are here now. We are going to look after you.'

I saw him off. He waved and said he would be back soon. I watched him go off down the path, his city shoes crunching on the weedy gravel.

Next morning I woke with my heart light for the first time in years. I walked into the kitchen, saw the half-scraped wall and the congealed pan on the stove.

'I won't ask where you've been,' said Katy.

I had walked home from the station through fields loud with birds. Katy wasn't in the cottage. I found her pitching straw and dung out of the Moron's stable into a barrow.

'You *know* where I've been.' I had told her that I was going to London to have lunch with Phoebe.

'I didn't expect you to be early,' she said. 'But I didn't think you'd stay out all bloody night.'

'I didn't mean to. Honestly. It got late. When I realised what the time was, it was just too late to get to Victoria . . .' How very feeble this sounded.

'I thought they ran all night,' said Katy, stabbing the pitchfork at a pile of droppings.

'No. Last one's just after midnight.' Thank heaven I'd checked.

'Midnight? It must have been quite a lunch.'

'It wasn't like that,' I said. 'She was taken ill. Someone needed to be there. Then it just got late.'

'Why didn't you ring, in that case? I was worried.'

'I thought you'd be in bed,' I said. 'The time just vanished.'

'I bet,' she said. 'So she was ill. In the restaurant? That must have pleased them. Where did you take her? To a hospital?'

I shook my head. What credible answer could I have given?

'Spend the night with her?'

A meteor shower of dung flew past me.

'Not exactly.'

'Not exactly? What does that mean?'

'Not in the sense you mean,' I said. 'I took her back to her hotel. She went to bed. Out like a light. I slept on the sofa. I promise you nothing happened.'

'Well, I believe you, Bhalu.'

I was curiously piqued. 'Why? Do you think I'm past it? Not capable?'

'What are you telling me now? That you *did* sleep with her?'

'No, I just told you I didn't.'

'Well, what are you saying? Did you or didn't you?'

Encore, the rain of dung.

'I don't think I'm exactly her type, do you?'

She paused, leaned on the fork and brushed a strand of hair away from her face. 'Women like her don't care about what a man's like, just what they can get out of him.'

'That's ridiculous. What could she possibly get out of me?'

'You've always talked about her, ever since I've known you, as a little angel. Well, can't you see what your angel has grown up to become?'

'I see a perfectly normal woman.'

'Oh, do you? Open your eyes, Bhalu. All that make-up. Hair straight out of a bottle. Dresses ten years too young. Come on, this isn't your angel.'

'You make her sound irresistible.'

Katy turned away and resumed her work. Scoop, twist, chuck. Scoop, twist, chuck. She did this every day, in all weathers.

'If you're going to stand there watching, you may as well do something. You could do his water.'

So I fetched the hose and ran it into the Moron's blue bucket. Tiny bits of straw pirouetted in the stream, were whirled round the sides in a watery waltz.

'There's something about her . . .' said Katy, swinging her fork, 'She's damaged goods, Bhalu. Don't get involved. Whatever may have happened to her, it isn't your affair.'

The word hung in the air, crackling with sulphurous fire.

'I'm already involved,' I said. 'I have been since I was eight.'

'Damn it, you're not *children* any more!' said Katy.

I turned off the hose and watched the last few drops from its little green mouth plink into the bucket. 'Am I supposed to stop caring about her just because she's grown up? If she *is* damaged, as you put it, doesn't she need her friends?'

'But it's not *just* friendship, is it?'

I didn't want to let it go at that. I said, 'When you have loved someone as a child, I think the feeling doesn't ever go away. It's there for ever. It doesn't change. That's the point, Katy. The feeling *doesn't* change. It's as if we were brother and sister . . .'

But even as this pious utterance left my lips I knew it was a fraud. It never had been quite true, not even when we were children.

'Liar!' said Katy. 'She's no more a sister to you than she is to the men she makes her money out of. You don't have to tell me what she does for a living, it's written all over her.'

'What the hell are you talking about?'

'She's a woman who lives off men, Bhalu.'

'We're safe, then. What have I got that she could live off?'

'She's the sort of woman who sleeps around. And she doesn't care if they're married. She had an affair with a married man. She told us herself.'

Oh you hypocrite, I thought, remembering coming home once to find our cottage filled with exotic birdsong.

I said, 'That's unfair. She didn't know.'

'So she says. But she *is* the sort of woman who asks someone else's husband to lunch in order to seduce them.'

Exotic birds clamouring in my mind.

'Bhalu, I do trust you.'

We were sitting at the kitchen table.

'She wants something from you. Okay, so it can't be money.' She gave a cynical little laugh. 'Somehow I don't think it's romance. So what is it?'

I said nothing. I was trying to decide to which idea that laugh had attached. Money, haha? Or Haha, romance?

I said, 'She wants me to go to India with her.'

Instead of the outburst I would have predicted, Katy sipped her coffee and looked thoughtfully at me over the cup.

'Phoebe does?'

'Yes.'

'Why?'

So I told her the story. Everything from *Retribution* to Sybil's *Last Journal* and the revelation that Mister Love was Prem Ahuja.

'This isn't just about Phoebe. My mother was involved too. In some way, she was mixed up in it. And it has affected all of us. Katy, I think this is the reason why Maya left India, something to do with threats and blackmail. I want to find out what.'

'But Bhalu, this is nonsense. What good will it do going there? It's forty years too late. Let it alone.'

She got up and went to the stove, stood stirring a saucepan with vigorous circular strokes that made her bottom wobble.

'Well,' I said. 'You're probably right.' I stood behind her, placed my palms on the voluptuous trembling hemispheres.

She said, 'Not now, Bhalu.'

'Let's go upstairs.'

'No! I'm in the middle of making lunch.'

'Afterwards then.' I put my arms round her and pressed up against her back.

'Goodness.' She squeezed round to face me. 'You *are* serious. Well, you'll just have to wait till tonight.'

For a moment we stood, arms round each other, faces almost touching, then she pulled away and turned to the grill, under which two chicken breasts lay tanning, side by side.

'This going to India . . . do you think she really means it?'

'As far as I can tell, yes.'

'In that case,' said Katy, 'I'm afraid there really is something wrong with her. I mean, why now? Why not years ago? Why didn't she go with her mother? Wouldn't that have made more sense?'

'I don't think they got on. Her mother seems to have gone a bit batty.'

'It gives me the creeps,' said Katy.

'What does?' I asked, setting out plates.

'She said her mother still talks to her. Don't you remember? And then she dragged you off to see that medium. If you ask me, she's madder than her mother was.'

A spasm of disquiet fled through my body. I remembered the terror on Phoebe's face when she thought Sybil was in the room with us.

'And Bhalu, suppose she finds this man. What will she do?'

'She says,' — it was something I had been wondering myself — 'that she just wants to *see* him. To let him know that she knows.'

'And then what?'

'What do you mean?'

'Suppose she looks him in the eye and says, "I know". And he looks back at her and says, "So what?" What happens next?'

'Nothing happens. She's done it. She's free. It's a psychological thing. Completing unfinished business. Laying the ghost.' I realised that I was quoting Sybil's *Last Journal*.

'You don't honestly believe that?' She was flitting round the kitchen, peering at the grill, stirring her saucepan. 'You said that at this lunch of yours, she was talking about revenge.'

'Only as a theme for a book.'

'How do you know she wouldn't pull out a gun and shoot him?'

'Don't be ridiculous.'

'How can you be sure? You hardly know her. No, let's be precise. You don't know her at all. She is a complete stranger.'

'A stranger I've known for only forty years.'

'A mixed-up, unhappy child you knew for a few weeks — that's all it added up to — forty years ago. A grown woman in whose mysterious company you have spent the grand total of three days. And one night. Whereas you and I have shared a bed every night for twenty-two years.'

Katy took a dishcloth and lifted the pot to the table. 'Voilà,' she said. 'Chests of chicken to the green pepper, à ma façon.'

A little while later, when we were eating, she said, 'If you go to India with her you're bound to have an affair.'

I said nothing. She let the silence lengthen, watching me. Her eyes were topaz blue. When she wore make-up, which wasn't often, she could make them look huge. To me she grew lovelier as she grew older. 'So,' she said, after enough of a pause had elapsed. 'I see you're not disagreeing with me.'

'Can't a man and a woman just be friends?'

'You tell me,' she said. 'You've had an affair. I never have.'

Again I said nothing. But this was not the same silence. This was part of a different silence. A silence thirteen years old.

One morning – it was during the worst of the bad times – I got to London to find our street closed, office inaccessible. Suspected gas leak, something like that. Golinkin was standing on the pavement thumbing through a Filofax. 'Going to take hours,' he said gloomily. 'May as well have the day off.' I caught a train back to Lewes and decided to walk home. A light summer day. I walked to the edge of town (riverside warehouses, warm brewery smells) and took a footpath by the river. The far bank was lined with poplars that stood on tall selves inverted in the quiet sliding green. Our cottage lay about two miles off, round the curve of the valley, hidden by a shoulder of downland. I struck out across fields in which the harvest was being gathered. The margins were crowded with poppies and cornflowers and in shaws and hedges, birds were calling. I recall thinking how good it felt to have a day unexpectedly to myself. I would surprise Katy, suggest we pack a picnic, some chicken, a cold bottle of wine, and take it up onto the Downs.

Came to the cottage. No one about. The twins, I & I, were at school. As I opened the back door I became aware of a strange music inside the cottage: a piano figure, glaring and dissonant, that took off into a run, a sort of stumbling arpeggio, and ended in chatter unmistakably like a bird call. Swooping clarinet notes, trills and calls. Piccolo piping. Groan of bassoon, oboe squawkissimo. A light intricate rhythm like a pencil rapidly clock-clocking in a wooden cup and a heavier regular soughing. I had never heard anything like it. This weird music was orchestrated — or was this not part of it? — with vocal sounds, odd low-voiced words, an exclamation, desperate mewing.

The living-room door was slightly ajar and from beyond it came the clamour of the musical birds. Katy must have the television on. She sometimes watched it while ironing. I was going to call out, but something, I don't know what, stopped me. I crept to the door and applied my eye to the crack where it was hinged. A blurred vertical stripe of living room came into view and with it the most incongruous sight. Over the back of our worn blue sofa a woman's naked legs were lifted in the air. Between them, a man's equally bare rump and shoulders were moving doggedly back and forth, as though he were leaning in to drive a plane along a plank. Their actions seemed curiously choreographic, now in time, now at syncopated odds with the bird calls. He would shunt forward, pushing the legs back as far as they could go. The legs would give a little shudder and the feet stretch till the toes were pointed. Her hands were clasping her thighs, greedily pulling them up and apart. Now the sounds resolved into what I had all along known they must be. Little soft cries, grunts, a low spoken word.

I don't know how long I stood, hidden by the door. Probably no more than a dozen heartbeats. I felt disconnected, unshocked. Far more surreal than anything I was seeing or hearing, was the fact that I found myself trying to remember terms from my daughters' ballet lessons. The twins, at nine, planned to be ballerinas as well as champion show jumpers as well as vets. They always wanted to show us whatever they had just learned, and would quarrel about the name of each step, or position. 'Iso, that isn't supposed to be *dessus*, it's *dessous*.' 'Oh, for God's sake Imo,' (they both had the habit of mimicking their parents' expletives), 'you did *devant* not *derrière*.'

What the woman's foot is doing now – what is that called? The toes extending, instep arching, there's a name for it. Allongé? Dégagé? He, en arrière, pulling back, and her leg slowly unfolding, en l'air, which is full of the invisible birds. His épaulement, quelques mouvements derrière, and here he comes again, en avance! Her hands, there's no ballet term for what they are doing, clutching at her knees, which, bending, plié doesn't do it, could now, no, *now*, at *this* instant, hardly be more fully pressed back. Again that little shudder, and a rapid fluttering of the foot (petit battement), all of this scored, for clarinet, or for the female dancer in this horizontal pas de deux, with throaty cries of surprise. On the thirteenth heartbeat everything stops. Silence. A word or two spoken in a low tone. She laughs. Her legs fasten round his waist. Then the resumption of their rhythm, his bass, her clarinet solo. By then I had no doubt what I was witnessing and, as quietly as I had come in, crept out again.

Stood in garden sunshine, wondering what to do. Old brick and flint walls soaking up the heat. Roses, planted by Katy, climbed upon them, raising creamy white and pink parasols against the sun. Zepherine Drouhan. Kiftsgate. Paul's Himalayan Musk. Alberic Barbier. Wedding Day. Pouring down scent. Odd how

Indian gardens, which have too much sun, love the rain, and English gardens, with too much rain, adore the sun. My father would have been proud of our roses. Katy tended them, pruning and dead-heading, always at the right times, to bring out the flowers. I followed the rose stems round the corner of the house, thinking that I must get far away. Headed for the back gate, a path to the fields. Nearby, low to the ground, was a wide open window and issuing from it came the extraordinary symphony of birds.

'It isn't Katy,' a very calm voice in my mind informed me. 'Katy has *lent* the cottage to someone – a friend – for the afternoon. Katy isn't here. At this moment, she is probably in Brighton.'

Then – of course! – I remembered her telling me that she was going to a client's house to supervise something. Something to do with walls! Some special paint effect! Scumbling?

There was a bush growing half across the window – in early summer it bore blue brush-like flowers, 'Ceanothus', I think it's called, something like that – which Katy had talked of cutting back, because it blocked so much light from the room. I turned back, crept up behind it, parted its branches. Sunlight falling like long larrups of golden syrup on floorboards, lighting up the corner of a Persian rug and lifting the eye onto the sofa, which no longer has its back to me. Now I see who is on it and what they are doing. I was going to say, I *know*, instead of I *see*, but knowledge implies understanding. I see what they are *apparently* doing. She, naked, is on her back, her head at the end of the sofa nearest me, her knees pressed to her breasts by the weight of the nude man crouching over her. I recognise him now. One of her interior design clients. Something to do with the music department at the university. We have been to his house and had dinner with him and his wife. *His* house she was supposed to be at. Musician. Explains why I have never heard this bird thing before. Must have brought it with him. Clever idea, scumbling to musical birds. This man, anyway, is the craftsman who has been keeping up that tireless to-and-fro. Now, framed by fading blue puffs of Ceanothus he rears up, catches her calves behind the ankle, pushes them back, stumbles (scumbles?) forward until he is kneeling, his knees wide apart. Catch myself thinking, he's going to come off that sofa. A rose-scented gust of wind, shoving rudely past the bush in which I am concealed, is ushered into the room by bowing curtains. It lifts the musical birds, sends them soaring, and sets the shaft of sunlight aswirl with dust motes, like the overhead beam in a cinema, projecting a scene which I could not accept as any more real than a film image, rhythm, music, to be experienced in detached incredulity.

How many times have I re-run this scene? Their heads are close together. Then comes that gust of wind, the dust motes spin, a branch sways, sunlight reaches out and touches their twin heads with gold. Now he rears up, adjusts his body and no longer is any detail hidden from my eyes. Her hips lift to meet his approaching body, they collide, draw apart and together again, moving in equal measure, a double-being whose two halves are joined by a fleshy umbilicum that lengthens and contracts, and sometimes vanishes altogether. Most men, confronted with this sight, of another man fucking their wife, might feel anger, pain, jealousy, grief. I felt none of these things, just a kind of astonishment lost in an immense calm. What I was seeing seemed at that moment to have nothing to do with me. And despite the pain that hit me later, I have never felt that there was anything sordid or even erotic about what they were doing, but something rather inevitable. There was a kind of tenderness in their mating, accentuated by the peculiar quality of the music, and her cries, lost in that abyss of birds.

I left the garden and went up the lane. A few hundred yards from the cottage, a car was parked. Shabby red Renault. I walked on the Downs, floating along cornflower and poppy planes. Sat on a hillside and watched light changing in the valley, sun and cloud chasing each other across the slopes, which came alive in dozens of pulsing greens and blues. I could see our cottage, a tiny toy, set among fields, the trickle of the lane, the red car.

When I went back it was evening and everything was normal. The twins were home from school. Katy greeted me with a kiss and said she'd tried to phone me at the office, but had had no reply. I said I'd been in meetings. Somehow, the evening passed. We sat on the blue sofa, watched television and talked about the twins. In bed that night I approached her, not knowing how she might respond, but she was willing enough. We made love with a passion that appalled me. Few times had been so intense. Katy seemed to open completely. There came a point where I pushed to the limit, felt her melt, and was admitted further, deeper than seems possible, and we lay breathlessly joined, as close to being one as two people can be. 'That was amazing,' I said afterwards. She replied, 'Like the night we made the twins.' I never mentioned what I had seen, never for a moment stopped loving her, but for that last remark neither could I ever quite forgive her.

It must have been two years later, when I was settled in the bookshop — the man having ceased by then to be a threat, he and his wife had moved to a university in Wales — that I turned on Radio Three and was startled to hear again the sounds of that afternoon. I listened until the end of the performance. It lasted less than a quarter of an hour. Then the announcer: 'In that performance of Olivier Messiaen's *Oiseaux Exotiques* . . .'

In bed, Katy renewed the attack. 'You'll be making a big mistake, if you get involved with her,' she said out of the darkness.

Our two forms were humped, back to back, under the quilt. Outside in the field some animal was uttering staccato cries. Vixen, perhaps. I turned over and ran my hand along her hip. 'I love this sexy curve. Just here, where it drops down and becomes your waist.'

'Too sleepy,' she murmured. Then, reaching behind, in a wide awake voice, 'Oh I say, that bitch has got you all razzed up.'

She rolled to face me. Our mouths were so close, we inhaled each other's breath. She put her arms round me and said, 'You and I are strong together. You're my rock.'

'I love you.'

'Bhalu, nobody could be closer than we are,' sighed Katy. She kissed my cheek. 'Now let's go to sleep.'

Next morning at breakfast she said, 'She'd get on your nerves, you know. You'd find her absolutely infuriating.'

I said, 'I promise you. I am not going to run off with her.'

My man in Bombay was efficient. Hardly two weeks after the lunch with Phoebe, a courier came into the shop with a large, heavy parcel which he dumped on my desk.

'Was wondering what you'd got in there,' he said, looking around. 'Now I know.'

But it wasn't books. The package, duly disembowelled, proved to contain transcripts of court proceedings from the Nanavati trial, a few cuttings from various newspapers, photocopied sections from a book in Hindi about the case, and, most importantly, photocopies of every relevant page of *Blitz*. Upwards of two hundred pages of thick curling paper. My man apologised for having found nothing during his previous search. *Blitz* had not reported the murder when it occurred and only began covering the case once it came to court in October 1959.

With the strangest feeling of déjà vu I began reading the story of the Ahuja murder. The reports spoke of 'the eternal triangle', but I knew there had been two triangles, interlaced and inseparable. In *Retribution* (which by now I knew almost well enough to quote by heart) Mister Love trifled with Sybil and S, and was shot by an unknown hand. In the *Blitz* account, Mister Love, now known by his proper name, trifles with S alone and is killed by her husband.

The press reports of forty years earlier had for me the haunting quality of being like, yet simultaneously unlike *Retribution*, near-identical twins. *Retribution* was the hidden, distaff face of the legend. So far as I knew, Phoebe and I were the only people left alive who knew the whole story. The public had only ever been told half. How odd that, as stated in *Retribution* the women had also been alike as twins, resembling each other confusingly closely not only in appearance but in name. Sybil had always referred to her rival as S. I now knew why.

In the early afternoon of 27 April, 1959, Commander Kawas Nanavati of the Indian Navy, an officer who had been marked for high promotion, drove his English wife Sylvia and their young children to the Metro cinema to see *Tom Thumb*.

Other cinemas in the city were showing, variously: Regal – *Vertigo*; Strand – *Escapade in Japan*; Maratha Mandir – *Amar Deep*; Excelsior – *This Happy Feeling* (the previous week it had been *Limelight*); Opera House – *Hira Moti*.

Commander Nanavati did not stay for the film, but drove to the naval dockyard and boarded his ship, the cruiser *Mysore*, ex-HMS *Nigeria* and now Indian flagship. He went to the armoury, said he was driving to Aurangabad (some reports say Ahmednagar) and needed a weapon for protection. He signed out a revolver and six bullets.

At 4.10 p.m., Nanavati rang the bell of Prem Ahuja's plush flat in the Jeevan Jyot building on Nepean Sea Road. Ahuja's servant Anjani, who knew Nanavati, was setting out a tray of tea. He told Nanavati that his master was resting. Nanavati pushed past him into the bedroom and slammed the door. The servant heard angry shouting, then shots. He ran into the room to find Ahuja dying in a pool of blood.

Nanavati, still holding the revolver, left the flat saying he was going to a police station, but instead he went to the Naval Provost Marshal, Commander Samuel.

Ten minutes later, Deputy Commissioner Lobo of the Bombay Police received a call from Samuel, who said he had sent Nanavati along to give himself up at Gamdevi police station.

'Are you sending him under escort?' Lobo asked. A couple of months earlier a naval rating from Nanavati's ship had strangled a woman in a cheap lodging house, and the Naval Provost had sent him to the police under guard.

'Of course not,' replied Samuel. 'He is driving himself. Kawas Nanavati is a gentleman.'

On the fatal morning, Nanavati had had a row with his English wife, Sylvia. His ship was not long back from a cruise and instead of the enthusiastic lover he must have hoped would welcome him home, Sylvia was withdrawn, distinctly moody. They had gone away for a few days with his brother and sister-in-law and Sylvia's behaviour continued to be odd. On their return, she refused an invitation to dinner with his brother because, she said, of a prior engagement with a friend, Mamie, Prem's sister. The Nanavatis had known Ahuja and his sister for some years. They occasionally made up a bridge four. Nanavati knew of Ahuja's reputation as a playboy with a penchant for the lonely wives of serving officers.

There are various versions of what happened on that morning, the twenty-seventh. Nanavati had some chores to attend to. He had to take the dog to the vet. In the afternoon, the family planned to go to the cinema. Another report describes a trip to the Metro, to buy tickets for the film. On the way home they apparently stopped to do some grocery shopping in Crawford Market. The atmosphere in the car was tense. If *Blitz* and various rather more fanciful accounts are to be believed, the following scene must be imagined when they got home.

The Nanavati living room, a large comfortable room with an airy sea view. SYLVIA *is seated on a sofa, with a magazine,* Eve's Weekly. *She pretends to be absorbed, but can't concentrate. Her husband,* KAWAS, *a handsome man in his thirties, is nervously pacing the room. He sits beside* SYLVIA.

HE: Sylvia, please. What is the matter?

She is silent, flipping through her magazine.

HE: Please. What's wrong?

SHE: Nothing. Why do you keep badgering me?

He puts his arm around her shoulders.

HE: Darling, something is wrong. Please tell me.

SHE: *(shrinking from his touch)* Don't do that!

He leaves the arm where it is, tries again.

HE: Sylvia . . . *(Hastily withdraws arm as a servant enters.)*

SERVANT: Sahib, memsahib, lunch ready.

Exit servant and Nanavatis. The room remains empty for half an hour, during which we are obliged to imagine them eating lunch at the family table. SYLVIA *re-enters, sits on the sofa and picks up her magazine, flicking the pages. Several more minutes pass before* KAWAS *comes in.*

HE: Oh, there you are. I was waiting in the bedroom. I thought you might like a rest after lunch.

She ignores him, continues flipping through her magazine. He sits on the other end of the sofa.

HE: Look Sylvia, we must have a proper talk.

She looks away.

HE: Sylvia, do you still love me?

Silence.

HE: *(hoarsely, or gently, according to various accounts)* Are you in love with someone else?

Silence.

HE: *(presumably hoarse by now)* For God's sake, you must tell me.

SHE: Yes.

HE: Who is it?

She shakes her head and will not answer.

HE: Is it Ahuja?

SHE: *(after a long silence, murmurs)* Yes.

HE: Did you remain . . . honourable?

She bows her head, then shakes it. He jumps up and paces the floor in great agitation.

HE: Oh God! Oh God! Oh my God!

SHE: What are you going to do?

HE: What is to be done any more?

He comes to a decision. Stops. Sits beside her.

HE: Look, is he prepared to behave honourably? Will he marry you? Will he look after the children?

SHE: *(hangs her head)* I don't know.

HE: Sylvia, listen, I can forgive you. I am prepared to forgive you. But you must give him up. Now tell me truthfully, darling, will you give him up?

SHE: I can't answer that at this moment.

He starts up again, this time in anger.

HE: I must go and settle the matter with this swine.

SHE: No, no. You must not go there. He may *shoot* you.

HE: Don't bother about me. It doesn't matter anyway as I am going to *shoot myself.*

SHE: *(jumps up and grabs his arm to calm him down)* Why should you shoot yourself? You are the innocent one in all this.

HE: By God, look at the time. Get everyone in the car or we'll be late for *Tom Thumb*.

The trial, at the Bombay Sessions Court, proved as sensational as the murder. There was huge public support for the wronged naval hero, and universal loathing for Ahuja the seducer, destroyer of wifely virtue.

Sylvia appeared in court wearing a widow's white sari and played to perfection the role of the naive, penitent wife, led astray by a scoundrel. She described the day of the murder. How she had had to nerve herself to give her husband the bad news that she was in love with another man. She could not bear to deceive him about what had been happening in his absence.

She told how Nanavati had found her moody and distracted, how under his gentle questioning she had confessed to being in love with another man and no, she would not lie, she had not been faithful. Her husband declared that he would go to talk to Ahuja. He would ask Ahuja if he intended to marry Sylvia and – this drew oohs and ahs in court – to look after the children. Sylvia begged him not to go. She said that Ahuja might shoot him (thereby claiming that Ahuja had a gun). That, said Nanavati, was why he went to get the gun from his ship. For his own protection. Or to shoot himself. Or both.

What a story! ALL THIS AND A SKULL TOO! shrieked *Blitz*.

Crowds have been stampeding the Court compound to catch a glimpse of Nanavati appear and disappear in his smart naval uniform displaying an array of medals and decorations. Cheers rend the air

every time he enters and leaves the Court. Numerous college girls are said to have lost their hearts to the handsome Commander. Some have swooned after seeing him. Others have reportedly sent him 100-rupee notes marked with lipstick. A few love-lorn nymphets have even made him offers of marriage, anticipating a divorce. While the overcrowded courtroom listens to the counsel, there is another mute and eyeless 'spectator' present – AHUJA'S SKULL, an exhibit in the case, which stands on the table near the press benches, grinning sinisterly.

The jury, like the crowds outside, was rather obviously in favour of the defendant and listened, nodding, to every point the defence elicited from the shamed, but repentant wife. The hero was going to see Ahuja for the *honourable* (yes) and *thoroughly responsible* (yesyes) motive of asking his intentions towards Sylvia and the children. And Sylvia had warned him that Ahuja might *shoot* him. (Obviously Ahuja had a gun – one can't shoot people without.) So Nanavati took a gun for *self-defence* (yes). Besides which, he also needed the revolver to *shoot himself* (oh yesyes), a most *honourable* (Roman, Japanese, tragic, heroic) way out of dishonour, despite the fact that *he was innocent* in all this.

Unfortunately for the defence, the judge in the Sessions Court was not willing to entertain the concept of a Wild West type shoot-out between these two revolver-toting rivals in love. No gun had been found at Ahuja's flat. Dozens of bottles of liquor had been found, a box of love letters had been found, but no gun. Ahuja could never have shot Nanavati. In any case, as learned counsel for the prosecution pointed out, for the defence to be valid, the act that causes death must proceed directly from an overwhelming and ungovernable impulse which in turn must proceed directly from the grave and sudden provocation. The prosecutor observed that three hours had elapsed between the wife's confession and the shooting. During this time Nanavati drove his family to the cinema, went back to his ship, drew a weapon, tidied up some official business, and only then set out for Ahuja's office and, not finding him there, his flat. There had been plenty of time to cool down. Drawing the weapon then waiting three hours was premeditation, ergo it was murder.

So the defence called Nanavati to the stand and the aghast and dumbfound court was asked to imagine another scene.

The Ahuja bedroom. A room with an airy sea view. It is entirely dominated by the bed. A dressing table with large mirror stands nearby. Also a wardrobe, and a radiogram. One door leads off to the bathroom. Another to the rest of the flat. AHUJA *is lying on his bed naked. Or in some versions is clad in a bathtowel, combing his hair at the mirror. A doorbell rings* (off). *A confused murmur of voices can be heard* (off). *The door of the room is flung open and* NANAVATI *stands there, holding a bulky envelope which, unbeknownst to* AHUJA, *contains a revolver (brought purely for self-defence in case* AHUJA *tries to shoot him).* AHUJA *snatches up a bathtowel to cover himself, or in languid disdain, continues combing his hair, according to whichever version the audience may prefer.*

NANAVATI: You low dog!

AHUJA *is startled, but arrogantly defiant.*

NANAVATI: Are you prepared to marry Sylvia and take care of her and my children?

AHUJA: Do you really suppose I'm going to marry every woman I sleep with? Get out of here right now, or I'll throw you out!

He takes a threatening step towards NANAVATI. NANAVATI *(not wanting to use the revolver) places the brown envelope on the radiogram and raises his fists.*

NANAVATI: By God, I'm going to teach you a lesson!

AHUJA , *declining the challenge of fisticuffs, makes a grab for the envelope (which he somehow knows to contain a revolver), but* NANAVATI *snatches it up, knowing that* AHUJA *will mercilessly shoot him if he gets it first.* AHUJA, *nothing daunted, grabs* NANAVATI'*s hand and begins twisting it to make him drop the envelope. For his own clear self-defence* NANAVATI *extracts the revolver and (not aiming it at* AHUJA), *orders him to stand back.* AHUJA, *in crazed and violent rage, does not do so. Instead he makes a grab for the gun. A struggle ensues.* NANAVATI *fearing for his life, but desperate not to use the gun, manages to push* AHUJA *back to the bathroom door.* AHUJA *rains blows on* NANAVATI *and pulls him into the bathroom.* AHUJA *now tries with all his strength to grab the gun from* NANAVATI. *He is very strong. So powerful is his grip that it crushes* NANAVATI'*s hand onto the gun.* NANAVATI *cannot let go of it even if he wants.* AHUJA *swings on* NANAVATI'*s hand. During this struggle a shot rings out.* AHUJA *looses his grip and falls to the floor.* NANAVATI *immediately leaves the bathroom.*

It was obvious, the defence contended, that from first to last the responsibility for Ahuja's death lay with himself alone. Nanavati had shown the utmost restraint. His civil (given the circumstances) and reasonable enquiry about Ahuja's intentions met only with abuse and threats. He did his best to settle the matter as men should, as written in the Gospel according to John (Wayne), with fists. But Ahuja, proving himself a contemptible coward as well as an impetuous arrogant hothead, tried to seize the envelope. Nanavati *had* to grab the gun, or without a doubt Ahuja would have shot him down in cold blood. He tried hard *not* to use the gun he had brought with him only for self-defence (did Ahuja's actions not prove how wise a precaution it had been?), but Ahuja kept Nanavati's hand clamped to it so tightly, whilst simultaneously raining blows on him and swinging from his wrist . . . The rest was karma. At the same time, of course (in case anyone remembered that three shots, not one, were fired) Nanavati had suffered further intolerable provocation in the form of the grossly insulting remark made by Ahuja, to wit: Did Nanavati really think that he, Ahuja, was going to marry each of the (numerous beyond counting) women he had slept with, including his, Nanavati's, wife? So it was an *accident* in *self-defence* in response to *an intolerable provocation*. In short, three defences rolled into one, but there can, m'lud, be only one possible verdict.

The establishment, just as fervently as the public and the 'yellow' press, wanted Nanavati acquitted. The Navy, to avoid scandal, had asked for a discreet court-martial. Deputy Commissioner John Lobo was obliged to explain to the Chief of Naval Staff that as Nanavati had killed a civilian in Bombay city, there was no way out of a public trial. Still the Navy did its best for its man. Appearing in his defence were Captain Kohli of the *Mysore*, who had given permission for him to draw the fatal weapon. Chief of Naval Staff Admiral Katari and Defence Minister Krishna Menon also took the stand on behalf of the gallant Commander. He was of course loudly championed by *Blitz*, which devoted much of each issue to demanding that sentiment should prevail over law.

The trouble was that nothing in the Nanavatis' story rang true.

Not Sylvia's painful honesty. She'd been deceiving her husband for more than a year without pangs of conscience. Why would she suddenly be morally unable to tell a lie? Much more likely that she'd got tired of waiting for Ahuja to make up his mind, and decided to force the issue. How could she guess that her gentle, kind husband would grab a gun and go hunting?

Not the need for the gun. The notion that Ahuja had a gun and was dangerous depended on the word of Sylvia alone.

Not the struggle in the bedroom. The servant outside the room said that mere seconds separated the crash of the bedroom door from the triple boom of the gun.

Not the intolerable provocation. Ahuja's alleged insult was the sort of thing a bully says, not to an angry husband waving a gun, but to a crying woman.

Blitz reported that when the jury filed back into court with its verdict, one pretty juror winked at the hero.

Not guilty!

'In schtuck with Katy?' breathed Piglet as we sat in Charlotte's and emptied a second brace of pints.

'How do you know?'

'She rang the other night. Late, it was. About eleven. Asked if you were with me. Should I have lied?'

'Of course not.'

'It's that blonde, isn't it? The one who lives at Sleeman. The mystery place no one has heard of.'

I didn't tell him, but I had already solved that mystery.

Maya's books were stacked upstairs, great piles of cardboard cartons, filling most of the two small rooms above the shop. Whenever I could, I did a bit of unpacking, classifying. Some of them would go into stock, most would join my private collection.

A few days after the lunch with Phoebe I opened a box full of books that had lived in Maya's rosewood bookcase. Among them were several titles on the Indian Mutiny.

The Indian War of Independence, 1857 (Veer Sarvarkar, Karnatak Printing Works, Chira Bazaar, Bombay, 1947. No. 252 of limited edition of 1000 copies. pp 552 including frontispiece of Sarvarkar and his famous jaw. Many colour plates. First published in England in 1909 and immediately proscribed).

The Tale of the Great Mutiny (W. H. Fitchett, Smith Elder & Co, London, 1901, pp 384, 1st ed, with portraits and maps).

Journey through the Kingdom of Oude (Major General Sir W. H.

Sleeman, Richard Bentley, London 1858, 2 vols with maps, pp 424).

Sleeman?

Now it came back to me. After Maya's funeral, when Piglet was pressing Phoebe for the name of her village, she had been staring at the rosewood shelves. And she had said Sleeman.

Ever since our lunch, I had been struggling with excitement, fantasy, hope, regret and doubt. Already Phoebe had told more lies than ever there had been between Katy and me. Only one thing lay unspoken in our marriage bed and probably because Katy had not wanted to hurt me. The pain of what I had never been meant to see, now dull, now exquisite, had faded over the years, just as we two had faded. I had long since forgiven her as she had forgiven me. I too had strayed. It had been a bad time for both of us. Katy was good, kind, loving and, yes, faithful in the sense that matters most. She loved me and had stayed with me.

And Phoebe? Katy was right. I knew nothing about her at all. Not about her husband, her marriage, not even where she lived. But Katy was also wrong. Phoebe was more to me than a grown-up stranger. In her face, I could still see the child I had loved, as she could see the child in mine. Now that we had met again, I knew what had been missing from my life all these years. Aristotle believed that love is the soul's yearning for a lost part of itself. She was the other half of the self I thought I had lost so many years ago. I could not just let her go. A resolve was shaping in my mind. The child I had been had not died. It was still there, still alive, waiting for a call. I would somehow find Phoebe, confront her. One way or another, resolve the mystery. What might follow I didn't know and did not want to think about.

This isn't foolish, I told myself. I had good reason for wanting to see her again. What I had been reading explained a great deal about her mother's torment.

The Nanavati verdict was rapturously acclaimed by the waiting crowds outside the Sessions Court, but their joy, like one of those butterflies that fly during the brief hot interludes in the monsoon, was brilliant but short. Word soon spread around the city that the judge had overturned the verdict. Declaring that a miscarriage of justice had taken place, he sent the case to the High Court and Nanavati to prison. The re-trial was scheduled for February 1960.

According to Phoebe the blackmailer had already begun his extortion before the first trial. By the time the High Court hearings began he was really turning the screw. The papers spread across my desk told me why. He was running out of time. Sybil's letters, found in the box under Ahuja's bed, had not been mentioned during the original trial because the Sessions Judge had ruled them irrelevant. But Nanavati's lawyers needed something new to take to the High Court. They had to give Nanavati a stronger reason for going to see Ahuja. What if it could be proven that Ahuja was in the habit of promising marriage as a means of seducing women? Sybil was about to be dragged into the case.

Twenty-six letters had been found under the bed. Three were from S, the rest were from five other women, each of whom must have been living in dread of being exposed. What was it Sybil had written? '. . . the ammoniacal taint that clung to me in those months after his murder, the constant terror that I would be uncovered.'

Only three letters were from Sybil, but these were the letters which Mister Love had so disobligingly read to S. Perhaps this is why the one woman S chose to expose was Sybil. Why she chose to make an issue of none but Sybil's letters.

Sybil, in her *Last Journal*, wrote that she could almost hear her rival gloating, 'You really thought you'd got away with it, didn't you, dear Sybil?'

MYSTERY MRS ? INTRUDES INTO NANAVATI TRIAL

BOMBAY: A mysterious woman – Mrs ? – who wrote three frantic love letters to Prem Ahuja at a crucial moment of his intimacy with Sylvia Nanavati dramatically crashed into the sensational trial this week when Defence Counsel Mr A. S. R. Chari began his argument before Mr Justice Shelat and Mr Justice Naik at the Bombay High Court.

WHO IS THIS MYSTERIOUS LADY? WHAT RELATIONS HAD SHE WITH AHUJA? WHY DID SHE WRITE THESE LETTERS TO HIM – ALL ON THE SAME DAY? WHAT WERE THE CONTENTS OF THOSE LETTERS? WHERE IS THIS WOMAN NOW? WILL SHE COME FORWARD TO REVEAL HER IDENTITY?

All that has been revealed at the moment is that Mrs ? is a married woman with children. She has reportedly admitted that she has had no relationship with her husband for a long time and she talks about 'five years of celibacy' in her letters. Mr Justice Shelat, after reading the letters, remarked, 'She must be a voracious writer.'

Submitting that the handwriting of these letters written by this mysterious Mrs ? had been identified by Sylvia Nanavati, wife of Commander Nanavati, who stands charged with the murder of Ahuja, Defence Counsel Chari, in his loud, stentorian voice, argued that the Sessions Judge Mr R.D. Mehta had committed a grave error in wrongly ruling out those letters on the

Sybil's letters were passed round in court, the latest prodigy in this case of skulls and scandal. She was identified only as 'Mrs ?', but the letters were hers, without a doubt. Long extracts were published in *Blitz*. In places they match, word for word, passages from her 1958 diary. The defence, seeking to prove that Ahuja had played fast and loose with S (as indeed he had), pounced on the letter in which Sybil ironically gave L permission to sleep with S. She had talked of 'marriage'. This was obviously a euphemism, but nobody could build a legal argument on what it might have meant. Sybil's letters made no difference to Nanavati. There was never any point in dragging her into the case. It was a needless piece of cruelty.

To whip up popular support for the failing defence, *Blitz* held public meetings and organised a petition signed by thousands of readers. But this time there was no jury to be swayed. Justices Shelat and Naik, agreeing with the judge of the lower court, found Nanavati guilty of murder and sentenced him to transportation for life (to the penal colony in the Andaman Islands). His lawyers promptly announced an appeal to the Supreme Court and, pending the outcome of that appeal, Mr Sri Prakasa, Governor of Bombay State, promptly suspended the sentence. Some editors and lawyers were worried by this apparent disregard for the court's judgement.

Blitz wrote:

**Wails of 'Democracy in danger!' are being raised by editorial writers and
legal pundits forgetful of the fact that their campaign seeks to demolish the
very basis of Democracy which is the Sovereignty of the People as expressed**

through the Jury and other manifestations of Vox Populi in the Ahuja Murder Case.

. . . All we propose to do here is to underline the *human* and *democratic* aspects of the incident. These are based on that greatly derided and heavily ridiculed thing called *middle-class morality*. The plain fact is that almost every other person belonging to the middle-class and indeed all the other classes exclusive of the sophisticated upper-class strata of society or the amoral minority of the intelligentzia [*sic*], *hails Nanavati as the man who fired those shots on* HIS BEHALF – that is, on behalf of the sanctity of his home and the honour of his family – against the plague of corruption, be it of the financial or moral variety that is eating into the body, mind and soul of the nation.

> Somehow Prem Ahuja, much as we regret and condemn his killing, has become a symbol of those wealthy, corrupt, immoral and basically unsocialist forces which are holding the nation and its integrity to ransom, while Nanavati, despite public repudiation of the violent solution he found to the tragedy of his shattered home, has come to represent in the popular mind the avenging conscience of humanity.

Nanavati's appeal was rejected by the Supreme Court, which confirmed the life sentence. However he served just three years. India's Defence Minister had appeared in his defence and now the baying of Vox Populi disturbed even the Prime Minister's peace.

Nehru's sister, Mrs Vijaylakshmi Pandit, was the new Governor of Maharashtra, the Marathi-speaking part of the former Bombay State. She gave Nanavati a State Pardon. He emigrated with his wife and children to Canada and vanished from history.

I finished reading as the calm light of a Sussex summer evening was touching, one by one, the spines of the books in my sanctum sanctorum, lighting them like candles.

I was thinking, Why do I feel such anger?

A few days later I had occasion to ring Srinuji. Maya had appointed him as executor of her will – the will she had had no time to execute herself. The flat in Sloane Square had finally sold, there were things to be discussed. He said he had a cheque for me and some papers to sign. I offered to come to London, but he said no, he would visit me. When I arrived to open the shop next day, I found him waiting outside. Strange to confess, when I saw him, in his guru's get-up, shawled against the morning air, I experienced something akin to affection.

'So Bhalu,' he said in his beautifully-modulated Urdu, after I had brought him in and given him a cup of tea, 'how have you been keeping?'

'I miss her.'

'As do I,' he said. 'I suspect none of us realised how remarkable she was. One of the things you and I have to discuss is a modest sum to be sent annually to a bank in Ambona. It seems that all these years, without saying a word to anyone, she's been paying the salary of a village schoolmaster.'

He opened a battered briefcase, a relic presumably from his time as an accountant, and brought out a sheaf of papers.

'First, here is your cheque.'

I stared at the enormous figure in disbelief.

'And I will need your signature on these.'

I began reading through the papers. Srinuji picked up a copy of *Blitz* from my desk, looked at it and put it down as if it had bitten him. At first I thought it was odd that he made no comment. Then it struck me.

'You *knew* about this business, didn't you?' I said, putting down the pen. 'This murder, in Bombay. The Nanavati case. You knew that Maya was mixed up in it.'

A curious expression flitted across his face. What was it? Alarm?

'Yes. But may I ask how *you* know?'

'Phoebe Killigrew had a diary of her mother's.'

'I should have guessed it would happen, once Mademoiselle Phoebe appeared on the scene.'

He had actually used the word *bibi*, which rhymed with her name. It sounded odd, Phoebe-bibi.

'She said her mother, Sybil, was blackmailed.'

'Not just Sybil,' said Srinuji.

'What?'

Thus, at last, I came to hear the hole-shaped story.

'I do not know his name,' Srinuji told me. 'Only that he was an official in government service. Whether police, judiciary or some political department, I can't be certain. My impression, and it is no more than that, is that he was a senior policeman.'

Within three days of Ahuja's murder, this man called Sybil to his office. Sybil recalled later that the place she visited was in 'a big government building'. An unremarkable room, a table covered with manila folders, a couple of chairs, a fan revolving slowly in the grimy air.

The official was extremely polite. He offered Sybil a cup of tea and expressed regret at having to inconvenience her. He showed her the letters she had written Ahuja and asked her to confirm that they were hers. Sybil, in great fear, asked if she was going to be exposed. The man replied that since there was no question about who had killed Ahuja, he saw no reason why her letters should be made public. (In fact, apart from S's, none of the letters ever did figure in the prosecution case.) But he could guarantee nothing. It was not his decision. He could not predict what the defence might do. Sybil, filled with dread, left his office and fled to her friend, my mother, in Ambona.

For a few weeks there was quiet. Then one day, a phone call came from Bombay for Sybil. The same man, the same obsequious regret. He had bad news. Her letters. Certain unscrupulous types. Impossible to control. He very much feared . . . No need to spell it out. In Sybil's imagination, tormenting spectres were already doing his work. Disgrace, they whispered, public humiliation. Not just her own, her husband's and daughter's. Sybil begged him to help her. He was reassuringly sympathetic. Of course, he said, he would do whatever he could. And while *officially* he could do nothing, there was an *unofficial* possibility, which he had hesitated to mention . . . It was abhorrent, went against his principles. It made him ashamed to say it, but Sybil understood, did she not, the way things were done in India? 'Oh thank God,' she cried. 'If it's just a bit of money he wants, tell him. No, please settle it for me. I'll pay you back.'

'She told your mother what she had done,' said Srinuji. 'It was Maya who informed her that she had just been blackmailed.'

'"No, he's a friend," Sybil insisted.

'But Maya said he would prove to be a devil. She called him Mr Shaitan.'

403

'You were wrong,' Sybil told Maya as the summer passed with no more calls. But Maya shook her head.

It began again after Sybil returned to Bombay. Alas, said the official, the forthcoming Nanavati trial was arousing huge interest. It had revived the trouble. He deplored the venality of his unscrupulous colleague, and hated to suggest, but . . . The demand, once again, was relatively modest, but after this he called frequently. Sybil paid and paid. When she had nothing left, she stole from her husband, and borrowed from friends. The first trial passed and her letters had not been mentioned, but the blackmail did not stop and as the second trial approached, the official's demands became more and more rapacious. Then Sylvia Nanavati identified Sybil's letters – *Blitz* announced the existence of 'Mrs ?' and Sybil had to cope with the prurient interest of Killy, who commented on the case at breakfast. 'An Englishwoman, mark you. Serves her bloody well right. Should never have married an Indian in the first place.'

Sybil thought she would go mad. Her love affair had collapsed. She had been jilted in the most contemptuous way by the man she had idolised. She had lost her baby and the foetus had been disposed of on a garbage heap. Her escape to Europe with her husband brought the unlooked-for hope that her marriage might revive. She was struggling to put the traumas behind her. Nanavati's bullets shattered her illusions as surely as Ahuja's skull.

The second trial finished as inconclusively as the first. Nanavati was at liberty, pending the appeal to the Supreme Court. For *Blitz* it was a dream come true. The public queued to buy each new issue. New angles were needed. It was at this time that Ahuja's ghost began to stalk the city in its bloodstained bath towel. The identity of 'Mrs ?' was a secret worth its weight in blood. The blackmailer called almost daily. Gone was any trace of politeness. There was a new, leering tone in his voice. He was peremptory, rude, no longer pretending that he was acting in her interests. His demands increased. Maybe the man sensed that Sybil was at the end of her tether. The goldmine was about to be exhausted. She tried to make a last stand. In desperation she told the man that if he did not stop calling she would go to the press herself. His reply was to take Phoebe from school one afternoon. It must have been the day she went swimming at the beach of the Governor's House. Bringing Phoebe and the ayah with her, Sybil fled for the third time to Ambona.

'This is when your mother intervened,' said Srinuji. 'And this was the act which determined the future for you all. A phone call came. The usual voice asked for Sybil. Your mother saw her friend's hand shake as she took the receiver. Maya seized it and said, in a rage, that the man had done enough, that he should not only leave Sybil alone but return the money she had paid him. Or else she, Maya Sahib, would personally see to it that he was exposed . . . Maya said that she had got Sybil to write down everything: his name, the things he had said, the amounts he had extorted, dates, times, methods and places of payment. Sybil could describe the inside of his office. She knew things that would ruin his career. All this was in writing, your mother said, and unless the calls stopped, it would be used.'

The man's reply filled Maya with fear.

'You are foolish to threaten me,' he said. 'Your own position is not impeccable. Your connections with foreigners and subversive elements have been noted. We are aware of your latest activities, stirring up discontent among villagers. You should be careful. A woman like you can make enemies. You live in a wild place. Your son roams all day over the hills unsupervised. Who knows what might happen?'

Some weeks later, Rosie fell to her death.

'Your mother did not believe it was an accident,' said Srinuji. 'And neither did Sybil. Immediately after the Killigrew ayah's death the police ransacked your house in Ambona. Why? What were they looking for? Sybil could bear no more. Within days she and her daughter were on their way to England . . . Once Sybil had left, things quietened down. Nanavati ran out of appeals and in the end – after the judgement of the Supreme Court had been set aside by politicians determined to free him – he too left the country, unaware of the second crime, blackmail, built on the foundations of his own. Bhalu, no one was aware of it. Not the lawyers, the courts, the press. Only two people left in India knew. One was the blackmailer and the other was your mother.'

It was soon Maya's turn to feel the pressure. Calls came asking her to 'deliver the package' or face the consequences.

'She refused, believing, I think,' said Srinuji, 'that safety lay in holding on to it . . . You, Bhalu, were sent out of harm's way to a boarding school a thousand miles away.'

Over the next few years Maya continued to receive calls, but fewer in number and the message now was 'glad to see you are still demonstrating sense'.

'Actually, she was not,' said Srinuji. 'She had written a script for a movie. One that would tell the whole story of the blackmail. It would be woven as fiction around the Nanavati murder. She had planned to call it *Gunah-e-ishq. The Crime of Loving.*'

'What happened to it?' I asked.

'No one was willing to produce it. Your mother believed it was the influence of this man she called Shaitan.'

'But who was he, this Shaitan?'

'Whoever he was, he was a very powerful man.'

'There is no sign of it among her papers.'

'Let me finish the story . . . You went on to university in Delhi, and it was many years before you returned to Bombay. One night you became involved in a fracas in a Muslim bazaar area. You were arrested and spent a night in the police station.'

'Yes, but I was released after a few hours.'

'What you did not know was that your mother received a phone call. The same feared voice. "Your son is in custody, arrested last night in a Muslim area. Seems he is a troublemaker like you. Forget your stupid script, your film career is over. Give me the thing I want. This is your last warning."

'And that, Bhalu, is why your revels were cut short and why you were sent, with a speed which must have surprised you, to study at a university on the other side of the world. It is why your mother followed with your sisters and would not go back. She wanted none of you to set foot in India again until this man was dead.'

'And is he not dead? He must be very old.'

'From the way she spoke, I would guess he is still alive.'

'His name is in a notebook. But where is the notebook?'

'Who knows if it ever existed?' said Srinuji. 'It may have been that she invented it to scare him off. But once she had mentioned it, the fact of its existence or non-existence made no difference. It *could* exist.'

'Maybe it's what Sybil was looking for,' I said. 'When she went back to India to find Maya.'

'It may be,' he said. 'Suffering. Desire for revenge. These things can be carried not just for one lifetime, but many.'

A picture came to my mind. Phoebe at our lunch, saying, 'What happened was so evil that it can *never* be forgotten, or forgiven.'

So I took a deep breath and decided to tell him. 'Phoebe wants me to go to India with her, to find the man who did this.'

'And will you go?'

'What is your advice?'

'I have already given it. Remember our game of moamma?'

'Hello?' I said into the phone. 'My wife and I were staying with you recently. About three weeks ago – Phoebe Killigrew.'

There was a pause. 'Oh yes?' Slight surprise in the voice.

'She left her lighter behind . . . a gold lighter, with her initials on. You were going to post it, but it hasn't arrived. Can you tell me, what address did you send it to?'

'Just a minute, sir.' Susurrus at the other end.

'We were in the white bedroom. The Corfiot, I think.'

Pause. A murmured conversation. Was it my imagination or did I hear a giggle?

'Yes sir, I remember you now. And your address?'

'We have two. My wife booked and I don't know which one she gave. Was it . . .' I cast about for an imaginary address. '17 Sleeman Road, Crediton, Devon?'

'No sir, that is not the address we have here.'

'Well, what address do you have?'

'I'm afraid I can't give guests' details over the phone.'

'Damn it, I'm her husband!'

A long pause. 'In which case, sir, surely you don't need to ask *me* for your own address.'

Wife, I had called her, and wife so many people had thought she would be. Ben, the stationmaster's son. Jula's mother, laughing till she choked, over her smoky hearth, asking to be invited to our wedding. Maya's and Sybil's faces, when Babu the driver told them they were destined to be joint-mothers-in-law. They had laughed too. Maya said, 'Destiny is not *what-will-be*. Destiny is what I do *now*.'

Was our destiny what *she* had done? Or *he*, that man whose name I did not know, whom Maya had called Shaitan, devil? Suppose he had been honest, and done his duty to protect the innocent and vulnerable, instead of breaking the laws he had sworn, and was paid, to uphold, what might my life have been like? Well, I would not have lost Phoebe, first love, childhood sweetheart, *jaan-e-janaan*, life and soul, but neither would I have met Katy.

I love two women. Which of them is my soulmate? Can a soul have more than one mate? Must I choose? I recognise, with a sense more of dread than of irony, that I am caught in the same dilemma that had trapped Mister Love all those years ago. How strange that I have also found myself in that other situation, which Nanavati, the man of honour, found so intolerable that it drove him to kill. Was I dishonourable to have felt no murderous urgings? At the time I had blamed myself, rather than Katy or the other man. Now, looking back to that day through the gulf and abysm of time – 'gulf and abysm', where did that come from? I thought it was Shakespeare, but it isn't, therefore probably Piglet – I understand why I was not angry, but moved and awestruck.

About five years ago I was looking at illustrations in one of the few genuinely valuable books that has passed through my hands, a seventeenth-century work on alchemy, whose splendid title began: *Amphitheatrum Sapientiæ Æterna, Solius Veræ, Christiano-Cabalisticum, Mageicum, Physico-chymicum, Tertriunum, Catholicon: Instructore Henricus Kunrath Lips. Theosophiæ Amatore Fideli, et Medicinæ utriusque Doctore,* and ended: *Hallelæ-Iáh! Hallelæ-Iáh! Hallelæ-Iáh! Phy diaboló!* The book contained a number of loose plates from some other text, hand-coloured by a long-ago owner. One of these pictures, whose beauty took away my breath, depicted the universe as concentric rings containing a rainbow, the sun, clouds and flames, encircling a central sphere of luminous night filled with stars and the crescent moon. Under the stars stretched a peaceful landscape and in the middle of this lay, coupling, a reddish-brown man and a white woman, by whose feet appeared a golden sun and silver moon. Underneath were the lines:

> *The white woman, if she be married to the brown man,*
> *presently they embrace, and embracing are coupled.*
> *By themselves they are dissolved*
> *and by themselves they are brought together,*
> *that they which were two, may be made as it were one body.*

I remembered that eerie, unearthly bird music, and it came to me: this is the music that accompanies the creation of life. Thus, thus, had it been when I & I were made. The honeyed movement, bodies pairing in equal consent, joined by that integument that seemed to belong to neither or both: it was all there in the picture. What I had witnessed in such pitiless detail was an arcanum being revealed: I had seen the alchemical marriage of souls. The meaning of that vision was at once clear and obscure: the man should have been me. But who was the woman?

I caught a train to London and hung about near the hotel. My patience, eventually, was rewarded by the approach of a familiar lugubrious face: the waiter who had served us three weeks earlier, on his way to work. I stopped him. We had a brief conversation. A note changed hands. He told me to wait in a café at the end of the street. I ordered a coffee and noticed, when I stirred it, that my hand was trembling.

There was a young couple huddled at a nearby table. The boy pulled a pack of cigarettes from his pocket and opened it. What looked like a condom fell out. The girl gave him a shove. Burst out laughing. About half an hour later the waiter came in. I gave him another £20 and he slid a scrap of paper in front of me. It was a London address less than a mile away. Bright's Lane, W8.

Kensington, just south of the High Street, is an area of smart town-houses. She, or at any rate her husband, must have pots of money. Well, that much was already clear from her smart clothes, the car, the expensive hotel. Bright's Lane sounded very desirable. I was imagining one of those chic little mews where off-duty stock-brokers can be seen at weekends with their sleeves rolled up, tinkering with Aston Martins and old E-types. But Bright's Lane was a surprise. I found an alley, lined with dustbins, that ran behind the back doors of the High Street shops. Number 12 was a black-painted door, half-ajar. There were a couple of bells, but none bore a name. Inside was a dark hall, bare floorboards and black plastic rubbish sacks stacked along the wall. Everything was filthy. I could not believe she lived here. I went up to the first floor. Two doors, the paint on them peeling. From behind one came the thudding of a bass, which stopped when I knocked. The door was opened by a young guy with stringy hair. Beyond him in the flat I could see a battered sofa against which leaned the guitar he had been playing.

'Phoebe?' he said, in answer to my enquiry. 'Upstairs. Top floor. Don't know if she's about. She's away mostly.'

'Is her husband here?'

'Husband? Sorry mate, no idea.' He gave me a peculiar look and shut the door. As I climbed the stairs I heard the bass resume.

The second and third floors were like the first. Outside one door stood a rusting pram filled with empty cornflake packets. It didn't feel like the sort of place she would live. What about her husband? The downstairs neighbour – neighbour? weird thought – didn't seem to know about him. Was this some sort of pied à terre? Had she chosen a place so unlikely that no one, for instance her husband, would think of looking for her here? The stairs to the top floor were as bare and dingy as the rest of the building. They led up to a small landing and a single door painted in faded rainbow colours. A moment's panic. I was no longer sure I wanted to find out what lay behind it. In my mind I heard Katy's voice: 'She's damaged goods, Bhalu. Madder than her mother was. You don't know her at all. She is a complete stranger.'

Summoning my courage, I knocked. No reply. I knocked again and the sound seemed to echo in the building. From downstairs came the faint thump of the bass.

Half an hour later found me, in a state of confusion and not a little funk, sitting in a wine bar that was doing its futile best to ooze continental charm. At least there was no young man spilling condoms from his cigarette packet. Without much enthusiasm, I scanned a long list of overpriced, indifferent wines and decided on a coffee. Would soon be awash with the stuff. What a bizarre day. I had decided to wait an hour and then go back. It was 5.45 p.m. If Phoebe worked – why not? I could no longer be certain of anything – there was a chance she might be home soon. So I got a table in the window and watched the street. Across the road was a salon called *The Laser-E-Razor* (for that carefree hair-free look). Three girls with near-identical tans and streaked-blonde hair came out and stood waiting while one of them locked the door. They crossed the street to the bar and took the table next to mine. I caught fragments of their conversation.

'. . . this hairy back. So he asks if we can do his arse.'

'No way!'

'That's what I said, but he drops his knickers . . .'

One of the girls, looking around for a waiter, caught my eye and realised I was listening. I gave her a sympathetic smile.

'. . . bends over and parts the bloody cheeks. There was a bit of *paper* stuck to the hairs.'

'God! Gross!'

The girl whispered to her colleagues. Three blonde heads turned and looked at me. I raised my coffee cup. 'Dirty old man,' I could almost hear them thinking.

Then I saw Phoebe. Surely it was her – fair as any of these three, T-shirt, faded jeans – on the other side of the road with a bag of shopping. She turned a corner towards the alley. I gave her a couple of minutes then paid my bill and left.

The building seemed darker and emptier than before. Silence, from behind the bass-player's door. My footsteps seemed to crash up the stairs. I came to the rainbow door. A line of light now showing underneath. Faint music, a radio or television switched on. I took a breath and knocked.

'Who is it?' called Phoebe's voice.

I dared not reply.

'Mario, is that you?'

A lock was turned. The door opened.

She screamed and tried to shut it. I put my foot in the jamb, behaving like a character out of a cheap thriller. My own detective, in fact.

'Wait! Phoebe, I must talk to you.'

'Take your foot out of the door.'

'No. Phoebe, please let me in.'

'I can't,' she said.

'Why not?'

'Because you've got your foot in the door!'

'Oh.' I withdrew my foot. The door closed, there was the clink of a chain falling away, then it opened again. Phoebe stood in the doorway, with her hands on her hips.

'Upon my life and soul, if it isn't my little friend Bhalu.'

But she was smiling. 'Well,' she said, when we had stared at one another for what seemed like an eternity, 'you've gone to all the trouble of finding me. Don't you want to come in?'

The room was enormous, with large windows that overlooked the High Street. Its floors were of polished wood overlaid with Oriental rugs and it was filled with heavy furniture of a kind I had not seen for years. Indian furniture, from an era that is hardly remembered, even in India. In a corner stood a carved rosewood sideboard. There was a writing desk, also in rosewood, and a sofa upholstered in pale silk, its back carved into branching trees full of monkeys and birds. This was surely no pied à terre. The walls were crowded with photographs and paintings in heavy gilded frames: a portrait of an Englishman in Hussar's uniform; a plump brocade-clad raja wearing strings of pearls and emeralds that would have bankrupted a small nation. Half-finished canvases were stacked against a wall.

'Don't look so alarmed,' said Phoebe. No kiss this time. She was still standing, hands on hips, apparently amused by the gaping figure revolving slowly on its axis in the middle of her floor.

'Forgive me, I am just a bit . . . flabbergasted.'

In a far corner of the room was a thing I had not seen since childhood, a tiger's head, yellowed ivories opened in a snarl.

'Better get you a drink then. Do sit.' Then, following my eyes, 'Don't worry. I shan't bite you.'

'*This* is where you live?'

'Yes.'

'On your own?'

'Yes. How did you find me?'

'I bribed someone at the hotel.'

She raised an eyebrow. 'Resourceful,' she said. 'But that's you all over, isn't it?'

'Is it?' I felt a stab of annoyance. How could she be so casual about having lied to me?

She sighed. 'I'm sorry. I was going to tell you last time, but . . .' She opened the sideboard, revealing a glass forest within. Bent to extract something, presenting to me a denim-clad rump and long dancer's legs. Ouch! Those laser-blondes were right. Dirty old man. Appalling. I was unable to look at her without my feelings being muddied by lust. The green butt of a bottle appeared between her thighs. Cork's small, rude noise. She straightened up, poured with her back to me. 'Bhalu, I'm very embarrassed. About the hotel. What happened . . .'

I thought, which *bit* of what happened?

'Did you manage to catch your train?'

'Oh yes,' I said at last.

'I'm so glad,' she said, returning with two glasses of red wine. 'I was worried about Katy.'

It was a decent wine, earthy, dark as her rosewood.

'Phoebe,' I said. 'Does your husband know about this place?'

She looked at me and did that little thing with her head. 'No.'

'But why?'

'Well,' she said, 'I'll give you one guess, my dear.'

'Look, I know about Sleeman,' I said, a little desperately.

'Sleeman?'

'It isn't a village in Yorkshire, near Richmond. Sleeman was a man who wrote a book called *A Journey Through Oude.* You saw it in my mother's bookshelf when Piglet was pestering you to say where you lived.'

She settled herself on the sofa, crossed her legs and patted the cushion beside her. 'Come and sit down, Bhalu.'

'Well? Is that true or not?'

'I had forgotten the name,' she said. 'Clever of you.'

Again I felt that stab of irritation. No, something hotter.

I said, 'You must have had your reasons for . . . well, to be blunt, for lying. I won't ask what they are, but . . .'

Her eyes held mine for a long moment. Then she said, 'Oh shit, I was afraid you'd see it like that.'

'Phoebe, what am I supposed to be seeing? All this.' I gestured round the room. 'I'm lost. What about Peter, your husband? If you live here, alone, where does he live?'

'Bhalu, there *is* no Peter!'

'You mean you're no longer together?'

'No, I mean there never was a Peter. I made him up. I'm not married. I never married.'

'I've lived here since I was a student.'

'Has *anything* you told me been true? I thought you went to the Caribbean. Or was that a fantasy too?'

'No! Bhalu, you can't understand. What it was like, when I went back to live with Mummy. She wanted me to give this place up, but I didn't, because I had to have somewhere of my own, to get away. And then when I was living in the Caribbean, I hung onto it. I don't know why, some sixth sense. Besides . . .' she swept her arm around the room, 'I had nowhere else for all this. It was just one room then, this one. But I'm the longest-serving tenant now and the landlord can't get rid of me, so he gave me the whole of the top floor. Here. Come and look.'

She got up and opened double-doors in the far corner. Light poured in from a huge, raftered room with a ceiling that was at least half skylight. In the centre was another of those heavy relics from old India, a carved four-poster bed, hung with Tussore silks.

'This place is a palace.'

'A palace hidden in a slum,' she said. 'The landlord thinks that if it gets bad enough I'll leave. But it suits me to have it the way it is. Who would want to burgle a place like this?'

'What about the other tenants? I met a chap with a guitar.'

'Mario. He's at the Royal College. Studying Baroque violin. Most of the people who live here are friends of mine.'

Looking at the bed's ancient cream and brown Tussores — wild silks, not spun by common mulberry-crunching silkworms, but unravelled from the hen's-egg-sized cocoons of huge cinnabar and ochre moths with owl's-eyes on their wings, and of long-tailed moonmoths whose phosphorus wings used to batter against our windows in Ambona — I was reminded of the marital four-poster Sybil had found so daunting as a young bride.

'Phoebe. Your furniture. Where did you get it?'

'My daddy,' she said. 'It's all he left and all I have left of him.'

Now that I looked again, the apartment was full of pictures of the same man. I recognised him, tall, with bushy eyebrows. The stern man who had stood beside Phoebe at Rosie's funeral. There were faded pictures of him as a young man in uniform fresh from Burma. On his wedding day, with the young Sybil, and a guard of honour of fellow officers. Smiling, standing with one foot on a supine tiger. Black and white pictures. Daddy photographed with Pandit Nehru. Looking rather grim, receiving an honour of some kind from a politician dressed in the Congress style, white cotton cap and kurta. Daddy in swimming trunks by a large pool which might have been Breach Candy. Daddy in a jeep, with Indian farm workers standing all round. These pictures hung on every wall, stood along every surface. How had I missed them before?

Apart from the wedding picture, there was not a single portrait of her mother. There were a few pictures of Phoebe as a young woman. Yes, she had been stunning. Phoebe in a bikini on a beach, probably the Caribbean. Phoebe and a man sitting on the steps of a house. One other photograph I recognised. A fair girl and a dark boy in a garden in Ambona, with the high cloud-cutting ridge of Bicchauda rising behind.

But the pictures of Killy were everywhere. The largest painting, an oil of him seated wearing tweeds, with a shotgun across his lap and spaniel at his feet, must have been done late in his life. It hung in a massive gilt frame in the centre of a wall. I saw that a garland of dried roses depended from it. On a table below stood a pair of small portraits and two silver candlesticks with half-consumed candles.

The place was a shrine to her dead father.

Phoebe's father, garlanded with roses dead as he, studied my face
from his pigment world. He was frowning slightly. I had never
known him as a child, never met him bar that one time, in the
exceptional, dripping circumstances of Ambona cemetery. Had he
minded that his little daughter's best friend was an Indian boy?
Sybil's diary noted the advice he gave her as they stood at the rail
of their steamer and the smell of Bombay came out over the water
to greet them: 'We have a *duty* to be friendly to Indians, but we
must never forget that our souls are different.' Deeper relations
were out of the question: 'Fish cannot marry tomatoes' (an idea
today's bioFrankensteins struggle to refute). Killy might not have
disapproved of me as a boy, but his gun-toting portrait disliked
the idea that I might be her *boyfriend*. Its eyes seemed unnaturally
living. In horror movies one is used to seeing eyeballs glaring from
behind holes cut in a canvas. The portrait's eyes had something of
this quality, but the holes were painted holes and the dimension
beyond, from which her father so warily appraised me, was some
brushstroked eternity.

The painter had added a touch to signify Killy's life in India. A
painting within the painting. The dull gleam of a gilt frame
behind the sitter enclosed a Mughal tomb, its dome ruined, grass-
covered and half-fallen, in a plain where a herd of wild asses
grazed. No whim, this, but a reference to the power of the British,
who ruled now where once Jamshed had gloried and drunk deep,
and who shot tigers where Bahram the Great Hunter (where is he

now, the wild ass stamps o'er his head?) had roved unchallenged. Fitzgerald's translation of Omar Khayyam had presumably been a favourite of Killy's. I wondered if Killy knew that in the original Persian, the line about Bahram, the king who loved hunting the wild ass, contains a deadly irony. *Gur*, the wild ass, and nickname of Emperor Bahram, also means the grave.

Killy the Mighty Hunter, where was he? The British in their turn were gone, along with their allies. Crumbling, grass growing from its cornices, was the palace in Kumharawa where poor Nafisa Jaan was entombed. Killy's portrait was itself grave-goods. I sat heavily back on the sofa. The things in the flat seemed suddenly sinister. A shrine, I had called it, but it was really a tomb, filled with the funerary treasures of a dead king. A tomb into which was sealed the high priestess of his cult, his daughter.

'You only just caught me,' said Phoebe. 'Another couple of days and I'd have been away.'

Yes, and I'd caught her off guard. Surely that was consternation on her face, just for a moment, when she saw who it was. Now she was back to that lighthearted nonchalance which, I increasingly realised, was an affection. I had glimpsed her soul, superstitious, terrified that her mother's spirit might be near. She had cried in the steamy Brighton café, when she told me about the last time she saw her father. In the hotel, she had become hysterical. But . . . perhaps she read the annoyance in my face because she said, 'I was going to get in touch, Bhalu, when I got back. Promise. I have something important to tell you.'

'Phoebe,' I said. 'Stop this now. If you have any respect for me at all, stop this play-acting. Why did you tell me you were married?

Why didn't you give me your address? Why take me to a hotel? And this place – is it *safe*? Why stay here? You obviously have money . . . Or perhaps,' I said as the idea struck me, 'you *do* have another home somewhere. Is that it? Mario said you're away a lot. Where do you go? What do you do?'

She had a way, that I had noticed in the restaurant, of holding her wine glass with both hands, like a medieval drinking-cup, and peering over the rim with those startling eyes. She listened politely as the pent-up questions of several months poured out.

'Why do I live here? Okay. First, because I always have. Next, because it's cheap. Last, because I don't plan to stay in England. One of these days I'll have enough saved, then I'll disappear and never come back.'

'You're always disappearing. Are you going to tell me where to?' She didn't reply.

'This woman-of-mystery act is wearing a bit thin. You know everything about me. You've been to my house, you've met my wife. You asked me to go to India with you. Now tell me the truth! Where do you go to? How do you make a living? That hotel . . .'

'Stop! Please!' she said. She looked suddenly tired. 'The hotel is owned by a friend. Natasha. An old friend. We were at the Slade together . . .' She stopped and I waited, determined that this time she would explain herself.

'So if I want to treat someone special, that's where I take them. I never have to pay. At least, not with money.'

'Not with money?'

She was going to say something but changed her mind. I waited. Her head drooped as if some spring within her had abruptly wound down.

'Bhalu, when we were at the hotel, remember I said there was something I wanted to tell you? But I was afraid. In case I was the sort of person you wouldn't want to know.'

'Yes,' I said, 'but you were talking about your mother's diary. I can understand why you were afraid.'

'It's mixed up with that, Bhalu, but it isn't that.'

I had no idea what she might be going to say. All sorts of wild ideas ran through my brain. Katy's flat statement, 'She's the sort of woman who takes men for what she can get.' What sort of woman would take men to a hotel like that? Why did she not have to pay? What was she — some sort of call girl?

Phoebe went over and knelt before a chest of some red wood, streaked with crimson, around whose periphery carved dragons chased one another.

'Come here,' she said.

She opened the lid. Inside was a tray, divided into small square compartments, in the same strange timber. The chest had an incense-like fragrance, like the dry spice of a cigar box.

'Is this some sort of sandalwood? I've never seen it before.'

'It's toon tree wood. The dragons are done in coconut.'

'What is it?'

'An opium chest. It belonged to my great-grandfather. How do you think the Killigrews made their fortune?'

More fantasies. Phoebe away for weeks at a time in Pakistan to collect opium? Drug smuggler? Opium dealer?

But it wasn't lumps of opium that sat in the compartments. They were full of cassettes, neatly labelled in date order. There were also some packets of photographs. An idea occurred to me.

'When you said, just now, that you didn't pay with money . . . Is this how you pay? With things? Objects?'

'Oh no,' she said. 'Every so often, I give Nat a painting.'

'A painting?'

'Yes, I'm sure I told you. I'm a painter.'

'You said you'd tried painting but given it up.'

'I never gave it up. It's all I've done for a living, ever.'

She opened a packet of photographs, sifted through it and handed me a print. A large man with a fair beard gazed out at me.

'This is Wulf. He's a friend. He has a wonderful name, Beowulf Cooper.'

'Is he your boyfriend?' Ouch. It had jumped out before I could think. Instant reversion to type. Behaving like a jealous Indian. Nanavati. I had not felt like that about Katy.

'Why do you leap to conclusions?' said Phoebe. 'Wulf is a good friend. Just a good friend. He runs . . . a sort of community. Up in Scotland. One can go there to rest, and think, and meditate . . . and paint. Look, I'll show you.' She pulled out more photographs. 'It's an island, just off the west coast. Not very big. There used to be a farm, but now it's just the community.'

I was looking at a low green island rising out of a calm sea of intensest blue. The picture had been taken from a boat, and the lines of its wake were carved like ridges in blue wood.

'There's these few little houses,' said Phoebe, pointing out a cluster of white boxes in a valley. 'A boat calls from the mainland once a week, in good weather. In winter you have to send for one, which can be difficult, because there's no phone. Wulf won't have one.'

So that was why she had never phoned, nor given a number.

'What happens in an emergency?'

'We have a radio, which is kept locked up. Once, we needed it and it wouldn't work. So we lit a fire on top there. Luinne Bheinne. The hill of laughter . . . It can also mean hill of anger.'

Another picture. Phoebe, in jeans and a thick sweater, standing on a hilltop. Beyond her the sea, a blue plate, stretching to an open horizon. 'There's a beach. You can't see it. In the summer the sea is warm enough to swim in.'

'What do you do up there?'

'I paint. When I've got enough paintings, I come back down to London. There's a little gallery in Cork Street which usually will take a few . . . It pays for this place and I can send Wulf some money . . . I stay here, a week. Perhaps two. At most a month. Then I'm off again.'

'What else do you do?' There was something she wasn't saying.

'Work hard. There's lots to do. Cooking, cleaning, repairs . . . gardening. We grow a lot of our own food.'

'Phoebe, what sort of community?'

'Well . . .' She took a deep breath. 'This is what I've got to tell you, so I may as well get it over with.' But she stopped.

'Go on, please. You can trust me.'

'It's a place where people can go, if they need to get away from things . . . if they are feeling disturbed. I mean, mentally ill.'

'Okay.' My mind was working like a propeller fouled in weed. 'But *you* go there – why? To help Wulf?'

'Bhalu, I go because I need to.'

We were both still kneeling by the opium chest. At least half a minute had passed and I had not responded.

Phoebe said, in a small voice, 'Oh, don't look at me like that, Bhalu. I shouldn't have told you.'

I put my arms round her. I held her. I hugged her. I cradled her. I said, 'I'm here now. I will take care of you.'

Outside, the long summer evening was beginning to fade.

'Since Mummy died, that's when it started . . . If you've never had bad depression, Bhalu, you cannot imagine what it is like.'

'Tell me then,' I said. 'Tell me, what is it like? I will help you get rid of it. I must.'

(God forgive my ignorant pomposity, I meant it.)

I am lying on Phoebe's four-poster bed, the skylight above me a deep royal blue. Shadowy half-light in the vast room. No longer day, not yet night. A woman's voice, Phoebe's, close by my ear, says '. . . hiding in sullen sheets all day?' A deep Scottish voice, equally close, replies, 'What are you hiding from, in *sullen* sheets?'

PHOEBE: It's me, isn't it? Realising I am still me.
WULF: Who are you anyway?
PHOEBE: *(Rather bitter laugh)* A woman growing old without a lover. *(Long pause)* I know what love is. I knew when I was a child, when I was a girl, when I was young. I knew what love was . . .
WULF: And now?
PHOEBE: All those selves trapped inside one another, knotted and twisted up together . . . the little girl who doesn't understand why Daddy sent her away. The art student who ran away to sea but never learned to paint like Gauguin, the daughter who tried to escape from her mother . . . but there's no escape, is there? *(He doesn't respond. Loud lamenting of gulls. A distant murmur which may be the sea. One can*

427

imagine them, sitting on a hillside, perhaps the hill of laughter and anger, with the tape running.) This is a paradox. I sleep in the day because I can't bear to be awake. At night, I daren't sleep for fear of dreaming. I leave on my bedside lamp, then wake in the small hours, terrified to see the light shining on familiar things. Clock. Book. Glass of water. Ordinary things are monstrous . . . proof that everything is still as it was . . . *(wind blowing across the microphone intermittently blots her out)* . . . a kind of twilight between waking and sleeping . . . *(wind is ruffianly)*. Then the whispering begins.

WULF: *Who* is whispering?

PHOEBE: You know who!

WULF: I know what you tell me. Who is whispering? *(Long silence with wind noise.)* . . . is whispering?

PHOEBE: *(Another long silence.)* My mother.

WULF: What does she whisper?

PHOEBE: Things I shouldn't know. I don't want to hear them.

WULF: What are you feeling?

PHOEBE: Terror.

WULF: What terrifies you?

PHOEBE: That she'll come back. That I'll *see* her.

WULF: Okay, so we're back to this . . . *(Female snuffling. Blowing nose.)* What does she say to you?

PHOEBE: Do I have to?

(Wulf does not reply. Long silence broken by the sound of gulls.)

PHOEBE: She says she must go to India. This is what keeps running through my mind, the conversation I had with her, before she went. She asks me to lend her the money for her ticket and for a hotel. She says, 'All I need is a cheap hotel.'

WULF: And what do you do?

PHOEBE: I give it to her. The money. In fact, I buy her ticket. She is gone about five weeks. Then a postcard arrives. It gives the date of her return . . . asks me to go to see her.

WULF: What happens next?

PHOEBE: I *don't* want to talk about it.

WULF: You don't want to, but you are going to because you are strong. You're strong enough to look at this.

PHOEBE: No, no, look at me, I'm a fucking mess.

WULF: I am looking at you. I see an attractive woman, well groomed. I see a good, decent person. I see a friend for whom I have respect. No fucking way are you a fucking mess . . . What happens next?

PHOEBE: The date comes. Of her return. I know I should go to the airport, but I don't. I feel horrible, mean, because she'll be broke . . . she has to go all the way to Lincolnshire on her own. But I don't go. I find something else that must be done. And in case you think . . . I wasn't depressed then, just guilty and miserable as hell.

WULF: Okay. So what happens next?

PHOEBE: The day arrives. She must have returned. I know I should go to see her, but . . .

WULF: But?

PHOEBE: I put it off. I find excuses.

WULF: But you *do* go. I know. So what changes your mind?

PHOEBE: I remembered the dream. She told me she'd had a dream that made her decide to go to India. *(Distress.)* She was so lonely . . . I left her there, alone.

WULF: So you go. What happens?

PHOEBE: Yes, I go. At last, I bloody well go.

WULF: You sound angry. That's good. This anger that you've been holding down, it turns into depression. Let it out! What happens next?

PHOEBE: I get in my car and drive. Every mile gets harder. While I'm far away, I can cut myself off, or cut her off. She's there, in a sort of bubble. She's *always* been there, she'll always be there. She's there in her house, reading, or cooking. She is so poor. I used to send her money, when I could – a bit here and there, sometimes a lot, hundreds of pounds. It would last for a while, but it was never enough.

WULF: You did what you could for your mother. You're going to see her . . . You're driving . . .

PHOEBE: Yes, I'm driving. I'm in my car. I'm leaving London, heading north. I'm leaving my world, entering hers. With every mile I can feel the misery growing, but . . . how can I describe this? It's not *mine* – I'm already as unhappy as I can be. It's *hers*, reaching out to me. The signs by the roads . . . *A1: The North, Grantham 54 miles* . . . are messages of loneliness from her to me. Gradually the whole landscape, and everything in it, become her messengers. The names of villages and towns I pass through accuse me. Bitchfield, that's a good one, Ingoldsby, Humby . . . their name signs shout out as I pass, 'We didn't leave. We stayed here, near her.' *(Sound of crying.)* 'We didn't abandon her.'

WULF: It's painful for you. But don't stop. You must go on.

PHOEBE: I can't . . . I don't want to see . . .

In her car, Phoebe is crying, remembering how her mother was when she was little. She is thinking, I'm her child, it's my duty to look after her, and I left her on her own. Outside, the flat Lincolnshire levels are passing, big wide fields. From some, smoke is rising, stubble burning after the harvest. She can see for miles, and each redbrick barn, farm, pub she passes reminds her that just over the horizon, her mother is waiting. She is crying as she drives, her slim hand reaching down to change the gears, slowing down behind a tractor whose driver waves as she passes. She does not turn back.

At last, there is relief from the monotony of the fen, a green ridge rising ahead. The road winds across a marshy valley and climbs up to a village whose buildings are outlined against the sky.

She comes to the first houses. It's a tiny place. Quiet. The car crawls past a pub, an old windmill. One more mile. Then ahead of her, she sees the opening in the hedge, the track that leads to her mother's bungalow. She bumps along the pitted ground. Birds are quarrelling over a ploughed field to one side. The car stops, its engine shuts off. For a few long moments silence descends on the scene: the small building, uncared for, in a wild garden. Dark trees behind. Then the car door opens and Phoebe steps out.

Nothing has changed. The path to the door is covered by weeds. She can hardly make it out. Here, in great abundance, are the dandelions her mother claimed to eat. There are brambles up round the windows. Thickets of them, loaded with fruit. The windows behind are rotting, falling to pieces. Phoebe is in tears. She is ashamed. She knocks at the door, glances at her watch. No reply. The bell doesn't work. She goes to look in a window. The drawing room is empty. Perhaps Sybil has gone out.

Phoebe stands for a moment, one hand on her head, wondering what to do. Then goes round the corner of the house, into a part of garden enclosed by a crumbling wall. Her mother's bedroom window is guarded by a screen of brambles. Carefully, she pulls

431

one thorny stem aside, another, peers through. Suddenly she is tearing at the brambles with her bare hands, fighting to reach the window. The brambles fly back, rip her arms. Her hands are bloody. A thick green stem rakes her across the cheek. She reaches the window. Puts her face to the glass. There is no one near to hear the sound that begins as a moan and becomes a howl.

The room is in green twilight. Phoebe can see the bed and, lying on it, the dark shape of her mother. She's hammering at the pane. 'Mummy! Mummy, wake up!' Glass shatters and Phoebe's hands are wearing crimson gloves. She reaches in . . . oh God . . . the smell . . . and the sound, a great buzzing. She wrenches the window open and climbs up. For a moment she wavers, seems to tumble inside.

Phoebe's scarlet hands clutch a handkerchief to her mouth. Her deep in-sung breaths turn to sobs of terror as she approaches the bed. Then horrible, dry retching. Sybil no longer has a face. Where it had been is a black, shiny pullulating surface. Her daughter stands beside her. The front of her jeans is turning darker, a spreading patch of darkness. She squats down by her mother's bed. Sybil's face disintegrates. It explodes into a swarm of blue-bottles. They settle on Phoebe, and she is slapping at them, screaming like a crazy woman.

Above me, seen through the architecture of Phoebe's great bed, the skylight was dark except for a few ragged smears of light, clouds lit by a hidden moon. A glowing green pinprick marked where the cassette player stood on the floor. Phoebe's voice, punctuated by sobs so violent they sounded like retching, had abruptly cut to the hiss of virgin tape running through the heads. Eventually this was ended by a faint click, since when there had been silence and darkness. I don't know how long had elapsed. I was thinking of something my father had told me about my grandfather's last days. The old man had been ill for some time. His heart was weak. He had difficulty breathing and ordered his bed to be brought out into the courtyard, the same place where half a century earlier the scorpion had fallen off the roof onto my sleeping father. The women of the household fussed around him with decoctions of fennel and nutmeg. They brought Nepalese comb-honey from the bazaar and used it as a treat instead of sugar to sweeten the glass of milk which was the only food he would take. The old man grew impatient with them. He waved them away and demanded his hookah, swearing at them until they brought it, and again when the bowl was not correctly filled, the coals were improperly placed, and when they forgot to freshen the orange-water through which the smoke gurgled during its long passage from the brazier to his lips.

The women smoothed over the courtyard floor with a thin wash of clay and cowdung, inscribed yantras and sigils around it with coloured powders and performed pujas for his recovery.

When this had no effect they called in a brahmin, who ensconsed himself like a living portrait in the frame of mystical emblems and immediately went to work, muttering the myriad names of God, stubby fingers working round his rosary of scrotal rudraksh seeds.

Grandfather was insufferably rude to him. 'Why are you wasting my time with this bakwaas (nonsense)? Are you determined to spoil my few remaining hours?'

The priest, mindful of the dignity of his calling, or perhaps of his fee (one hundred and fifty rupees a day plus two full meals), swallowed his pride along with his rice, curd, dal and two sorts of vegetable, accompanied by home-made pickle and potato-stuffed parathas made with best ghee, and maintained his thankless vigil, ready to begin the whispering, the sky-map the old man would need in the beyond. His soul, once freed from its skull prison by the kindly blow of his son, my father, would rise from the funeral pyre, up into the air, which would open, like the hole in the hub of a bullock-cart wheel, like the bowl of a hookah, like the mouth of a hungry child. Grandfather had no time for suns and moons and godlings. All his adult life he had been a member of the Arya Samaj, a reformist Hindu movement which was impatient of ritual mumbo-jumbo, disapproved of idol-worship and campaigned for the emancipation of women and the abolition of the caste system, whose incantating representative now sat before him. So he lies on his bed, scowling and puffing smoke at the shaven-headed brahmin, who is provoked at last to complain, somewhat absurdly, 'Baba-ji, smoking is very injurious to the health.'

'But good for your bald pate,' retorts Grandfather, determined to squeeze what enjoyment can be had from his final moments, and calls for last night's hookah scrapings to be boiled up with mustard oil to make a hair-engendering poultice. The household chitter and chide him and the brahmin says, 'Anxiety is making you bad-tempered. That is natural. Try to look forward to the next life, because whatever your karma, for that split-second before you are reincarnated, your soul returns to God in a realm without pain.'

'To hell with you,' Grandfather says. 'There is no world without pain. And if there were it would not be worth living in.'

The picture in my mind changes. I see my mother. She is lying propped up on pillows. We — Ninu, Suki and I — are with her, kneeling beside her bed. Maya's face is gaunt, her breathing harsh. She can no longer speak. Maybe she can't hear what we are saying. Maya is terrified of her karma. But why? For her karma is not a question of reward or punishment in some future life. How often has she said this? Not for her the weighing of the heart in the feather hall of Osiris, or judgement before the great white throne of *Revelation* where the just and unjust are sorted, like the fit and unfit on the railway sidings at Auschwitz. Maya needs no gazetteer to the afterlife. She knows she will not have to go alone into the high windy places of the bardo: its naked rock, cliffs and desolate screes (this is the Tibetan, not the Hindu, vision, but Tibet is, by crow-flight, not very far from our village; from the roof of Grandfather's house the Himalayas can be seen as a dirty smudge above the northern horizon). Like Grandfather, she does not fear being challenged by monsters, mocked by obscure, second-rate divinities, or lured towards dark cave mouths that lead to further births.

Maya does not believe in any kind of life after death, much less in life after life after life. She used to quote Nietzsche, who said, 'The final reward of the dead is to die no more.' To which she would add, 'If he had been born a Hindu he would have phrased it differently. He'd have said "to live no more".'

For Maya, karma is experienced in the here and now. She is still 'here', but only just, and there is not much 'now' left. Soon, she will stop experiencing her karma, but it will continue to work itself out through our lives. Hence her fear. When her eyes open to scan each of our faces for the last time, that look says, 'I'm not afraid for myself. It's you I worry about.' We kneel by her bed, whispering words of love and comfort; assurances that she has done well for us, that she can depart with an easy mind, because we are happy and strong and impregnable. My mother dies with her children around her and a small strange smile on her face.

Then I think of Phoebe, squatting on her heels in a storm of flies.

There was a troubling scent in the air. The sweetness of incense, but something else as well. Under the double doors to the other room, a line of yellow light showed. It wavered. Flickered. Alarm, the accumulated force of the day's revelations, propelled me off her bed and hurled me at the doors. I threw them open and stood amazed.

In the darkness of her big front room burned two rings of fire: concentric circles of candles glued onto saucers, stuck into wine bottles hung with waxy stalactites; there were paper lanterns with nightlights inside, and clay lamps whose wicks balanced steady yellow flames. At the centre of this weird luciferan collection,

Phoebe was seated on a rug cross-legged. Her eyes were closed. She appeared to be meditating.

Her voice, out of the candledusk: 'Come here, Bhalu.'

I advanced, but was halted by the first ring of flames. A demon conjured from hell by a medieval sorcerer could no more have penetrated that charmed circle. My feelings were in utter confusion. Shame, that I had doubted her. Pity, for what she had suffered. She was my oldest friend. I wanted to go to her, take her in my arms, stroke her hair, comfort her, but did none of these things. I stood, paralysed by the peculiarity of the scene, or perhaps by some instinct akin to self-preservation.

After a while she said, 'I'm sorry I told you lies.'

'It doesn't matter now.' Nothing could matter, after what I had just heard.

'Unfortunately, it does. If you have to lie to someone it means you don't love each other enough.'

'We've always loved one another,' I said. 'Ever since we were small children. Nothing can change that.'

She did not turn her head or open her eyes, but I heard her sigh.

'What was I to do, Bhalu? If I'd told you about myself – about this place, all the other things – what would you have thought? Would you have wanted to know me?'

'Of course I would.'

'How could I be sure, Bhalu?'

'How could you *not* be sure?'

'People change.'

'No!' I cried, with a vehemence that surely must have astonished her. 'People don't change, deep down.' I hadn't changed. I was still the boy who had led her to the Kathodi's sacred grove, and to the haunted temple on Bicchauda mountain.

She opened her eyes. 'Sit here. Opposite me. So I can see you.'

Like someone entering unknown territory, I stepped over the flames and into the realm of her madness.

'Mummy changed,' said Phoebe. She hunched forward and hugged her knees. In the uncertain light, with shadows changing the contours of her face, it was hard to make out her expression.

'Phoebe, I am so sorry . . . about your mother. It must have been . . .' Oh, the destitute vocabulary of solace. 'If only we – that is, all of us, Maya . . .' But now it was caution that tied my tongue, stopped me saying, lest it sound like a reproach, that had we known, Sybil need not have felt so alone.

'It would have made no difference,' Phoebe said in a harsh voice. 'You've no idea how bad she was. I would go to see her and she would sit – look, like this . . .' She began rocking back and forth as people do sometimes when they are disturbed. 'Sometimes she wouldn't talk the whole time I was there – two or three days at a stretch. It made me angry. I should have been kinder.'

She lifted her face and looked at me, and I could see the wet tracks on her cheeks. 'Bhalu, people who talk of the *blackness* of despair don't understand. Despair isn't just darkness, the absence of hope, a night without stars. It's worse. Bhalu, try to remember what the nights were like, in Ambona . . .'

I looked, and saw a landscape in utter darkness, a sky lit by a vast river of stars.

'Despair is being afraid of the stars.'

I remembered what she had said on the tape, about being filled with nausea by the monstrous reality of everyday objects.

438

'When she died, her depressions passed to me. My sole inheritance, the only thing of hers I kept. The house was sold, but the things in it . . . I never knew what became of them. I left everything. I could never go back. One cupboard, I heard later, she had filled with books. The walls were damp and the books round the sides and on the bottom had rotted together into a pulp. They had to be scraped away with a spade . . .'

Her body convulsed and her hand jumped to her mouth. She was no longer thinking of books. I sat helpless, unable to enter this further realm of pain that she and her mother had shared. I was remembering a day, long ago, when a woman wearing dark glasses got off a train, followed by a little blonde girl in an Alice-in-Wonderland dress.

'Bhalu, I used to think I was a good person. But I can't be. How could I have abandoned her?' She covered her eyes with her hands, and resumed rocking to and fro. It was no longer a demonstration of her mother's misery, but of her own. Looking at the wretched figure before me, I knew she had been right not to tell me her secrets.

'Despair is like emotional suicide, Bhalu. Anger turned against oneself. Wulf said, you do this when anger can't be directed against its proper target. He asked who *else*, other than myself, I was angry with. I said, Mummy, but then realised that I couldn't be angry with her any more. She'd suffered too much. Wulf kept pressing. So I said I was angry with Daddy, for abandoning us . . . but he had suffered too.' She fished a handkerchief from somewhere about her person (women are infinitely resourceful about handkerchiefs) and blew her nose. She looked so forlorn, sitting in her circle of candles and lamps. I wanted to hug her, squeeze the grief out of her.

'You never knew my father, Bhalu. He wasn't the monster that Mummy made him out to be. He was a kind man, Bhalu, my father. He did his best to save their marriage . . . Do you know what the real tragedy was? She need never have worried.'

I suddenly realised what she was now going to tell me. That Killy had known all along, about Sybil's affair.

'He told me, that time he came to England. He blamed himself. He would have stood by her if there had been a scandal. He was prepared. He knew about everything except the blackmail. If only he had spoken to her . . .'

The irony of *if only*! Had Killy, forty years ago, opened his heart to Sybil, she could have told the blackmailer to fuck off! No – they would have done it together. Exposed him. Probably ruined him. Maya would not have got involved. We might never have left India. Sybil's slow, lonely disintegration – Phoebe's pain – all would have been avoided. But Killy had chosen *not* to speak, and from that choice proceeded the consequences. Could there be a clearer demonstration of the futility of Maya's view of karma as a guide to moral action? It was nothing more than ironic hindsight.

'Why didn't he tell her?' I asked.

'He thought it was kinder not to. If you found out something someone didn't want you to know, what would you do?'

I thought of Katy, and said nothing.

'It was a kind of lying,' said Phoebe. 'Pretending he didn't know. He didn't love her enough to clear away the lies.'

'Why do you keep insisting on this?' I asked, feeling suddenly irritated. 'Your father lied *because* he loved your mother. Perhaps she wasn't ready to receive the truth. It takes two.'

'Yes,' she said. 'It takes two. Bhalu, do you know what love is?'

Even at the best of times there is never an adequate answer to a question like this, so I made a noncommittal motion of the head.

Phoebe said, 'I've read all the authorities on love and not one from Ovid to Stendhal, from John the Beloved Disciple to Fromm has said what it really is.'

'What is it?' I asked, unable to resist.

'It's a fire,' she said, 'in which one must be prepared to sacrifice everything. It's a blowtorch to burn off the secrets that cake the chambers of the soul. It's being totally truthful, giving oneself completely, withholding nothing . . .'

'Did Wulf tell you this?'

'We've talked about it.'

'Do you love Wulf?'

For the second time, she looked directly at me. All traces of tears were gone and she was smiling. 'Not like I love you, Bhalu.' She leaned forward and said eagerly, 'When two people accept each other completely, there is no further need for secrets. Nothing need be hidden. We can accept each other just as we are. And who are we? What's in here . . . and here.' She tapped her head and laid a hand on her heart. 'Wulf says, "With nothing we come into the world and with nothing we leave it." That's who we really are.'

I listened with astonishment to this jejune philosophising. At any other time I might have said something cynical, but not now.

'Bhalu, could *you* trust someone that much? With anything? Can *you* love someone so much that you refuse to hide from them? That you are willing to be yourself completely?'

'I thought I could,' I said, thinking of Katy.

'Can *we* two be together as we are, fundamentally? Nothing but ourselves. Can *we*?'

'Yes,' I said, not knowing what she meant.

'Take off your clothes.'

I thought I had misheard, but she stood, crossed her arms and pulled off her T-shirt. The white line of her bra fell away and was tossed on the sofa. She undid the waist of her jeans and must have stepped out of them and her underwear together, because then she was naked. I looked again on the body I had seen before, this time with more terror than desire.

She sat down again on the rug, cross-legged as before. Closed her eyes. Paid me no attention at all.

Candle-flicker. Oh Lord, I was thinking, this is the weirdest moment of my life. How have I, from my humdrum existence, come to this? This person, whom I have loved since she was a child, has lied and lied to me. Everything she has done since we met again has been calculated, staged, a series of initiations through which I have had to pass in order to be close to her. Now she admits her lies, and by doing so turns them into evidence that she loves me. But what is the meaning of such a love?

I sat, watching the soft light sculpt her body, moving on its planes and hollows. I took in every part of her, without desire, just seeing a human female, heavy breasts — almost too heavy for the narrow ribcage — the dimple of the belly-button and smooth swell of flesh around it, the faint swatch of hair where her belly curved below. I did not know what to do. One part of me was saying, 'This woman is confused and perhaps not quite sane.' Another, 'This is something to which I have been destined since a child, when we played under the waterfall, and were scolded.'

I bent down, took off one shoe, then the other. Socks, shirt. Undid trousers. Hesitated. Then the last bit of clothing. Stepped over and laid them all neatly on the opium chest. Stepped back into the circle of flames, self-conscious about my body. One year short of fifty. But I stood before her and she opened her eyes and let them pass over my body: lean, for the most part, scrawny, some might say. Ribs showing, slight belly, from lack of exercise. The eyes descended, did not linger, and passed without any change of expression to thin shanks, big feet.

'Sit down, Bhalu. Opposite me. Over there.'

Her white body, my brown one.

'Now,' she said, 'there's just you and me. No more bookseller, no more painter. No more married, no more unmarried. Just you and me. Bhalu and Phoebe. There is a beautiful story from India about Siva and Kali. They say that when Kali dances, it is Siva who moves within her limbs, and when Siva dances, it is Kali whose power moves inside him. That is what love really is, two people who have surrendered completely to one another's wills, who act as one . . . Bhalu, we are together again like years ago. The things that started then have got to be resolved.'

'Phoebe,' I said, 'where is this leading?'

'Imagine how powerful that love is, then imagine a hate just as powerful. Bhalu, I can't forgive that man who tortured my mother. I still feel terror when I think of him. And rage. Wulf said this was my despair. When I understood it, it would vanish. But it hasn't. Then he said confront it and let it go. So I told you, that day in the hotel, I was planning to go to India to find the man. I want to look him in the eye and show him that he no longer has any power over me. Remember? I said I couldn't do it alone. I asked you to come with me.'

I was silent. Yes, she had said these things, and also told me that she wanted to slit the man's eyeballs and tear out his throat.

'I remember,' I said at last.

'I knew you'd agree. Now, don't be cross. Bhalu. I said I'd got something important to tell you. It's this. I've made the plans for us. I've bought our tickets to Bombay and booked us into the same hotel where . . .'

I had to stop her. I said, 'Phoebe, I'm sorry. I'm very sorry, but I will not go to India with you.'

VI INDIA

I am studying a map across which a giant river wriggles, joined
by tributaries as wide as itself, all inter-connected in curious,
gravity-disdaining patterns, each flowing into and out of several
others, some even flowing *through* one another. 'A story is a river,'
says my mother's voice in the tone she reserved for her profun-
dities, 'made by the joining of many streams.' This recollection is
greeted by a rude scoffing sound, a contemptuous raspberry that
compels my eyes to focus. I am lying on my back on a damp bed.
What I had taken for riverine chorography is an Amazon-basin
of cracks in the plasterwork of a spectacularly unclean ceiling.

Again, that insulting noise.

A black face is peering down at me. The face splits, pokes out a
pointy charcoal tongue.

'Kraaark!'

The crow, leaning down from the open window, gives a little
sideways hop. Ducks lower to look at me. 'Kaaark!'

The harsh cry unblocks the ear. Other noises rush in. Familiar
sounds, not heard for almost thirty years. Clip-clop gharry, whoosh
of taxi, swish of another taxi, putter of motorbike, horns. Voices. I
jump out of bed, go to the window. The crow panics and dives off
in a crackle of black wings. From the window: dazzle over Bombay
Harbour. Green water. Sun on ships anchored out in the stream.

India returned to me in a rush. Instantly. The heat. The smell, a
heavy oily odour compounded of truck exhausts, jasmine, smoke

and fish. Crowds outside the airport last night, although it was so late, past one o'clock by the time I exited. A man with a gold chain shining against the dark skin of his neck, who asked for a hundred rupees so he could buy himself 'a good shirt'. Urchins demanding to carry my bags to the long line of battered black-and-yellow cabs.

My driver was a large man who smelt of coconut hair oil. He ground his gears into reverse and the taxi juddered backwards, to the accompaniment of a loud electronic version of 'Jingle Bells'.

'You've returned from where?' he asked in Hindi, accelerating away through bodies that seemed to melt aside at the last possible instant.

'England. First time back here in thirty years.'

I was thinking how astonishingly recognisable everything was. The car was an ancient Fiat that must have been on the road since I was a child. Painted onto the dashboard in shaky white letters was the legend HYPOTHECATED TO DENA BANK. To every available surface were glued garish cards depicting Hindu gods and goddesses: Siva, blue-bodied, ash-smeared, with the moon on his brow and a huge cobra wrapped round his neck; Kali, dancing on a headless corpse. Her eyes were glaring mad and the tongue that protruded from her gaping mouth hung almost to her navel. She wore a necklace of severed heads, from which dripped carefully painted blood. The strangest feeling of relief came over me, at the familiarity, the utter normalcy, of these things.

'I live in England now, but Bombay's my home town.'

The taxi squeaked and rattled in a most pleasing way. My feet, I saw, were resting by a hole, whose corroded edges were gently flapping. Nine inches below, my native tarmac was speeding by.

'England? I thought so. When I heard you talking back there, I thought, this gentleman looks Indian, but speaks like a foreigner.'

'Is my accent that bad?'

'Bad? What meaning does *bad* have, in this town? You should know, in Bombay, "sub kucch chalta hai". Anything goes. "Aapun ko chai maangtai." Me wants tea . . .' He laughed. 'You were talking Hindi, but it sounded like an English movie, "Hawhaw kissmiss".'

He reached over with his left hand, and flicked a lighter under an incense stick fixed somehow to the ashtray. The taxi swerved into a blare of oncoming horns.

'Things have changed round here,' I said, enjoying the novelty of conversing in my true mother tongue, by which I do not mean the Hindi I spoke to Maya or Srinuji, but the city patois, which is a rowdy, grammar-less and atrociously mangled mixture of Hindi, Marathi, Konkani and English, with many words that have never been heard outside the city. 'What happened to the old airport?'

'The old airport? You mean Santa Cruz? You *have* been away a long time. It's been domestic-only for years. And they've changed the name to Chhatrapati Shivaji Airport.'

Shivaji. My old hero. Founder of the Maratha empire. The man who kept the Mughals out of our hills, who defeated the great Afzal Khan, who climbed the implacable cliffs of Sinhagarh by tying ropes to giant ghorpat lizards.

'So which airport did I just fly into?'

'That's the *new* airport. International-only. It used to be called Sahar, but a couple of months ago, they renamed it to guess what?'

'How the hell am I supposed to guess?'

'Well, it's now Chhatrapati Shivaji *International* Airport.'

'What? They're *both* called Chhatrapati Shivaji? Isn't that rather confusing?'

The driver turned in his seat to look at me. 'You came back here expecting to find *sense*? This is Bombay! Well, actually it isn't Bombay any more. They renamed it.' We were bearing down on a listing truck, heavily overloaded with lashed-on sacks.

'Watch the road!' I shouted.

'It's now called Mumbai,' said the driver, flicking the wheel as the truck blared past. 'I'd be all for it, if changing a name made anything better. But all it does is keep the fucking politicians happy . . . The same day they renamed the two airports, the government announced that it was renaming its big poverty scheme. The only trouble was, they'd already only just renamed it – a month earlier – so they were actually renaming the renamed scheme.'

'What's the point of all this renaming?'

'You're an educated guy. Figure it out. The politicians changed the name and also the way they did the sums. That's all, yet they said the new re-renamed scheme would "change the face of village India". But of course nothing really changed. At least not for the better. Nothing ever does.'

A sudden rattling on the roof reminded me that I had come to India during the monsoon. Within moments, rain was falling so hard that the road ahead vanished. The driver stopped the car.

'Wipers not working. No problem.'

He got out and cleared the windscreen with swipes of his hand. We started off again, but it was not long before the performance had to be repeated. In this way we proceeded slowly, in fits and starts, through dim streets, long stretches of gloom lit by sporadic street-lights. The rain stopped as suddenly as it had begun. I sat and stared at the passing city – the walls of buildings dirty, streaked with grime and mould, mottled, cracked, peeling; brown bulbs in windows, an oil lamp flickering behind the sack door of a humble dwelling. As the aircraft had made its final approach I had seen no bright lights below, only feeble glows as if people were burning candles. Tiny glimmers in a huge darkness.

The bazaars in Mahim were crowded although it was 2 a.m.; a stream of people were entering a Hindu temple, garland-sellers outside its door. The driver pulled up again without any explanation, got out and disappeared into the crowd. A minute later he reappeared with a garland of marigolds and draped it round the mirror.

At Worli Naka we stopped at a cross-roads marshalled by a policeman with a long baton. A family crossed the road in front of the cab, the man clad Bombay style, narrow trousers encasing stick legs, billowing shirt belted round a tiny waist. Behind him walked two women in drab saris, equally thin, with jasmine sprigs in their hair. One of them turned and gave the policeman a dirty look.

On an impulse I asked, 'What do you think of the police?'

'The pandus?' He gave a short laugh. 'There's another thing that doesn't change.' He lifted his hand and rubbed the fingers together in the sign that means money.

Near the centre, the streets were deserted, traffic lights flashing on continuous amber. We were approaching VT Station. VT! The Victoria Terminus where Mister Love's ghost had gone a-haunting, whence trains departed for Ambona.

'They renamed VT,' said the driver. 'It's now called Chhatrapati Shivaji Terminus . . .'

I was staying at the Rudolf Hotel, Apollo Bunder, the same place that Sybil had stayed in six years earlier. It was Phoebe who had decided that we should stay at the Rudolf. She thought we might learn something. Sybil had had a definite purpose in coming to India and it had not been simply to find my mother. The place was uncannily as she had described it. We pulled up to find Arabs in long kaftans sitting on the sea wall. The first thing I discovered was that Shankar, the room boy, still worked at the hotel. I recognised him instantly from Sybil's *Last Journal*. The red dot on his forehead, paan-smeared mouth. He showed me to my room and departed backwards, bowing low with folded hands and servile protestations, but a hard glimmer in his eye told me I'd already been weighed up, by the standards of his Arab customers, and found wanting. I would not ask about Sybil until I knew him better.

Now he appeared at the door with the breakfast I had ordered on my arrival the night before. An omelette, Indian style, thin as a pancake, flecked with green chilli, and toast which was already wilting in the muggy heat. I had no very clear plan for the day, but the first thing I had to do was ring Katy. Ten in the morning. It would be five-thirty at home. Katy would still be asleep, curled up in our bed. Another half hour before the old copper alarm clock on the bedside table rattled her awake.

I ate sitting by the crow's window. The harbour was heaving to a gentle sludgy swell. Barely a hundred yards from here, Mitra, Dost and I had sat, twenty-eight years ago, on the night war broke out between India and Pakistan, and watched the rigging of dhows in the harbour turn to blue fire. There were no dhows now. Out on the water, sightseeing launches were busy, coming and going from the steps below the Gateway of India, the giant arch of yellow basalt planned to commemorate the first ever visit by a reigning British monarch to India, but ironically remembered as the place through which the last British troops left the country. Immediately to the north of the Gateway, but invisible from my window, was the naval dockyard where Nanavati had gone to get the gun from his ship. Stretching beyond that was the commercial port where Killy had brought Sybil ashore just over half a century ago and warned her that India would not be as she imagined. Poor woman, how could she have imagined what lay ahead? The city was full of ghosts. How appropriate that I had been greeted by a crow, guardian of the gateway between the landscape of the living and the realm of the dead. (Indian villagers say that a crow cawing from a window is a sure sign that you will have visitors. They also believe, however, that whooping cough can be cured by riding a bear.) Ghosts notwithstanding, I felt elated. I was back! I would do things I hadn't enjoyed for three decades. Stroll along Marine Drive, eat pani-puri at Chowpatty beach and pau bhaji wherever it took my fancy. I would look for my old friends Mitra and Dost.

Floating up from Apollo Bunder, under my window, came a glorious cacophony. Raised voices: 'Ey! Ey! Ey!' Cries falling like music, overlaid by the chugging of diesels, burring of scooters and the horse-cloppy gharries. These were lined up further along the street, outside the Taj, hoping to catch foreigners. Every so often one passed beneath, carrying a covey of Arab women clad from head to toe in black, drawn by horses whose ribs protruded like those of carcasses, and who endured the lashings of their drivers with miserable stoicism. I thought of the Moron in his comfortable stable at home, where it would already be light, where Katy would be waking, going down to the kitchen, pulling the kettle onto the Aga. I would leave it fifteen minutes, then ring. I wasn't looking forward to the call.

'Oh, hello,' she said coolly, as if surprised, and not particularly pleased, to hear from me. I waited, but there was no more.

'Well, I'm in Bombay,' I said. 'It's eleven in the morning here. I've been waiting to phone you. What are you doing? Making tea?'

'I've just put the kettle on,' said Katy, still in that cool voice. 'Why? Do you want one?'

I felt an odd jubilation. My calculations had been correct. My other life was still working normally. I said, 'I was just imagining you at home.'

There was a long silence at the other end, then she said, 'I was about to go out to the stable.'

'What's the weather like? How's the Moron?'

Without waiting for an answer I began telling her about the horses at the Gateway of India. She cut in.

'Bhalu, this call must be costing a fortune. You needn't go on pretending to be interested in me . . .' Her voice was very far away. I was surprised by how *foreign* she sounded.

'I'm not pretending.'

'Is she there with you now?'

'You know she isn't.'

'So you say. If she's there, listening, please don't bother to call me again.'

'Look, Katy,' I said. 'She's in London. At least, so far as I know. Check if you don't believe me. I'll give you her number.'

'Bhalu, if I have to check on you, I've already lost you.' There was a click, and five thousand miles of cable and ether went dead.

'Phoebe. I'm sorry, I won't go to India with you.'

Before she could say anything, I held up my hand. 'I don't mean I won't go at all . . . I'll go, but on condition I go alone.'

I told her I would discover what I could. If I could find any way to trace the man who had blackmailed her mother I would report back, and we could then decide what to do next. I don't know what I was expecting. Tears, certainly, a tantrum maybe. She surprised me. She said, 'Bhalu, I think that's a very good idea.'

'Well, that's settled then.'

She smiled and closed her eyes. We sat in silence for a while.

'The thing is,' I said, thinking aloud, 'I started by assuming that if I went, I'd be doing it for you. But I want to go for myself. My life has been shaped by what that man did. And I think I've met him too. It keeps hammering at me that it was him – must have been – who gave me a hard time when I was arrested. In Dongri.'

'Thank God!' she said, 'At last, we're doing something!' She jumped up and went over to her sideboard, fetched another bottle of wine and, quite unselfconsciously, went through an unclothed version of her uncorking procedure.

We were both still naked, with the candles guttering all around us. The scene, which a few moments ago had seemed almost

455

threatening, was now . . . well, there is something comical about nakedness. We sat drinking wine and looking at each other.

'Phoebe,' I said. 'All this . . . it's a bit silly.'

'Yes,' she agreed. 'But only a little bit.'

She stood up and pulled me to my feet. Then she took my face between her hands and kissed me. I am not tall, we were about the same height. Her breasts were pressed against my chest. My arms went round her and she relaxed into them. My hands slid down her long back, found her rump and squashed her to me. She must have felt how aroused I was. Perhaps because of this, she disengaged, gazed at me fondly from a distance of about four inches, and kissed me on the nose. 'And you're a poppet,' she said. Then she picked up her clothes and disappeared into her bedroom.

I dressed, awkwardly, not really able to think. Walked round the room looking at pictures and came across a shelf of old books.

Books, books, books, always a fascination.

Lays of Ind by Aliph Cheem.

Bullet and Shot (in Indian Forest, Plain and Hill) by C. E. M. Russell.

Medical Hints for Hot Climates by Charles Heaton.

Notes on Stable Management (with glossary of Hindustani words) by Col. J. A. Nunn.

These were her father's books.

A further title caught my eye. Killy's 'miraculous little work of prophecy'. The 'hate-filled tome' Sybil had so despised.

India in 1983.

The year 1983 was a memorable one in the history of England . . . the two claims which it professed to make on the attention of posterity were that, during its span, Home Rule was at last granted to the irrepressible aspirations of the Irish People, and that what had long been denounced by all thoughtful politicians and advanced thinkers as an unspeakable anomaly, the British Empire in India, suffered final and official extinction . . .

Thus the opening of *India in 1983*, borrowed from Phoebe and carried back by me to the land of its inspiration.

'A farcical account of an imaginary evacuation of India by the British and the subsequent Government by a Babu Raj', a note on the title page explained. The book had been written in 1883, only twenty-five years after the Mutiny, and its anonymous author had to project himself a century into the future before he was able to imagine Ireland and India as free nations. But as he reassured his readers, it *was* only an 'imaginary evacuation' and the insulting term 'Babu Raj' expressed his opinion of the chances of Indians ever successfully governing themselves. 'Prophetic', Killy had called it.

The evenings hung heavily that first fortnight in Bombay. I read a lot. *India in 1983* mostly, and Sybil's *Last Journal*. My days were spent dodging through streets in which brown water laked after each downpour, tramping from one library to another, in search of anything I could find about the Nanavati case. I was collecting the names of everyone connected with it – investigating officers, court officials, lawyers and their assistants, journalists, politicians and their staffs, military officers — anyone who might have had access to the letters found in Ahuja's flat. In the evenings I would review my haul. The names stared at me, flat and meaningless. Sybil and Phoebe thought the blackmailer had been a government official of some sort. Maya, according to Srinuji, had believed he was a senior policeman. But we did not know for sure. Only women could be excluded with any certainty.

Then it occurred to me that blackmail is a crime of the head, not of the heart. The box under Ahuja's bed had contained letters from six women. Wouldn't the blackmailer have put the squeeze on all of them? Why pick on Sybil and ignore the rest? But who were the other women? Who might know?

'Bhalu! You?'

What astonishment and delight the voice at the other end of the phone poured into those two words.

'Here in Bombay? Arré! When did you come?'

Zafyque, Maya's old friend. He had known Sybil. *La Cantatrice Chauve* in 'faute de mieux' French.

'You're staying *where*? What made you choose that place? It has a reputation for being rather . . . how shall I put it . . . shady.'

'It's a long story,' I said.

'Why don't you come over for dinner? We're not far.'

'Okay, when shall I come?'

'Come now. Shahnaaz is away. I am alone. I'd enjoy company.'

'Now? But it's almost ten.'

'So? Who in Bombay eats before ten?'

*　　*　　*

I walked through a quarter of tiny shops, some of them housed in corrugated boxes scarcely bigger than phone booths. One cupboard-like establishment had nothing but a bunch of green coconuts hanging on its bright blue walls. Another, the MAHA-RASHTRA PLUMBING COMPANY, displayed bits of piping arrayed according to gauge. A bare room of surpassing filthiness described itself as RESTAURANT PARADISO. A man in a singlet squatted inside, cooking on a small kerosene stove. His customers ate at tables in the street, ignoring the dogs that picked through garbage at their feet.

A few twists and turns, following the directions he had given, brought me to a high wall studded with broken glass, above which rose the scarred façade of an old mansion. A chowkidar dozing by the door (huge and studded with ironwork), confirmed that Zafyque sahib did indeed live here. He let me in. I mounted a wide stair to the fourth floor and was shown by a servant into a hall stacked high with books, and papers dun with age, most of them untouched for years, judging by their veil of dust.

'Bhalu, welcome home, my boy!' bawled the rich, thespian voice. 'Through here!' I found him sprawled in a cane armchair sipping a drink, on a terrace where flimsy curtains were being lifted like dancers' skirts by a sea breeze. Zafyque must have been as old as either Maya or Sybil, but his hair was black and his beard still possessed a vigorous Shakespearean jut. He rose to greet me, and we embraced.

'Come, sit,' he said. 'Scotch.' Statement, not question. 'I am so sorry about your mother. She was a wonderful woman. She had *something* . . .' He did not seem very certain what it was. 'She wrote to me about a play. What was it called? To do with Jerusalem?'

'*Via Dolorosa.*'

'That's right. Did you ever see it?'

Of course I had not. A nurse with painted toenails had opened Maya's door and the tickets had remained, unused and forgotten, in my pocket. Katy later found them and propped them on the mantelpiece in our bedroom where they probably still were.

Zafyque told me he was engrossed in a new production and began outlining the difficulties he was having with his leading lady. I listened, noticing how the lights of the bazaar spread to a dark, hard line that marked the edge of the sea.

'So anyway, what brings you to Bombay, after so many years?'

I said, 'You remember an Englishwoman called Sybil Killigrew? She did *La Cantatrice Chauve* with you.'

'Ah! Bazaar! Balzac! Bazooka!' His hands flew up into the air and he declaimed:

> '*Une pierre prit feu*
> *Le château prit feu*
> *La fôret prit feu*
> *Les hommes prirent feu*
> *Les femmes prirent feu . . .*'

I was reminded of his performance in the bistro in Battersea, chatting up the waitress in his best buongiorno accent.

'Forty years I've remembered those lines!' he said proudly. Then, as the significance of this struck him, 'But how can this be connected to your visit?'

So I told him.

* * *

A servant laid the dinner out on a table between us, naming each dish as he set it down. There must have been a dozen dishes, for the two of us.

'My dear young man,' said Zafyque when we had eaten, 'this is a preposterous tale.'

'But a true one.'

'It's correct that Sybil had an affair with Ahuja. We all knew that. But the rest? This allegation of blackmail?'

'. . . is also true.'

'So you believe, and I'm sure you're sincere. All right, let it be true. How will you prove it?'

'We can't, without the notebook – the one that names him, that Maya and Sybil hid. But we can confront the man.'

'Leaving aside the difficulty – actually I'd say impossibility – of finding him, okay, suppose you succeed. What will you do?'

The question Katy had asked.

'Phoebe's idea is that we should document the whole thing and make it public.'

'Isn't this rather near the knuckle?'

'Why?'

'Her own mother – the scandal. Would the family want it dug up again? What good can it do, after all these years?'

'It can bring my friend peace of mind.'

'This friend, Phoebe. You speak as if she's very close to you. Are you . . . excuse my asking?'

'No,' I said. 'Just friends.'

'Bhalu, you're asking me to remember things that happened half a lifetime ago. Many of those people are dead.'

'If you can remember lines from that era, why not people?'

'I never knew Ahuja well. Only by reputation. I remember Sybil getting mixed up with him, but I don't know who the other women were . . . There is another thing,' he said. 'Your mother had a bee in her bonnet about a theme of this sort. A famous murder, police corruption. She was trying to get a movie made. She wrote script after script. But she got nowhere. Nobody would touch it.'

'It was called *Gunah-i-ishq*. Was her script no good?'

'It was a story nobody wanted to hear . . . I don't think anything has changed. I seriously advise you to drop it.'

Later, he said to me, 'Do you know what the real significance of the Nanavati case was? Nothing to do with the *Blitz* tale of romance and murder. The passion! Adultery! Jealousy! What a play it would make! Now if only Nanavati had shot his wife first and then himself, we'd have had our own Indian *Othello!*'

I wondered if he remembered that other reversal, Othello in lacy undies, strangling the hulking muscular Desdemona.

'In fact,' Zafyque said, 'there *was* a movie made of the story. I have it on video – I will lend it to you. But as I was saying, the real impact of the case was different. First, the behaviour of the jury made the politicos realise that juries were dangerous, they could not be controlled. So they abolished the jury system in India.'

'With no jury, there's just the judge to manage?'

'We have many good judges. Thank God this country is not completely rotten. There are even rumours of one or two sincere politicians. But bribery is a subtle thing. One hears stories about judges. Before a case opens, His Honour receives two brown envelopes. One is from the plaintiff, the other from the defendant. He hears the case, gives a fair judgement. The loser's envelope is returned, unopened. The question is, can that be called a bribe?'

The servant came in and silently began clearing up the meal.

'. . . The second thing was this. Nanavati was found guilty of murder by three separate courts, up to and including the Supreme Court. Yet he was pardoned and set free. This called into question other life sentences. There was a guy called Gopal Godse, who had been in prison since the death of Mahatma Gandhi. Gopal was the younger brother of Nathuram, who did the actual shooting . . .'

The Case of the Fan-Dancer's Horse. Nathuram Godse, the Perry Mason fan who had assassinated Mahatma Gandhi.

'It's fifty years since Gandhi's death, but the hatred that killed him is still at work in the world. The controversy is not over. How do I know all this? Because last year there was a play written about Nathuram. A Marathi play. It caused a huge tamaasha because it gave his, the assassin's point of view. It was banned. Many people, me included, think that was wrong. Works of art should not be banned. What made the play dangerous, was that it articulated a different version of history. One that does not fit with what we were taught at school, or what was preached by our politicians after Independence. But it's that view of history that is coming to be accepted now . . . Once Gandhi was a hero. Now, you might find it difficult, at least in this town, to find two people who have a good word to say about him. The thing is, people forget. Gandhi was anti-bigotry, anti-communalism, he stood for Hindus and Muslims, both. People in those days saw that for themselves. They had his moral example in front of them. They heard him speak. What's left now? Garlanded portraits in public buildings? Lip service by generations of tainted, self-seeking politicians who betrayed everything he stood for. Nowadays his even-handedness is interpreted as anti-Hindu. Of course, we have our history books, but there is such a thing as rewriting history.'

Zafyque looked grim. I remembered that during the communal riots in Bombay in 1993, he had kept an iron bar inside the door of this flat.

'Our modern politicians are a very sorry breed, Bhalu. Most of them see public office as a means to line their pockets. They will do anything for power. In Britain, Enoch Powell got drummed out of the Tory Party for his remarks on race. Here, every thug who can raise a communal rabble is able to stand for office . . . See, the thing is, Gandhi was wrong. Not in what he said and practised – that was noble. His mistake was believing that other people would have the guts and the strength to follow him. Also, he was naive about certain things. In 1930, when Gandhi's followers went on the salt march, they walked unarmed, bare-headed, straight into the lines of police with their lathis . . . They were hammered down. Gandhi said that we should not blame the police who did the beatings, who were Indians. They had been led astray by their British masters. Once we got our independence, he said, there would be no further need for police. They would melt back into the people. There would be a loving relationship between police and people. That is a sick joke. I belong to a human rights organisation. A few years ago, a report written by Amnesty International on India came into our hands. It contained nothing we did not already know. Suspects in police stations being beaten, tortured, sometimes even killed. Women raped. When I read this report just one thought was thudding in my mind: Gandhi, thank God you never lived to hear these stories.'

It was one o'clock in the morning. Past time to go. Zafyque saw me to the door. He said, 'Sorry I am not able to help you . . .' He held on to my hand for a few moments longer. 'Bhalu, if you are determined to go round asking questions, especially about the police, please be careful.'

The tumbledown quarter through which I had come earlier was bunkered down for the night. Despite the fact that it was the rainy season, some people were sleeping, wrapped in sheets, on the steps of shops. On charpays under inadequate roofs. My home town was a vast slum, where the rich hid in palatial boltholes, with the poor camped at their gates.

Near the hotel a drunken man stumbled out of a doorway and accosted me. 'Hey, sir! Sir! Want a girl? Anglo-Indian? Virgin!'

Above his grinning head, a sign over an antique shop caught my eye. LIVE IN ORIENTAL GLORY OF GRANDEUR.

I had a video player delivered to my room and played Zafyque's tape. The film was *Yeh Raaste Hain Pyaar Ke* (*Such Are the Ways of Love*). The video player, like everything else about the Rudolf Hotel, was comically wretched — what had Zafyque meant by 'shady'? The image was poor, bands of noise zigzagged across the screen, the vertical hold was precarious, every so often losing its grip and flipping the picture rapidly upwards, but under the opening song, I could make out a woman in a white sari, lying at the foot of a shrine. This surely was the hero's penitent wife, S, transformed by the magic of the camera and the rewriting of history to a noble, if flawed, Hindu woman. White for mourning, for regret, for grief. Yet what grief, what regret had the real S felt, who could calmly deliver testimony that the Sessions judge had rejected as false, in the presence of her erstwhile lover's bullet-holed head? How had she changed so suddenly and completely, from a woman who could hardly bear the sight of her husband, to the repentant, loyal wife? How could she bear to see Ahuja's skull grinning at her perjuries?

One thing truly puzzled me. Why had she decided to drag Sybil into it? To save the husband she had been desperate to abandon? Sybil's letters could never have saved him. Or did the memory of those letters still rankle, those literate, infuriatingly funny letters that Mister Love had so cruelly read to her? Was it simply a final act of spite? She had successfully got rid of Sybil from Mister Love's life. For a year she had him to herself. Still, he did not seem to want her. Did she blame Sybil? Why should you get off scot-free when I am suffering? Is this what she had thought? Facing disgrace and disaster herself, had she decided to take Sybil down with her? Whatever passed through S's mind, whatever her motive, what she did was hideously cruel. Sybil had suffered enough at her hands. There was never any need for a second family to be dragged into the maelstrom and destroyed.

A slow violent anger kindled inside me. That image of Sybil's deathbed. Phoebe kneeling beside it. Phoebe's despair. I thought, I feel nothing but disgust for the Nanavatis and their sordid débâcle. Disgust also for Prem Ahuja. I don't want them in my life any more. They can fuck off out of it. What do I care about a jealous man with a gun and a temper he couldn't control, or for a playboy with a roving eye, or an empty-headed bitch who fucked up so many people's lives? 'Thought you'd got away with it, didn't you?' S had said.

'Your husband got away with it,' I shouted at the white figure on the screen. 'But you made bloody sure that Sybil didn't.'

At about 2 a.m. the heavens opened and sent down a heavy shower across the harbour. The Arabs on the sea wall outside the hotel began their cavorting and yelling. I picked up Sybil's *Last Journal*, written here, in this hotel, perhaps in this very room. Sybil had struggled against the impossibility of language to convey the terror of the sounds that assaulted her, out of the hubbub of the street – soft calls, muffled voices – she often heard her own name called: 'Ey Sybil mem.' 'Oh, Sybil mem.' 'Oh, Killymem.' Except that it could not be, because nobody knew she was there. Echoes of what? Terrified, Sybil crouched in her hotel room and covered her ears. Unable to move. Unable to leave. There was a scratching at her door, as if an animal were raking it with claws. Then a soft, urgent tapping. Shankar, the housekeeping boy was standing outside.

'What do you want?'

'You called me, madam?'

'No.'

After a few minutes it started again, scritch-scratch, tap tap, tap tap tap. She put a pillow over her head and tried to sleep.

I woke, still angry. My morning paper contained a rich nugget of irony-ore.

ONE HUNDRED YEARS AGO TODAY.

LONDON 1899: Crime of Passion. A terrible tragedy is reported from Bandora, near Bombay. Captain Iremonger, late of the Durham Light Infantry, was shot by an engineer named Gregory, on the staff of the Great Indian Peninsular Railway. Mr Gregory afterwards shot his wife dead and blew out his own brains. Captain Iremonger lies in a precarious condition. Jealousy, says the *Central News*, is alleged to

When Shankar came to take my breakfast tray I asked him if he
remembered Sybil staying at the hotel.

'An elderly English lady. On her own. It would have been about
six years ago.'

He did remember, because she was such an unusual guest.
Rarely did English people come here to this hotel, and never one
so old. She stayed in her room, he told me. Hardly went out.
People would ring and leave messages for her. He brought her
those messages. He did not forget her, because one evening, at her
request, he had brought her a bottle of whisky. She got very drunk
and was shouting in the middle of the night. Some of the Arab
guests complained.

'Sahib, one thing I remember. After she came back from her
trip, the police turned up here. They talked to her. That was just
before she left – when she went back to England.'

'Her trip? What trip? Where did she go?'

'I can tell you that too,' he said. 'I went to buy the ticket.
First class on the *Deccan Queen*, VT Ambona return.'

I questioned Shankar about the policemen. Who were they?
From which police station? Had they given a name? I did not for
a moment believe that they had come about the whisky bottle.

But Shankar did not know, did not know, did not know.

'The English memsahib, which room did she have?'

'Why, this one! This room we keep for non-Arab guests.'

Ah, so that was why the ceiling was cracked, the carpet reeked,
and when you turned on the air-conditioner, it gave off a smell

like a dead animal. Later, I telephoned Phoebe to give her the news. Apart from the discovery that Sybil had gone to Ambona, I had drawn a complete blank.

Tap tap tap. Two nights later, very, very late. Tap tap tap. Tap tap tap. It was happening to me. These sounds that had scared Sybil. There was definitely a soft tapping at my door.

'Bhalu? Are you awake?'

She crept in and without a word, removed her shoes and climbed into my bed.

'You're not cross with me for coming?'

I shook my head. We lay together a long time, close. She must have been able to tell what my feelings were, they were shamefully apparent. Then she undressed, her long body naked in the light coming in from the street, and slipped, not into my bed, but into the twin bed next to mine.

She reached out across the gap and touched my arm.

'Bhalu, will you give me twenty longs?'

She said, 'I worked it out. I *know* where the notebook is. I realised when you rang me and said that Sybil had gone alone to Ambona . . . Do you remember that day, of Rosie's funeral? The cemetery in Ambona? Well, there was a tin that was buried in the grave. I wanted to give Rosie's locket back to her. We all put something in.'

'It was buried,' I said, 'but not with the coffin. It was just placed under the earth and covered up.'

'That's where it is!' she said. 'Bhalu, that's what they did with it. It was a place nobody was going to disturb. I bet Mummy thought she could get it later. Except that Daddy stepped in and suddenly we were on a ship heading for Aden. Bhalu, that's why she came back to Ambona. To get it. And I am sure it didn't come home with her. So unless your mother removed it, it is still there!'

'Are you suggesting we dig up a grave?'

VT might have been renamed Chhatrapati Shivaji Terminus, but its smells and sights had not changed. Last time I'd been here was when I travelled up to Ambona to see Jula. Now Phoebe, wearing dark glasses, hair pulled back under a scarf, stood beside me in the bustle of porters and fellow travellers. We were drinking tea, the *real* Indian Railways tea. That too, thank God, had not changed.

'How do you find it? To be back in India?' I was consumed with curiosity about her feelings and wanted to see everything through her eyes. I was excited that we were returning to Ambona together, but at the same time I was afraid that going back would threaten our old, precious, carefully-preserved memories.

A small gaggle of beggar children had gathered round us, attracted by the firangi lady. She opened her purse and solemnly gave each of them a coin. They smiled their thanks, then sent their brothers, sisters, cousins and friends to see us.

Phoebe said, 'I know I shouldn't give to the children. Isn't that what everyone says? . . . Do you have any more coins?'

Don't give to beggars. That was the standard wisdom. You may feel sorry for the children, but the money will only be taken off them. They work for grown-ups, criminal gangs, they get nothing for themselves. To give these children a chance, eradicate begging. But how likely was this, in a country where to give alms is a sacred duty, where the world's poorest people uncomplainingly support a population of five million wandering ascetics? It was also a fact that thousands of homeless children worked desperately hard, scavenging rags and plastic, shining shoes and doing anything, including begging, that could buy them a meal. I knew with what shame I had sat in taxis determinedly refusing to see the pleading faces and tiny fingers at the window.

On the way to the train Phoebe's charity faced a sterner test. A ragged man – he might have been drunk, drugged, or ill – lay on the platform, urinating through his clothes, the pool of his piss spreading away from him. Nobody was paying him any attention. Phoebe clutched my arm. We would have to step over the yellow stream. The man groaned and rolled over.

'Bhalu, we must get help.'

'There isn't any. We'll miss our train.'

'There must be someone. You go and find someone. I'll stay here with him.'

'Phoebe,' I said. 'Nobody is going to help this guy. No doctor will come out for him.'

'Then you wait here,' she said, and was gone.

A few minutes later she returned with a small elderly gentleman carrying a briefcase. He was a doctor, she said. She had found him by going to the crowded booking hall and calling aloud for help.

The doctor bent down by the man's head, then drew back sharply.

'Madam, this man has been drinking.'

By this time a small, interested crowd had gathered, offering comments and advice.

'Leave him alone.' 'No, make him go outside. Filthy devil.'

The doctor said to Phoebe, 'At J.J. Hospital this man could get help. I will ask if he can be taken there.'

'What about money?'

He smiled at her. 'No, no, the treatment is free. Now dear lady, you may take your train.'

Phoebe knelt beside the man, opened his hand and folded a banknote into his fingers.

To me the doctor said in Hindi, 'Take her quickly. Because she's a foreigner and made a fuss, the railway police will come. I'm afraid they'll throw him out into the street. Certainly they will beat him. She is a tender-hearted lady, it would be hard to bear.'

As the train began its sliding run through East Bombay, I took her arm and said, 'Phoebe, I'm ashamed.'

She said, 'Don't be. If you open yourself to the pain all around you, you'll go crazy. That's what they say, Bhalu. But what if you're already crazy?'

*   *   *

472

Bombay had grown. The train rumbled past vast new housing developments. What once was just mudskipper marsh, now housed rows of new apartment blocks. They were building a whole new city on the mainland. The centre of gravity was shifting northward and the old town, already known as South Mumbai, would one day suffer the strange fate of becoming a distant suburb.

Beyond the new city, not much seemed to have changed. The countryside spun away, flooded fields, lines of women bending, plunging fistfuls of rice-paddy into the ooze. I knew exactly how that mud felt, soft and squelchy between the toes. The field edges would be alive with crabs, black and yellow, and there would be small inexplicable fish among the paddy stalks. The twenty-six tunnels re-enacted themselves exactly as I remembered. Then we were out, among hills clad in monsoon green. Vast drops, waterfalls roaring down the escarpment. Then the familiar shape of Duke's Nose came looming to the right. I felt a huge upwelling happiness: this would always be the centre of my world, the place where I was completely and utterly at home.

Ambona was unrecognisable. The town had expanded across the railway line and large hotels and shops lined the main road. The small market with its old houses was still there, but was now just a corner of a much larger bazaar that stretched away as far as I could see. The statue of King George had gone, replaced by a woman holding a water pot. The lanes were thronged with men on scooters, threading their way between puddles. Village women. Cows wandering through the crowds. Bustle, commerce. No one wearing poverty like rubies.

Phoebe, in her jeans, T-shirt, and dark glasses, attracted a small crowd. 'Where from? Where from?' the children yelled.

'From India,' she replied. 'I was born in India. I'm Indian.'

The Christian cemetery in Ambona is off a back road that runs away from the bazaar towards the lake. A sloping hillside full of trees, overgrown to waist height by elegant plants with drooping spade-shaped leaves. Green light. Rain falling through the trees. Graves submerged in a sea of leaves. Here and there a marble angel or an urn poked through the jungle. We brushed back the leaves, trying to read the names on the gravestones and wooden crosses. Some of them had names, most did not. The place didn't fit at all with my memories. Surely we had stood over in *that* corner. But now it looked completely different.

In the midst of the wilderness was a small chapel, green with moss and mould. The door was locked, but round the back was an open wooden shed. Wooden crates were ranged about its walls with utensils, tools and a few clothes strewn about. Towards the back of the hut, a pot was bubbling on a blackened kerosene stove. In the centre of the floor was a large boxed-in wooden chair with arms, like a throne. A naked man suddenly stood up from where he had been crouching, behind the chair. He was very thin, very black, with a round amiable face that aimed to please.

'Just a minute, uncle, I was having a bath. Oh my! Aunty too! I'll just put on my pants. Come, come, sit. Uncle, madam. Yurr. Sit yurr, sit sir, sit.'

His accent was old Anglo-Indian, like Ben's parents. I had heard nothing like it for thirty years. He vanished again and we caught the rustle of clothing. In a moment he called out and told us his name was Frances. He was the caretaker. He said he lived in the tiny hut.

A couple of minutes later, we were following him along rainy paths between the graves, looking for poor Rosie's tombstone.

'Now what name you said, Richards? We got a Richards over yurr, came in las year. Richards?'

'Not Richards,' said Phoebe. 'De Mello. Forty years ago.'

All over the cemetery, gravestones and monuments peered out of the sea of tall plants. At their bases grew the strange succulent flowers I remembered from my childhood. I asked their name.

'Dese flowers, they call dem Gauri, the Hindus call dem Gauri. Dey buy de flowers twenty, thutty rupees each. Dey take them and use them in a puja. A Ganpati puja, sir, yes . . . Sorry, what name you said just now?'

'De Mello.'

Frances said vaguely, 'Look yurr sir, don't walk on bare earth, it's been raining, raining, raining tree days, de ground is soaked, you'll sink. Walk yurr, sir, walk dis way. De Mello is it, come den, dis way.' But after another round of graves, all smothered in the tall drooping gauri lilies, we were no nearer finding Phoebe's old ayah.

'Come sir, come, dis way, I want to show you . . .'

He stopped in front of a grave which was covered with a bed of cracked sand. 'Look sir, it was nice marble. People come at night, dey jump over de wall, dat side dere, the Bori side. They have taken away the marble. What name you said?'

On some graves, the mounded red soil of the ghats had been drilled away by rain, leaving mud sculptures like miniature termite mounds.

'De Mello.'

'We got a Da Silva. I remember. Come, come, I tink over yurr. Came recently? Dis year?'

'A long time ago. Nearly forty years.'

'Fotty years, oh my! She was Protestant?'

'Catholic.'

'Okay sir, I'll look dis side, you look dat side . . .'

We heard him crashing round in the undergrowth, still talking. 'Boys come over de Bori wall. Trow stones for the fruit. I shout, chase dem, but dey just run way. Den dey come back trow stones at me too.'

'Not quite all there,' I whispered to Phoebe, and was surprised to see the anger that jumped into her face.

'He's lonely! How would *you* like to live in a graveyard on your own? I bet he has no family. Poor man.'

'I'm sorry,' I said, kissing her. 'You're more compassionate than me. You were right to get help for that man, on the platform.'

'It wasn't just compassion,' she said. 'What he was doing, I've been there.'

I remembered then, the tape, Phoebe squatting beside her dead mother. That evening, her bedroom, candles, Kensington, London, all seemed improbably far away.

'De Mello? Boxer, is it? 'Bout five years ago,' came the voice of Frances.

'No,' said Phoebe patiently. 'She was an ayah. Forty years ago.'

'Ayah. Fotty years ago. Fotty years ago, I was not even born. Ah, dey mus' have put her wid another one.'

'Another one?' Phoebe and I said together.

'What name? Da Silva?'

'De Mello.'

'Oh sir, it's coming to me now sir, I am getting her now. I seen dis one. De Mello?'

He led the way back up the hillside to a new site. 'I am starting to feel her now, sir. Dis way, over yurr, dey brought her dis year only, opened another one and put her in. De Mello, ayah from fotty years ago. Look for a blue cross, sir.'

But the grave we stopped at was marked JOSEPHS.

'Sir, I'll ask the registrar, sir, at the church. He has the records. In the morning I'll ask, sir. How long will y'all be staying yur? Till tomorrow. I'll just go and ask, sir.'

We could not find the grave.

'I'm sure it was about here,' said Phoebe, stopping by an angel with a broken wing, covered in green mould and monsoon slime.

'I'm sure too,' I said. 'We were standing just here, in a line . . .'

But there was a strange name on the grave.

'What did you mean, put her with another one?' Phoebe asked.

'What I said, madam?'

'You said she might have been put with another one.'

'All de old graves been changed now, madam. No space left. Since maybe about seven, eight years back. Before my time.'

Sybil had come six years ago. So she'd been too late. The graves had been reorganised. God knows what had happened to the tin.

'What happens when you run out of space?' Phoebe asked.

'Each person get tree tree years,' said Frances. 'See suppose I die, madam, so I go in. Tree years later uncle dies, dey open it and uncle here's going in . . . Den tree more yurs, you die, auntie, we put you in same. Plenty of room, dere is, madam . . . Come, come, I'll show you. Dis is de oldest ting sir, see sir, see madam, see de angel with de broken wing? Dat's the oldest ting, goes back to 1861.'

He led us back past his shack. Phoebe stepped inside and had a quick look round.

'Bhalu!' she said. 'Poor man. He's been drinking kerosene.'

The day, which I had imagined as a joyful homecoming, was turning out to be anything but. We walked back, defeated, to the bazaar, followed by gawping locals.

'Batlibhoy's shop has gone,' I said. 'It used to be there. Do you remember? Babu would bring us and we'd buy sweets.'

'I don't remember.'

By the time we found ourselves a rickshaw, I was dreading going back. What else had changed?

'Do you know an Abdul Razaq?' I asked the young driver. 'Friend of mine, used to drive one of these things.'

'Sorry, no idea. It's a big town.'

'It didn't used to be, when I lived here.'

'Ambona is a big tourist area now,' said the rickshaw driver. 'People come up from Bombay. Lots of big hotels. Five stars too. They come for the scenery. Nature.'

But what was left? As we came out along the lake road – the old crumbling bungalows with their rose gardens still there – I caught my first glimpse of our home mountains. There was the line of the dam, and beyond it the hither slope of Bicchauda. It was monsoon, and the slopes were green, sliced by waterfalls. A shiny slide of rock marked the point where Rosie had fallen. But the mountain had changed. The forest had gone.

By the monsoon lake (Ambona Lake), now fenced off from the crowds of tourists, we stopped, near the foot of a waterfall, by a bamboo and matting stall, in which a man with kind eyes and a thin woman were crouched over a stove. We ordered tea.

'He kaay ae?' asked Phoebe, with that little drop of the head, pointing at a plate of snacks. I wanted to kiss her.

'You speak Marathi!' said the man. 'They're vada pau.'

Their names were Kali Das and Mangala. They lived in Ardau village. He was younger than me, I guessed. Might have been one of those tiny children with kohl-rimmed eyes and round bellies, naked save for a string round their waists, who used to gather round with tin mugs when Maya arrived, the urn of Red Cross milk carried on a pole by two Karvanda villagers. I began to ask if he remembered the milk deliveries . . .

'The woman who brought milk?' he interrupted. 'She would come with huge cans, like this.' Indicating a four-foot can. 'I remember,' he said. 'My sisters and I, we used to drink the milk, when I was a small child.'

It was in my mind to say that the woman was my mother, but for some reason I did not.

Phoebe was looking at the large mountain on the far side of the lake, which was half-hidden in cloud.

'What was that hill called?' she asked. 'Ask Kali Das.'

'They have no names,' he said.

'But they do,' I said. I knew their English names at least. The big one was called the Sugarloaf, a throwback to British times, when a Mrs Atkinson had lived in these parts and earned herself a reputation for shooting tigers. 'There are three of them, the big one, Sugarloaf, then a smaller one, then comes Duke's Nose.' How many times had we stood on top of Bicchauda and looked across the lake, admiring that view.

'No, no,' he said. 'There are only *two*. This one, and Duke's Nose.' He pronounced it Dyoosnooze. Was I going mad? Had I really forgotten these hills so completely? He had lived here all his life, since a small child. He should know.

But in the rickshaw on the way to Karvanda, and our old house, I worked it out. As we went past Ardau village, Duke's Nose, with its hooked double peak, was unmistakable. But the smaller central hill appeared to be no more than a spur of the Sugarloaf opposite. From Bicchauda, above our house, they were clearly three separate hills. Kali Das had counted only two, which meant – incredible thought – that he had never in his life travelled as far as the road to Karvanda. Either that, or he had not used his eyes. Why had he, not I, been privileged to live here all his life?

We rattled through the cutting we used to call the Khyber Pass. The road to Karvanda was once a cart track that wound up the mountain from this point. If you walked on it barefoot, the red dirt pulsed up between your toes and rinsed your feet with a softness like that of talc. Now it was a tarmac road that twisted steeply up a series of hairpins. The rickshaw chugged on through mist – actually cloud – blowing past, the hillside cradling dozens of tiny pools, marshy pools, from which arose the frenzied creaking of frogs. There was more forest here. A tall tree was being shaken in the most alarming manner by a troupe of monkeys. At the point where we should have turned east and up, the new road veered off in a different direction and drew near the edge of the stupendous cliffs opposite Tiger's Leap. A clearing appeared, a viewing point. I told the driver to stop. We would ask the way. Hawkers pestered us, offering tea and bhuttas – corn cobs roasted and sprinkled with lime juice and chilli powder.

'Hataanich jevto,' smiled Phoebe, at her most charming. The bhuttas were very delicious. From a small boy we learned that the old way to Karvanda village was still there, it was just accessed at a different point. He also told us to watch out for tigers.

'What? Are there tigers here?'

'Why d'you think this place is called Tiger's Leap?'

'I thought it was just a name.'

'It *is* a name,' he said. 'But that's why it's *this* name and not Deer's Leap or Squirrel's Leap.'

'Have you seen the tigers?' I asked him.

'There's a cave, a tiger's cave, in the cliff right below where you're standing.'

'Really? And have you seen one yourself?'

'Of course. Lots of times. I'm not afraid of them.'

I translated for Phoebe, who said, 'He's just like you used to be.'

The morning mist cleared and a hot, bright day blew in from the sea. Up the road we went, the views opening out below. And there it was, climbing up into the blue, our home slope of Bicchauda, what was left of its jungle steaming on its flanks. There were fewer trees, more bare rock showing, bigger pastures. But it was still there. And so was the rough track that broke from the road and led up the hill, round that corner, past those trees . . .

We asked the rickshaw to wait and walked up in silence, too consumed to say a word. The last time I had been here was thirty years ago. Then, not much had changed.

The gates to the house were closed, rusted together, padlocked with a length of rusty iron chain. Weeds were growing through them, just as before. But now, I noticed, a small tree had forced its way between the bars. No one could have lived here in years. It was surreal. As if nothing, but nothing had changed here. The wall crumbled a little as I scrambled over it. Tired limbs now, nearly fifty. How easily I would have leapt that when I was ten. And yet in my mind, in this place, here, in my kingdom, I was myself again.

'Come on, Fever,' I said, with only the faintest sense of absurdity, and she climbed up after me, no longer middle-aged, but my lithe supple love.

We dropped down the other side into a garden overgrown with trees of considerable size. Why had the garden been allowed to get into this state? Then we saw the house — shutters half off their hinges, missing doors, jungle trees poking branches into window-less rooms, the courtyard overgrown above head height in lantana, the pond cracked and empty.

What had happened here? We went inside, and stood in silent amazement. The house was derelict. Its rooms were empty, its walls rain-stained, with plaster crumbling off. A furry black mould grew on every surface. It had not been lived in for years.

'Bhalu, look!'

In what had been our bedroom, faint traces of a wall-painting. Not just any mural, but one of an old woman with glaring eyes done by a little girl who was learning to paint.

'Bhalu, no one has been here since we left!'

Karvanda village was still there, not much changed, except for some newer houses beginning to crawl towards the slope of Dagala. I noticed a couple of scooters parked in sheds beside old bullock carts. A television aerial fixed to a dead branch high on a mango tree, a row of small green birds perched on it. Above us, the Kathodi cliff reared, still thickly jungled. Jula's family had all left. Dhondu had died long ago, his wife followed not long after. The sisters were both married, one was in Mumbai, the other in Pune. The brothers were working in Pune for the Forestry Department. These things we learned, over glasses of thick tea, from an elderly man who turned out to be Rameshbhai, the teacher I had met all those years before. The school was still running.

'We have government funding now,' he told us. 'And we need it, because the school's twice the original size. But the money from your mother still comes. Not once has it failed to arrive.'

'Are you in touch with Jula?' I asked hopefully, thinking of his plans to publish enlightening educational books.

'Mitra? Haven't seen him for years. He's in Mumbai still, I'm sure. I heard he had got mixed up in politics. I'm afraid I don't have any address.'

We asked about the house and learned that it had been shut up and decaying for as long as anyone could remember.

'It was bought by some big person from Bombay, but he never came here. It has been falling apart for years. There have been offers to buy it, but the owner won't sell.'

We returned to Bombay defeated. To the Rudolf Hotel and Shankar-of-the-Red-Dot, who eyed us curiously, this pair whose passports bore different surnames, who had taken separate rooms, who ever since Phoebe's arrival had slept in the same room, but – as far as the room-boy's experienced eye could tell – in separate beds.

'Two rooms, two rents,' he said with a smirk. 'We could put a double-bed in yours.'

My reply was a smirk, the mirror image of his own.

A few days later, in my room. A muggy afternoon, windows open, fan full tilt. She was lying on her bed watching television.

I said, 'Phoebe, your mother's diaries . . . do you remember a party given by a man called Sub? Must have been in the late fifties. There was a long list of food and other things.'

'Hmm?' she said, her eyes fixed on the screen, across which brightly coloured shapes were flashing, accompanied by dramatic music. 'Oh look, he's getting away!'

'I'm sure it mentioned a bootlegger they all used.'

'Did it?'

'Do please listen to me for a moment.'

She rolled over and fastened on me those great eyes of hers. She was wearing shorts and a top that showed much midriff. Almost my age, how on earth had she kept so trim? I wish I had a picture of that moment. She looked lovely. Kind, sad eyes, green-grey, like the long-ago brahmin's wife.

I said, 'Look what we've got. No notebook. No name. No idea who the other women were . . .'

'No hope at all,' she said in a babyish voice. 'Oh *dear!* Does Bhalu need a nice bootlegger-man to give him a dwinkie?'

'Stop it,' I said, taken aback by this sudden childishness. 'Listen, I've thought of another possibility. What did the police find in Ahuja's flat, besides the letters?'

'Women's knickers?' she asked, still in the same annoying voice. 'Lots of frilly panties? Suspenders? Dildos?'

'They found a lot of bootleg liquor.'

'Oh what a naughty, naughty man he was.'

'I've just thought . . . isn't it possible that the blackmailer put the squeeze on the bootlegger too?'

'Naughty, wicked blackmailer,' said Phoebe.

'From what I can make out, everyone in this town is on the take. So it's a fair bet that the bootlegger, whoever he was, was already paying off the cops and magistrates . . .'

'Yes?' she said, one eye on the television set. 'Ooh look, he's doing it again!'

'Will you listen to me? Our blackmailer wouldn't be put off by that, would he?'

'Sorry, put off by what?'

'By the fact that the bootlegger was already paying the police.'

'No,' she said, reverting to silliness. 'Mister Shaitan is not a very nice man.'

'No, he's a complete bastard.'

'Naughty Bhalu, said a wicked word.'

'Will you be serious for one moment?'

She thought about this. Then shook her head.

'Right! That's it!' I jumped on her and began card-indexing her ribs with nimble bookseller's fingers.

'Nooo!' she screamed, wriggling, breathless with laughter. 'It tickles! Stop it! Help!'

'Only if you promise to be serious.' I was lying on top of her, crushing her, my weight forcing her to speak in little grunts.

'I don't *want* to be serious. I'm sick of being serious. Oh please! I can't always be serious. It'll kill me.'

So I tickled her again into hysterical half-sobbing laughter.

'Help!' she gasped. 'Naughty Bhalu-alu! Stop! Mother!'

Something dark flew through her eyes, then they steadied.

'Now,' I said, through clenched teeth, 'will you listen?'

She struggled silently, furiously, then gave up and lay still. We were looking into each other's eyes from that point-blank range. Suddenly she smiled and I felt her hand reach down between us.

'Oh Bhalu,' she said in her baby voice, 'I think you like me.'

I rolled off her onto my back, and closed my eyes.

A moment later I felt her hair brush my face. 'I love you, Bhalu,' she said. 'I really love you.'

She laid her head on my shoulder. We lay for a long time with our arms around one another, as we so often had when we were children.

All day we'd been arguing about what to do. I was ready to give up and go home. Phoebe, not long arrived, wanted to stay and keep looking. 'People leave traces. The things they do leave traces.' It was like listening to Maya. She reminded me that I had studied, albeit by mail order, the science of detection. 'There must be some clever thing you can think of. If anyone can, you can.' Her faith in me was unnerving. As a child she had followed me trustingly through jungles and along the edges of cliffs, never conceiving that I could lead her into danger. Now she expected me to thread the labyrinth of Bombay. The city, vast, inapprehensible, mocked us every time we left the hotel. The sheer number of people crowding its streets, clinging to buses, hanging out of the packed trains that arrived at Churchgate every minute, crammed into teeming mohollas and overpopulated chawls, was overwhelming, yet each person's tale was unique, intricately connected to all the others. How was I to unravel the single clue we sought from this huge web of stories, that not only extended over hundreds of square miles of city, but stretched back forty years through time? In England it had seemed somehow logical, the idea that she should find and confront the man who had tortured her mother, but here, in Bombay, or rather, Mumbai, it seemed hopelessly naive. Our quest was a waste of time. I had been stupid to come. I realised that I was actually here to close a gyre, to end my own exile. To see Bicchauda again. The breath had caught in my throat, as we bumped along those last few miles, and the old familiar horizons began to open, but things I'd have expected to delight me – an old man approaching under a rainhat (and Phoebe remembering it was called an 'irrla'), peering into puddles and catching the flick of tiny fishes, seeing lads with bamboo rods squatting by pools where we had caught catfish – these things did thrill me, but it was a bitter pleasure. I found myself trying to assert proprietorship of the land in a dozen small ways. 'Remember this?' I asked Phoebe. I picked up a rock and dashed it against another, breaking it like a stone coconut, to reveal the quartz crystals within. 'That sulphur smell?' But she did not remember. My longing – it was not nostalgia, but a desperation to belong – forced its way out in conversations with people like the chai-wallahs Kali Das and Mangala, about the naming of local hills, and the old boy in the rainhat, whom I had greeted in rusty Marathi on the pretext of confirming that we were on the right road, but really in order to inform him that I had once lived here. I had been afraid that going back would ruin the old memories, but they remained – distant, inviolate, untouchable. This fear was replaced by another, harder to bear, that were it not for the memories, the place would hold no particular magic for me at all.

As for Phoebe, what was she thinking? I had worried about what she might do if we ever found the blackmailer. That now seemed ridiculous. Apart from her odd outburst of childishness, she had been cool and controlled ever since her arrival, quite the elegant memsahib in her loosely belted jeans and crisp suits cut just above the knee. I felt a guilty pride when she took my arm in the street.

About Katy I hardly dared think. I had phoned her only once after that first call. She had been as unfriendly as before, convinced that Phoebe was with me. Since Phoebe's arrival I had not rung again because I hated lying to Katy. It would have been pointless to say that I had not expected Phoebe – I had been glad to see her – dishonest to say there was nothing between us. How could I tell Katy we had not been to bed together or slept together when Phoebe had often lain in my arms, and slept in the bed by my side? Had we made love? Well, what else are kisses and murmurs of affection? When applied to our peculiar relationship, the usual euphemisms for sex failed utterly. The only truth was the brutal four-letter fact that we had not actually fucked. I was ready to go home, but first I wanted to find my old friends. It was thinking of Dost that gave me the idea about the bootlegger.

'Black Market Services?' said Phoebe into an imaginary phone. 'Is that Mr Legger? Hello, this is Mr Shaitan, from the insurance agency . . . No, not your usual branch . . . I am calling about this new situation. Your premium is for day-to-day matters, you are not covered for this. A further one-off premium will be payable.'

'Exactly. Now, given just how extraordinary the new situation was, wouldn't Mr Legger remember Mr Shaitan? In your mother's diary, Sub named the bootlegger they all used. I don't remember it, but I'm sure his joint was in Char Null.'

'How does that help?'

'Char Null is a place in Dongri. Where we used to smoke hash. Where Dost used to brag that he knew everyone.'

'Well then,' she said. 'We just have to find Dost.'

'Put some clothes on. I am taking you to Dongri.'

Once upon a time, before ever the English, or the Portuguese, or the Muslémeen came to India, before there was Bombay, or Born Bahia, before the caves of Elephanta were carved, there were seven islands, baking in sun, salt and silence. At high tide, they were separated by a sluggish sea, but when the tide ebbed they reached out to one another through overheated malaria-marsh where eels coiled among the mangroves, and across mudskipper flats printed by the feet of birds and crabs, as if they, the islands, already sensed their destiny. So close-knit were they that from a mile offshore one would have seen an unbroken undulation of coconut trees, under-lined by beaches where fishing craft leaned on outriggers and nets were hoisted to dry.

Seven islands, whose first inhabitants, simple fishing folk, skins burnt almost black by the sun, called themselves Kolis and lived in villages whose names were their histories: Colaba, 'Koliground', Mazgaon, 'Fishville'. The chief place in the archipelago was a very old temple to a goddess, Mumba Amma. She was made of stone, had wide eyes, an orange complexion and no mouth. Through whatever depths of language one dives to retrieve the meaning of her name, it always reduces to the pearly syllable 'Ma'. From her, the home island derived its name, the place of Mumbamai. The temple stood among groves of tamarinds, beneath a hill which the Kolis called simply, 'Hill'. In their language, Dongri.

Life in the Mumbamai islands conformed to the rhythm of the tides, which brought in, and swept away again, drowned birds and dead sea-snakes, bladderwrack, coconuts, driftwood, the keel-bones of cuttlefish, spars from shipwrecks (whence, over the centuries, a small hoard of Mauryan kharshapana coins, a silver tetradrachm of Bar-Kochba, copper shivrais struck by Chhatrapati Shivaji, plus sundry copperoons, bazaruccos, half-dudus and pice), and while the Kolis worked the tides, bringing in their catches of mackerel, shrimp, pomfret, seer fish, king fish, ribbon fish, swordfish, tuna, dory, squid, lobster and of course the infamous double-bummalo, kings, dynasties and empires came and went unnoticed. Dongri and its temple survived the Satvahanas, Chalukyas, Rashtrakutas, Silharas, Yadavs, Ahmadshahis and the Portuguese. But when the English built their fort at the south end of the temple-island, its northern-most bastion extended to Dongri hill.

Beyond the fort was an esplanade, an empty space which could be raked with grape and roundshot in case of an uprising, and on the far side of this, a 'native town' began to grow. Dongri was soon swallowed up. Warehouses replaced tamarind trees, and tall square-riggers docked where the Kolis had sewn their lateen sails. New arrivals from all over India brought their trades and set up shop in the narrow, crooked lanes (which still exist, I told Phoebe, as our taxi drove there, often still specialising in the same goods). In and around Dongri the newcomers were mostly Muslim. The Hindus camped to the west and north. As for the dispossessed Kolis, they were put to work by the British, building roads through the marshes, breaking and carrying rock to make sea-walls and close up the tidal breaches between the islands. In accepting this work, which all but destroyed their old way of life, they gave the English language a new word. They were no longer Kolis. They had become 'coolies'.

Bombay bazaars at night, lights and dazzle. I told the driver to do a tour of the Muslim mohollas and felt like a tourist, pointing out to Phoebe things I thought would please her – open-air cook-shops dishing out biryani and kebabs, a man frying jalebis in a huge pan. Near Masjid Street in Bhendi Bazaar, I asked the taxi to wait, and took her for a walk through crowded lanes lined with shoe- and cloth-stalls, to the building where Mitra had once worked. The printing works, as I knew, was gone – the first thing I had done on arrival in the city was look for it in the *Yellow Pages*. In its place was a veterinary clinic. However, in a nearby lane we found the shop of Dawood Khan, who Dost used to insist was the only tailor in Bombay who knew how to cut a shirt. To me, starved of such sights, the walk was bliss, but Phoebe was uncomfortable. 'People are staring.'

'Well,' I said, 'you won't see many foreigners here at night.'

'Choop,' she said in a terrible accent. Shut up. 'I'm not foreign.'

So we returned to the taxi and carried on to Dongri. I told the driver to slow down as we neared Char Null. I was looking for an

491

alley that led off the main road. Would I recognise it after thirty years? The streets here were gloomier. The bazaars had given way to an area of small businesses. Some Dongri trades: auto repairs, switchgear dealer, leather goods, paper-maker, relegious (*sic*) books, sanitaryware supplies, embroiderer (fancy stitching), ship-chandler, industrial chemicals (spice oleoresins, essential oils), fashion accessories (exporters of eyelets, mannequins, dummies, undergarments), dozens of road haulage firms.

Alley after alley passed, dark openings lined by shabby wooden buildings. Trucks and handcarts parked for the night. That one? No. This one? 'Stop!' I told the driver.

'Are you sure we should get out here?' Phoebe asked.

A broader than normal opening, narrowing abruptly where the corner of a building jutted into it. This surely was where they had tied the ropes to erect the cinema screen. I dismissed the taxi. At that moment I had no fears about our safety. This dark anonymous alley was, like Ambona, one of the magical places in my life. After the circle of hills, the circle of charpays. How often had I imagined turning up out of the night, and finding Dost sitting here with his chillum, in a tamarind-sour cloud of hashish smoke.

There! There it was! Moosa's! The shadowy archway with its wrought-iron gates. Here we had sat, the string beds arranged in a rough circle in the street, and the goat had watched the movie with me. A street-lamp stood just where I remembered. There was the old warehouse across the road . . . but something had happened to it. A huge scorchmark flared across its face. The SAURASHTRA TRADING COMPANY was still there, but its sign was charred, nearly obliterated. Now it simply read CURRY . . . YARNS.

Then it struck me that there were no string beds in the street.

Nobody had come out to greet us. The alley was deserted.

'Bhalu, I don't like it,' Phoebe said. 'Can we go?'

I said, 'I don't know what's happened here. I'll ask someone.'

'Please!' she said, tugging at my arm.

'Ey! Yes? What do you want?' A voice from a doorway. A thin man about my own age. Phoebe was still pulling at me. I said I was looking for a friend I had not seen for a long time.

'He lived here? What's his name?'

His real name, Mohammed Khan, was like searching London for Peter Smith. 'His friends called him Dost,' I said. 'We used to meet in this lane. Years ago.'

'Really?' the man asked, staring at Phoebe, who could not understand what was being said. 'What did you do here?'

'Drank chai. Chatted. Debated . . . we were students.'

'Oh I see,' he said politely. 'Whereabouts?'

So I pointed to Moosa's dark gateway.

'Well, I don't know,' the man said. 'Sorry.'

I had an idea. 'Is there still a tea shop round the corner?'

'This is a city of tea shops.'

The Café Jam-i-Jam (Cup of Jamshid), which had once belonged to Dost's uncle, seemed unchanged. Memorable, the meals I had eaten here, in those days when the city was at war, the time of blackout and sirens, when we sat, stoned as mystics, and watched orange blobs of tracer float slowly up into the darkness. But no one remembered Dost. We gathered a small crowd before it was clear that nobody could help us. The adda was gone. I could not find my friends.

There was a taxi parked a few yards up the street, its driver dozing in the back. Bombay is full of taxis. In Sewri, where taxi-drivers seem to flock at night to roost, the lines of parked cabs are five miles long. I told the cabby to head for Mahalaxmi, more or less the opposite direction to our hotel. I didn't want to go back to Apollo Bunder, to sit and brood. Our latest failure was somehow the most depressing. There had been – what was it? amusement? impudence? insolence? – in the manner of the people we had talked to. We would enquire again, I told Phoebe, at that other haunt of our youth, the adda on the shore by Haji Ali's tomb. But I knew we would find no trace of Dost.

'Go via Zaveri Bazaar,' I told the driver, so we wound at a snail's pace through little lanes clogged with handcarts and bicycles and people until we found ourselves in the goldsmiths' quarter.

'Stop here a moment.'

Above the clutter of roofs and awnings rose the pink-and-white tower of a Hindu temple.

'Mumba's temple. This is where it was rebuilt after the first one was destroyed.'

'Why was it destroyed?'

'The English,' I said quite unconscious of the fact that they included her forbears (there had been Killigrews in India since the early eighteenth century). 'Deep down, they always feared us natives. Smiling faces, knives in the dark. We were devious, treacherous, sly, on no account to be trusted. That's why they cleared the ground round the fort. To give their gunners an uninterrupted field of fire in case of trouble. Mumba's temple was in that zone, the Esplanade. It was demolished to make way for fortifications of some sort. Mumba Devi moved here, and has been here ever since.'

'How do you know all these things?'

'I'm a bookseller. What else do I have to do all day but read?'

We asked the taxi to wait and took a walk along Mumbadevi Street: stalls hung with rosaries of rudraksh beads – Srinuji would have felt right at home here – posters of exuberant gods and goddesses. Siva, moon-browed. Kali doing her victory jig on his decapitated corpse. Hundreds of times I must have seen this image, but had never noticed before that the severed heads in her necklace all belonged to men. At a flower stall by the temple gate – jasmine, marigolds, roses, lotuses – I bought Phoebe a garland of jasmine, wound it round her neck like a triple necklace of pearls.

In 1888, about a hundred years after the original temple of Mumba was knocked down – and about the time that a disgruntled Englishman was correcting proofs of his futuristic fantasy *India in 1983* – its old site began swarming with coolies carrying bamboo scaffolding poles, marble, decorated tiles, stained glass, metal, bricks. Where, for centuries beyond memory, the goddess had dispensed her fishy blessings, they built a railway station and named it after the Great Mother Over The Sea. Victoria Terminus. VT. It was renamed Chhatrapati Shivaji Terminus by the same politicians who, in a bid to reinvent their missing history, to fill a history-shaped hole, had renamed the city after the goddess.

The adda at Haji Ali was also long gone. No one there but a few beggars and a steady stream of faithful returning across the causeway from the sea-mosque, where the day's last namaaz had just finished. Waves were breaking at their feet. They looked as if they were walking on water.

We sat on the sea-wall and watched the tide swell round Haji Ali's dargah. White marble on troubled darkness.

'Would you like to go out to dinner?'

I had in mind to take her to one of those little places in the bazaars, a café like the Jam-i-Jam, where we'd sit at a table in the street and eat whatever was good and hot and ready.

She shook her head. 'I'm tired. But I don't mind sitting here. The mosque is beautiful.'

'Yes.' Was it my faulty memory, or had this lovely old building once been disfigured by a huge neon sign advertising SHALIMAR BISCUITS? After a while I said, 'Really precious experiences can't be recreated or shared. One shouldn't even try. It's impossible.'

'Why do you say that?' she asked, lighting a cigarette. 'You sound cross.'

So I told her about the meals I remembered so well, at the Jam-i-Jam, the pleasure of sitting in the street . . . 'But it wouldn't be like that for you. You'd be pestered. People would stare. You'll never be able to share that experience.'

'I've already shared it,' she said. 'It was in the story you gave me to read. About you and Jula and Dost . . . at that place where we've just come from.'

'Yes, where you saw only a depressing and frightening alley. How can I bring it back to life for you, what it was really like?'

'You already have,' she said. 'You wrote about it.'

'Such things can't be captured in words. You have to feel them for yourself.'

496

'I can't relive your memories,' she said. 'I don't expect you to relive mine.'

I wished she would say again, as she had earlier, 'I love you,' but she sat on the wall, smoking a cigarette, looking out to sea, where the lights of a ship glowed distantly, on a horizon lost in night.

Some evenings later I returned to the Rudolf alone, exhausted from trudging the streets of Dongri visiting printing works, and going to see every political party I could think of, to ask whether anyone knew a Shambhumitra Kashele, alias Mitra, who had once been our old friend Jula. I'd ask for some tea, I thought, then go to Phoebe's room and see her. For the last few nights she had been sleeping in her own room.

In reception were the usual gaggle of white-robed Arabs. Among them was a large man with a fleshy face who stared at me as I entered. Not an Arab. His shirt, unbuttoned to halfway down his chest, disclosed a gold chain nestling on a great deal of hair. Several rings flashed as he folded his paper.

The desk clerk said, 'Sir, this man has been waiting for you.'

'This is him?' said the man, standing up. He gave a great bellow of laughter. 'Never. Not a hope. I don't believe it.'

'I'm sorry, are you looking for me?'

'Wah, what an English gentleman you've become.'

'Do I know you?'

'You mean you don't recognise me?'

'Should I?'

'Put it this way,' he said. 'If I hadn't been circumcised . . .'

The hotel clerk, disconcerted by this strange remark, was quite dizzied to see me run forward and embrace the stranger, who spread his own arms in generous welcome.

'How on earth did you find me?' I asked, when we were in my room, and a pot of tea stood on the table between us.

'I didn't find you. You found me,' he said, looking round at the shabby furnishings. 'Bhalu bhai, what are you doing here? Don't you know this is a rather shady place?'

'But I couldn't find you,' I said. 'I've been trying for days. I went to Moosa's but it has all changed. What happened there?'

'All that later,' he said. 'First, where is *she*?'

'She?'

'Your girlfriend! Or forgive me, maybe she's your wife . . . The blonde with the sulky mouth that everyone's talking about.'

'But how do you know? And who is everyone?'

'The tea-drinking elite that hangs out at my uncle's place. Only it isn't his place any more.'

'Whose is it then?'

'Mine.'

'Yours?!'

'Mine,' he repeated, evidently enjoying himself.

'But I went there and asked for you . . .'

'You certainly did – the most exciting thing that's happened there for years. I've lost count how many people have come sidling up to me and said, "Dost miyah, an old friend of yours came from England with . . ."' He made an hourglass gesture.

'I must have asked a dozen people. Nobody knew you.'

'Nobody knew? Everybody knew! Most people in the street would have known. I've lived in that area all my life. My whole family is there. Of course they know me.'

'But . . .'

'. . . But they don't tell you that, eh? Well, Bhalu, take a look at yourself. You come to Dongri. Do you look like a Dongri-wallah? No! Do you even look like a Bombayite? No! You're someone from outer space. A Martian! Look at those trousers, those shoes. Your face is a normal brown colour, but everything else screams *phoren*'. (The last word was English, he was otherwise speaking Urdu.)

'Not only that, but along with you is this woman. Is she a woman you might pass in the street without a glance? No, she has a pink skin, hair the colour of butter and blue eyes . . .'

'Green,' I said, laughing. 'She's very clear on that point.'

'I like green better,' he said. 'So you and green-eyes have already attracted the attention of every loafing idiot on the street. Okay, this is no big deal. You might be a pair of lost tourists, except . . . what do you do next? You ask for me. Mohammed Khan, used to be known as "Dost" — well, that was in my youth, my dear, a time of indiscretions and things best forgotten. Still, out of sheer curiosity they might have brought you to me, but then you really excelled yourself. Aapne saari duniya-jahaan mein dondi pitwa di (you banged the drum to the whole world), saying — "Dost and I used to meet at a place around the corner." And not just a vague round-here-somewhere, but *that* corner, over *there*, in *that* lane. And then, as if that isn't specific enough, you inform everyone. "It used to belong to a man called Moosa Ali."' He began to chuckle. 'But the funniest thing is that you told Moosa's nephew we were a debating society.' Dost laughed until his eyes were wet.

'Arré bhai, you always were a bhola Bhalu.'

*　　*　　*

'So,' he said, smiling at me. 'Say.'

Old friend! For a moment I could *say* nothing. A salty tide rose inside me, and hung, poised to overwhelm. Say? What could I say? He seemed to understand what I was feeling, because for quite a while we just sat and smiled at one another.

What's the story? Where did you go? What happened?

Stories begin before their beginnings. A blue room. A Ganesh calendar on the wall. A plain-clothes cop who interrogated me.

'Remember the night we were arrested?'

I began to tell him what had followed – my life in England, Katy, the twins, the lost years, the bookshop. He listened carefully, rarely interjecting, except when something puzzled him.

'This bookselling,' he said. 'If it doesn't make money, what good is it?'

'I'm happier since I stopped making money.'

'Over here that kind of happiness can kill you. You know the first rule of life in Bombay . . . *Agodar potoba, nantar vitthoba!*

First Mr Gut, then Mr God.

'I see you follow your own advice,' I said, indicating the swell of his kameez. Quite a belly, had Dost. Doing well, clearly. Glitter of gold round his neck. On his knuckles.

'Takes time and money to make one of these,' he said, patting Mr Gut. 'After marriage, children, I quit fooling about. Settled down. Took over the Jam-i-Jam . . . must be fifteen years ago. Now I have two restaurants. Some side businesses too.'

I said, 'Well, I'm afraid with me it's quite the opposite. Katy's the earner in our household.'

'So she's not your wife.'

'Of course she is,' I said, thrown by this.

'Your wife is Katy, and she is at home,' Dost said patiently. 'So who is *she*, this other woman, the one you're here with?'

'Just a friend.' I had not yet broached the subject of Phoebe.

'*Just* a friend? But you fancy her like hell, don't you?'

'Why should you think that?'

'Because, my friend, why else would you take her to Haji Ali and sit on the sea wall holding hands like a pair of young lovers? Also, on the way back to the hotel, you put your arm round her and called her "darling"!'

'How do you know these things?'

'The taxi you took, from outside the café . . . my Cousin Murad. Speaks no English, but has seen enough movies to understand "darling".'

Then I remembered that as we left Haji Ali, the same taxi had drawn up beside us and the driver said he'd waited because he had a feeling we might want to go on somewhere else. At the time I'd thought nothing of it. Just a cabby hoping for a tourist-sized tip.

'What about Mitra? Do you see much of him? We're looking forward to meeting him. Phoebe hasn't seen him since we were all about ten. In those days he was called Jula . . .' I spoke on happily into what I soon realised was a lengthening silence from Dost.

'We are no longer close,' he said at last. 'Things have changed.'

'How do you mean? Has Mitra changed?'

He smiled. 'Will he ever? He's still the same serious, shit-faced old fly-killer, determined to set the world to rights. Still got that chip on his shoulder.'

'Then what . . . ?'

Dost sighed, spread his hands. 'Difficult to explain . . . It's not

Mitra. It's Bombay that's changed. Politics has got into everything. Like mildew. Ruins whatever it touches.'

'I don't understand. I heard that he got mixed up with politics, but how could that affect a friendship?'

'You really have been living on Mars,' said Dost. 'Don't you get news over there in England? Are you really unaware that—?'

But before he could establish the precise nature or extent of my ignorance, there was a tap at the door. Phoebe came in, wearing an evening dress that appeared to be upheld only by her breath.

'I'm tired of slumming it!' she announced, pirouetting to reveal a back scooped to the waist. 'Tonight we're going somewhere where the menu is in French—' She stopped when she saw the stranger, who rose uncertainly to his feet.

'Phoebe! Guess who this is!'

They stood staring at one another. Never, in all the times I had imagined this meeting, had I realised there would be such a gulf between them. Nor had I remembered that they would not speak each other's languages, so when I cried, 'It's Dost!' I was unprepared for her to step forward, hold out her hand and say, in a manner absurdly English, 'How do you do?'

'Zahé kismet!' (My good fortune!) replied the dumbfounded Dongri-wallah. His hand, arrested in the act of rising to touch his breast, reached hesitantly for her hand: a peculiar sight, my two old friends, trying to harmonise their rituals of greeting, negotiate the difficult passage that had opened between their worlds.

I began explaining to Phoebe how Dost had found us, while he stood by, looking unwontedly shy.

'So the taxi-driver was your cousin!' she exclaimed.

'Sorry, not speaking too good English,' he said in that language.

'Better than my Hindi!' was her practised reply.

'Bhalu explained me about you. Meeting you is for me a very pleasure . . . Bhalu,' (to me in Urdu) 'it's sickening not being able to express oneself properly. She must think I'm a peasant.' To Phoebe, from whose breasts his eyes could not unfasten themselves: 'Please you will take food . . . dinner . . . at my place . . . ?' To me: 'Come on, lad, I've got my car outside. You're expected, everything's prepared. We'll make a real night of it . . .' To a hesitating Phoebe: 'So you please come? We go now.'

She looked at me. I nodded.

'Thank you,' she said, 'I'd love to.'

Not wanting to embarrass her in front of him, I said, 'Il faut que tu te change. Ta décolletage est délicieuse, mais pas appropriate.'

'Et ton français,' she snapped back, 'ne s'est pas amélioré depuis l'école! On ne dit pas "appropriate", c'est *approprié*. Alors moi, je le suis toujours! . . . Please excuse me,' she said to Dost, and left the room. When the door had closed behind her, Dost burst out laughing and clapped me on the shoulder. 'Yaar, tumne kamaal kiya! Kya maal laaye ho!' (Lad, you've surpassed yourself. What goods you've brought!)

It was eight, dark outside. Lights of ships on the black harbour water. A strong shower earlier had cleared the air and it was, for Bombay, almost cool. Dost, giving his collar an upward flick and donning a pair of dark glasses, led us across the road. By the sea wall was a parked taxi, with a familiar figure snoozing in the back.

'Your chauffeur?'

'Who needs to own a car, when there are taxis in the moholla?'

'Might have guessed,' I said, feeling a great relief. Rough and ready Dost might be, a Dongri-wallah from his upflipped collar to the tips of his flashy shoes, but with him around, things would be taken care of. Handled. Ho sakta hai. Can do. At Zafyque's house I had felt he was as baffled as I was about our mission. Dost wouldn't have to *think* about what to do, he would *know*. It was his city.

'This is Murad . . . Murad bhai, these are my friends.'

'Salaam aleikum,' said Cousin Murad, giving a knowing smile as 'darling' and I slid into our familar seats. She had changed into a long skirt and a blouse that buttoned to the neck, giving her the air of a louche schoolmistress. 'Memsahib, take back.' Murad the driver turned and pressed some rupees into her hand. 'No, no, no,' he said, when she protested. 'My brother friend. No charge.'

'So Phoebe, first time coming India?' Dost asked.

'I was born here,' she said.

'Born India? Then why you left? Why not stayed here?'

In bits and pieces, with me acting as interlocutor, the story began to emerge. With each new detail, Dost grew more delighted.

'Childhood sweethearts? Meeting again after so many years? Just like a filmi romance.'

'Bhalu isn't the least bit romantic,' Phoebe told him. 'I asked him to come to India with me, and he said no!'

'You said no?'

'That's right.'

He laughed. 'Yaar tu kab sudhrega? (When will you improve?) So you struck a pose and said, "Nahi, main nahi aaunga." (No, I won't come.) And then you came after all. You know what you two remind me of? There's a movie — have you seen it? *Dilwale Dulhaniya Le Jaayenge.*'

I was translating for Phoebe. 'We remind him of a couple in a film. You could translate it as *True Heart Wins the Bride.*'

'Please,' she begged Dost. 'Tell me the story.'

'I telling Bhalu. Bhalu telling you.'

But she wouldn't allow that. 'Your English is perfectly good. You tell me.'

'Okay, so this is the fillim of Yash Chopra. *Dilwale Dulhaniya Le Jaayenge* is — kya kahte hain (what do you call it?) — mega-hit! This fillim was shooted in Europe first-half and second-half Punjab. One hero actor Shah Rukh Khan plays a boy Raj and actress Kajol . . .' (to me, aside, in Urdu 'My God, that Kajol, what a minx!') . . . 'Kajol plays a girl Simran. They both living to England.'

As he talked, the middle-aged man receded and he became again the film-crazy youth of three decades earlier.

'So Raj misleads his life and goes to college at Cambraj with a long tall genie, very fast. He's not so good chap . . . aankhen-milaana, usko kya bolten hain? . . . thank you . . . flirting with girls and making fun. Simran is a bilkul aap jaise pretty girl . . . just as you, waiting to meet a dream guy.'

'What is this long, tall genie?' *Lambu-djinni* was what he'd said.

'A car, yaar. Lambu-djinni is a fast car.'

'Lamborghini,' said Phoebe.

'These two, girl Simran and boy Raj, he don't know her, she don't know him, go to see pahadon . . . mountains . . . in Swizzerland. One-in-crore chance they meet on train. She seems not to interest in him. She asks to Raj that would you come to my shaadi, wedding, in India. He say her, like Bhalu say you, "nahi, main nahi aaunga". From this she know he in love with her.'

'Oh!' said Phoebe. 'Is that how you tell?'

So we left Apollo Bunder, passed the Taj Hotel, haunt of those who think they run the city, to return to the place where the city began. We drove north through the old Fort past VT (CST) where the original temple of Ma had stood, back to the bazaar area named after the hill the Kolis had called 'Hill', and returned to the Jam-i-Jam where this time the tea-drinkers and hangers-on crowded round to say hello, each one wanting to slap my back and shake Phoebe's hand, and when we sat down at a table in the mirrored inner room, people drew up chairs and crowded round us on all sides.

'Come on, this is a celebration! What will you drink?'

'Tea,' I said, hoping Phoebe would not ask for alcohol. 'Tea,' she agreed, to my relief.

'Okay, bring some tea!' And the word passed back through the ranks. 'Tea! . . . Arré bring tea! . . . Hot tea!' So tea came, brought by the obligatory small boy. Glasses of tea, milky, sweet, warmed by cardamom. 'Snacks!' cried Dost. 'Snacks!' the echoes chorused. 'Samosé . . . and khichda! Give them some khichda like yesterday's . . . corianderful!' So plates came, and everyone sat and watched us eat. No one else touched a thing.

'Ey, *jukebox* chalao!' Which turned out to be a CD player rigged through a pair of decrepit loudspeakers that sounded as if they were hissing the singers.

'Phoebe,' said Dost, 'you eating nothing! What you will have?

507

Will you like to eat mutton biryani? . . . Ey, kitchen!'

'Fish biryani is nicer,' called someone. And the chorus began again. 'Or how about chicken! Jamjammy special! . . . Brain egg masala! . . . Will she like it? . . . Sheekh anarkali is great . . . Arré forget sheekh anarkali, bring some gurda kaleji! . . . Mahi-e-aab! Nice fresh pomfret . . . What about rotis? . . . Try a baida roti. Chicken! . . . Kheema? . . . Bhalu miyah, you must *definitely* have some nalli nihari . . . But we don't do it . . . A-bé! I *know* we don't do it! Let the boy run to the Noor Mohammadi, tell them to send four half-plates.'

So we ate, and gradually others around us also fell to. We had to stop them ordering more food and even, when Dost and his friends thought of some choice thing the kitchen didn't have ready, sending out for it. Impossible even to contemplate the sweets, kheer, ladwas, falooda, sutarpheni, they pressed upon us.

'You know what I wish?' Phoebe said to me. 'I wish Jula could be here with us now.'

Dost must have caught enough of this to understand. 'Tell her, I'll take you to meet him. He comes here, occasionally. We still say hello. But it isn't the same. Too much trouble. But between you and him there will be no problem. He'll be delighted to see you.'

'What happened? You never explained.'

'Aie, baba, it's a bad story.'

Phoebe, as was her habit after a meal, got out her cigarettes. It was not really done for a woman to smoke in public, at least not in that area, but Dost, without batting an eyelid, produced a lighter and flicked it.

'Hey, maybe Phoebe would like some wine. I got some, just in case . . . Ey, bring the wine!' A bottle was duly placed in his hand

and two large tumblers, wet from the tap, were set before us. Phoebe, who had not been consulted, watched as Dost unscrewed the cap and filled the glasses to the brim, upending the bottle, until a bloody trickle ran down each one onto the marble tabletop.

'Best Indian wine,' he announced.

'Aren't you having any?'

'I am Muslim. I don't drink alcohol.'

She lifted the glass with both hands, took a sip.

'You like it?'

'Lovely.' Through a smile of startling insincerity she whispered, 'C'est comme un sirop anti-tussif.'

My French was not sufficiently amélioré for this, but I told her with a straight face, 'Dommage, mon amour. Il faut boire tout le vin, ou il serait insulté.'

Dost once again caught the drift. 'You don't like? Then leave! Leave!' To me, Urdu: 'We have no corkscrew. I got that one because it was the only bottle with a screw-top . . . Ey, bring more tea!'

The small tea-boy came up — he could not have been older than nine or ten — and set down a clutch of tea-glasses. Phoebe said, 'He's so young and he works so hard. Would it be all right if I gave him a tip?' She fished in her purse for some coins. 'This lady wants to give you a tip,' Dost told him. 'What do you say?' The boy gazed into Phoebe's eyes, levelled his palm at her, wiggled his hips and sang, in a high quavering tone, 'Aati kya Khandala?'

'Arré! What battameezi is this? Ey! Chal!' Dost cuffed the lad affectionately. 'Little sod thinks he's sadak chhaap . . . acting tough like a street kid. Really he's just a poseur, aren't you? Don't I see you going to school every morning with your satchel?'

The significance of the boy's song was lost on me.

'Bhalu, I have something for you as well,' Dost said. 'To bring back memories. Or perhaps make new ones.' He opened his hand to reveal a beautiful little chillum, turned from a single piece of hardwood, with brass rims on the bowl and mouthpiece.

Later, Dost took us to his house. A narrow passage led from a door in the street to a small courtyard, entirely enclosed, off which various rooms opened at ground- and first-floor level. We climbed a stair wet from a passing shower, and went into a room with a balcony overlooking the street. It contained a maroon sofa of some plush material, covered in clear plastic, upon which Phoebe and I sat, while Dost lounged opposite, on a bed with white sheets and a bolster, tamping tobacco into the chillum. How many pipes? Two? Three? The room was lit by a fluorescent tube which flashed in the mirrors, inscribed with green and gold Arabic phrases, that hung on every wall. A fan whirred in a corner, turning its moon face from one to the other of us, as if following our conversation. From a further room came the sound of a movie on TV, laughter and voices . . . Phoebe was lying back with her eyes closed. Asleep, or magic-carpeted away? Last time she had mixed hashish and wine was in the hotel in Kensington. Natasha nasha. A million miles.

'It comes to this,' I said. 'We're hoping you can help us trace the bootlegger . . . if he is still alive.'

For the past hour I had been telling him our story. The whole thing. Sybil's love affair. The death of Mister Love. The revelation that he was the Nanavati victim. The letters and bottles found by the police. The blackmail. The man who abducted Phoebe from school. The death of her ayah. The cop who had interrogated me.

The threats made to Maya. I told him about our failure to find Sybil's notebook, or trace any of the other women who had been involved with Ahuja. The tale, as I related it, sounded to my increasingly stoned ears more and more fantastic, like something I might have picked off one of my shelves in faraway Lewes. I told Dost of my meeting with Zafyque and how he had advised me to drop the whole business. Finally, I presented my hunch that Mr Mailer, as Phoebe had called him, might also have got his hooks into the bootlegger.

Dost heard the story in silence. He said nothing even when I stopped speaking. The room filled with a profound quiet. The fan's breath stirred the leaves of a spray of red roses too perfect to be real. They stood on a small table between us, on which also were glasses of water, a bag of tobacco and the lump of hashish which, albeit somewhat diminished, was still the size of an apricot. The quiet thickened, laminated by layer upon layer of silence until it grew quite impregnable. My own thoughts were shouting in my mind.

Then the silence shattered. 'I don't blame you,' I heard my own foolish voice saying, 'if you find our story farfetched . . . Zafyque said it sounded like a plot for a movie.' But Maya had tried to make this story into a film and nobody wanted it. No, the Bombay film world had cried. We don't want to know!

'Zafique knows nothing,' said Dost, the assonance setting up an eerie echo. (We were guftagooing in Urdu and in that tongue, therefore, was the faintly reverberating goonj: what Dost actually said was 'Zafique kucch janta nahi,' after the crowd of producers had bayed 'nahi, nahi, nahi.')

'Where does he live? Colaba, you said? Big house, no doubt.

511

Chowkidar. Servants, of course. Car . . . Business . . . Nariman Point . . . A different world . . . see them every morning in Mohammed Ali Road sitting in their status symbols, queued up in the smog. The air is brown and stings your eyes . . . they are listening to their business reports and western pop music, they don't see what's on either side of them. Must be people living in Bombay who have never heard of, for example, Madanpura . . . who have never set foot in Maulana Azad Road . . . don't know the half of the things that go on in this city. On the streets outside here, every passing life could be a movie . . .'

I did not want him to get sidetracked into movies.

'You never answered my question. About the story I told you. Do you think we're fantasising?'

'On the contrary,' he said. 'It doesn't surprise me at all.'

'It's a true story.'

'The police in this city are like maggots. They feed on filth. I doubt if there's anything they wouldn't do for a buck.'

'So can you help us?'

'Forty years ago? Your bootlegger would be an old man . . . if he's still alive. And you have no name.'

I closed my eyes and tried to visualise Sybil's diary, recall the list of provisions for Sub's strange deathday party, written in his bold, sloping hand. Suddenly, with utter clarity, it came back to me.

'It was Saqi Baba!'

But Dost seemed unimpressed. 'That's it? Saqi Baba?'

'He supplied a lot of that circle. That's the name we should at least start with.'

'But Bhalu, you know as well as I do that Saqi Baba means nothing. It's just a way of saying "liquor-wallah". Could be one of dozens of people. Bombay is bootleg city. And our area, Dongri, they call the Palermo of Bombay. Mafialand. Smugglersville. In, out. In, out. Whisky. Gold. Tobacco. Hashish. You name it.'

'But you have connections . . .'

'You must be joking,' he said, loosing a huge gush of smoke into the room, handing me the chillum. 'I'm not into that stuff. I'm a café owner. I don't want to get mixed up with all that.'

So what had happened to the youth, in his fine Lucknowi kurta, curling round the chillum long fingers which in those days weren't encumbered by rings, who used to tell me, 'Whatever you want, it can be done yaar, peacefully.'

'I thought you knew everyone in the rackets.'

'Probably I told you so. It wasn't really true. I was trying to be a cool guy. Like some idiot tapori, you know what that means? Walking the streets pretending to own them. I talked big, and shat my pants, that's the fact.'

But remembering how bravely he stepped in front of Mitra and me that night all those years ago, I could not believe him. I said so.

'You've always been a romantic,' he said. 'It's funny. I look at you and underneath your English gent I see the same old Bhalu. Bhola Bhalu, Bhalu-the-innocent. You used to look with such wide eyes at the filthy street. You'd find magic in anything. Goats, dung, peeling walls.'

'That wasn't me, it was this,' I said, handing back the chillum.

'This doesn't change you, it just opens windows,' he said, taking it and holding it up. 'You know what this is? It's what my uncle named his café after. This is the Jam-i-Jam. The Cup of Jamshid. They say that Jamshid's cup reflects the entire world, the whole universe. Everything that can be seen, smelt, heard, touched or in any way known by the mind. It is all there at once. Totality. All the answers to everything, all at once. You just have to make sense of it. Give me one fact and a goli of Moosa's . . .'

So when the exquisite little pipe came again to me – it was a hundred and fifty years old, Dost told me, he had got it in Jodhpur – I shut my eyes and tried to *see* the crucial fact that must lie at the heart of the mystery. A romantic, Dost had called me. Maybe he was right. I was stuck in bholaness. I looked inside myself. Yes, he was still there. Still alive, waving feebly at me. There he was, the child of Ambona, with his constant reproach, 'Why have you not lived up to my promise?' Sitting beside him was a slightly older iteration, who could glory in gutter smells and read scripture in the flakings of paint. Mired in Bhalu-dom I was and always had been. I travelled to the other side of the world, but never left Ambona and Dongri. When I had first thought of trying my hand at fiction, years ago, all my ideas revolved around these two places, as if no others existed. I never had a linking or encompassing narrative, just a chaplet of stories. To each character their own tale. Babu the hunter's tale. Jula the cowherd's tale. The stationmaster's tale. The screenwriter's tale. The rose-grower's tale. The Kathodi's tale. In Dongri, the beggar's tale. Moosa's tale. Dost the ne'er-do-well's tale.

Once – it must have been the influence of hashish even then – the idea occurred to me of writing a book whose primary, Dostian, *fact* was a one-paragraph letter of complaint addressed to the SAURASHTRA TRADING CO at 6 Panwallekigalli, Dongri, as follows:

Dear Sirs, the consignment of tea you had invoiced to us on 8th March inst. reached us yesterday itself and same were immediately examined, but we regret our inability to accept them. We ordered a first quality tea, but you have sent us the damped leaves, which we are unable to sell and most of the cases are in very injurious condition. For this reason we telegraphed you this morning as follows: TEA GREATLY DAMPED; CAN NOT SELL. ACCEPTANCE REFUSED. HOLDING AT YOUR RISK. LETTER FOLLOWS. We confirm our above telegram, and request you to dispose off the goods at once, and refund to us our disbursement of Rs. 433/- for railway freight and octroi paid by us. Kindly do the needful, and oblige.

This dull message would have been copiously footnoted (eg 'Panwallekigali', 'Dongri', 'tea', 'damped leaves', 'your risk', 'octroi', 'kindly do the needful, and oblige') and these footnotes would have further footnotes (eg k.d.t.n.&o. identified as a Nelsonian usage), which in turn would be footnoted until the footnotes to footnotes to footnotes to footnotes had spread the story across much of the world and several centuries. I planned (of course) to call it *Foot Notes, or Pad Yatra, A Pilgrimage In Words*, but made the mistake of describing the idea to Maya, who simply reached down from her shelves a copy of *Pale Fire*, her way of letting me know, without having to utter a word, that there was room only for one writer in the family . . .

Yes, how hard it is, confronted by the pile of tangled threads that constitute a story, to identify the loose ends that can be called beginning and end. I thought of poor Sybil's list of false starts, her endlessly recycled openings, the mind refusing to be coaxed on excursions into new territory, returning stubbornly to the same start points, what were they now? Selim's apology for a gharry? The blonde Taj-dwelling tart? Poor Marlene Dance, who found love in a shower of rain at Gorai Island, where the villagers provided eggs, rice and arak smooth as . . . Inhaling, inspiring, drawing deeply, soughing, I drew upon the Jodhpuri (the same provenance as Katy's riding britches) chillum and searched and searched for Dost's primal fact. But all I found were stories. Stories, and cycles of stories, told and untold, lying in vast tangled heaps, impossible to unravel. Somewhere among them a clue that would lead to the Blackmailer's tale.

'. . . and I can infer the world,' concluded Dost.

This whole tortuous thought process had occupied less time than it had taken him to finish his sentence.

'. . . Will you at least tell us whom we could ask?'

'Bhalu, it's not so simple. It's not like there is one set of people to know. In the old days, when we used to go to Moosa's, there were a few big names. Karim Lala, Haji Mastan. Nowadays there are dozens of gangs. Freelancers. Entrepreneurs. A chap who was in one gang one day, breaks away and takes people with him. Then he's at loggerheads with his old boss. They are at one another's throats. People who were friends become enemies. Alliances shift. Who should I talk to? Where in all this do I fit in? The answer is, nowhere. I don't want to know.'

'But what can we do then?'

'Your friend, Zafyque,' said Dost, 'did talk some sense. To hell with the past. Let it go. Something from forty years ago? Forget it. Leave it alone. Whatever happened, let it go. Shouldn't we be thankful that we are here now, alive, that we have our families, friends, food on the table?'

Phoebe, who had no family, leaned on my shoulder, our first intimate contact for days, and murmured, 'What is he saying?'

So I told her. She woke up and (like the fan) looked from one to the other of us. Me, still holding the chillum, Dost veiled by clouds of intoxicating smoke.

'Say to him, you don't understand. Do you suppose I like this eating away at me? I *want* to let it go. I *want* to forget. But what am I to do when it invades my sleep, drops me down deep wells? I can't politely ask it to go away. Tell him that one way or another, with his help, or without it, I will find the man who blackmailed my mother. Then, maybe I'll be *able* to forget.'

Her eyes closed and she remained there, head on my shoulder.

'Take care, she is a real phataaka,' said Dost. A bombshell. Did he mean blonde or boomplosive? 'She should forgive, make a clean start. Half the trouble in the world comes from not letting go of the past. It's like history. Why do we need it? Why the fuck do we care about it? We'd all be a damn sight happier if we didn't know any. Then we'd have to judge the man next to us by his smile and his character and his actions, not because he happens to belong to one community or another. You ask Mitra about this, when you see him. Ask if in his heart, he doesn't agree with me.'

My eyes were heavy. I was trying to listen to what Dost was saying, but my own thoughts kept intruding, and there came a point where it was no longer possible to distinguish one from the other . . .

You wanted to know what had happened to that building across the way from Moosa's. The one that went on fire . . . Une pierre prit feu. La maison prit feu. L'arrondissement prit feu. La cité prit feu. Les hommes prirent feu . . . A mob came one night and threw a petrol bomb at it . . . Why? Because it was owned by a Muslim, in a Muslim area, and the mob was Hindu . . . how could this be in a city which regarded business as its religion? First Mr Gut, then Mr God. But on the sixth of December 1992, three hundred thousand Hindu fundamentalists, many of them stark naked, began with bare hands to tear apart the Babri Masjid, a mosque in Ayodhya. They claimed that the mosque had originally been a Hindu temple, and not just any temple, but the birthplace of the god Rama . . . a claim consistent with the work of Mr P. N. Oak, an historian, place-of-domicile Pune, who founded the Institute for Rewriting Indian History to demonstrate that the Mughals built nothing of note in India, but merely hijacked and converted earlier Hindu buildings . . . Oak published such works as *Taj Mahal Is Really Tejo Mahalaya* (a Shiva temple). One may take it then that after the destruction of the Babri Masjid, an act which startling numbers of Indian politicians failed to condemn, the precedent has now been set for dismantling the Taj . . . Bhai sahib, within hours, when news came about the masjid, rioting began in Bombay . . . it started right here in Dongri . . . the previous riots in Dongri had been over the *Satanic Verses* . . . a stone-hurling mob gathered near the Murgi-mohalla (Chicken bazaar) Masjid on Memonwada Road. Next day the Muslim youths attacked and damaged the Hindu Shaneshwar temple . . . then the Hindu youths struck back . . . they came down that street. They had stones and swords. They were breaking windows and setting fire to buildings . . . Shameful to have to admit this, but wasn't he right, that Victorian bigot who wrote *India in 1983*? Hadn't he known just what would happen if you gave Indians the power to govern themselves?

> There were a few riots where some Mussulmans considered that killing a cow and sprinkling Hindus, who happened to pass by, with its blood was a not-inappropriate way of testifying their feelings . . . and when this expression of opinion was met by the counter-device of slaying a pig and throwing the corpse into a mosque, some slight disturbance of the peace usually followed.

Ah Mr Bigot, whoever you were, you couldn't have imagined how bad it would actually be. Dost told a tale of mayhem and murder: a friend's daughter, on her way back from school, caught by a sword-carrying mob who cut her throat; young men beaten to death, set on fire, row upon row of corpses in the morgue. What changed afterwards? Everything and nothing. There's a wariness, a mistrust, that wasn't there before. Mitra and me, that's what came between us. How could it have happened? How could people who had lived together for so long, suddenly start slicing each other's windpipes . . . Maya, on what turned out to be her deathbed, had asked these very questions, but she was remembering 1948 . . . What caused the deaths? Not religion, that was just an excuse. The cause was, as it always is, the greed of politicians for power . . . Gandhi, thank God you never lived to hear these stories . . . gangsters and politicians joining hands to fund Bollywood movies . . . Ordinary people are fed up with immoral politicians, their criminal friends and the corrupt police who do their dirty work. Any leader who dares to tackle this will be a national hero . . . if he survives. It isn't wise to threaten these people. In this city, at least half the murders are committed by the police. Open your paper. Almost every day you see the same item. It'll say something like. 'Police kill three in encounter.' Only the names change. The story is always the same. 'Criminals' (attributed to some well-known gang) are challenged. Invariably, they refuse to surrender and open fire on the police. The brave pandus return fire and the hoods are killed. Everyone knows these stories are fairy tales. How many people ever witness the gun battles? Most people believe the bullets are fired in the back yards of police stations. Are the dead men really gangsters, or just people the police want out of the way? Bhalu, tell Phoebe, don't pursue this vendetta. Let it lie. Do not stir up this wasps' nest. If your man was a high-ranking police-wallah, he will have powerful contacts. His finger can reach out of the past and touch you. It costs five hundred rupees to have a person killed in this city.

I worked it out. Just under £7.50.

It was well after midnight when we got back to the hotel. Still very stoned. The sea-wall was lined with white-clad rain Arabs. As was my habit, I sat down to my diary, but wrote nothing. Dost's lump of hashish lay in front of me. The scrap of newspaper in which it was wrapped informed me that C. Khilar, of IIT Bombay would deliver a lecture on *Nanoparticles Formation in Reverse Micellar Systems*.

A snatch of song below. The Arabs began a slow hand-clapping. I went onto the balcony and looked down. There was a crowd of them inside the hotel compound, gathered round a slim Indian girl. A singer with a good strong voice. She had a baby clamped to her hip, and with her free hand was knocking a merry cross-rhythm out of a pair of castanets. The Arabs danced round her, clapping, singing along, enjoying themselves. Soon there were coins bouncing at her feet, but burdened as she was by her child and the castanets, she could not pick them up. So one of the Arab men held up the corners of his long nightshirt and went round taking a collection. It was soon heavy with silver and banknotes. Even I was moved to wad up a fifty-rupee note and throw it down. When the song ended, the girl, without letting go of her child, tucked her castanets away and found a cloth bag, into which the money-man poured her reward. No sooner had she taken it than a khaki-clad and lathi-wielding policewoman arrived at a run and began haranguing the girl who stood sulkily, looking to her audience for help. 'Leave her alone,' I heard the Arabs saying. The girl was emboldened to make some reply. Then – I could not believe what I was seeing – the policewoman slapped the *baby*. The mother screamed. Angry Arabs surrounded the cop. Everyone was yelling at once. I too lost my temper and rushed downstairs, but by the time I joined the crowd, the girl was already being led away. Little doubt what would happen to the money. On the way back in, I was surprised to find Phoebe, in black silk pyjamas, arguing with the hotel manager.

'It happened on your premises,' she was saying. 'If I see anything like this again, I'll report you to my friend . . .' The last few words were nearly lost in a hubbub of Arabic. They might have been 'the way she was hitting her,' or, it must have been the hashish twisting my senses, but I could have sworn she said '. . . my friend *the Deputy Commissioner*.'

Next day Dost rang to say that he had contacted Mitra. 'The saala is overjoyed. He even sounded pleased to hear from me. He apologises that he is tied up with meetings today, but asks you to his house tomorrow. I will send Murad.'

'I'm going shopping,' Phoebe announced. 'You needn't come with me, Bhalu. Men are so tedious in clothes shops.'

Over the previous few days, there had been a noticeable coolness between us. Why, I didn't know, but it dated from our first visit to Dongri: the day of tickling and baby-talk, Moosa's poker-faced nephew and the amused regulars at the Jam-i-Jam. After that, until Dost's surprise appearance, I had not seen much of her. She took to going out by herself. Where to was a mystery. In the evenings, I would knock on her door and hear the silence echo behind it, or be told she felt unwell and wanted to be left alone. What had opened up the 'deep well' of depression, for such it obviously was, she would not say. She rebuffed my attempts at support. 'No one can help. It's best to be alone. It goes, in the end.'

But how far away was the end? I was restless. I had been in India almost a month and our quest had got nowhere. I knew I should go home and mend my marriage. I had tried several times to phone the cottage and the bookshop, but there was never a reply.

The morning of the day we were to meet Jula. We breakfasted on my balcony overlooking the harbour in the kind of clear light you get after a night of heavy rain, the sky washed clean by storms. The hills on the mainland were distinct and very green. Sunlight fizzing in a glass of orange juice, greening the flecks of chilli in my (Rudolf special) omelette. Happiness is in the details.

'Seven pounds fifty? I don't think so. He'll have to pay a lot more than that to get rid of me.'

I had expected her to be scared, or upset by Dost's warning. Instead she seemed to regard it as a joke.

'If we do manage to get close to this man,' I said, 'if he feels threatened . . . Dost was genuinely worried.'

'Well, I'm not running away,' she said. 'And I know you won't either. After all, you're my hero.'

Phoebe, in a new flowery dress and effervescent humour, was her old self. The evening at the Jam-i-Jam, or perhaps the prospect of seeing her childhood playmate Jula-Mitra, had restored her spirits. We were friends again.

'Aren't you excited, Bhalu?'

Of course I was. I hadn't seen him for nearly thirty years. Not since our indigent Moosa days. But for her it was the first time since Ambona. Since they were both small children. Last time they saw each other she was a little Muffety Mai, and he was a cowherd wearing an irrla.

As usual, we found Murad's apology for a cab waiting by the seawall. He welcomed us with a smile and insisted on opening the door for Phoebe, and dusting the seat with his handkerchief before she got in. The address to which we were to go was in a Hindu area abutting the Muslim quarter. The same district Mitra had lived in when he worked at the printer's in Dongri.

'What will he be like? I hope there's some old Jula left . . . I hope he still likes *me*.' Phoebe was babbling like a child. Since we had been in India, she had constantly been switching between sophisticated woman and little girl.

The route Murad chose took us through areas unfamiliar to me. We left a main road clogged with ancient, gaudily-decorated trucks listing along under impossible loads, and entered a maze of crowded lanes. Tumbledown jopadpattis, hutments, stretched away along every alley we passed. White dog with a pink sore between its ears. Man in filthy rags, with matted hair, by the side of the road, mango cock hanging out, pissing into black mud.

'I have to ask the way,' Murad said, adding as if in explanation, 'Leather workers' area. What a disastrous place this is.'

Mitra lived in an old chawl, a grim Bombay tenement originally designed as cheap housing for mill workers. Its walls were cracked, and streaked black by a century of rains. Nearby, at a tap by the roadside, women were filling pots and buckets. They stopped and stared at us when we got out of the cab.

'Ey! Where is Mitra Kashele?' Murad asked, and the women all pointed at once, up towards the third floor.

Small children followed us, gazing at Phoebe with wide eyes, up the flights of an outside stairway and along a balcony, still soaked from the storms of the previous night. Down below, the women were tracking us. Their voices chorused up to us, calling in Marathi, 'The next one! Yes, that one! That one!' Mitra was obviously well known. We came to a doorway above which was a swastika daubed in vermillion. A string of withered mango leaves hung from nails on either side of the door, exactly like the one that had looped across the entrance of his parents' house in Karvanda.

The door was opened by a man whose stoop hid his height and made him seem more elderly than his years. But I had no doubt it was Mitra. He wore glasses now, but still had the worried frown I remembered so well. It was a kind face, for all its seriousness. He was dressed in a simple white shirt and trousers and his feet were bare, horny as his father's had been. He looked at me briefly, began to smile, then his eyes passed to Phoebe.

'No! This cannot be Fever.'

Phoebe (she who was toujours appropriée), rushed into his arms with a wild shriek. 'Jula!'

Mitra laughed out loud. 'Yes, this is me, but can it really be you? And Bhalu too? Out of the blue! After all these years! Oh, this is a wonderful day!' His English was improved beyond recognition. He must have worked hard.

Then he held out his arms to me and said, 'Brother!'

On what point of this turning earth could I stand?

Deep inside everyone is a lake of raw, nameless emotion, whose occasional explosive uprushing we experience either as grief or as joy, sometimes both at once. A kind of catharsis, a temporary breach of the carefully rehearsed personality. I had laughed when I met Dost, but when I saw Jula again, I cried.

The flat was very small and very bare. Two string charpays occupied much of the floor space. There was a table covered with papers, an ink-stand with old-fashioned ink bottle, penholder and nibs. A calendar of Ganesh, rotund and rat-riding, supervised things from a wall. The most surprising thing was the books. There were hundreds of them, on homemade shelves.

'Please come in, come in . . .' It touched me that the first thing he said, after we had been made comfortable on the charpays and offered tea, was that he was sorry to hear of my mother's death.

'Maya-ji was an unusual person, Bhalu. It is no exaggeration to say that I have always taken her as my inspiration.'

'She would have been proud of you, Mitra.'

'Jula! Jula! Jula!' cried Phoebe. 'I'm sorry, I just can't call you Mitra. How good your English is!'

'I studied. I learned. You can do anything if you try. Well, most things . . . One cannot always succeed.'

I knew from Dost that Mitra had started a printing business which had failed. Some time after this he joined his political party, the one about which Dost would not speak, because it was part of the nationalist-fundamentalist alliance which had destroyed the Babri Masjid.

So we talked, about when, and who, and what, and where. He told us how he had left the printing works and taken a loan to start up on his own.

'What I wanted to do was make books. You remember? It was your mother who encouraged me. This was after you had left for

England. She helped a lot. So I began publishing books which retold our stories, from *our* point of view. I don't just mean an Indian point of view, I mean the view from ground-level. As the people in my village saw it. History is written by rulers and the hirelings of rulers, but the only history worth recording is the struggle of the ordinary people.'

It was like listening to Maya.

'The trouble is, bhai, that people at ground-level, at least in India, often cannot read, and in any case don't have money to spend on books. I had great difficulties trying to get schools to buy my books, because they were perceived as being political. Money was short, the business was in trouble. I felt defeated. I was bitter, full of resentment. At that time I was subsidising the work by printing political pamphlets. It turned out to be my future.'

Through political work, Mitra said, he had rediscovered his self-respect. 'But not ordinary politics. I am not talking about fine-sounding principles and promises made to win votes, but sincere practical work. Your mother believed that, Bhalu. And that is why I chose to join the party. Where is the real social work being done, in politics? Congress Party? BJP? Forget it. Join those who get in among the janata (common people) and roll their sleeves up.'

He told us that he spent much of his time fighting for clean water and electricity to be made available to the shanty-dwellers, to control rents and the depredations of slum landlords.

'I've heard that your party is anti-Muslim.' It had to be said.

'This is a misconception.' He looked genuinely unhappy. 'We work for our own people. I mean Maharashtrians. Most of the people living around here have similar backgrounds to me. But that does not make us against anyone else.'

527

'Dost told me about the troubles.'

He made that little gesture, snatching at the air. Invisible flies.

'Which troubles? Of troubles there is no shortage. 1993? The riots? What did Dost bhai tell you? It was all Hindu-instigated and the Muslims were the innocent victims?'

'Someone started it. We saw the damage, the marks of fire, in Dongri,' said Phoebe suddenly.

'What has happened in this country?' I asked. 'How could the two of you be pulled apart? You used to be inseparable.'

'It's lifestyle, not politics, that divides us. Dost is a sweet fellow, but he's what you might call a tapori, a time-pass man. Lack of gaandmirch.' (No chilli up the arse.)

At least he still had that foul mouth which used to get him into trouble as a child.

'Jula, I can't believe you would condone violence,' said Phoebe.

'Come here,' he said. 'Let me show you something.' He opened the door and led us out onto the balcony, causing the group of women and children who had been clustered outside to scatter in alarm. 'They are curious about you,' he said, laughing. 'Fever's beautiful golden hair. Now look . . .' He pointed.

Stretching to the south was a desolation of huts and shanties. It stopped abruptly on the edge of a wide area of waste ground, marshy in places where the rainwater had pooled. On the far side, the slums began again.

'Over there is a Muslim area, just as desperate as this. During the riots men on both sides started shooting across the no-man's land. There are still bullet marks in this building. Yet I know my counterpart on that side. He is doing the same work as I do here and we often co-operate. Phoebe, I don't condone violence. I don't like it. But I have to live with it, just as all the people around here do. There was fault on both sides. Did Dost tell you about the Hindu family burnt to death in a chawl just like this one? I am not a bigot. But it must also be said that the Hindus in this country feel they have not had a good deal. What kind of democracy is it where the wishes of the majority are constantly ignored in order to appease minorities?'

'What sort of wishes? Do you mean the ban on cow-slaughter?' I asked. 'I read somewhere that cowdung can cure stomach upsets.'

'Yes,' said Mitra. 'And prevents heart attacks, improves memory, plus the mooing of cows alleviates certain mental conditions, the smell of a cow's excrement kills tuberculosis germs. Also, it is pointed out that Lord Krishna was a cowherd and Buddha attained enlightenment after eating kheer.'

'A sort of milky sweet pudding,' I explained to Phoebe.

She said, 'We had it at Dost's restaurant the other night.'

'Not only this,' said Mitra, 'but a Russian scientist whose name I forget has claimed that milk is helpful in combating the effects of atomic radiation. And that houses covered with cow dung are protected from radiation . . .'

'And you believe all this?' I asked.

'I do believe,' he said, 'that if our leaders in Delhi and elsewhere cared as much about fundamental human rights as those of cows, they might be worth voting for. On the other hand,' a mischievous smile crept over his face, 'I am very fond of cows. Remember, like Krishna, I was a cowherd too . . . although Gaulan and Chandri and that naughty wandering Pandri never inspired me to utter the *Bhagavad Gita*.'

There was a knock on the door, and a woman came in, with dishes of food, which she set on the table. Smiled shyly, drew her sari across her face, and went out again.

'My wife is at work,' Mitra explained, 'so the neighbours kindly look after me. Come, let us eat.'

The meal was very simple. Rice, dal and a little vegetable, with chapattis wrapped in a cloth to keep hot. A complete contrast to the rich biryanis and gurda kalejis of the Jam-i-Jam.

'The pickle is homemade,' said Mitra. 'Do you recognise these little green things . . . they look like peas?'

Karvanda berries.

'Jula, we've been to Ambona and seen the house,' said Fever. 'No one has lived there since us . . .' I liked that *us*. 'My painting of Rosie is still on the wall!'

He said, 'It's been left to rot. Nobody knows why. They say it was some senior police-wallah who bought it, many years ago. After your parents left, Bhalu.'

So, at last, our story came out. As he listened, Mitra grew amazed, then angry. He made us tell the story again, going over each detail. Every incident. At last he said, 'I would love to nail the bahinchod who did this to your mother, Phoebe. And *your* mother, Bhalu. But I'm afraid I agree with Dost. It's a waste of time raking up the dead past. And it *could* be dangerous. Better to forget it.'

'Wait,' she cried, 'how can I just forget it? How can you just ignore everything we've told you?'

'I don't ignore it, behan, but there's nothing I can do.'

'By doing nothing, you allow it to go on. You encourage it.'

✻ ✻ ✻

On the way back, Phoebe was silent. Glum. Murad took us back by a different route. Somewhere in the Girgaum area, we were held up by a traffic cop. From ahead came the sound of chanting.

Ganpati bappa morya
purjya varsha laukarya
Ganpati geley gavala
chaiin pade re amhala

A truck appeared, fantastically painted and carrying an even more fantastic cargo, the huge elephant-headed Ganesh, perhaps fifteen feet tall, decorated with ornaments, flowers and lights. Two old conical speakers were blaring out religious songs. Walking behind came men banging double-ended drums and cymbals. In a few more weeks it would be his annual festival and this image would be carried again in an even bigger procession to Chowpatty beach, taken out into the sea and submerged for ever. Strangely enough, this most popular of festivals (for India's most popular deity) was more or less invented by the Independence campaigner, Lokmanya Tilak, who saw in it a way to rouse nationalist fervour disguised as religious celebration.

'Stop!' said Phoebe, suddenly. 'I want to walk in the procession.'

There was no arguing, so Murad and I watched her disappear into the throng of celebrants following the truck, and crawled along behind. From time to time I caught a glimpse of her among the crowd, laughing, a flash of blonde hair. But then I lost sight of her. I thought she would be gone no more than a few minutes, but half an hour passed and she did not return.

'I'll get out and look for her,' I told Murad. 'You follow.'

So I found myself in the middle of the Ganesh worshippers, smiling faces, women distributing prasad. I could see no sign of Phoebe. I ran from one end of the procession to the other, and threaded my way across it a dozen times, but could not find her.

By the time Ganesh, on his truck, reached the open space where fund-raising speeches were to be made, the crowd had thinned and there could no longer be any doubt. Phoebe had vanished.

Several hours later, back at the hotel, there was still no sign of Phoebe. I did not know what to do. Dost telephoned me, after a sheepish Murad carried the news back to Dongri. 'Don't panic,' he said. 'There is probably some straightforward explanation. Maybe she decided to go shopping.'

But I knew that was impossible. It got to seven, eight o'clock. Five hours since she had disappeared. I felt sick. My mind was churning with awful things that might have happened to her. I kept thinking of cases Zafyque had described to me, that his human rights organisation had investigated, of people who had gone missing in custody; how their relatives had to go and plead for news from the very men who had possibly murdered them. Finally, I rang the British Consulate, but got a message saying the office was closed.

Nine o'clock. News time in England. I turned on the television, thinking that if Phoebe had been involved in an accident, it might have been reported. Endless channels of Hindi film music with all-singing-all-dancing videos. A business report. Flipping through, looking for news, it did nothing to lighten my mood when I heard a voice ask, 'Are you seriously saying that if the police are corrupt it is *we*, not they, who are to blame?'

Two men sat facing one another in a studio: the interviewer, who had put the question, and his guest, described by a caption as LUKE ORTO, JOURNALIST, a man whose pleasant demeanour seemed to me wholly at odds with what he was saying.

ORTO

> I am saying that corruption is an evil of society as a
> whole, not of any particular profession. It only exists
> because people are willing to offer bribes.

INTERVIEWER

> And the police themselves bear no responsibility for
> taking bribes?

ORTO

> Would they be corrupt if we did not tempt them? If
> you were a constable or subinspector with fifteen
> years' service, living in a rundown chawl, earning a
> pittance — less than a municipal peon! — you might
> be tempted too.

Our blackmailer, was he one of these underpaid slum-dwelling unfortunates? Had Sybil gone to him and begged him to take money in order to keep her name out of the papers?

INTERVIEWER

> Honest people living in equally bad conditions say they do
> not want to pay bribes. The police demand them. We hear
> endless stories of police cruelty.

ORTO

> We know there are a few policemen who will do anything
> for money, even act as hitmen. The answer is not to damn
> the whole force. We must bring the culprits before the
> Anti-Corruption Bureau.

INTERVIEWER

What about these 'encounters' we hear so much about?

ORTO

Cops don't become 'encounter specialists' because they *like* killing. It's their job and it becomes second nature. Someone has to do it.

INTERVIEWER

What? Go out looking for gunfights? Like the Wild West? Like Wyatt Earp?

ORTO

Our police have no choice. They are *forced* to resort to encounters because the court process is so long and tedious and the rate of conviction is so low. The laws we inherited from the British favour criminals. But our police boys are winning the war. Terrorists and gangsters have been taught, bullet for bullet, that if they come to Bombay, the only way they are leaving is in a coffin. I believe that if our police were freed of political shackles and given a free hand, overnight they would turn Bombay into a law-abiding, crime-free city.

'Luke Orto,' said the interviewer, concluding the session, 'is the editor of *Society Samachar*.' Then, with a Freudian slip of the brain, added, 'He writes on many subjects but with authority and passion only on the police.'

I dreamed that I was lying in my bed at the Rudolf Hotel. The room was in darkness. There was a scratching, a scrabbling at my door. Something with claws trying to get in. In the dream, I lay in my bed, not wanting to wake, terrified of whatever was outside. Again it came, the sound of nails scraping on old wood.

'Bhalu, it's me. Let me in.'

I jumped up and opened the door. She staggered, almost fell, into the room. I caught her and she flopped against me. 'Phoebe! What happened? Are you all right? I was beginning to panic.'

'Mustn't do that. Panic is vulgar,' she said with a strange chuckle and I realised that she was drunk.

I turned on the bedside light. It was past three in the morning. Outside, incredibly, there was still music: Arabs sitting on the sea-wall, having one of their all-night parties. Phoebe looked a mess. Her eye make-up had run. She sat on the end of my bed, in the summer dress she had worn to visit Mitra.

'Got a drink?' she asked. 'We need to celebrate.'

Underneath the raffishness, there was something defiant in her tone, like a child that knows it has done wrong.

'Why did you run away like that?'

She got out a cigarette, found her lighter, and struggled for an infuriatingly long time to produce a flame. 'You should be proud of me,' she said at last, exhaling smoke. 'I've solved the problem.'

'How? Where did you go?'

'To the police headquarters.'

'What?' If she'd said Shaw's Bookshop, Lewes, I could not have been more surprised.

'Now you're cross.' She rasped my cheek with a nail. 'Where do you keep your whisky?' She got up, did an unsteady little dance over to my suitcase, and began rummaging among my underwear. 'Honestly Bhalu, how many weeks and you still haven't unpacked.'

I didn't say so, but I had just *re*-packed. I had decided that I must go home. Almost a month and there had been no word from Katy, no reply whenever I had tried to phone her.

'We'd run out of ideas,' Phoebe said, splashing a gargantuan measure into my toothmug. 'I knew you wouldn't agree. So I had to do it myself.'

'By *do it*, you mean go to the police?'

'Yes. Sorry I tricked you, but you'd only have tried to stop me.'

She's lying, I thought. 'You don't even know where the police headquarters are.'

'True. So what I did was, I nipped into that noisy carnival and out the other side and found a taxi. Just asked it to take me there.'

'But why? What did you do there?' Visions of her lobbing bricks through windows.

'I laid a complaint.'

'Against whom? For what?' The ephemeral hope presented itself that perhaps she'd been cheated by a shopkeeper. Or subjected to the harassment that the press euphemistically (thereby mitigating its nastiness) called 'Eve-teasing'.

'Against the man who blackmailed my mother.'

Her story, so far as I could follow it (she kept interrupting herself with irritating and irrelevant digressions) was this: after giving Murad and me the slip, she got the taxi to drop her outside the police HQ (rifle-toting constables at the door – did you call them pandas? – no, pand*us*), walked in and demanded to see the

Commissioner. The bemused officials at the reception desk told her it was impossible, but she refused to leave. She said that she had a serious complaint and only the Commissioner himself could hear it. So they put her in a room where she waited until, eventually, an officer came to talk to her.

'He was very sweet,' she said, having as much difficulty uttering the word as I had believing it. 'He said he was sorry to have kept me waiting and asked me if I'd like tea, or a cold drink. So I had some tea and I was quite impressed that it came in a pot – on a tray with a blue-and-white china milk jug . . .'

'Yes, yes,' I said, desperate to get her back to the point. 'So what did you tell him?'

'Don't be silly What do you think? The whole story.'

'The *whole* story? Everything?'

'Yes. He listened very politely, but he seemed a bit embarrassed. As if he was too nice to say he didn't believe me.'

'Well, why are you surprised?'

'Don't be cross, Bhalu. I have got it all sorted out. Anyway, my first officer said it was a very serious matter and he would have to call in a senior colleague. So they sent for more tea. And samosas. And this other policeman came. *Very* good-looking. Big brown eyes, and one of those absurd moustaches they all seem to have . . .'

The new arrival – she seemed very struck by his looks; each time she mentioned how handsome he was I experienced a stab in the ribs from that monster whose eyes matched hers – asked her to repeat her story while he took notes.

'So you told him why we are here?'

'Of course. I had to tell him everything.'

'Was that wise?'

She thought about this, drawing deeply on her cigarette. 'What else could I do? We had got nowhere. I was disappointed when Dost refused to help us. Then, when Jula told us to give up, I just couldn't bear it any more. I said to these policemen, "It may be a long time ago, but a horribly cruel crime was committed and the person who did it has never been brought to account".'

'So what did they say to that?'

'That they were very sorry such a thing had happened. Not all policemen were like the one who had dealt with my mother. I still had the feeling they didn't believe a word, but they said they'd look into it and get back to me.'

'They'll get back? How? You told them where we're staying?'

'I didn't have to. They already knew.'

If I had sentiments about what she had done, the craziness of walking into the lion's den and informing the lion that it was under investigation, I kept them to myself. There was only one other question.

'Why are you so late?'

'Oh.' She laughed. 'The Chief Inspector I talked to – the good-looking one – he took me out to dinner. Then afterwards we went dancing . . . Oh, look at that face! What a scowl! Bhalu, you can't go on being a big brother to me for ever.'

She shifted herself up the bed until she was leaning over me.

'Don't be jealous, silly boy.'

She bent down and kissed me, and I could taste the brandy, or whatever it was, uncoiling on her tongue. She was quivering as if a thin current of electricity were running through her body.

'Bhalu, can I stay with you tonight?'

'Of course.' She had not slept in my room for several days.

She reached behind her back with the contortionist ease that women seem to possess, buzzed down a zip, and lifted the dress over her head. The bra came off in almost the same movement and the scrap round her hips did not survive much longer. All this I had seen before, but she was behaving in a particularly voluptuous way. She passed her hands under her breasts, then slid her fingers down her abdomen (slight swell of middle-aged tummy) and scratched for an absent-minded moment at the top of her pubic tangle, as if alleviating some momentary itch. Usually she slept in the other bed, but tonight she climbed in alongside me, her body warm, still fluttering with that strange energy, like a myriad moth wingtips.

'You too,' she said. 'Nothing between us.'

So I, beginning to be infected by whatever excitement possessed her, got out of bed and my pyjamas and, careless of my visibly engorged state, lay down beside her. But by then she was asleep.

Tousled dreams. Tango, tormaline, troubadour, turbine, terrine, dreams beginning with t, ending nonsensically. It must have been an hour later when the phone rang. I had fallen asleep again. Groggily I picked up the receiver. There was no one at the other end, only a sound like an animal's harsh breathing. Perhaps I dreamed it. Maybe I dreamed also that there came again a faint tapping at the door. Next morning, Shankar, bringing breakfast, ostentatiously averting his eyes from the blonde curls on my pillow, told me that two men had been round earlier, asking about me. Which country's passport did I hold? Who had been to visit me? What was my home address?

Phoebe was still sleeping when a call came from Dost. He

had news to discuss. Not over the phone. Murad would collect us. I repeated to him Phoebe's tale of her adventures with the good-looking Chief Inspector and Shankar's report about the two men who had visited the hotel. Dost seemed agitated.

'Your girlfriend is bad news. Make sure your wife is all right.'

So I called home again. Half-past four in the morning in Lewes. The earliest light blueing over the Downs. Katy was bound to be in bed. She must hear the phone downstairs. But as before, there was just the endless ring ring ring, until at last the hotel's operator cut in and informed me what I already knew, that, 'Party is not replying, try again later.'

Phoebe, woken by my phone calls, yawning, stretching, rubbing her eyes, refused to worry. She stepped into her dress, picked up her underwear, and departed to her room.

Murad said, through a mouthful of paan: 'Bhalu, there's a guy following. Do you see? About a hundred yards behind? Thin saalaa on the motorbike?' He directed an expert stream of crimson juice through his window, narrowly missing a pedestrian, and spoke into a mobile phone. I glanced at Phoebe, who was lying back, her eyes hidden by a pair of very dark glasses – last night's junketings must have left her with a sore head – but of course she had no idea what we were talking about.

A few minutes later we were crawling through a Dongri lane towards a narrow cross-roads. Out of a side turning appeared the blue and yellow nose of a venerable truck, engine cowling banging loose. I thought, We're stuck now, we'll never make it. Somehow we slid past. Murad laughed. Behind us the truck, inching across the junction, was completely blocking the road when it appeared to stall. The driver jumped down and stood looking at the bonnet, shaking his head. A couple of hundred yards and several turns later, Murad swung the car into a warehouse whose tall gates immediately closed behind us.

Phoebe gave a litle snort and woke up. 'Where are we?'

I had no idea, but in any case did not answer, because as we passed through the gates I had had an unexpected, overwhelming jolt of homesickness. I could almost hear Katy's voice, as I let myself in through the back door of our cottage, calling, 'No need to ask where *you've* been.' The huge, dim space reeked of furniture polish and sawdust. Pure Pigletry. All around us were stacked pieces of furniture, ornate carved Indian almirahs and four-poster beds, Chippendale chairs and tables, in various stages of completion.

'We make antiques here,' said Murad, with no sense of irony. 'All for export.'

He led me and a faintly protesting Phoebe through a door at the back, into a chartless maze of passages, archways, balconies, chambers, antechambers, across courtyards, up stairways and over flat roofs. At one point we came out on a parapet and saw the old bazaar area with its red-tiled roofs spread out beneath. All around us, from coops, came the fluttering and cooing of caged birds. 'Racing pigeons. They can fly from here to Delhi.'

Dost was sitting with a small man, who wore glasses perched on top of his head. He had a refined and somehow otherworldly air, as if he were a scholar rather than what he actually was, a tailor.

'Bhalu, my friend,' said Dost, 'you must not go back to that hotel. In fact, it's time for you to quit your British gentleman act and become an Indian again.'

The little tailor went to work with a tape-measure, taking my naap, which is to say, the measure of a man. With great delicacy, he performed the corresponding service for Phoebe, who, I noticed, was wearing yesterday's sun dress, very likely still with nothing on underneath. I was experiencing the most contradictory feelings about her, finding it harder and harder to revive the memory of our old friendship and reconcile it with my constantly thwarted desire. She for her part, I was convinced, no longer saw her hero when she looked at me, only the weakness my mother had so despised. It was a relief when a woman appeared in the doorway and beckoned her away.

'I went to see a man,' Dost said. 'You need not know who. A very old man, half blind and so fat he can hardly get out of bed. What a stench! Poor fellow suffers from some disgusting condition that makes the room stink of piss. Anyway, he gave me a name. I wrote it down . . .'

He passed me a slip of paper. The name written on it was not one I recognised. It meant nothing at all to me.

'Are you sure this is the man?'

'I am not sure about anything. Least of all that you should be pursuing this. If you want my sincerest advice, take Phoebe and go back to England.'

'How can we get this man's address?'

'I can't help you there.' After a moment's thought he said, 'Mitra could help, if he wanted . . . His political friends.'

An hour later I was dressed like a native of Dongri. Pyjama trousers held up by drawstring. Long kameez in Afghani green. White lacy skullcap. A woman, veiled from head to toe in black burkha entered the room with a tray of tea. She set it carefully on a table, then made a little obeisance in my direction. 'Thank you,' I said, in Urdu. The woman emitted a giggle and said, 'Bhalu, you look just like Ali Baba.'

The strangest thing was that, in the street, in the bazaar, I felt, for the first time in years, completely at home. Nobody looked at me twice, nor at the dark-robed Muslim woman by my side. We were going to Dost's house, Murad, a few steps ahead, leading the way. The street no longer looked foreign, it was an everyday place where ordinary people were coming and going about their business. People entering a mosque to make their midday prayers. In every city between here and Tangiers there would be similar scenes. It struck me how odd it is that in England, people who live in neat, well-kept houses, catch trains into the City every morning and buy a new car every four years, honestly believe that they are leading *normal* lives.

Some hours went by. It was sweltering afternoon when Murad appeared carrying suitcases. 'Your belongings. It was not easy to get them. The police have been there again, asking for you. I found a room boy who said he would pack your suitcases. I thought I'd have to bribe him, but he refused to take money.'

'Did he have a red tikka on his forehead?'

'He did,' Murad agreed. 'He said to tell you he was glad to help, because he would do anything for madame.'

Madame was resting, recovering from her long night. From the next-door room where she was asleep came the gentlest of snores. How typical that she should be oblivious to the worries seething like a knot of worms in my brain. Why were the police looking for us? Was it because of what she had done? Perhaps they were only responding to her complaint, wanting to tell her the result of their investigation. Perhaps not . . . Why did Katy never answer the phone? Amidst the guilt a pulse of terror. What if something had happened to her? I remembered the threats made to Maya. Should I ring Piglet? But how? He did not believe in telephones. Couldn't afford them, he said, and did what calling was necessary from a phone box in the High Street. Perhaps I should ring the White Hart and leave a message with Charlotte. One part of me wanted to get the next plane home but then I thought, in a moment of tenderness, of the sleeping woman next door, and was surprised to discover that the majority of conflicting voices that constituted the democratic republic of Bhalu were urging me to see our strange mission through.

I stationed myself in a chair directly in front of the fan, and looked for some way to divert myself until Dost came home. Apart from a pile of filmi magazines, at which I could not bring myself to look, the house was devoid of reading material. How different from our cottage, where no nook was without its pile of books and the loo was a small library of things currently being studied. In my suitcase was Killy's favourite work of fiction, the one which he was fond of quoting at dinner parties. *India in 1983*. As I turned its pages I was assailed by a familiar feeling of dismay. I had come to hate the author's sneering tone. Yet the more of it I read, the less like fiction it seemed.

> In the first place, a native board having unlimited control over funds was an institution, whose proceedings every native could thoroughly understand, whereas the notion of an unsympathetic and incorruptible Englishman had

long been acknowledged to be quite incalculable. Here was an administrative body, which could be touched with the feeling of one's infirmities – which could lend an ear to the uncle who wanted employment for his nephews, to the poor man with the large family, who had six brothers-in-law and thirty-six cousins all desiring appointments, – which could sympathise with the fraudulent contractor, the neccessitous builder – and in whose bosom the swindling overseer, who had been declared incapable of serving government again in any capacity, could find a congenial haven of rest not unaccompanied by profit. The souls of all these innocent and worthy men were rejoiced, the money was blandly divided, and if no improvements were carried out, it was probably because the Boards knew, what no Englishman had ever been able to grasp, that, as a rule, the inhabitants of Hindustan prefer going along a bad road to going along a good one, and discern charms in a tumbledown and filthy serai which a cleanly and well-kept building can never afford. The great thing was, you knew where you were with the Committees. Matters were arranged orientally, and at the bottom of the native character there is a profound sympathy with oriental methods of administration. It was perfectly certain that the larger part of the funds would stick to the palms of the members of the Committee, that their relatives and friends would compose the entire administrative staff, that no contract would be given unless a handsome commission had been paid to the President and Secretary, and that any works that were constructed would be exclusively adapted to the improvement of the President and members. All this was thoroughly understood, and the feeling it aroused was not one of indignation, but a simple desire to participate in the spoils.

I thought, this man's prejudice is given the lie by the generosity of ordinary people, but the politicians and police chiefs of India are doing their utmost to prove him right.

Evening came, the time of pigeon flight. Outside, the heat was still growing. One of those stifling mid-monsoon lulls. An uncomfortable night lay ahead, unless a storm broke and cleared the air. In my wallet was the piece of paper with the name on it. When Dost returned, I would ask him to arrange another meeting with Mitra. Darkness fell, with bursts of filmi-music from the street below. Dost did not return.

It must have been about eleven when there was a knock on the door of the room. The young tea-boy came in, he who had flirted with Phoebe. He had a message from Dost. We were to leave the house immediately. 'Go to the place you used to know many years ago. Dost-uncle will meet you there. He said don't delay, don't ask questions. Come with me now, I will show you the way.'

I went next door to wake Phoebe and found her long black robe lying discarded on the floor. She was curled up on the bed naked. Light filtering in from outside stroked her cheek and touched the hills and valleys of her body. She looked defenceless and utterly lovely. I shook her shoulder gently, then harder, till she stirred.

'Phoebe,' I whispered. 'You must get up.'

'I'm so tired,' she said, still full of sleep.

'We have to leave here straight away.'

'But why?' she protested 'We've only just got here.'

'Dost says we must go. The police are looking for us.'

She sat up and opened her eyes very wide, as if they could cast a light in the gloom. 'The police? Why should that worry us?'

I thought about this, and admitted that I didn't know.

'They're our friends now,' she said. 'They're going to *help* us.'

Was she so utterly naive, so convinced of her allure, her ability to charm men, that she really believed this? This was one of the moments I recall best from that whole time, when it became clear to me that I would never understand her.

'Come here,' she said. 'Lie down. I love going to sleep on your shoulder.'

She looked so appealing that despite the huge urgency of the moment, the boy waiting next door and heaven knows what on its way to Dost's house, I felt a desire to take off my clothes and make love to her. It puzzled me that we had so often come so close but that always something happened to prevent it.

She held out her arms. 'Come here,' she repeated. 'Let me cuddle you.'

Even as the reply formed in my mind, I thought it was a stupid thing that I was about to ask – insane, given the circumstances – but in a voice so coarsened by emotion that I hardly recognised it as my own, and through a violent drumming in my ears, I said, 'Phoebe, don't cuddle me. Fuck me.'

Slowly she lowered her arms. An expression almost like pleading came over her face. She smiled and said, 'Bhalu . . .'

My heartbeat became a hammering coming from somewhere outside my ribcage. Commotion downstairs. The boy next door called, 'Bhalu-ji! Men are here!'

What followed was so strange that I often doubt it actually happened. Perhaps it was not real at all, but a dream . . .

We were waiting in the darkness of what had once been Moosa's doorway, our backs pressed to the wrought-iron gates that used to guard his kingdom. Inside was the courtyard I remembered, with its lime bush and frangipani tree, and stairs leading to a storeroom that Mitra, in another life, had told me was air-conditioned to keep the hashish fresh. Half an hour, at least, since the boy had led us here and left us, saying, 'Stay hidden. Keep quiet. Don't move till Dost-uncle comes.' Phoebe pressed close to me. Under her black robe I could feel that she was naked. She had her veil pushed back. Light ran down her profile, kindled a strand of hair. Her head was cocked in that questioning manner of hers. Despite the mugginess of the night, she was shivering. Beyond, the alley was all angles of shadow, a solitary street-lamp caught in a whirling mist of flies.

Ever since I uttered those words, to which her reply had been cut short, she had behaved like a lamb. All the feistiness had gone out of her. She pulled the robe over her head and followed me, her hand clutching mine. She clung close at every step. At times, as we followed the boy, down a back stair, along a passage, out of one of the house's myriad doors – the place was like a rabbit warren – I would catch her face turned up towards me. It was as if she had once again become the trusting child, content to place her safety in my hands.

Distantly, from somewhere deep in the bazaar, came a shout. She started, gave a little exclamation of fear. I placed a finger on her mouth. I was scared too, but the melodrama annoyed me. Nothing, surely, but a late-night roisterer. I forced myself to think of something other than fear. I stared at the familiar building across the road, its architecture, rotting frames, layers of flaking paint – and the charred sign that read CURRY YARNS.

It had been a spice warehouse. On still evenings, Dost had told me once, you could catch the tang of cinnamon dust. Or was it the scent of her hair? How could the loops of history, of story, have brought us back here, in danger, to this place where I had once sat on charpays, inferring the universe? Her trembling had grown worse, she was shuddering. I put my arms round the woman to quiet her and she buried her head in my shoulder. I bent and kissed her forehead and she lifted her face to me. In the faint light, I saw tracks of tears on her cheeks. I said, with a bravado I was far from feeling, 'Don't worry, Fever, I'll look after you.'

Of what was the architect thinking when he designed those windows? The wooden shutters recalled the buildings of earlier ages. To me, remembering how it had looked when I was stoned, the street wore an ancient Indian air. It was an alley in the thousand-year metropolis of Pataliputra, capital of the Maurya and Gupta empires. Mitra and Dost and I were nagarikas, young men about town. The nagarika had certain daily duties, most of which involved his own amusement. Among his pleasures were amours with interesting ladies. The sage Vatsyayana wrote a book called *Kamasutram* which gave detailed instructions on how infallibly to seduce other men's wives. From Sybil's diaries we knew that Mister Love had kept a copy by his bed – Mister Love, whose murder hid a second, monstrous crime, which had remained undiscovered, its perpetrator unpunished. Wasn't this the message Phoebe received at the séance – the second séance, which she attended alone after I had left for Bombay – from dead Maya and dead Sybil? My mother and hers, directing our destinies from beyond, respectively, the pyre and the grave. Be careful, they warned, the 'threats' are still alive. Mister Love is dead, but not at rest.

A whistle from the darkness. The tea-boy. 'Murad is waiting at the corner. Hurry.'

Phoebe and I left the doorway and began walking.

'Run,' hissed the boy. So then we ran, and saw the taxi, with the boy holding the door open. He slammed it shut on us and climbed into the passenger seat beside Murad.

'Holy Moses,' he said. 'Do you want to die?'

We were pulling away from the mouth of the alley when I saw the figures arriving at Moosa's door. Blurry shadows holding what might be sticks. But in the lamplight, the gleam of metal.

'What is happening?' I asked. 'Where are we going now?'

'Dongri is not safe for you,' said Murad. 'Word has gone about. Not everyone here is our friend.'

'How did they know . . . ?' But I could answer the question myself. That night we had gone round the area, asking for Dost and talking about Moosa's.

'You have to go to Mitra,' said Murad. 'Dost phoned him. He knows you are coming. There you will be safe. But you must leave Bombay as soon as possible.'

The area through which we were travelling had become dingier and poorer. There were hutments by the side of the road, roofed with corrugated iron and black polythene.

'It will be safer if I drop you here,' Murad said. 'You can do the rest on foot. Follow the boy. He knows the way.'

We alighted at a spot where a number of handcarts were pulled up by a wall. Perched on the end of one of these, a pretty woman was trying to persuade her baby to drink something from a steel glass. The baby chuckled and threw the glass into the gutter. The woman reached down, retrieved it, wiped it on her sari and tried again. Again the baby threw it down. A black-cowled Muslim woman stopped, picked up the glass and handed it back to the mother, who uttered a word of thanks to which the woman in black did not reply.

We started after the boy, who was walking slowly ahead of us, already some distance away, from time to time turning to make sure we were following. As Murad had taught us, Phoebe was one step behind me. I could not tell what she was thinking. After a while, the boy stepped into a side lane, its first few dozen yards brightly lit, shops on either side: cloth merchants, an emporium full of pots and pans with a row of aluminium buckets hanging above its entrance, a café from whose open front film music issued, where a man was frying pakoras in a deep curved pan. A small group of street children, true sadak chhaap, stood nearby, calling out to the cook, who ignored them. Our tea-boy was already some way past this group when the cook reached down with his ladle and flipped a pakora sizzling through the air towards the children. A small girl caught it, cried out in pain. The man laughed to see her juggling to save it. She ran into the night, chased by her friends. Behind me, Phoebe muttered something I could not catch. I turned. She was hobbling, and for the first time I realised that her feet were bare. The road surface here was pitted, with sharp stones protruding from the tarmac. There were large puddles left in the potholes from the last shower and her bare feet trod through the slush. Ahead of us the boy continued without hesitating, a small figure caught now and again in the glow of a street-lamp. A haze of woodsmoke spread across the road. The street-lamps grew fewer, their dull spillages of light at first one, then two hundred yards apart, until at last there were no more. Now the only illumination was the dim flicker from doorways. People passing were shapes in the gloom. Five men were sitting on a string bed with their knees drawn up, backs to a brick wall, five points of orange fire in the darkness. Suddenly the sky rumbled. Somewhere, a dog howled. A flicker of lightning in clouds hanging low overhead, a stirring in the turgid air. The boy, with a glance behind to make sure we were still at his heels, ducked into an alley, a few feet wide, margined by clogged gutters, that led away between shacks made of wood and beaten-out tin cans. Inside one of these, glimpsed by the smoky light of a kerosene lamp, a woman with a cruel face was nursing a baby. In a brighter hut, lit by a naked bulb, a man was chopping meat with a cleaver, casting lumps of flesh into a pile. Blood had pooled on the floor. It trickled out of the open doorway and leaked in black veins into a drain full of furry growths. I noticed that where a patch of light fell through a door, the boy stepped round it, passing on the shadow side. Some distance ahead of us a single bulb emitted a feeble tobacco glow. Beyond it, the alley dwindled to a muddy path and the plank-and-can shacks gave way to dwellings hung with rags, plastic sheets and torn sacks. It was growing hard to see. The boy hurried on, and then he was gone. The alley had come to an end, debouched into darkness. Blind air thick with the stench of garbage reached my nostrils, and nearby, incongruously reminding me of Maya, the scent of cobra-jasmine. My eyes acclimatised to a wide, rubbish-strewn space, across which smoke was blowing. Lightning sparked again, a downward flash, illuminating more wasteland ahead. I took Phoebe's hand. She did not speak, but I could feel again that she was afraid and guessed from her sharp exclamations that her feet were being caught by thorny weeds and broken bricks. Without a word I swung her up into my arms and carried her. She said something, lost in a huge rumble of thunder. The first drops of rain struck my face. Phoebe was surprisingly light and I stumbled forward at a half run, looking for the boy. There was no sign of him. He was somewhere far ahead, gone into the night, leaving us lost in the middle of nowhere. I could not decide what to do. Should I turn back? Behind us, I could still distantly make out a light flickering here and there among the shanties we had left. I had my wallet and credit cards. Perhaps if we worked our way back to the main road we could get a taxi and hole up in some out-of-the-way hotel where nobody would think of looking for us. From somewhere in the district behind us arose the sound of shouting. Probably it was nothing to do with us, but it made up my mind. Rain was falling in earnest as, slowly, I picked my way across the uneven ground towards a well of deeper darkness, a round hole in the night. It was the empty mouth of a concrete sewer pipe, a yard across, that must have been lying there a long time, for beneath its curve a lantana bush had grown. As we approached, moths flew up in a cloud from its tiny, bitter flowers . . .

I said, 'Fever, we're going to stop. Shelter from the rain. The boy will come back and find us.'

She said in a small voice, 'When I was little, I always thought we'd get married. But I never thought you'd be carrying me across a threshold like this.'

A little later, we were squeezed well inside the pipe, our faces so close together that I could feel her breath on my face. She was still trembling and our arms were wrapped round one another. I could feel her heart beating. She said, 'Bhalu, what you asked, earlier . . .' 'I shouldn't have said it. I'm sorry.' Her mouth found mine in the darkness, and gave the answer to that earlier question. She took my hand and guided it onto her breast, then after a little, pushed it further down. She wriggled until the long robe rode up, and my fingers touched the soft skin of her thighs. Again she took my hand and placed it where she wanted it. 'Now my dear', she said, 'do you doubt?' She kissed me again, disengaged, and said, her fingers meanwhile fumbling with the drawstring at my waist, 'I wanted to do this since the first time I saw you again, but I daren't because you were married and you love Katy.' But even as she said this, her fingers were at work on me. 'I've never loved anyone like I love you . . . we're so close we don't *need* to do this.' Her words rushed out in clusters. 'Do you *really* want to? Darling, I'll do anything you want, but maybe we should stop now . . .' I did not stop. Somehow in that narrow space I clambered on top of her. 'Our parents . . . Bhalu, isn't this what got them in trouble?' She was still babbling, urging me to desist as she tugged down my pyjamas and her thighs parted. I thought of Katy, and betrayal, but then I thought of exotic birds. Outside it had begun to rain hard. Water drumming on the hollow pipe created a roar that drowned first her protestations, then our joy- and shame-filled cries.

Morning light entered the pipe and found two people huddled together, their clothing in disarray. How many times during the night? Our passion, fuelled by terror, seemed inexhaustible, as if we needed to express in a single night everything we had ever felt for one another. We stank of sex.

'Bhalu, where the hell are we?'

'In a sewer pipe somewhere in the middle of Bombay. Being chased by desperados.'

She laughed. 'How strange that I feel so happy.'

We crawled out. A blustery wind was blowing sheets of rain across the waste ground we had traversed the night before. To the south, the direction we had come, was the low line of a hutment. Ahead stretched a deserted land of stagnant pools, and ruined buildings. The desolation looked smaller than it had in the dark. In the other direction, only a little more distant, was another line of ragged roofs.

Phoebe said, 'Someone's coming.'

From southward, two figures, one much taller than the other, were approaching under an umbrella. As they drew near we saw that it was last night's boy, accompanied by a worried-looking Dost.

'Thank the Lord you're safe,' he said to me.

'They didn't follow,' said the boy. 'It wasn't my fault. I came back to look for them, but they had disappeared.'

'It really wasn't his fault,' I said. 'We got ourselves lost.'

'So where did you spend the night?' asked Dost.

'What is he saying?' asked Phoebe. So I translated.

'Oh,' she said. 'We found a most charming hotel.'

Looking from one to the other of us he said, 'I daren't ask what you two have been up to. She's an amazingly bindaas woman.'

'Is that a compliment?' The word was new to me.

'It means . . . well, it's difficult to explain what it means. But yes, it probably was a compliment.'

I was still feeling protective of Phoebe. In her loose black robe, nothing on underneath and no shoes, she seemed a little thing, not at all the daunting woman she could be, and what we had done together had filled me with tenderness.

'Okay, well your girlfriend has to change her clothes. Over there –' he pointed to the north – 'is where Mitra lives. But it's a Hindu stronghold, so she's going to look a bit conspicuous if she goes there dressed like that.'

'She can't change.'

'Why not? Can't she just take off the burkha?'

When I told him, he sighed. 'Truly bindaas.'

Half an hour later, Dost and the boy, followed by two rumpled creatures – by their dress a Pathan from Dongri accompanied by his wife, hidden from head to toe in a burkha, the pair of them, judging by the way they held hands and clung together, obviously much in love – entered the lanes of Mitra's community, drawing stares from women filling water pots at roadside taps and men about their early business. When we mischievously asked how to find Mitra Kashele, a dozen amazed voices told us the way.

Mitra's face, when he answered his door, was a mixture of relief and anger. He pulled us inside and said to Dost, 'Are you out of your mind? Why have you brought them here dressed like this? We'll have to get them out of here.'

'Yaar, is this a way to greet an old friend? The lady has nothing on underneath.'

Mitra took this in his stride. 'What about Bhalu? He looks like some Kabuli camel-shagger. They'll have to change.'

An hour later, Phoebe reappeared wearing a long skirt, and I found myself – none of Mitra's trousers would fit me – in the dhoti and coarse-spun shirt of a Maharashtrian villager.

Dost said, 'They must stay with you. It isn't safe in Dongri. Men are scouring the place looking for them. The hotel in Colaba has had another visit. They have got to get out.' To me he said, 'Now you look every inch the bloody Hindu.'

Mitra said to Dost, 'I have got the address.'

Dost said, 'For God's sake don't tell Phoebe. Just let's get them out of the city as quickly as possible.'

Mitra said, 'Don't you think they should have the choice, after all they've been through?'

I said, 'Don't talk about us as if we aren't here. What address?'

'The address of Mister Shaitan,' said Mitra. 'I have found out where our blackmailer lives. It's a few hours' drive from the city, but I know the area well . . . I think we should tell Fever. But let's hope her experience of last night –' he gave me a wry glance '– has taught her a lesson.'

'So it's four of us in the car then,' said Dost, after Phoebe had expressed her opinion.

'How four?' asked Mitra.

'Murad the driver. Bhalu, Phoebe and me,' said Dost.

'Five,' said Mitra. 'I've also got a score to settle.' To me he said,

'I'm doing this for your mother.' Turning to Dost he added, 'And of course your famous cock.'

The events of that day run and rerun in my mind like a film. Going up the ghats in heavy rain. Jula — Phoebe refused to let us call him Mitra — sitting beside Murad. She in the back between Dost and me. There was a lorry jam stretching all the way down the mountain. 'This is nothing,' said Murad. 'Last month, there were landslides. They caused a jam sixty miles long that took a whole day to clear.' We passed several overturned trucks, upset by steep cambers and tight hairpins. Ahead of us, heavy lorries were crawling up the pitted surface in clouds of diesel smoke. Congestion, or something broken down up ahead, often caused them to stop. They found it difficult to get going again, dragged backwards by their heavy loads, wheels spinning until they smoked. A man would jump out of the cab and shove a large rock, the size of a watermelon, under a rear wheel. The lorry would leap forward, like an athlete pushing off from starting blocks, and the lad would rush to jump back in, leaving the stone obstructing the road. The ghat was littered with stones like these. Perhaps the truckers left them for each other. Anything rather than call in the men on small motorbikes who swarmed up and down, weaving among the slow uphill traffic, looking for breakdowns. 'To get a lorry going again, one thousand rupees,' Murad told us. When a car ahead of us developed some trouble and stopped, the roving mechanics were on it like flies to rotting offal. 'He won't make it to the top,' said Murad. 'They'll spike his fuel supply. Then come back for another fee. They'll make a killing out of him.' Slowly we climbed, among a stream of antique lorries, up past the Hanuman temple, until at last Duke's Nose appeared, looming to the right, its cleft peak shrouded in cloud. A few minutes later we were on the edge of the escarpment, staring into the endless view from Khandala. All around us, the mountains, strange rain-green shapes, were cut by waterfalls like slashes of ice.

'Jula, where did you say we were going?' asked Phoebe. 'Because after Khandala, doesn't this become the road to Ambona?'

'Aati kya Khandala,' sang Dost suddenly. It was the song our tea-boy had crooned to Phoebe.

> 'Ambone mein chikki khaenge
> Waterfall pe jayenge
> Khandala ke ghat ke ooper
> Photo kheechke aaenge
> Haan bhi karta naa bhi karta
> Dil mera deewana
> Dil bhi sala party badle
> Kaisa hai jamana
> Phone laga tu apne dil ko jara
> Pooch le aakhir hai kya majra
> Arey pal mein phisalta hai
> Pal mein sambhalta hai
> Confuse karta hai, bas kya?'

'What does it mean?' Phoebe asked. For someone on the verge of confronting her nemesis, her sangfroid was astonishing.

'It's a useless song,' said Jula. 'Hardly needs translating, since it's half in English anyway. Waterfalls ... photos ... a woman who can't make up her mind ... Confusion of the poor heart.' Turning to me, he said, 'Majrooh, the lyricist – remember, Bhalu, he was a

561

friend of your mother's — said this song was a disgrace to Hindi poetry.'

But obligingly, he sang to Phoebe:

'In Ambona chikki eatenge
To waterfall goinge
Khandala ke ghat ke on top of
Photo clickke comenge
Yes it alsos, no it alsos,
This mad heart of mine
Switches parties, bloody heart,
(Just like a bloody politician)
Oh what an age we live in'

We passed the turning for Ambona. Several miles further on, a small, inconspicuous road climbed away through a forest of teak and sal and bamboo. Before long it became heavily rutted. Finally the tarmac gave out and we were skidding along a rough track, kicking up clouds of red dust, raising around us the smell of my first night in Ambona.

Murad parked the car so that it was hidden behind a grove of bamboo. He and Dost would stay with it, while the rest of us went on foot through the forest. We would spy out the ground before walking into the home of our enemy.

How beautiful it was, that early afternoon hike over hillsides and along ravines, the forest in these parts still thick, untouched, streams alive with rainy-season fish. There were birds I had not seen since I was a child and whose existence I had forgotten. Fork-tailed drongos, green bee-eaters. The morning's rain had stopped, and as we walked, our mood seemed to lighten. We were walking back into our childhood, where nothing could touch us. Three of us, marching in single file, just as we had when we were children and making just as peculiar a sight. Jula, leading the way, was now the one wearing trousers and a shirt. My turn, in the dhoti, to be the villager. Phoebe followed behind, skirt hoisted to the knees. She was quite nerveless, in high spirits. Perhaps she was savouring the imminence of her revenge. On a hillside we came across some cows, spread out grazing the rich grass. Jula said, 'Fever, do you remember how to call them?'

'Hamba!' she cried, and the cows looked up. 'Haalya!'

Our walk seemed to last hours, but we had probably covered no more than five miles. The end of our quest came suddenly and was quite unlike I had expected it to be. It was late afternoon, the same day we had crawled out of the pipe. We passed through a thicket of karvanda bushes on top of a low hill and there, below us, was the road again. Set back from it was a gateway, a drive leading through a well-tended garden – banana plants, a guava tree, a fountain with goldfish – to a large bungalow surrounded by a verandah in which, sitting reading, was a very old man.

Phoebe led us through the gates and up the drive. The man looked up from his book and saw us. He took off his reading glasses and stared.

'Good afternoon,' Phoebe said. 'I think you know who we are.'

'I'm afraid I don't,' he replied politely. 'Are you lost?'

'No, we've come all the way from Bombay to meet you.'

'Really? On foot?'

'Our car is nearby,' said Phoebe. 'With other friends waiting for us to return safely to it.'

'Safely? Are you in some danger? Did you say you were looking for me?'

'You were in the Bombay police, weren't you?'

'I was,' he agreed. 'But I have been retired for twenty years.'

'A man was blackmailed,' said Phoebe. 'It was a long time ago, in the 1950s, while you were still in the force. The man was a bootlegger. He supplied drink to society people.'

'I see. Is this a case I should know about?'

'Yes,' she said, 'because the bootlegger had a customer you must surely remember. A man called Prem Ahuja.'

I was searching his face, but caught no flicker.

'Ah,' he said. 'The Nanavati case. Well, what you've said about the bootlegger does not surprise me. That sort of criminal is always in some kind of trouble. But I don't understand why you have come to tell me this.'

We were still standing under his verandah, looking up to where he was sitting. I said, 'Sir, are you aware that one of the women involved with Ahuja was also blackmailed? By the same man?'

'The Nanavati affair was a long time ago. It's hard to remember things accurately. I believe I was out of station when it happened.'

'I don't think so,' said Jula, speaking for the first time. 'It's my understanding that you were involved with the case.'

'So I was,' he said. 'With the investigation. One of dozens. Unfortunately that does not change the fact that memories fade.'

'I doubt if memories of that case could ever fade,' I said.

'You speak remarkably good English,' said our host, taking in my village apparel. 'Don't stand in the hot sun, please. Come in. Sit down. May I know your names?'

So we went up onto his verandah and sat on wicker chairs, in a semi-circle, facing him. Phoebe said, 'My name is Phoebe Killigrew. Perhaps my surname will ring some bells with you?'

'I am afraid not, dear lady,' he said with a smile. 'But please do enlighten me.'

So Phoebe began to tell the story I knew so well. Sybil's ill-fated love affair with the man she called Mister Love, her abortion, the murder, the trial of Nanavati, the blackmail. As she talked she never took her eyes off his. This was the moment for which she had waited so long. 'I wonder if the blackmailer ever realised,' she said, 'how cruel, how evil, his action was? For the sake of a few thousand rupees, he destroyed my mother's life.' She described in detail Sybil's suffering, and her death. 'This man, if he is still alive, needs to know that what he did was unforgivable, and that he will never be forgiven.'

'I am shocked,' the old man said. 'I offer you my sympathy. But I don't believe anyone I knew could have done such a thing . . . How can you be sure this blackmailer was a police officer? Isn't it much more likely to have been a journalist? Or some corrupt official of the court?'

'I never said he was a policeman,' said Phoebe. 'You have said it. But court officials don't generally kidnap children from school and frighten them with murders they've investigated.'

'Nor,' I added, 'do journalists interrogate people who are being held in police cells.' I was trying desperately to remember the features of the policeman who had threatened me. I could not see them in this old face.

'Nor,' said Jula, 'do journalists or court officials have the power to put people in such fear that they leave the country which needs them far more than it needs bahinchod gangsters and corrupt cops.'

The old man endured all this with a polite smile. 'It seems you are convinced that your culprit was a policeman,' he said. 'But why come to me with this story? What do you expect me to do?'

'Tell us the truth about what you know,' said Phoebe, with an earnestness that wrenched my heart.

The old man picked up his reading glasses and polished them for a long time on the corner of his shirt. 'Are you suggesting – I hope you are not – that I am the man you've been describing?'

'No,' I said. 'But you might be. We're not yet sure who he is.'

'Not *yet*? Then what is the good of making accusations?'

Phoebe said, 'The man who blackmailed my mother thinks that he is safe. He thinks a crime committed so long ago can never be traced to him. He believes that any evidence we have against him is hearsay and that no court would admit it. But that man also has a reputation, and a family. He is near the end of his life. The last thing he would want now is for his old crimes to be dug up and gossiped about in the scandal sheets.'

'This man,' he said. 'Without proof, what can you do?'

Pheobe gave a giggle and then began to laugh. I felt suddenly fearful. There was something so inappropriate, fiendish almost, in the sounds she was making. Pray God, I thought, let her not somehow have got hold of a gun. Let her not shoot him. We have no proof that it was him. Then it occured to me, if this really is the blackmailer, he knows that there was a notebook that could sink him. He thinks we haven't got it.

I said, 'There is a notebook. It was written in shorthand. It contains everything we need. Dates, times, places, amounts. His threats written down verbatim and witnessed. Even a description of his office.'

Once again from Phoebe came that unnerving laughter. 'Our man,' she said, 'was so desperate to find the notebook that he actually bought the house where he thought it was hidden.' To my amazement, she winked.

Our host had lost his smile. 'This is all nonsense,' he said. 'Without this supposed notebook you can do nothing. Even with it you could do little.'

'The notebook,' said Phoebe, flying now on the wings of invention, 'never left my mother's possession. It is in the safe of my solicitor in England, who has instructions to make its contents public if anything unpleasant happens to me or any of my friends . . . Soon we will have that information, and then we will decide what to do with it.' She paused. 'The man named in the notebook — *whoever he is,*' she said, looking him in the eye, 'would like to spend his last years in peace. But my message for him is that he is going to have no peace from this day onwards. Soon the evidence of his crimes will be decoded. Since it involves a famous case, it will be of interest to the press. I may release it to journalists. I may not. This man will live from day to day never knowing when his name might appear in a headline. He will face the constant dread of being uncovered. He will feel sick with dread when he wakes up each morning. In fact, he will hardly dare open a newspaper. He will suffer exactly the same fate he inflicted on my mother . . .'

The old man clapped his hands and a servant immediately appeared from inside the house. I thought, This is where we get thrown out. Or worse.

Instead he said, 'You have come a long way in the heat to tell me this interesting story. Won't you have some tea?'

'It's him. I know it is!'

The five of us were in the house on the slope of Bicchauda, where my family once had lived. We had wandered round rooms now beginning to be invaded by trees, and were sitting around the edge of the crumbling fountain, once full of goldfish, now dry and packed with leaves. Outside, the car waited. Murad had parked it in exactly the same spot where Babu used to station the Humber.

'I wish I was so sure,' I said. 'The old man didn't behave like a guilty or a worried person. He gave us tea, and offered to help. Can you really see him as a sinister controller of thugs in a city a hundred miles away?'

'I *know* it was him,' she repeated. 'It *was* him. The same man who stole me from school!'

'If it was the man,' said Jula, 'his rectum must be turned inside-out by now. You have done what you came for. It's over. Now go home and forget. This is finished.'

'For once the bugger is talking sense,' said Dost, to whom Mitra repeated his remark in Hindi. 'Let the past officially be declared dead.'

'Oh but it isn't,' she said, when I translated this for her. 'He was the same cool bastard he's always been. I want him so terrified he can't breathe.'

'Fever,' I said. 'Jula is right. If this is the blackmailer, he now believes we have the evidence to damn him. Let's go home and leave him to ferment.'

'But we don't have the evidence,' she said. 'It was a lie.'

'In this case,' I told her, 'lie or truth, makes no difference.'

'It's not enough!' she cried. 'You don't understand! None of you! I haven't been through all those years of misery just to let him off the hook. He was smiling when he said goodbye!'

'Well, dear,' I said, 'the truth is we *haven't* got the notebook. And we've failed to find it, so there's nothing more that can be done.'

'Nothing more!' she mocked. 'If I'd left things to you, Bhalu, nothing at all would have happened.'

The venom in her voice astonished me. Could this be the same person who had clung to me all through last night? Who had told me that I was the only person in the world she had ever really loved? She went on, apparently unaware that she had upset me, 'You know what I think. The notebook is here. In this house.'

I was too shocked to reply. It was left to Jula, who missed nothing, to ask why she should imagine such a thing.

'Because Mummy came to Ambona,' she said. 'At first I thought it was because the notebook was in the cemetery, but now I think perhaps it's been here all along.'

'Why would Maya have left it behind?' I asked, as calmly as I could.

'I don't know about that,' said Phoebe. 'But why else did that man buy the house then allow it to go to rack and ruin? Why did he make sure nobody else ever lived here?'

'This is all just speculation.'

'Did you see his face? He looked really rattled. I *know* he is the man, and I feel sure the notebook is here somewhere. It's here right now, probably within a few feet of us.'

'Fever is right in this much,' said Jula. 'The house *was* bought by a police bigwig, who *did* allow it to fall apart. It's also a fact that no one has lived here after your family.'

'It seems obvious to me,' said Phoebe, 'that the notebook must have had something really damning in it. Something even worse than blackmail. If we could find it, we would know why he was so desperate to get his hands on it.'

'We do know,' I said. 'It named him and recorded every detail of how the blackmail worked. It even described his office.'

'What is a worse crime than blackmail?' she asked. 'Think!'

'Rosie!' said Jula.

'Yes, poor Rosie. Remember the blackmailer threatened them over the phone. Not just Mummy, but your mother too, Bhalu. Suppose Mummy recorded those threats, with Maya as a witness? A few days later, Rosie died.'

'It was an accident, Phoebe. You and I both know that. It was our fault that it happened.'

'It wasn't our fault,' she said angrily. 'We were made to feel guilty about it, but Mummy believed she was murdered.'

'Isn't this just a little too far-fetched?' said Jula.

'No, Jula, it isn't. Maybe you don't remember that day, but I do. How quickly the police were here. They searched the whole house. What for? Didn't you see the fear in that man's eyes when you told him we had the notebook?'

'Probably just afraid we were loonies,' I said.

'Oh, for God's sake!' she screamed. 'Why are you trying to let him off the hook?'

'I've had enough of this,' I said. 'Tonight we return to Bombay and tomorrow I'm booking my flight home.'

Instantly, her mood changed. 'Bhalu, please don't let me down.

Won't you help me look for it? It's hidden here somewhere. We can surely find it.'

'I'll go with her,' Jula said. So they went together round the house, exploring the rooms, just as Nina and I had done on our first day, while I sat on the fountain with Dost and Murad, whose lack of English had kept them out of the controversy, but who had been unable to miss the tone of our debate.

'It seems,' said Dost with his usual perception, 'that our Phoebe has got you all churned up again.'

I did not know what to reply. I was thinking that I had been mad ever to listen to Phoebe. Crazy to come to India in the first place. Why had I done it? Perhaps because I wanted to prove that I was not *just* the dull, middle-aged man I appeared to be. That the adventurous child I had once been was still alive in me. Perhaps because my marriage had grown too humdrum, and it appeared that I could captivate a beautiful woman. How baffling now seemed last night's passion. Had I just been ridiculously gullible? Viewed in a certain unhappy hindlight, the events of the last few weeks carried the hallmark of all my actions, the bhola-ness for which I had always been celebrated. Bhalu the Bhola. Bhalu the Simpleton. Bhalu the Fool. Bhalu the Innocent-No-Longer.

'Bhalu, look at this! I found it in a cupboard in our old room!'

Phoebe was back, restored to bouncing optimism. I recognised at once what she was holding out to me. It was a torn-off cover, now heavily mildewed, of a book bound in what had once been red cloth. The front endpaper and flyleaf were still attached. *Puck of Pook's Hill.* An engraved frontispiece showed children playing on a Sussex hillside.

'Damn,' I said. 'That was a first edition.'

'Is that your only reaction?'

'Well, how do you want me to react?'

'I wanted you to realise,' she said, 'that if a piece of this book could survive here, and still be legible after all these years, so could the notebook.'

She resumed her search.

It would be dark in an hour or so. Jula said to me, 'Bhalu, let's all walk to Karvanda. We ought to visit the school and look up Rameshbhai.'

But Phoebe refused to come with us. She said, 'The notebook is here somewhere. I don't want to leave till I've found it.'

Dost did not want to go to Karvanda either. 'Persuade Phoebeji to pack it in,' he said to me. 'I'm hungry. Think of the kebabs we're missing at the Jam-i-Jam.'

I remembered that a couple of miles away, on the Tiger's Leap clifftop, there were hawkers selling roasted corncobs. Dost said that he and Murad would drive down there and fetch some.

Watching the car disappear down the track, Phoebe looked thoroughly miserable. I asked, 'Are you sure you'll be all right here on your own?'

'Yes, of course,' she snapped. 'Why wouldn't I?'

It was as if our intimacy of last night had never been.

As we were walking along the twisting track, down Bicchauda and up onto Dagala mountain, Jula said cryptically, 'I'm afraid Fever is not in the best of health.'

'What do you mean?' We were speaking in Hindi.

'There's something about her. Can't put my finger on it, but it's disturbing.'

'She gets excited,' I said. 'She also suffers from depressions.' As he made no reply, I said, 'She was hurt badly when she was young. You and I never even knew.'

'She uses people, Bhalu. She uses you.'

No. I did not want to believe it. 'She's had a bad time,' I said, 'but she has courage. Lots of guts. She's loyal.'

'I've seen you together. When she knows you're looking at her she's all games and girliness. But the moment you look away, she goes blank. Just seems to lose interest. As if you'd ceased to exist.'

And what you don't know, I thought, my reservations about bhola-ness already forgotten, was that last night she proved to me that she loved me. Over and over. With a passion that shook my heart. But this I could not say to him.

At Karvanda we found half the village gathered to watch a game show on TV. One of those instant-rags-to-riches fantasies, hosted by an ex-film star. But it was switched off when Jula arrived. He was soon deep in conversation, surrounded by old friends.

'People here are proud of him,' Rameshbhai told me. 'Because he started with nothing and has achieved so much. So much good he does. He is always working, working, on other people's behalf.'

A politician, I thought, who gives the lie to *India in 1983*.

Dusk was already blueing the sky when we came back down the mountain. Ahead of us at the house, we saw the car. Its headlights were on, pointing into the ruins. Why would Murad do that?

'Something is wrong,' Jula said, and began to run.

As we got nearer we could hear Dost and Murad. They were calling out, 'Phoebe! . . . Phoebe!'

'What has happened?' shouted Jula. 'Where is she?'

Dost came to meet us. On his face was an expression of such misery that it cannot be described. 'She is gone,' he said.

'Gone?' shouted Jula. 'Where could she go?'

'I don't know. We came back and she was not here. There was no sign of her at all. We have searched everywhere, in the house. Around about. Nothing.'

I felt sick. How could we have been so stupid as to leave her on her own? But what danger could there have been here, in these familiar surroundings? When I began to think of it, there were many dangers. Cobras in loose stonework, particularly during the monsoon. Dusk falling over the mountain. Perhaps she had gone for a walk. There were crevices you might miss in the gloom. Not far away were the terrifying cliffs from which Dost and Murad had just returned. One false step and you would tread thousands of feet of empty air. There was one peril of which I dared not think. The enemy. Had we underestimated him? Had he somehow guessed where we would go after we left his house? He lived barely twenty miles further into the mountains, among the hills of beyond and a day. Had he come here? Or one of his hirelings? That scream, caught on the wind, the night Rosie died. From westward, where the dark bars of cloud were streaked with pink, came a rumble of thunder. A tongue of green lightning licked the distant Duke's Nose.

Jula said, 'I'll go to the village. We'll get people out searching. We must find her quickly. There'll be an almighty storm.'

'Wait!' I said. 'I know where she has gone.'

I would not let them accompany me. If she had gone alone, so must I. It was forty years since I had last climbed up Bicchauda mountain, but the old path was still there, stretching palely into the dark. I climbed through clumps of karvanda thorn flung into strange shapes by a wind which was already keening in the grass and in the trees higher up the mountain. The lightning was nearer and the air was full of the scent of coming rain. This was the way. It was the way she must have gone, because it was the way we had climbed before, all those years ago. The path winding up between groves of trees on the higher slopes. Fewer of them now. Wide spaces where once forest had stood. The view opening out to the west, above the vast blackness of the lake below, now full and probably churning. When the wind blew hard, as it was doing now, the lake produced breakers that crashed against its shoreline in bursts of white foam, like the sea. Rain began falling. Far to the west, the lightning was at play again, over the Sugarloaf and the nameless mountain beside it, the one whose existence Kali Das the tea- and vada-pau-wallah had denied, though he had lived by the lake all his life. For the first time I hesitated. Ahead of me stretched the slippery rock slope, drenched by steadily dropping rain, where Rosie had fallen to her death. For the first time I hesitated. I was so high up the mountain that the lights of the villages in the valley below were tiny glimmers. I had been hoping to catch sight of Phoebe, sure, filled with a certainty beyond any doubt, that she had come up here. Had she passed this way? Crossed the dangerous rock? We had done it before, when we were children. Slowly, very carefully, I began to inch forward, not daring to look anywhere but at the ground right under my feet. A bright blare of lightning lit up the entire rock face. I jumped back, slid, fell to my knees, my fingers scraping desperately at the treacherous surface. I thought I had seen a snake writhing just in front of me, but it was a current of cold water, coiling over the rock, on its way to become a waterfall hundreds of feet below. Gradually, the angle of the rock eased, became gentler, gave way again to grass. I was near now. There was still no sign of Phoebe. But I knew where she must be. Close by. And we would be close, when we met again, in this place. When she knew that I had come after her, proved that I had read her mind and did, after all, share her deepest wishes. Already, in a part of my own mind, I was rehearsing the words we would exchange, and the knowledge, too deep for words, that we were one, could never be parted. Here, we would renew the solemn vows to one another that we had made when we were children. It was our destiny, this night. I was looking for a clump of tall trees, a glade, but the mountainside was different. Eventually I came upon what at first I had taken to be a pile of rocks. It was the little shrine. Still there. But now it stood in the middle of a grassy field. No tree to be seen for dozens of yards. The forest had gone. Lightning again, dancing all round Bicchauda. Inside the shrine, the eyes of the little goddess glared out, as they always had done, surveying with no change of expression a scene changed beyond all recognition.

This was where I had expected to find Phoebe. But she was not there. It then came to me that she really had vanished, and that I was alone on the mountain.

Nearby, the stone still reared. In one of those lightning tremors when the whole sky seems to light up for a moment like a faulty fluorescent tube, I could see that its tip was still thickly coated with vermillion. So the villagers still came here. The old gods were still alive. And on a night like this, the spirits would be dancing.

I did not know what to do. So I sat down with my back pressed against the stone and closed my eyes.

In my mind, but quite clear, as if the words were spoken out loud, I heard my mother saying, Hamari kahaniyan apné aaramb sé pahle aaramb hotin hain, aur apné anta ké baad tak jaari rahtin hain. Our stories begin before their beginnings and continue beyond their ends.

Mother, you craved too much responsibility. You took upon yourself the guilt of millions. Maybe you could not bear to be insignificant. I should never have listened to you.

You always were a foolish boy, comes her reply, delivered by the booming of thunder off basalt cliffs. Look at you, sitting on top of a mountain getting soaked when there are important things to be done in the world.

What things, may I ask? How do I know what is important and what isn't? How are we to act — isn't this your famous impossible question — when we can have no idea what the result of our actions will be? Judged solely by outcomes, it's impossible to determine whether any act is moral. Or immoral. According to your logic, in fact, since consequences fan outwards and onward without end, everything we do must be both infinitely good and limitlessly evil.

Don't be so stupid, roars the downpour, conveying her reply. It means we must act with the best intentions. We must try, try, try to be good. Have you tried to be a good boy, my little Bhalufer?

I have not, not, not, been a good boy. That's why I am soaking here on this humpy hill. I mustn't have done my lessons because I

577

still don't understand how to live in the world. I do not catch on or get-it-in-one and have never done the right or clever thing. I drove poor Katy to exotic birds. And last night I fornicated in a sewer pipe with a woman not in the least my wife.

Bhalu, murmured a gentle voice near my ear, what's to be done with you? You have behaved like an irresponsible shyster. Aren't you just like Mister Love, who could not decide which of two women he loved and lost them both?

It is cold. I am shivering. The spirits come here to dance at the time of lightning. I can see the shadows flying around me, leaping to the beat of an enormous drum. They are all here. Maya is here. Sybil, young and pretty, cradling a baby whose body bears the marks of dogs' teeth, happy at last. Killy is with her. I see Grandfather with his hookah. Nafisa Jaan, whose fingernails were torn off clawing at the inside of a brick wall. Rosie, smiling now, dancing on her Haadal feet. And look, here is Mister Love in his bloody bathtowel, with his empty whisky bottle and half-emptied skull at the centre of a crowd of elegant women. Over there is Noor, waltzing fit to break your heart with her faithful sub-human.

Here comes Gandhi, all smiles, the wounds in his chest scarlet as Remembrance Day poppies, laughing with Nathuram, whose neck is still twisted from the rope. Here is Lord Mountbatten, mangled by the explosion that killed him, chatting to Nehru, who alone of his dynasty, died intact. All those who were killed in the riots are here. And those who died in the Partition. And here is dear Manto, looking for a pencil. A sea of ghosts, crowding to the stone, waiting to be released.

EPILOGUE

FREDDY THE TAXI DRIVER
(LEWES, SEPTEMBER 1999)

Jula found me and brought me down from Bicchauda. He stayed by my bedside for the three days I lay in the cottage hospital in Ambona. In Bombay we went to the police and reported Phoebe missing. Weeks went by and there was no sign of her. My money had run out and I was staying with Dost.

So at last I came home. Caught a morning train from London to Lewes. It was a fine late summer day. I walked from the station through fields loud with birds. The harvest was in and the fields were blonde stubble dotted with hay bales. I passed along the river, noting the perfect symmetry of poplars, entered the lane that led to our cottage with a feeling of wild expectation. I had not been able to contact Katy. My return would be a surprise. I came to the cottage and let myself in. It was empty. I ran from room to room, my feet thudding on bare floorboards. What would I have given for a blue sofa and the music of birds? But there was nothing. I ran to the stable. Oxymoron was not there. Nor was he grazing in his paddock. His saddle and tack were gone. The concrete floor was swept bare and washed down. They had gone.

Eventually, I came out and sat on the grass. By the living room window the ceanothus had long since finished flowering.

I walked back up into the town. The bookshop was closed and locked up. I had no key. When I went to the bank, the manager told me apologetically. 'The account is closed. Your wife withdrew all the funds, as she was entitled to do. She told me that you had gone abroad and that she was joining you.'

I could not even afford to visit Charlotte, but found Piglet in his workshop, chary of meeting my eye.

'Been wondering when you'd return, lad. I've got a couple of things for you.' He handed me an envelope in Katy's handwriting and a package that had been addressed to me at the cottage.

Her note said: 'I have bought a cottage and a field in the South of France. The Lot Valley. The twins helped me move. We did it in several trips, in the horsebox. Your things are here. If you want to come home, I'll be glad to see you. But I won't expect you, Katy.'

Went to the bookshop, broke in through the back door and made myself a cup of tea. Everything was as I had left it on the day of my departure to India. The boxes of Maya's books still occupied the centre of the bindings room. I picked up the phone and asked the operator to connect me to a number in France.

It took weeks to sort out the things I wanted from the stock I would leave for the new owner. I slept meanwhile in one of the storerooms, on a camp bed lent to me by a kindly and anxious Piglet. A letter arrived from India. A note from Jula.

Bhalu, I found Phoebe. She is staying in Candolim in Goa, with an Italian chap. I think she just met him. She says to tell you that she is grateful for everything you did . . . As far as I can tell, on the night she disappeared she walked down the hill, took a lift from a passing truck and went back to see the man we had left. They appear to have come to some understanding because she now has no plans to leave India. I make no comment. If you want to contact her, the only address I have is c/o Freddy the taxi driver, Outside Summer Villa Hotel, Candolim, Goa. Dost and I are meeting next week. We have joined forces to start a community liaison group. He and I will chair it. For some reason Dost calls it our debating society.

The day before I am due to leave for France, I find the parcel that Piglet had given me on the day of my return, still unopened. Inside is a package wrapped carefully in brown paper and a note in Panaghiotis's small, beautiful copperplate. *My dear Bhalu, your mother had left this book with me for safekeeping. I meant to send it to you after she died, but unaccountably, I find I still have it. So I am posting it to you. I miss her greatly, as I am sure you do . . .* Some courtesies followed and an invitation to visit him when next in London.

I undo the wrapping and a slim brown volume comes into my hands. An odd volume of *Robinson Crusoe* in early eighteenth-century binding. Something about it looks wrong. I open it and immediately see why. The covers from an old book have been bound round an elderly notebook. Lined paper. I recognise the handwriting immediately. It is not in shorthand, but in plain English. Everything is there. Dates, times, places and amounts, listed in rupees. The dates begin in 1959 and continue through to mid-1960. There are passages of narrative too.

I turn a page and the name jumps out at me. For a long time I sit staring at it. What should I do? Send it to Phoebe, c/o Freddy the taxi driver, Candolim, Goa? Return to the hills of beyond and a day?

I am shivering. There is a fire burning in the grate.

ACKNOWLEDGEMENTS

To all those friends who gave their time to read and comment on an apparently endless series of manuscripts: to Sathyu Sarangi in Bhopal, who knows what it is to struggle against injustice; to Shreeram Vidyarthi for always being there when I needed to pick his brain about this or that aspect of Indian cultural life; to Anil Thakraney, who helped me obtain many documents pertaining to the Nanavati murder and in whose company I made two very enjoyable visits to the 'Ambona Hills'; to Gulab Rao, headman of Ardau village, for giving me an 'irrla'; to Simran Shroff who provided me with Sub's list of party suppliers (with one or two exceptions it is a current list, its usefulness, I feel, outweighing the anachronism); to Alyque Padamsee and Sharon Prabhakar for introducing me to Mrs Rita Mehta who kindly opened up the *Blitz* archives to me; to Mohan Deep for giving me access to his research on the Nanavati case; to John Lobo, for generously sharing with me his memories of Commander Nanavati's arrest and trial; to Graham Johnstone, who introduced me to calypso and sent me the lyrics of 'Pussyistic Man'; to Jonathan Harvey who talked to me about bird calls and the music of Oliver Messiaen; to my sister Umi Stoughton for her many valuable insights; to old friends in 'Ambona' and Dongri; to all the people, far too many to mention, whose kindness sustained me during my trips to India; finally, to my editors at Scribner, my agent Carole Blake and of course my family: thank you, and as Maya would have said, 'May God, in whom of course I don't believe, bless you!'